Hopes and Horse Feathers

Written by

L. M. Van Zandbergen

Edited by   Cover Art by

Steven Moore   George Patsouras

D1444554

Dedicated to my nephew, Dimitri.

Chapter 1

Look for the *Setting Sun* at Dawn

Shail sat at the end of an otherwise empty pier. He hugged his knees close to his chest, and rocked slightly from side to side. The *Setting Sun* was very late. The wind carried the sounds of laughter, music, and waves lapping against the shore. Shail turned around to look behind him. The sight *should* have been enough to lift his spirits.

It was a perfect late summer day. In every direction there spread an unmarred expanse of brightest blue. The waning sunlight made the countless green leaves glint silver as they swayed in the evening breeze. Every inch of earth that wasn't paved or plowed was covered in lush grass, with lots of dancing dandelions and bouncing buttercups.

Every house Shail had passed on his way to the pier was a bustling hive of activity. People were gathered in pairs and groups, and young children dodged between the adults as they ran squealing after one another. The air was filled with the background hum of conversation and collaboration, occasionally punctuated by triumphant shouts from those who had been victorious in their chase. There was an air of excitement that lent an energy to their various activities.

The beauty was lost on Shail. It was only a matter of hours before the setting sun, or *lack thereof*, brought an end to another day without his grandmother. At this rate, Gran Rox would miss the most important occasion of the season, so far as Shail was concerned. Grey-winged gulls glided close, calling to each other as they spiraled effortlessly up and down the ever-varying air currents. The swiftly flowing river was dotted with scores of ships ranging from small fishing vessels that needed few to crew her, to giant three masted galleons with dozens of men to man her decks. None bore sails like the ones Gran Rox had described to Shail in the letter she had sent before beginning her voyage downriver.

"The top edges are so dark, they appear almost black, but they lighten towards the base until they are a near-match for your eyes. A great, orange half-circle dominates their bottom quarter, with long, thin, rising streaks. That's how you'll recognize the Setting Sun. She's scheduled to arrive a week before the summer festival. That will give us plenty of time to catch up, and we can reprise our roles as the household's resident healers. If you help carry my luggage home, we'll stop by that lovely tea shop with those lemon lotus you love!"

The day before the *Setting Sun* had been due to dock, a lone dragon borne courier had delivered a single, brief message from the ship's captain. It had simply said, "Delayed". Neither it, nor the rider, had offered any further explanation. What did '*delayed*' mean? A day? Two, three? More? What if *delayed* meant Gran Rox would be so late, she missed the festival entirely?

Shail had dutifully spent his free hours during the past week watching for the *Setting Sun*, seeing its namesake disappear at the end of each disappointing day, but never the object of his search. At first, Shail had been hopeful the setback would prove short, but as the time that remained before the summer festival had dwindled, his impatience had given way to a gut-gnawing anxiety as the sun slowly arced across a sky whose calm cerulean seemed at odds with his mounting unease.

Shail's small figure, silhouetted against the horizon as he continuously paced back and forth, had attracted sympathetic attention from some who also spent their days by the river. A friendly fisherman who regularly sat nearby, whistling tunelessly while he mended his nets, had not only loaned Shail an old wooden cup, he refilled the container with fresh water whenever it was emptied. Shail kept it sheltered in the shade of a nearby piling, and there was usually something small to nibble on sitting companionably close. Shail's mother Lisasin would drop off a biscuit or apple, thoughtfully wrapped in an embroidered cloth, whenever she took a break from organizing the decoration of their household. But neither the scent of the bread, baked fresh each morning, nor the sight of the plump red fruit

7

could tempt him. Shail had unfortunately forgotten the protective paste his uncle had given him on the first day of his vigil. The parts of him that had been exposed to too much sun, chiefly his face and forearms, prickled uncomfortably, but Shail felt no inclination to return home early.

Shail sighed, stretched, then shaded his eyes with both hands, scanning the water from the end of a dock usually reserved for the boarding and offloading of passenger liners. Few of the ships he could see sported sails with only a single pigment; most flashed no fewer than four complimentary hues. One of the strangest was a schooner whose creamy white canvas was littered with large, lurid spots. Shail's eyes stung from the ludicrous sight; he blinked and rubbed them, deciding to get a drink to break the monotony of his thus-far fruitless search. As he drained his cup of its contents for the countless time, Shail heard his name being called from the landside. He turned towards the voice, recognizing it, and the smiling face, as belonging to his paste-providing uncle, Wengsper. Shail waved, but could only manage a grimace in greeting.

Shail assumed his uncle had stopped by to chat for a few moments, as he did periodically when his duties as the Dockmaster's assistant allowed. While Shail paced restlessly back and forth, Wengsper would cross one polished boot over the other and lean the top of his shoulder against Shail's drink-shading dock piling. At such times, it was easy to see the resemblance between them.

8

Their eyes were the same shade of robin's egg, a trademark of the men in their family; their dark, olive-tinted skin was so similar, when his uncle laid an affectionately arm around Shail, it was difficult to tell where one ended, and the other began; and both were darkly tressed, although Shail wore his wavy raven hair loosely bound at the nape of his neck, stray tendrils framing his face, while his uncle's was cut short and kept in check by the stiff, brimmed hat he wore as part of his uniform.

To Shail's surprise, Wengsper did not assume his normal post, but instead strode purposefully up the dock, stopping squarely in front of Shail, his smile widening. "I have an early Feather's Day gift for you, nephew mine! Want to guess what it is?" Shail, irritated by such ill-placed humor, tried for a quelling glare, but the gravity of his disapproval was somewhat diminished by his having to look up at his uncle, who topped him by a full foot and a half. All the same, Wengsper visibly wilted. "Sorry, 'course you don't want to guess, not after waiting out here for so many days. Well, here 'tis. I got word of the *Setting Sun*, just come in from ...."

The rest was lost as Shail latched onto the larger man's arm, dropping his cup in his frenzy, causing it to roll off the edge of the dock and disappear into the depths below. "Someone's seen her! Where? When will she arrive? Why wasn't she here on schedule? Was there an accident? Pirates? Is Gran Rox onboard? Is she alright?"

Shail could not wait for an answer before asking another anxious question.

The big man gripped Shail's shoulders in his strong, steady hands, "Alright, easy now! Take a breath, and I'll tell you all I know." Shail snapped his mouth shut with an audible click, nodding as he collected his wits. Wengsper released Shail after one last, brief squeeze, then stepped back and regarded his nephew levelly. When Shail regained his composure, his uncle allowed his arriving grin to return to his bearded face, and gestured to Shail's reddened complexion. "I'm hoping your Gran will be so busy with all the going-ons she won't have time to track me down and tan my hide the same color as your own. T'would be a terrible embarrassment, a man grown turned over his mother's knee. I did give you that sunshield …"

"I forgot it. I'll tell her so myself. Now, what's the news?"

"The *Setting Sun* should be here by dawn tomorrow." Shail let out a joyful whoop, drawing a collection of chuckles from those with earshot on the surrounding water and neighboring piers. Gran Rox was safe, and would be here for Shail's ceremony, just as she'd promised! Wengsper waited for quiet, then resumed, "I don't know the specifics yet. I was sorting the missives for Dockmaster Colth. You know how he hates doing it himself, and I don't mind really, though it can get mighty tedious." Shail groaned, so his uncle hastened on, "Well, anyway, there was another message, dropped off by the same courier as before, and it's just as strange as the first. More than one word this time, but hardly any more helpful. 'All's well, details on arrival'. You'd think they could give a body a bit more to go on after disappearing for a week, without a whisper of why." Wengsper frowned for the space of a few heartbeats, but his face cleared as he continued. "Anyhow, knowing you'd be here, I came to tell you soon as I could get free so you could run home and let everyone know the good news." Wengsper hooked his thumbs into his broad, black belt, looking pleased as Shail performed a lively dance on the spot. "I wagered you'd find such news worth all the feathers on a winged stallion." Shail enthusiastically agreed, then jerked straight as his uncle's words sank in. He had to tell his family! They would have been nearly as worried about Gran Rox as Shail. There wasn't a moment to lose!

Shail set off running as fast as he could towards home, calling back over his shoulder, "Thank you, Uncle! I'll tell them sir, right now! Docked before dawn!" Wengsper laughed and waved to Shail's swiftly retreating form. As he followed, at a much slower pace, he lustily sang bits of an old waterman's song.

"I've sailed this river to the sea, with naught but stars and fishes,

To keep me comp'ny dark and day, far better than a missus.

Just I and me, to work these decks, I'm captain, crew, and cook oh,

I run the rigging, swab the deck, and bait all waiting hooks oh.

When back in port, with wink and nod, I'll bid myself good day sir,

To dance and dice, each one times thrice, and spend my hard-won pay sir.

Shore leave is short, my course is set, tide's out and so am I oh,

Port may be fine, for a space of time, but I'm a sailor 'til I die oh!"

Shail left a trail of dust in his wake as he tore up a path lined with gaily decorated shops, their flags and streamers snapping in the wind. A short time later, Shail caught sight of home; a two-story, light grey stone building, like its neighbors, with windows thrown wide, the long white curtains that lined each one billowing out in the steadily blowing south-western wind. Shail could see members of his extended family working outside, readying the house for the merrymaking that would begin tomorrow. The festivities would last for a full day, culminating in the Stallion Feather Ceremony.

There were four Stallion Feather Ceremonies a year, usually the finale of each season's largest communal celebration. All of the town's children with the corresponding birth season who had reached a particularly significant age would be proudly presented with a single feather by their relations. It was this ceremony that Shail had been most eager for Gran Rox to attend. It would mark his thirteenth summer, and everyone knew thirteen was a lucky number.

Shail leapt up high as he could as he passed through the front door, brushing its lintel with his fingertips, a feat he was justifiably proud of, having mastered it only within the last few weeks. He dodged in between a cousin carrying a tray with napkins that matched the ones Shail's mother had wrapped his snacks in, stacked so high his cousin had to peer around the side to see where he was going, and an aunt consulting a list she held close to her face, her reading glasses perched forgotten upon her head.

Tantalizing aromas were coming from the kitchen, and as Shail inhaled through his mouth, now watering with renewed appetite, he could almost taste the delicious dishes cooking therein. He had barely eaten the past few days, and his stomach rumbled in protest. The anxiety that had plagued him was gone, and now all the anticipation that had been deadened by worry filled Shail twice over.

Reaching the central staircase, Shail was careful to stop at the sixth step, not the seventh. He filled his lungs, threw back his head, and shouted, *"Hey, listen!"* All activity ceased, startled faces for once having to look up to see him. When he was sure he had everyone's attention, he continued, "Wengsper told me the *Setting Sun* will arrive at dawn! Gran Rox will be here tomorrow!" A joyful chorus went up from everyone in the room.

Shail's mother spoke warmly as she slowly descended the stairs, "That's wonderful! Everything should be ready, and now that we can rest easy on Gran's account, your feather ceremony should be perfect!"

Shail walked down the last few steps beside his mother. When they reached the bottom she drew him tightly into her arms, leaning down to rest her chin on top of his head. His mother smelled like flour, and after she'd released him, Shail could see a smudge on her nose where she'd scratched while baking. Looking closer, he noticed she looked pale, and there were dark circles under her eyes. She absently tucked a strand of hair that had come loose from her braid behind her ear, its blackness a stark contrast to the grey that had begun to grow at her temples.

She winced as she took in his sunburned skin, pulling a small bottle of salve from the apron she wore to protect her skirts, gaily covered in pink, palm-sized petals picked out in pale thread. "Try this, it should help ease the pain, and bring on a peel." Shail took it, grateful that his mother had not tried to apply the contents to him herself. He had begun to resent her treating him like a child; he was thirteen summers old now, after all (although he still loved it when she hugged him breathless, as she had done just now). "Have you finished preparing Gran's room like I asked?"

"Yes ma'am," he answered. "It's been ready since the day she said she would be here." Shail had made up his grandmother's bed with freshly laundered linens, swept the floor and fireplace, stocking the latter with several logs of dry wood, wiped down all the room's furniture and windowsills with rose-scented water, and dusted the clock that rested on the mantle over the hearth; he'd had to stand on a chair to manage that last task. He had avoided the room since then. Without its intended occupant, Shail had no further interest in staring at its walls, his thoughts circling between wondering where Gran Rox was, wishing she were there, and imagining what they would be doing if she were.

Gran Rox had retired after a successful career as a traveling healer, or Travealer as they were commonly called, which made her the go-to person for anyone in the house in need of patching up. Each time she visited, Gran Rox would set up in a sunroom at the back of the house, carefully laying out the items she always traveled with to treat basic illnesses and injuries. Shail had been her assistant for as long as he could hold a piece of clean cloth for binding an injury or wiping a brow. Gran had said she thought Shail would make a competent Travealer someday, and he was seriously considering applying for apprenticeship in two years. That would give him time to complete his journeyman's tour, the last stage of his formal training, before gaining his majority at age twenty, just as Gran Rox had done herself. Until then, he would enjoy helping his grandmother, and she would be here tomorrow!

Shail's mother gave him an approving pat, "I know she will appreciate that, thank you. Supper should be ready soon. Why don't you see if you can help in the kitchen until then?" Shail nodded, and his mother gave him a quick peck on the cheek before going back upstairs.

The rest of the evening passed quickly. The meal tasted every bit as good as it smelled, but the feast would not begin in earnest until they broke their fast tomorrow morning, lasting until after the Stallion Feather ceremony. There would be enough food to feed all of Shail's family who lived nearby, or, like Gran Rox, were in town to visit and enjoy the festivities. With a full belly, and the sure knowledge that with a little more patience, he'd have the double blessing of his grandmother, and his thirteenth horse feather, Shail sought out his bed on the second floor, wriggling under the covers in his excitement for the coming morning.

Chapter 2

Dragon Egg Lotus

Leeinn decided to take a detour and visit one of her favorite places before dinner. When she reached her chosen spot atop the abbey's wall, she breathed in deeply, relishing the varied scents of vegetation, both the fragrant generated by the green and growing, and the mildly malodorous of the dead and decomposing. Aside from the faint echo of a gong, and the far-off cry of waterfowl, it was quiet. Leeinn enjoyed a moment of silent reflection.

All the clouds spread along the far horizon were ablaze with the final rays of the setting sun, and Del Abbey was winding down for the day. It had been uncomfortably hot and humid all through the afternoon, but with dusk now approaching, the temperature had dropped significantly. The moisture in the air was settling into a low-hanging mist that beaded every grass blade, wreathing the ground in a gauzy vapor that seemed to contain countless sparkling stars. A fair breeze could be felt up where Leeinn rested, but closer to the ground the air grew still, checked by large clusters of willows with long, hanging branches, scattered about the landscape as far as the eye could see to the north, south, and west. To the east, a well-maintained, winding road led away from the abbey's main entrance. It was wide enough for three large carts to comfortably pass each other, with a pair of paved paths running parallel for pedestrians. The master road builders had taken the future need for shade into consideration as they constructed their creation, planting tall trees with wide, spreading canopies along its edge. There was enough space between their trunks for small stands selling abbey-made food and wares. The abbey bells rang out, signaling the end of normal working hours, and calling everyone to the dining hall for the evening meal.

Leeinn loved this place. The abbey was the only home she could remember, the only world she wanted or needed. She absently shifted her large woven basket full of dragon egg lotus, often called dels for short, back to the crook of her arm. Leeinn usually had this spot to herself when she visited, and this evening was no exception. There had never been a need for wall guards in Leeinn's lifetime; only the wooden watchtower, positioned between Del Abbey and the edge of the dragon's territory, was manned year-round, day and night, save when the very worst of weather drove everyone inside for safety's sake. She knew from her history lessons that the early settlers had found the tower crucial to their survival, but the long interval of peace had seen its watch relegated to the newly Accepted, rotated out every twelve hours.

18

Two options were available to residents and visitors wanting to travel between the outer wall's three levels: climb the switchback stairs, found at each of the wall's four corners, or wait in one of the lift lines. At first, there had only been a single suspension room to carry people and parcels alike. As the abbey prospered, a second had been added to the western wall. These days, the eastern elevator was primarily used by quick-paced passengers, leaving the other for the bulky items that needed to be transported to and from the ground.

In response to the upcoming Hopeful ceremony, there had recently been an increase in all manner of traffic, and it was the Liftmaster's prerogative to prioritize the loads. His authority allowed him near total control of lift-related operations, including the requisition of both for "official abbey business". Single riders, like Leeinn, he would label least important, forcing her to go last, if he did not deny her access entirely.

Leeinn preferred to trust her own feet anyway; the lifts had always felt cramped to her, even when she was the sole occupant. The stairs were a price she willingly paid, because from where she now stood, she could look out upon the land where the dels had grown long before the current human settlement had been built, tended by countless generations of dragon gardeners. The floating flowers allowed Leeinn only brief glimpses of the still, liquid surface beneath.

Leeinn looked down and saw one large dragon, obviously male because of the quail-like cream and chestnut pattern on his scales, lounging at the edge of the del meadows while watching a group of winged horses. Most were dun-colored mares, save for a pair of brilliantly plumed, white-haired stallions. They all waded sedately through the knee-high water, occasionally pausing to gently breathe on a del's rounded top. Their chosen bud slowly opened, revealing a small quantity of golden nectar cupped within. The winged horse would quickly slurp the contents before consuming the plump petals, mottled an unassuming grey and white on the outside, but as vibrantly rainbow-hued within as the stallion's feathers. Del abbey's outer walls replicated this facet; the face they showed to the world was plain and unadorned, but those within were surrounded by vivid color.

The pride Leeinn always felt for her home filled her near to bursting as she considered how it had become famous for the variety and quantity of its namesake it produced annually. She had met many Hopefuls over the years who had been inspired by tales that told of the unique relationship between the residents and local species, both flora and fauna. They had faced the trek to the abbey, despite the distance and dangers between; for although it was rich, by necessity Del Abbey was situated near the outskirts of the dragon egg lotus water meadows. She had never made the journey herself, but Leeinn had heard riders say even when flying fast with minimal breaks, it took three days to reach the nearest city. They had sympathized with those without winged mounts, forced to follow the twists and turns of the thoroughfare, and requiring triple the amount of time to reach the same destination.

The current abbey residents were a fairly even mixture of immigrants and children like Leeinn, raised by an Accepted parent or parents, accepted themselves when the time came, who spent their entire lives within the abbey's holding. *Trinity willing*, Leeinn mused, her home would soon welcome two new siblings. As she thought of the Hopefuls, Leeinn glanced down at her basket packed near to overflowing with dels. They were closed now, looking for all the world like the dragon eggs they were named for in miniature, but would be coaxed open by specially trained winged horses tomorrow morning, giving the blossoms most of the day to fill Hopeful Hall with their heady fragrance. Leeinn could hardly wait to see everyone's faces tomorrow evening when they first beheld the Hopeful Dais, which barely had room for the two candidates, so much of its floor was covered with flowers.

When she had celebrated her thirteenth spring, Leeinn's father had afforded her a small section of the abbey perfect for the cultivation of dels, which only they two had tended since. More than once, he had said the dragon egg lotus Leeinn grew there produced a sweeter perfume and nectar than any he had ever encountered in his life. High praise indeed, and an opinion held by many more than just her father. Every abbey ceremony and celebration saw Leeinn's dels in high demand, and she would always cheerfully oblige.

Leeinn realized she had lost track of time. She made for the stairs; she would have to hurry if she wanted to drop off her latest offering and get to her place at table before supper started. She wasn't worried as she took advantage of every shortcut and side passage she had memorized over a lifetime spent within the abbey.

Leeinn's first stop, conveniently close to the western wall, was devoid of people when she arrived. Leeinn arranged her dels among the display that already dominated the Hopeful Dais, a ten-foot-wide, circular platform at the bottom of a bowl-like depression. One side was lined with tiers of benches. The other side consisted of two immense arched doors that were only used during the Hopeful ceremony, allowing the Trinity access to the hall, and the people inside. The entrance was otherwise kept shut and hidden behind floor length curtains the same shade as the surrounding stone.

Her errand complete, Leeinn stored her basket in a tucked away closet and left the building, pausing only to pull the main door closed behind her. Her absence would already have been noticed, but so long as she was in place by contemplation, her father would overlook her tardiness.

When she arrived at the hall a short time later, breathing lightly, people hailing from every corner of the map lined the long wooden benches; fair-haired Heylothers rubbing elbows with midnight black Lodvidians, and giant Gieftari laughing merrily with child sized Isrenths. The hall hummed with their excited chatter. The Hopeful Ceremony was the following day, and no one could seem to talk about anything else. Leeinn slipped along walls hung with masterwork tapestries, sliding into her usual place at her father's table, which sat opposite the main entrance and was raised a single step above the rest of the hall. Her father Rumaru briefly paused his private conversation to smile in Leeinn's direction, despite the fact she knew the sound of her approach should have been drowned out by all the noise in the hall. Her father's extraordinary ability to perceive his environment unseen was a common source of amazement among guests. It was almost impossible for strangers to tell that he had been blinded as a young man, his other senses guiding him through the world better than many whose eyes worked perfectly. People were just as surprised to learn that Leeinn was adopted, for they looked similar enough to actually *be* parent and child. Leeinn braided her waist length locks the same way he did his; when she wound their hair together, as she did sometimes when feeling particularly close to him, they made a beautiful compliment, her black against his silver. Leeinn reached out and gave his hand a gentle squeeze in greeting, pleased that their skins were the same shade of sun kissed brown. He returned the pressure, then released her hand to pick up a mallet with a bulbous felted tip. He struck a small table gong, producing a reverberating sound that instantly quieted all the chatter.

Everyone turned their attention to the abbot as he spoke, his mild tenor voice pitched to carry to those seated furthest away from him. "Good evening, all. To those visiting, be welcomed, and please, treat this place as your own while you stay with us. To my fellow Accepted, I give thanks for your tireless dedication to this abbey, which we call home. And lastly, to our Hopefuls, I encourage you to use this time to consider what lies before you. Your lives will change tomorrow, one way or another. Let us all take a moment for contemplation before we enjoy our well-earned meal".

The hall went still, the only sound Leeinn could hear was the gentle susurrus of breathing. Leeinn mimed her father's position, back straight, eyes closed, and palms lying relaxed upon her knees. Rumaru had a gift for timing; just as the hall reached the point of breaking the imposed silence, he sounded the gong one last time, signaling the start of the meal.

Dozens of attendants brought out loaded dishes, placing them in the center of the tables. Leeinn glanced over at the two Hopefuls her father had just addressed. One was over six and half feet tall, her hair in long, thin braids interwoven with wooden beads and charms that clicked pleasantly together when she moved. Her tablemate barely reached her shoulder, and kept his head and face shaved clean. They both sat, eating and talking quietly, seeming to encompass an entire intimate world all their own between their closely bent heads. They had caused a bit of a stir

24

when they had arrived together, both humbly asking to join the abbey. While it was not unheard of for married couples to seek acceptance together, it did have the potential to end in tragedy. Leeinn would not envy the decision either would face if one became Accepted, but the other was refused.

Leeinn was startled from her train of thought by the guest sitting to her left, who had coughed politely to get Leeinn's attention. What had she said her name was? Gira, that was it, a daughter of the Trader seated next to Rumaru. "Priestess?" Gira's tone made Leeinn wonder how many times she'd already had to repeat herself. "Forgive me if I've interrupted your thinking, but I was curious what part you will play during the ceremony tomorrow?"

"Oh, the Trinity will carry most of the ritual. The attendants, myself included, mostly just open the Del Doors, present the Hopefuls, and award those who are accepted with a Del Abbey pin."

Gira looked down at Leeinn's habit, frowning quizzically, "But you're Accepted. Where is yours?"

"The pins are too precious to wear all the time. Each person is only given one, when they are first accepted by the Trinity. They're usually saved for special occasions. I'll be wearing mine for the ceremony tomorrow, all the Accepted will."

"Ahh, I see," said Gira. She seemed full of curiosity, a state common among visitors to the abbey, for

25

having gotten one answer, she at once asked "I'd *heard* that you call your winged horse *herd*," she quietly tittered behind a delicately manicured hand at her pun, "a treasure. Why is that?"

Leeinn replied, "It's because of the essential role they play. The dragon's diet consists of two main components. They need the dels of course, but equally important are the feathers from the winged horses, particularly those shed by the foals. The female dragons made the water meadows so the dels would flourish, attracting the winged horses, and enticing them to live here permanently. Because there are so many dels, and so many winged horses, the abbey can sell the surplus flowers and feathers to buy the few supplies we cannot make for ourselves. As you know, the rut feathers are considered the most valuable by people. We can take all those shed by our stallions because the dragons only covet those of the colts and fillies. So, we call our winged horses a treasure because they are treasured by both the abbey, and the dragons."

Her dinner companion clapped her hands together in delight, "How clever! You know, I've heard them called other things. I mean besides a herd or treasure."

Leeinn grew still, trying to keep her voice neutral as she said, "I know there are some who do not value the winged horses as we do here at Del abbey, and so give them less flattering names."

Gira seemed oblivious to the coolness that had managed to enter Leeinn's tone, for she blithely continued, "I wouldn't say less flattering, personally. The word I heard used was *fortune*, because just one would fetch such a sum. Feathers, hide, hooves, organs, bones; every part is said to be worth its weight in gold."

Leeinn's stomach gave an uncomfortable squeeze, and she put her fork down on her plate. She reminded herself that the world outside her abbey was very different from the one she knew and loved, but the thought did nothing to negate the nausea she felt at the concept of using, or even worse, harming, a winged horse for any reason, much less mere profit. "We harvest that which is not needed or wanted by the dragons, but we never hurt the winged horses. We only take the feathers that have been shed naturally. Even after a winged horse dies, its body is buried by a female dragon in the del water meadows, to replenish the nutrients in the soil."

Gira hastily apologized as she flushed with embarrassment, "I meant no offense Priestess! Please forgive my thoughtless speech."

Leeinn regained her composure and changed the subject. "I'm Accepted, but not actually a priestess yet. I'm too young, and still in training. Please, just call me Leeinn." Searching for a safer topic, she asked, "Is this your first time viewing the Hopeful ceremony?"

Gira's over-enthusiastic response caused all Leeinn's lingering misgivings to vanish; the poor thing really was eager to please. "It is! I've been looking forward to it ever since my mother told me our family would be attending!" Their dinner talk flowed easily from there, Leeinn answering as many of Gira's rapid-fire questions as she could, but otherwise allowing her companion to carry the conversation.

No, the dragons did not frighten her. Yes, they were quite large, but as they did not often eat meat, usually the worst an Accepted had to watch out for was being accidentally stepped on. Was there a place for the creatures to go for shelter? Well, the trees gave the treasure and dragons decent protection from sun and showers, but for those bonded to riders there were two main buildings, each one specialized for the species stabled there, as well as an infirmary, built further away, for the ill or injured in need of a quiet place to quarantine and convalesce. No, she was not particularly interested in becoming a bonded rider, but she had helped in the creature's care, feeding, grooming, and cleaning their stalls, since she had grown big enough to perform such tasks.

Leeinn occasionally tuned Gira out and focused on her father, who was speaking to Gira's mother, given the honor of sitting at Rumaru's side because she was the head of a family who shared a long and lucrative history with Del Abbey. Leeinn wondered if Gira took after her father, for she was already taller than her mother, with blonde hair rather than brown. Rumaru seemed to be regaling his guest with an amusing story, for she chuckled as she chewed.

The meal was eaten, and the evening came to an end. Leeinn bid her guest and father goodnight. Gira stammered something about having had a wonderful meal, and how she would pray for both the Hopefuls. Rumaru gave his daughter a parting hug, and Leeinn spent the hours until dawn dreaming sweet dreams, safe and snug in the same bed she had slept in since she was a child. Her last thought before she drifted off was for the Hopefuls, wondering whether they would still be together this time tomorrow.

Chapter 3

Arrivals, but No Answers

Shail awoke in time to watch Gran Rox disembark from the *Setting Sun* shortly after sunrise, just as Uncle Wengsper had predicted. Despite the early hour, his grandmother moved briskly, dressed in a loose cream-colored shirt and tan trousers, the latter tucked into latte-colored leather boots. She had cut her silver hair shoulder short again, brushing it back and then leaving it to its own devices. When she stepped onto dry dock, she crouched down and opened her arms to receive Shail as he threw himself at her, making a small, "*Umph,*" noise when he connected. They both clung to each other with all their collective might for several heartbeats.

When they finally broke apart, Gran Rox had tears in her eyes. She sniffed a bit, drawing in a shaky breath, and swallowing hard. When she had regained control of herself, she held Shail at arm's length, giving him a calculating eye up and down. "You've grown since last I saw you, grandson mine. You'll be taller than me soon."

Shail stretched until he was nearly standing tip toe, inordinately pleased that she had noticed. "Taller than you, and mother, and even Uncle Wengsper!"

Gran Rox nodded, "And have you brawn to go with your new height, young man? I've the usual luggage. The porters can handle the heaviest, but I could use your help with the two I keep close to hand."

Shail puffed out his narrow chest, "You can count on me Gran. I'm your man." Grunting in approval, Gran turned to signal a waiting sailor. The burly deckhand acknowledged her, and soon brought over two weathered traveling cases, placing them politely at Gran Rox's feet. He nodded respectfully to her, winked at Shail, and then returned to his ship, his gait retaining the rolling quality it had acquired from years spent on a shifting surface.

Shail picked up one of the bags, staggering only a little with its added weight, and Gran Rox hefted the remaining one herself with apparent ease. She turned her head to look up the hill, "I think I remember the way to that shop I promised we would visit, but I doubt it's open at the moment."

"It's ok Gran. I know it's too early. We can go another time." Recalling the way his uncle liked to escort his lady friends, Shail gallantly offered his free arm to his grandmother.

She smiled broadly, "My grandson is growing into a proper gentleman! I gladly accept, thank you kind sir." She curtsied, a comical gesture in pants, then accepted Shail's proffered arm, and they began making their way away from the river. "I hardly have to ask if everything is ready for tomorrow. Your mother has always been good at organizing those sorts of things."

Shail nodded, "Yes ma'am! Including your room. I took care of it myself."

Gran Rox smiled, "It seems I owe you a great deal. I wonder if just one lemon lotus will be enough to make us even. Perhaps a few sugar stallion feathers, or a couple of chocolate dragons are in order. Maybe a sampler consisting of all three?" Shail could not help wriggling at the thought of such generous compensation. "Is your uncle staying out of trouble?"

Shail considered, "Nothing out of the ordinary."

"Nothing he would want you telling me about, you mean." Shail ducked his head to hide his face and kept quiet, and Gran let out a bark of laughter.

As they strolled arm in arm towards home, they were greeted by the few shopkeepers that were opening that day. Shail was a common sight in town, and Gran Rox was well known in these parts for her healing expertise. The plump old woman who ran the apothecary was particularly pleased to see them, going so far as to leave her storefront to give Gran Rox a tight hug. Shail's grandmother hugged her back, and he tried not to be alarmed when she left her case sitting on the ground, indicating she meant to stay and chat for a while.

"Rox! We were afraid you weren't going to make it to the festival this year! I'm glad whatever it was that kept you cleared up in time."

"So am I friend! Cutting it close I know, but I'm here now, and I can't wait to start eating!"

The apothecary laughed merrily, and then turned her attention kindly upon Shail. "I've watched you walk to the dock and back every day this past week. Made my poor heart nearly break. I know you must be pleased your gran's finally here."

Shail nodded enthusiastically, "Yes ma'am, I sure am! Getting my feather without her there would have been just awful. She's been here for every one of my stallion ceremonies, I should have known she wouldn't miss this one." Gran Rox's eyes twinkled, and she graced her grandson with a grin.

Gran's friend comfortably rested clasped hands on her generous stomach, "I heard your ship went missing, and naught but a single word to put those waiting at ease." Shail thought he saw a shadow momentarily cloud his grandmother's features; it passed so quickly that he soon forgot it.

Gran said, "From what I gather, for none of us passengers were given much more of an explanation than you were in that missive, they kept the ship quarantined for some reason until they could be sure it was safe for us to dock. We were told to stay in our cabins, and all our meals were brought to us. I was lucky my room had a porthole. Got a lot of reading done when I wasn't staring at the river, I'll tell you that. Just before we all went batty with boredom, the ship started moving, and here we are."

The apothecary looked affronted. "They didn't give you a reason? None at all? I'm surprised you didn't track down the captain and demand answers. I wouldn't have left the ship until they explained themselves to my satisfaction, believe you me." She crossed her arms and managed to look surprisingly menacing for an elderly woman in a freshly pressed pinafore and lace cap.

Gran Rox shrugged once more, "They wouldn't say anything save to apologize over and over for the inconvenience; even refunded everyone's fare. I'm here now, safe and sound, and in time for Shail's feather ceremony. That's all that matters to me." Shail's patience began to wear thin, and he had begun to fidget as the two women conversed. Gran Rox glanced down at him, then back at the apothecary,. "We'll have to talk more another time. I think my handsome escort is eager to get home and start the fun." Her friend promised to catch them both later, Gran Rox made her goodbyes, finally picked up her bag, and the two continued on their way.

"Did they really not tell you anything Gran? Didn't you ask? You're a whole week late!" Shail tried to keep the accusation of out voice; he knew the delay had not been her fault.

"I'm afraid not. Let's not worry about it anymore. Tell me everything I've missed!"

Shail told his grandmother how he had waited at the dock for her while the rest of the family prepared their house for the festival. Gran Rox made a sympathetic sound as Shail showed her his sunburned skin.

"Why didn't you put on any protector, grandson mine? I should think a boy on the verge of becoming a young man should know better. Especially one taught by me."

Shail looked abashed, "I did remember it! The first couple of days anyway. After a while, I got so worried, I forgot."

Gran sighed, shaking her head. "Well, it can't be helped now. Be glad we don't hail from Heylother, or you'd look like a freshly steamed lobster. As is, you're going to shed like a serpent in a day or so, then have strangers believing you're half Lodvidian. At least you won't burn again until next summer. In the meantime, I have something in my packs that will help."

"Mother already gave me a salve. I think it's one of yours, the one with the aloe. It works, anyway. I used some last night, and the burns don't hurt anymore, although they are beginning to itch." They walked slowly, Shail catching

35

his grandmother up on all the recent goings-on. Gran Rox laughed and scowled at all the right times; she was a wonderful audience.

When they came into sight of the house, they were greeted warmly by everyone who was awake. Shail's mother met them at the door, this time in skirts that matched her lilac eyes, and the tears that had only threatened at the dock were spilled amongst much happy hugging. When Lisasin let Gran Rox go, Uncle Wengsper was next in line. He picked Gran Rox up and twirled her in a full circle before crushing her to his chest.

Many tried peppering Gran with questions, but she waved them all off. "Later! Later I say! I've only just arrived, let's just be glad I'm here. I'm starving! Where's the food?" Her family was forced to relent in the face of Gran Rox's legendary appetite; they gave up trying to get anything more out of her, and sat down to break their fast.

After a whirlwind day, Shail was ready to rest. He was hugged and kissed and made a general fuss over as everyone else also sought their beds. Gran Rox had been gregarious through the daylight hours, eating most, talking most, and laughing most, but had grown quiet as the evening drew to an end. Shail assumed she must be tired, like he was. Once or twice, over the course of the day, he had seen his mother and uncle trying to talk to Gran Rox alone, always to be put off. Each time they were rebuffed, Lisasin's face became strained, and Wengsper would get a drink to stare broodingly into. The dissonance was unlike anything Shail had ever seen between the normally thick-as-thieves trio. When he had attempted to broach the subject, their speech had been light enough as they assured him all was well, but he had thought their faces looked troubled.

Having changed into his bed clothes, Shail settled down to sleep, hoping that a good night's rest would give everyone clearer, calmer heads tomorrow. Gran Rox had not said how long she would stay once the festival was over. Shail hoped she would visit for another week, to make up for the one she had missed. Better yet, maybe Gran would take him to stay with her, then he could have her all to himself. If he was lucky enough to have that happen, he even dared to dream that he might get to make the return river boat ride by himself, no longer needing a chaperone when he was officially considered a young adult.

He was roused from his rest, what seemed like only a short time later, by the sound of a raised voice coming from next door. As that room was currently occupied by Gran Rox, Shail threw back his summer-thin covers and ran barefoot to investigate.

He arrived to find his grandmother, mother, and uncle all standing facing one another. Gran Rox was by a window with closed curtains, looking weary but wearing a resolute expression. Lisasin's hands were clutching her skirt, and her face was flushed; it seemed it was she who had disturbed Shail's slumber. Wengsper stood by the crackling fireplace, the largest source of illumination in the

37

room, looking grim. All three turned towards the sound of the door being opened.

"Is everything all right? I thought I heard shouting. What's going on?"

Shail's mother plastered a brittle smile on her face, forcing her hands to relax, dropping one to her side, and making a conciliatory gesture with the other. "Nothing, son of mine. It was nothing. We just got a little carried away in our conversation, that's all. Go back to bed."

Gran Rox spoke quietly from behind her daughter, but not so low that Shail could not hear her, "Perhaps he should stay. This concerns him, as much as it does us." His mother looked angrily towards Gran Rox, but the comment tempted Shail to disobedience.

He took a few steps further into the room. "What are you talking about? What concerns me?" When no one in the room answered him, Shail said, "I'm thirteen summers now, or will be tomorrow. Whatever it is, I can handle it. You can trust me." Shail bridled slightly at seeing all three adults share a brief, slightly patronizing look over his head.

Gran Rox noticed his reaction, and reached out to him. "Come here, grandson mine." Shail obeyed this time, afraid that any further refusal on his part would have him forced from the room, and she took his hand in both of hers as she sat in one of the room's two chairs. Uncle Wengsper remained where he was; Shail's mother stood near her brother with arms crossed tightly across her chest, staring pointedly into the fire. Gran began, "You like Tabirc, right?"

Shail was immediately confused by the seeming non sequitur. "Of course! He always tells the best stories about his days as a dragon rider."

Gran nodded slowly, "How would you feel about going to stay with him?" Shail's mother made a small noise, but offered no further comment.

Shail looked curiously between her and Gran Rox. Something was going on here. "That sounds great. But why would I do that?" There was another pregnant pause, and Shail was getting tired of the looks the three passed, clearly not being privy to an important portion of the plan. His uncle continued to look back and forth between the two women while wisely choosing to keep his own counsel.

Gran continued, "You've shown interest in becoming a Travealer when you've reached your majority. I happen to know the Masterhealer permanently stationed in the village where Tabirc has retired. His name is Conlun, and if you want, you could shadow him for a few weeks, maybe even a full season. It would give you good firsthand experience with a teacher, and patients, who aren't family."

Shail's eyes went wide, "I thought only Guild-associated apprentices and journeymen could shadow a master, and not until they're at least fifteen."

"An exception could be made, in your case."

Shail thought he suddenly understood the cause of his family's argument. "You set this up for me, but mother doesn't want me to go. Is that it?" He looked at his mother, whose face had become unreadable.

"That is part of it, yes." Gran Rox answered.

His mother sighed, holding her arms out to Shail, "You're still very young dear, and the place where Tabirc lives is not close. And a season is a long time for a boy to be away from home, from his family. For those, and other reasons, I don't think it's a good idea."

"Far away, and remote," agreed Gran Rox. "The only person you would know for miles around would be Tabirc. I would take you to him, then leave you there, and come back to get you at the end of your trial."

Excitement bubbled in Shail's chest. "But that sounds wonderful! Mother, please, I want to go! I'm not a child anymore, and if Master Conlun doesn't mind teaching me, I'll work hard to prove myself worthy of his time. Please say I can?"

Lisasin glared at Gran, "This is not fair, and you know it." Gran Rox simply looked at her daughter without speaking. Shail held his breath as he waited to see who would win this tiny battle of wills. He felt his heart surge as his mother finally dropped her gaze.

"If it's decided, we'll leave the morning after the Stallion Feather ceremony," Gran Rox said quietly. Uncle Wengsper sighed, looking resigned.

Shail's mother hugged him, kissed the top of his head, and gently pushed him towards the door. "Go get some sleep. You'll need your rest if you're to rise early and pack."

Shail squeezed her back. "Thank you, mother! You'll see! I'll make you proud! Thank you, Gran! Goodnight, Uncle!" Wengsper tousled his nephew's hair, gave his sister and mother a tired nod, and then he and Shail left them to make up on their own. Shail hoped his mother would not be too angry with Gran. It sounded like a once in a lifetime opportunity to him, his mother was just being over-protective. Gran would never set him up to fail; if she thought he could do it, then he would do everything he could to prove her right.

Chapter 4

Tiny and Tancer

Leeinn rose and dressed in an old, comfortable abbey habit. She decided to seek out the two Hopefuls, and offer her help if they needed anything before their big moment. Leeinn found the woman in the Dining Hall, sitting alone at her chosen table. She was stirring a bowl of oatmeal in a distracted manner, but did not appear to actually be eating. There was no sign of her spouse.

She looked up as Leeinn stopped and stood by the seat situated across from her. Leeinn arched one of her eyebrows as she gestured towards the bench, and waited. When she received the signal to sit, Leeinn rewarded the woman with a warm grin and the Hopeful smiled shyly in return. Leeinn busied herself with her plate, and her breakfast partner went back to playing with her food.

After eating in companionable silence for a bit, Leeinn tried striking up a conversation with her thus far silent associate. "I've seen you in passing since your arrival, but we have not had a chance to speak one on one yet. I'm Leeinn, daughter of Rumaru."

"Call me Tiny," answered the woman in a low voice.

Leeinn quirked her lips in amusement, for this woman would tower over most people when she stood. Even while sitting, she could easily look a full grown Isrenth in the eyes. "And your husband? Where is he? Is he not hungry?"

Tiny snorted, "Tancer has never been a morning person. Everyone else's lunch is normally his breakfast."

Leeinn giggled, "He sounds like my father. Did you have any plans for today, other than your ceremony tonight?" Tiny shook her head. "When you've finished your food, I can show you around the abbey until he wakes up."

"I would like that, thank you. Could you take me to see the winged horses or dragons? Either one, I don't care which, I'd just like the chance to see them up close."

Leeinn laughed merrily, "As you wish. Follow me."

Leeinn led Tiny out of the dining hall, chatting away as though they were old friends. Tiny easily kept pace with Leeinn's quick stride. She did not seem inclined to talk about her past, which was not unusual. Many people seeking acceptance were also looking for a fresh start. So long as a person was deemed acceptable by the Trinity, no

43

one was required to give more details than they felt comfortable sharing.

Tiny's focus seemed to be on the future, "If Tancer and I become Accepted, is there a chance we could work in one of the stables?"

Leeinn nodded her head, "I'll introduce you to Dragon Stablemaster Dooreg, and Winged Horse Stablemaster Wyntrin. They'll be the ones to take you on, if you can impress them." Leeinn eyed Tiny's not so tiny build. "I don't think you'll have much trouble convincing them."

Her friend looked pleased, "I don't mind working hard, and I'll do any job I'm given the best I can."

Leeinn and Tiny approached the winged horse barn amongst much hustle and bustle. Leeinn greeted each stable hand by name, quickly introducing Tiny to each person they passed. Every Accepted wished Tiny the best, and she always answered with a subdued '*thank you*'.

Leeinn remarked, "There should be a few mounts with their riders getting ready for their mid-morning patrol flight. And there's a mare who was due to drop her foal last night. If we're quiet, before we leave we can take a quick peek." Tiny's eyes grew large at this prospect.

The winged horse barn was large and airy, with thirteen open box stalls lining the left and right of the rectangular building, and a long stretch of open passage leading from the main door to the secondary exit at the opposite end.

"Do you really have so many winged horses, to need all these stalls?" Tiny asked.

Leeinn tried not to look smug, "The stable is just for those that are bonded to a rider, and each box has more than one mount assigned to it. But not all winged horses make for suitable mounts. Most live out their days in the del water meadows. The Stablemaster keeps an eye on all likely foals, and once they're weened, they are taken for preliminary training, to be completed if they show themselves capable as they grow."

Tiny tried to hide her horrified reaction, "You take the babies from their mothers? And they just let you?"

Leeinn was quick to explain, "No, no, nothing like that! Do you not know about the relationship between the winged horses and the dragons? The farmers and the fathers?" Tiny looked nonplussed, and Leeinn realized her companion had less knowledge of the abbey than she had thought. "Perhaps you should tell me what you do know, and I can fill in the gaps."

Tiny shrugged, "I know you need winged horses to open the dels. I know there are people here who pair with a winged horse, or dragon, to serve the abbey's needs." She looked up and chewed on her bottom lip, clearly searching her memory for anything else. "Oh, and both mares and stallions can fly, but only the male dragons, the drakes, are flighted."

When she offered no more to her litany, Leeinn nodded slowly, thinking of where best to start, "Most of what you said is true. No one has ever been able to figure out how to make a dragon egg lotus open without a winged horse. You can tear a del open of course, but the damage makes the nectar, petals, and fragrance go sour, ruining every part.." They were getting close to an occupied stall, so Leeinn said, "I'll tell you more about the dragons when we visit their stable. For now, let me introduce you to Rider Randoi. He'll be good to know if you want to work here."

They stood respectively outside the compartment, Leeinn rapping smartly on the wooden frame. A dark face with close, fluffy hair, like a black sheep, popped up suddenly from behind the stall wall. When he saw who it was, he smiled broadly, "Well, good morning, ladies. Nice to see you, Leeinn. Who's your friend? You're one of the Hopefuls, right?"

"Yes. Please, call me Tiny."

"You ever seen a winged stallion before?"

Tiny nodded, "I saw a long dozen at a city parade when I was a child. They were the most beautiful creatures I've ever seen."

Her words seemed a magic phrase, for Randoi slid open the stall door in a clear invitation for her to enter,

"This here is my mount Cloudhoof. He and I go back a couple years now. Sweet as sugar too, if you want to touch him. Just put your hand out flat, let him sniff you, and then you can rub his nose or stroke his neck; it doesn't really matter. So long as he's getting attention, he's happy. I warn you, once you start, he can be a regular nuisance if you stop before he's ready, which won't be this season."

The winged stallion turned from a hanging bucket on the far wall after hearing his name. His long muzzle dripped drops onto the clean straw that covered the floor, and both ears faced forward with interest. He was a gorgeous animal. He stood six feet at the shoulder, with fine white hair covering his body, rainbow wings, and yolk-yellow eyes. Most of his feathers were iridescent, separating into individual colors near the ends. Randoi gave his partner a thorough nose rub. Tiny watched all this with a look of longing. When Randoi stepped back, she hesitantly took his place next to the stallion. She did as Randoi had instructed, and Cloudhoof gave her hand a cursory sniff before lipping it in a friendly manner. Relief showed on Tiny's face, and giving a small, delighted laugh, she pat Cloudhoof gently on the nose. Unimpressed with her timid response, Cloudhoof ducked his head down so that her hand slid to the space between his ears.

"Ok, ok," laughed Tiny, "I get it! You want me to scratch *here*!" She obliged the stallion, and Cloudhoof half closed his eyes in pleasure.

Randoi said, "You're doomed now friend. He'll never let you leave now that he knows you're a good ear scratcher". They laughed, and Leeinn spoke with the Rider for a few more minutes while Tiny was absorbed with Cloudhoof.

Leeinn almost felt bad having to pull the woman away. "I'll bring you back to visit another time. We'll see you later Randoi. I'm taking her to see the new foal next." The three made their goodbyes, and the two left with Tiny looking back more than once in Cloudhoof's direction.

Leeinn led Tiny to the last stall on the right. She met Tiny's gaze, pressing a finger to her lips. Tiny nodded her understanding, and they simultaneously peered into the pen. The interior was slightly darker than the rest of the well-lit stable, but they were still able to clearly make out a dozing winged mare, with her foal sleeping at her feet. It had only bare stubs for wings at the moment; it could easily have been mistaken for one of its non-flighted cousins. Tiny made a slight, "*aww*", and the mare opened her eyes to look at them. She whickered softly in greeting, and her new babe awoke with a wide yawn. It began the laborious process of standing. Its mother leaned down to give it a light lick, and it nuzzled her back.

Tiny said, "The little darling! Is it male or female?"

Leeinn eyed the foal, then shook her head, "Can't tell from here, colts and fillies look the same until their first molt. This one will join the treasure in a week or so."

Standing on wobbly legs, the foal looked curiously back at the two women, completely unafraid in its new surroundings.

They watched for a while longer, until they heard the abbey bells sound lunch. Leeinn took Tiny back to the dining hall, and they found Tancer already helping himself. He waved when he saw them enter, and they both went to join him. Leeinn sat opposite the couple, shaking Tancer's hand when Tiny introduced her. Tancer hooked a thumb into the back of Tiny's belt; she was too broad for his arm to span farther than her hip, and she leaned comfortably into him.

He gave her a squeeze, "And where have you been hiding? I came down and couldn't find you, and I've had nothing to do but pine away."

Tiny looked pointedly at Tancer's half-finished plate. "Nothing to do but pine? Poor man, such trials."

"It will be nice once we're Accepted. I'll be able to find you a lot easier in this abbey than in the City. I'm telling you," with his fork, Tancer pointed first to Leeinn, then to Tiny, "This one can disappear like a shadow at noon when she has a mind to. Half our courtship was just me tracking her down day to day."

Tancer grinned at Tiny, but she turned her gaze to the table's top, the humor fading from her face. "There's no guarantee we'll both be accepted." She shifted on the bench to look at Tancer directly, "I know you said you would

49

leave with me if I was refused, but after seeing this place, I'm not sure I could ask you to do that." Tiny suddenly gave a great sigh, "I just wish you wouldn't talk like it's a given thing."

Tancer gave a conciliatory nod, "Alright, I'm sorry. I just don't have any doubts, that's all. I love you, and I know the Trinity will to."

"And what if they love me, but not you?"

Tancer shook his head, "Impossible. Have you ever known anyone who didn't love me?"

Tiny looked sad for a moment, "My father, for one. And mother, for two."

Tancer shook Tiny gently, "Only because I stole their beautiful daughter away. They don't count because their opinions are rubbish". Tiny gave a weak laugh. Leeinn cleared her throat, and her two companions broke off from their banter.

"Leeinn took me to see the winged horse stable. I met a stallion named Cloudhoof, and his rider Randoi, and even saw a day-old foal. You have to go with us if we get another chance to visit!" Tancer smiled at his spouse's renewed exuberance.

Leeinn said, "We were thinking of checking out the dragon stable after lunch. Would you like to join us?"

Tancer nodded affably, "Absolutely. Just as soon as I finish this plate."

Under her breath, Tiny said, "And two more." Tancer pretended to elbow her in the stomach, and she made an exaggerated *"oof"*.

Finished with lunch, Leeinn led the two Hopefuls to the dragon stable. The structure was both wider, and taller, than the winged horse stable, with each individual compartment being double the size of Cloudhoof's stall. Tiny had spent most of their walk describing her and Leeinn's morning to Tancer, but as they approached the building's main entrance, all of their attentions were drawn by a young copper-winged dragon closely following a much larger male towards a small group of people waiting inside the stable. There were three attendants, one adult woman, one boy, and one girl, the latter two both appearing to be around the same age as Leeinn. The two younger handlers went to the smaller dragon, and the woman went to tend the male.

"Do you remember when you said that only the drakes can fly?" When Tiny nodded, Leeinn continued, "That's not entirely true. Only the female dragons, we call them farmers, are unable to fly. Males, we call them fathers, and flyers, which are neither male or female, as you can probably tell from the name, can fly until they get too old, or become female."

Tiny looked startled, "What do you mean, 'become female'? Are they not born male and female, like all animals?"

Leeinn shook her head, "Dragons aren't born with a gender. They're sexless until they encounter enough unclaimed water meadow to make them female, or eat enough foal feathers to become male. We call our males '*fathers*', because their main job is to watch over hatchlings and foals alike, and the females '*farmers*' because it is they who tend the water meadows."

Tancer left off looking at the dragons in front of them, now being vigorously scrubbed with long-handled brushes, to add to the conversation, "But a dragon can switch between all three states throughout its life, right? A female can become male, and vice versa?"

Leeinn nodded, surprised that Tancer seemed so much more informed than Tiny, "It really comes down to their environment and diet. Water for farmers, feathers for fathers, and when neither are available, they become sexless again and search until they find a new home that has either, or both. It's how they keep the balance, each dragon becoming whatever is most needful."

Tiny pointed at the dragon, "So even that large ....
father there. He could become female, a farmer, and lay eggs?"

Leeinn hid a smile behind her hand, and stifled a small laugh, "That one has been female before actually.

52

Used to be one of our best layers, before he became a father." Tiny's eyes went wide, and she looked at the dragon with renewed interest. Tancer raised his hand like an eager schoolboy, and Leeinn pretended to call upon him for an answer. "Yes, Hopeful Tancer. You have something to add?"

"I believe the farmers produce two types of eggs. Once or twice a year, after mating, they will fill a nest with eggs that will eventually become dragon hatchlings. The rest of the time they're like really, really big beaver-chickens." Tiny gave an unbelieving snort. Tancer looked mock affronted at her lack of faith.

Leeinn giggled, "That part is true too. All adult winged horses love to eat the second kind of egg. I was taught that's why the dels look like dragon eggs when they're closed up. All part of a clever ruse to fool the winged horses into spreading the del pollen as much as possible. Even the nectar looks like yolk." A gong sounded, drawing their attention. "That's the signal to get ready for the Hopeful ceremony. I'll take you back to your rooms so you can change, then meet you at Hopeful Hall."

Leeinn was as good as her word. As she left the two Hopefuls at their door, Tiny gave her a quick hug, "Thank you. I want you to know I appreciate everything you showed me today. I hope we can soon call this place home".

Leeinn returned the embrace, "So do I, my tiny friend."

Chapter 5

Fishing, Without the Fish

Shail had risen early to wash, dress, and hastily pack a change of clean clothes, a basic first aid kit he had made himself, a few sheets of fresh parchment, two new quills, and a bottle of black ink. The last three were for notetaking while he shadowed Master Conlun; Shail wanted to impress him by arriving prepared. As he rummaged through the contents of his desk, Shail found the fishing kit Tabirc had given him for his tenth stallion feather ceremony. The sight of it made Shail smile. He opened the small pouch to check its contents. Hooks, lengths of tough line, a tiny reel, and a slim, extendable rod. They reminded Shail of the unlikely, but valuable lesson he had learned from fishing with Tabirc. He closed his eyes, and relived the memory.

When Tabirc had given him the kit, Shail had initially been rather confused, and more than a little dismayed. He had never shown an inclination for fishing. In fact, he hated to fish, because fishing usually involved killing, when you were successful. Shail thought he could defend himself if he were attacked, or fight to protect someone else, but otherwise, just the thought of intentionally causing pain made him feel sick. But Tabirc was Gran's oldest friend, and had long been counted among Shail's "uncles". Shail did not want to upset him by refusing his gift outright.

He reluctantly accepted Tabirc's invitation to visit the river and, "cook what we catch for supper." Tabirc chose his favorite fishing spot, a soft bank that was sheltered from the full brunt of the sun by the leaves of the surrounding trees in every season save winter, with a tangle of upthrust roots that supplied a convenient spot to recline and rest a pole while waiting for a bite. Tabirc sat down easily, resting comfortably cross-legged and bare footed. He had forgotten to shave that morning, and his face and chin were covered in a greying stubble that he absently scratched every now and then. Tabirc often groused that the hair on his head would soon end at his eyebrows. Still, he bore it well. When he and Shail had walked through town, a pretty woman half his age had greeted Tabirc with an affectionate kiss on his cheek. Tabirc blushed like a boy, and she had laughed with amusement as he stammered a greeting. He had politely turned down her offer to cook dinner for him, on any night he was free, hastily drawing Shail between them. He had held Shail by both shoulders like a shield as he made his excuses. She had given a disappointed sigh as they hurried away, Tabirc almost leaving Shail behind in his rush to the river.

Once there, Tabirc had relaxed, but Shail's anxiety had increased tenfold. He did not want to hurt a fish. He did not want to kill a fish. *Oh, all loving Amik,* Tabirc was handing him a live worm to use as bait! He expected Shail to pierce the worm with a hook! Shail woodenly took the offering. Was he being silly? It was just a worm, and it was normal for people to catch and eat fish. What would Tabirc think of him if he refused? Would he be angry? Would he tell Gran? Would *she* be angry?

Shail felt the worm wriggling between his pinched fingers. It was cold, and still wet with the earth Tabirc had dug it from. It desperately tried to escape Shail's grasp, thrashing wildly. Shail was struck with profound pity for the creature. It had no idea what was going on, nor could it guess its grisly fate; Shail wondered which would be worse, to drown or be eaten. It was just a frightened animal, and wanted to get away from the scary thing that held it. The scary thing that was Shail.

Suddenly, Shail could stand it no longer. He jumped up, "No! I can't! I'm sorry, but I just can't!" Tabirc reared back in surprise. Dumbfounded, his jaw actually dropped as he watched Shail release the worm in a nearby grassy patch. Shail felt his face flush. He knew he was behaving foolishly. He hung his head, and braced himself for Tabirc's rebuke. He could not have been more startled when the big man gently touched his shoulder.

"You alright lad?" Tabirc sounded genuinely concerned.

57

Shail shook his head, "I just ….. I don't like hurting things. Any living thing. Even worms." Tabirc furrowed his brow, and Shail rushed on. "And if I hurt the worm, I might have to hurt a fish, if I catch one. And if I don't catch a fish, then I hurt the worm for nothing. But if I do catch a fish, then I've hurt two things I didn't really need to hurt at all. We have plenty of food already, so fishing is just for fun. But I don't think hurting things is fun." Winded from his frantic explanation, Shail just stood, and breathed, and trembled. Tabirc looked at him for a long moment. Shail felt his stomach sink.

Finally, Tabirc spoke, "Alright, we'll fish without bait."

Shail blinked, sure he had misheard Tabirc, "Fish …. without bait?"

Tabirc nodded, "Then nothing gets hurt, and I still get to tell you my stories."

"So …. you're not mad?"

Tabirc cocked his head curiously, "Why would I be mad?"

Shail shrugged, unsure of how to phrase his concern, "Because fishing without bait means you definitely won't catch anything. Isn't that the point of fishing?"

Tabirc chuckled and shook his head, "The point is whatever you want it to be. If you're hungry, the point of fishing is food. If you're not hungry, the point of fishing is spending time with a friend. If catching a fish upsets you, then we just cut that part out."

Shail felt his stomach unclench, then he hugged Tabirc hard, "Thank you for understanding."

Tabirc laughed and hugged Shail back, "We're two wings on the same dragon, of course I understand." When they released each other, Shail returned the smile, before a niggling thought caused his expression to falter. Seeing this, Tabirc immediately asked, "Something else?"

"Will you tell Gran about this? Fishing with no bait I mean?"

Understanding lit Tabirc's eyes, and his tone turned reassuring, "What's to tell? We went fishing, and didn't catch anything. I've always had rotten luck, Rox won't take it amiss." Shail felt tears in his eyes. He scrubbed them away with his sleeve, not wanting Tabirc to think him a crybaby. Tabirc saw the movement, and rightly guessed the reason for it. "Never be ashamed to cry lad. Sometimes the best thing in the world is a good blubber. Anyone who says differently isn't someone you want to be around." Shail suddenly felt a calm come over him. Tabirc was safe. He was exactly what Shail thought a father would be like; not that he would know.

Shail nodded in response, "I was just really scared, and now I'm not."

Shail sat once more, and Tabirc gave him a long side-eye before casually saying, "Got a new story for you."

Shail instantly perked up, "Which dragon partner is it about?"

Tabi"I didn't say anything about a dragon." Shail gave him a *look*, and Tabirc relented. "My first, from when I flew as a scout for my homeland's air force."

"Her name was Indregas, wasn't it?," asked Shail.

Tabirc looked pleased, "So it was. Indregas,. Beautiful beast. Gleamed like a newly minted copper coin when I got her all cleaned up; a once-a-day chore she insisted I perform at least twice, if not thrice, daily, vain thing. Had more personality than most people give her kind credit for. They all have their quirks, of course, but Indregas liked to grief me more than any other dragon I've ever met."

Shail laughed, half convinced Tabirc was joking, "How does a dragon tease somebody?"

Tabirc held up the fingers on one hand, ticking them off one by one with the other, "She would steal my work vest and bury it in her favorite sand pit, leaving me to dig it out again. Let me tell you, sand is the worst. It's course, and rough, and irritating, and it gets everywhere! She thought she was the size of a lap dog, with no respect for personal space. Broke more than one chair, she did. And she had definite opinions on what she did and did not like, which I had to take into consideration, least I be faced with her fury." Tabirc completed his list of complaints by adopting a fierce expression of flared nostrils and gimlet glare. Shail supposed this was Tabirc's impression of his dragon, but ruined the effect by bursting into gales of laughter. At first, Tabirc pretended offense at Shail's lack of propriety, but soon began chuckling himself, his eyes taking on a faraway cast. "For all that, she was the best I ever flew. The others were good in their way, and I loved them all, but she was something special. She hardly needed training, just watched the other dragons, and then did what they did. Most you have to keep in harness with leads when they're that young, but my Indregas would follow me around in nothing but scales not a week after we were first partnered."

Shail tried to bring Tabirc back on course. "The story?"

Tabirc waved in a '*I'm getting there*' motion, "Well, Indregas liked the cologne I wore in those days. She'd steal the shirt right off my back and take it back to her sleeping spot, the little thief! I thought if I put some of the scent on her things, she'd leave mine alone. Bought a bottle just for her, tied with a little golden ribbon, 'cause that was her favorite color." Shail was touched to hear Tabirc had put such kind thought into a gift for an animal. Maybe that was why he had understood Shail's feelings about the worm. Tabirc continued his story. "I had intended to just give her bedding a few sprays, and repeat as the smell faded, but Indregas had a better idea. She snatched her present from my hand, ran to her stall, and up ended the contents, soaking everything." Tabirc shuddered, and Shail wrinkled his nose in sympathy. "When it was just a few dabs at my neck and wrists, the scent was pleasant enough, but a full bottle, all at once!" Tabirc pretended to swoon, falling limply back among the tree roots.

Shail had to ask, "What did Indregas think? I remember you saying a dragon's senses were all stronger than a man's. Was she affected like you were?"

Tabirc's face went still, his voice flat. "You'd think it'd be worse for her, wouldn't you?" Shail nodded obediently, and was rewarded with a swift, "*Wrong*! That silly scale belly loved it! And that wasn't the worst part!"

When the old dragon rider seemed content to let the tension build indefinitely, Shail finally begged, "Well? What was the worst part?"

Tabirc was obviously enjoying his audience's discomfiture. When Shail mimed a whack at his uncle, Tabirc finally answered, "My wonderful partner plucked me from the distant spot I had fled to, carried me kicking and cursing to the center of the mess, and dropped me." Tabirc scowled at Shail, daring him to find humor at Tabirc's unfortunate experience. When he was sure Shail was appropriately somber, Tabirc continued his lament. "The Stablemaster was furious! Unlike my wing mates, who thought it was the funniest thing they'd ever seen. I was made to throw out every stitch and scrub the floor beneath a dozen times at least. I never did get the smell out completely." Tabirc held his mournful expression for a moment longer, then took a seated bow, signaling the end of his performance. Shail applauded appreciatively, and Tabirc tipped him a gracious nod.

The sun had begun to sink by the end of Tabirc's story, and they decided to head home; Tabirc was staying with Shail and his family while he and Gran visited. They both slapped the dirt from their trousers, and Tabirc retrieved his fishing pole. They walked unhurriedly back; in the growing darkness, it was easy to see the town lights through the trees. They were welcomed back by Gran Rox, Uncle Wengsper, and Shail's mother.

"I don't see any strings of finned opponents bested in watery battle," joked Wengsper.

Tabirc winked at Shail in a conspiratorial manner, "Not today. Gives them the chance to fatten up for next time." Shail felt a glow of affection for Tabirc, but schooled his face into an appropriately rueful expression.

"No matter," said Gran, "Lisasin saved two plates, just in case you had your normal luck, Tabirc."

"Girl, you are Amik sent, and I blessed by his favor!"

Shail's mother laughed, "So you say every time I feed you." They had all laughed then, and Shail had known a moment of pure familial bliss.

Shail came back to the present. He dropped his fishing kit into his pack, figuring he could add anything else he thought of after his ceremony tonight, or before he and Gran departed tomorrow morning. He left his bag on his made bed, and went to knock on his grandmother's door. When she didn't answer, he cautiously stuck his head in to find the room empty and the fireplace cold. He decided the second likeliest place to find her would be the kitchen. He was right; she was sitting by a giant roasting pit that was large enough to cook a full-grown wild boar, sipping something that steamed spiraling curly cues. Already there were bubbling pots and pans on burning stoves, and sizzling meats on spinning spits.

She raised her drink to Shail when she saw him, "I came to get a cup of coffee before helping to bring breakfast out to the picnic tables. Want to help?"

Shail pumped a fist towards the ceiling, "Absolutely! What can I do?"

"You take those plates over there, and I'll grab as many forks and knives as I can carry." They each grabbed their assigned pieces, and headed out to the yard behind the house. It was a beautiful morning; pleasantly cool, particularly in the shade. The tables sat under trees Gran Rox had planted when she had first moved to this house, shortly before Shail was born. In his lessons on natural flora and fauna, Shail had been taught trees normally took twenty to thirty years to reach their full height, but Gran had used some kind of special fertilizer that made her gardens and orchards flourish in a way that seemed almost magical.

They put a set of their combined items at each place setting around the table, and people began to drift in in ones and twos, yawning as they greeted one another. One or two who looked particularly pale and bleary-eyed discretely asked Gran for a draft of her special "long night" tonic, which she doled liberally out of a skin slung over the back of her chair. They would swallow the entire cupful in one or two long drafts, thanking a grinning Gran before going to find their own seats. The morning sun was well up, and the leaves danced in the breeze, their shifting shadows dappling everything beneath. When everyone was gathered round, Gran Rox stood silently up from her place at the head of the table, and all speech slowly died.

When she had all of their attentions, Gran Rox spoke low but clearly, "Good morning, all. I'll make this short and sweet. Today is the summer festival, and our Shail will be getting his thirteenth horse feather tonight." Hoots and applause greeted this, many leaning over to pat whatever part of Shail they could reach. "So let us make the most of it. I plan to have the best time I can. Who's with me?" A roar of assent answered her. Those on breakfast duty brought out the fare, and the air was filled with the sounds of merry feasting.

Shail sat between his mother and Uncle Wengsper, leaving space in front of Gran for her many plates, bowls, and cups. Without further ado, she proceeded to sample each in turn, her expressive face making up for her silence while she energetically chewed. Lisasin went over the plan for the day, Shail only partially listening as he watched one of his smaller cousins pass half a sausage each to a black cat and blue merle dog sitting under the table. Shail's mother reached over to tuck a strand of hair behind his ear, smiling at him as she did so. His cousin raised her eyes until they met his. She looked guilty until he put a finger to his lips, and winked. She giggled, and then jumped slightly as the dog pressed its cold nose into her hand, looking for more food.

Shail's mother turned her attention to him, "Have you laid out your robe for tonight?"

"Uhh, not yet?"

His mother rolled her eyes while her brother snickered, "You are so like your uncle."

Wengsper made an affronted noise, "Hey! What's that supposed to mean?"

"Nothing, brother mine. Have some more toast." Wengsper pretended to huff, but could not quite keep the edges of his mouth from curling upwards. Shail could not imagine being happier. And the day was only beginning!

Chapter 6

Hopeful Ceremony

Leeinn found her father sitting near the entrance to Hopeful Hall. He leaned back against the wall behind him with his eyes closed, and his hands rested loosely on the knob of his walnut-wood walking stick. The small smile on his face looked especially tranquil; he almost appeared to be asleep. Leeinn delicately kissed his cheek, and the smile grew until it dominated his features.

"I hear your dels are a success, darling daughter. Not that I needed to be told. Even from here their scent is divine, my little wind chime." Leeinn dimpled, adoring all the affectionate names her father had called her for as long as she could remember. "Shall we go in?" he asked.

Leeinn laughed, "They can't start without you, father. If we don't go in soon, they'll probably come out to get you." Rumaru '*hmm'd*' in agreement as he got up easily from the low stone bench; at fifty-four, he was still limber as a man half his age. His long silken silver hair was in its usual plait, which he had garlanded with tiny del buds fresh from their garden. Leeinn linked her arm through his, and they entered the building in step. Her eyes were able to adjust almost immediately from the dwindling daylight outside to the interior of the hall. The benches were already filled, and everyone's voices were hushed in excited anticipation. Leeinn and her father filed down the shallow steps to the seat reserved for the Abbot or Abbess of Del Abbey. He returned Leeinn's affectionate cheek-to-cheek press, then arranged himself in a position similar to the one Leeinn had found him in only a few minutes ago. *'Such a dozer,"* Leeinn thought with tolerant amusement.

She went to stand by the curtains in front of the Del Doors. Leeinn looked to Tancer standing on the Hopeful Dais. Once they'd made eye contact, she held up both open hands just above her waist, palm out, and then waggled all ten fingers towards the ceiling, a common sign for good luck. Tancer smiled and waved back, but Tiny seemed rooted to the spot, her focus fixated upon the entrance that would soon admit each of the Trinity and their partners. The main lights were lowered, and there was a collective gasp as the darkness revealed the luminescent starscape that had been painted on the ceiling. The curtains began to slowly open, and all conversation within the hall ceased.

Two colored, lacquered wooden doors were revealed. Their arches were dominated by a frontal view of the head and torso of a green female dragon. Her arms hung down so that everything below her was within the protection of her claws. Next there was a brown male

69

dragon with wings spread protectively around the winged stallion standing within the curve of his front legs. In turn, the stallion's wings sheltered an unopened Sacred Twin dragon egg lotus, the only kind of del that was as colorful on the outside as it was within; the bottom half of the flower sat within the curled tail of the female dragon. The eyes of all three creatures were studded with gems: golden topaz for the stallion, dark-honey amber for the father, and exquisite blue diamonds for the farmer. They glittered in the dim light, making all three seem almost alive. The doors had been a labor of love, meticulously carved by masters alone. They mirrored the symbol on the Del Abbey pendants that adorned every Accepted robe in the room.

The pair of Hopefuls stood a few feet apart from each other, facing the Trinity's entrance. Leeinn pressed a cunningly hidden switch, and the doors began to smoothly, soundlessly open. She went to stand by the Hopeful Dais, watching as spotlights tended by hall attendants followed each creature as they entered the hall.

The female dragon was first, as was proper; the water meadows would not exist without the farmers. Leeinn heard startled gasps from those in the audience who had never seen a farmer before. She stood and walked on her two hind legs, balancing with her huge, paddle-like tail. Her front legs were only about half as long as her hind, and bore long, blunt claws. She still had wings, but they were small and fragile, obviously not used for flight. As she entered, everyone who had been seated stood and waited respectfully.

Next came the male dragon. Each of his four legs were tipped with four equally long clawed toes; his front feet had a single, smaller digit each, similar to a dog's dewclaw. His two large, leathery wings were currently held tightly against his body, their edges patterned to look like the feathers on a winged mare. He would not be able to easily open them to their full extent in the confined space of Hopeful Hall, but once outside, they would allow him to gracefully master the skies. He wore a decorative version of the saddle used by dragon riders when they flew with their mounts. It was made from polished leather, and sat just behind where the father's wings jutted from his back. Small silver bells were strung on the long, thick straps securing the padded seat to his body, and they tinkled musically as he moved.

Last came the winged horse. Leeinn heard Tiny draw in a quick breath, and then let it out in a choked laugh. It was Cloudhoof, looking splendid in his ceremonial harness. Behind him strode his rider Randoi in a dress uniform that complimented his mount's plumage. Next was the same woman who had given the father a pre-ritual scrub at the stable that morning, dressed to match the male, and finally a man nearly as tall as Tiny went to stand beside the farmer. He wore only a simple green abbey habit with his Accepted pendant on the breast. They arranged themselves in a row so that they and the Hopefuls faced each other.

71

Tancer couldn't seem to decide which to look at first, but Tiny only had eyes for the winged stallion. For a moment the tableau held, then a gong sounded, and the doors shut behind the Trinity.

The hall had been cunningly wrought so that the words spoken from the point of the Abbot's chair was caught and amplified to the entire assemblage, "Good evening, all. Please be seated." He waited until everyone had settled before continuing. "We have gathered here tonight to bear witness as two Hopefuls stand for judgement before the Trinity. Hopeful Tancer, if you desire to join Del Abbey, step forward." It had been decided beforehand that Tancer would be judged first, as he was the more confident of the two. That confidence was tested under the full weight of the hall's regard. He wavered for a single moment as a spotlight settled upon him, then lifted his chin, squared his shoulders, and carefully stepped in the small spaces between the open dragon egg lotus to stand at the point of the dais closest to his judges. Rumaru tilted his head slightly, as though he were listening closely to Tancer's tread upon the Hopeful Dais. The man and the farmer also stepped forward, close enough for the dragon to touch Tancer. She leaned over, and drew his scent deeply into her nostrils.

The man spoke, "Hopeful Tancer, my name is Uillhif, and this is my partner Deiga."

Tancer bowed before them, "It is an honor to meet you both." He straightened, and waited. Tiny looked on with an anxious expression.

"Why do you wish to make Del Abbey your home?" The two Hopefuls had been coached to have an answer ready for each question the human halves of the Trinity would ask as part of the ritual.

"This is a place of peace and plenty. My needs are simple. I only want my wife by my side, and a small space to call our own. If we are allowed to live here, I will work hard, and do all I can to make my brothers and sisters proud to call me family." Deiga looked at him for a long moment, then leaned down once more to give Tancer a long stroke of her tongue from his chin to the crown of his head, slicking his hair up in a comical dragon lick. Tancer looked stunned, but the rest of the hall broke into delighted laughter. A yes from the farmer! She and Uillhif returned to their waiting positions, to be replaced by the father and his partner.

"Hopeful Tancer, my name is Faydrah, and this is my partner Dehlawnay. What occupation would you seek here if you are accepted?"

"To be honest, the type of work does not really matter to me. I prefer to be outside if possible, but really, I just want to be near my wife. If I can work wherever she does, I will be content with the duties I'm given." While Tancer gave his answer, Dehlawnay had sniffed him, just as Deiga had done. He tilted his head, looking at Tancer first one way, then another, with obvious deliberation.

73

Tancer stood still after he was done speaking. Dehlawnay gave one final long sniff, then bumped Tancer's chest gently with his nose. The hall gave a muted cheer. Another yes! Only one to go!

Cloudhoof and Randoi took the center spot. They were formally introduced to Tancer, and then the stallion's rider asked the final question, "What will you do if you are refused?"

"I will leave Del Abbey. I will cause no harm upon my leaving, nor harm the Abbey or its folk by my actions in the future." This was the only answer that was the same for every Hopeful, and every applicant had to swear to stand by this oath before they would be allowed to become Hopeful.

Satisfied, Randoi turned to Cloudhoof, "What say you?" Cloudhoof walked forward, and Randoi motioned for Tancer to hold out his hand, palm up and fingers straight. Tancer did so, and Cloudhoof gave his hand a thorough inspection. There were murmurings of dismay when the winged horse turned away and returned to stand beside Randoi. Rider and mount shared a look, then Randoi expertly dodged out of the way as Cloudhoof reared onto his back legs, spreading his flamboyant wings wide, revealing brilliant, peacock-like eye spots and trumpeting loudly. Everyone was on their feet and adding their triumphant shouts to the stallion's. A third yes, Tancer was Accepted! A beatific smile broke over his features.

"I think you're in," Rumaru said dryly. His joke was met with appreciative laughter. "Daughter, will you do the honors please?" Leeinn had ascended the ramp built into the dais and held out a square, snow-white pillow with a Del Abbey Accepted pin placed upon its center. Tancer took the offering with trembling hands, turning it so the faint light reflected off its surface, making it twinkle like a new star. He stood stiffly, staring at his newly acquired pin as though it were a precious jewel. Leeinn understood, all Accepted did. Tancer turned and held his treasure up like a trophy. The audience loved it, and the roof tiles rattled from their returned roar. With dramatic emphasis, Tancer pinned his prize to his white Hopeful Robe, over his heart, and under the collar's four thick bands of blue, brown, beige, and brimstone. Tancer looked to his wife, and his smile faltered as he noticed she was openly crying. He started to go to her, but she shook her head and mouthed, "*Well done*," through her tears. Tancer nodded as he spoke without sound, "*Your turn*." Tiny gulped, then nodded resolutely. A spotlight followed Tancer as he walked back to his original position, then swung to Tiny. Silence filled the hall once more.

Rumaru spoke, "Hopeful Tiny, if you desire to join Del Abbey, step forward."

Deiga and her partner moved to meet Tiny at the edge of the platform. The farmer did not have to stoop nearly so low to sniff this Hopeful's head. Tiny stood

75

perfectly still, as though she were a statue carved from stone.

"Hopeful Tiny, my name is Uillhif, and this is my partner Deiga." Tiny bowed low, only able to whisper her greeting back. "Why do you wish to make Del Abbey your home?" Tiny tore her gaze away from the farmer in front of her to look at her husband, who smiled broadly when their eyes met.

Tiny's face melted, and when she turned back to answer Uillhif, she stood straighter and taller, as though bolstered by her beloved's belief, "I want to live in a safe place where my husband and I can grow old together. Del Abbey offers us the best chance at that life."

The tall female dragon lazily blinked, and gave a low, throaty call. Her partner said, "Deiga approves." Tiny gave the tiniest of nods to show she had heard. The farmer was replaced by the father. Tiny seemed a bit less tense now; her shoulders had relaxed slightly, but her breathing remained shallow and quick.

"Hopeful Tancer, my name is Faydrah, and this is my partner Dehlawnay. What would you like to do here if you are accepted?"

"Work at the stables!" Her enthusiastic outburst elicited sounds of approval from the spectators, and Tiny ducked her head in embarrassment.

Faydrah pat her partner's shoulder, and gave an exaggerated stage whisper, "Here that, another pair of hands to do your bidding." Another round of laughter, louder than before, and even Tiny joined in this time. Dehlawnay extended his wings to about half their full span, drawing all attention back to the matter at hand. Faydrah pretended to cough into her closed fist. "Well, we could certainly use someone with your size in the stables, if you please the masters of course."

A huge man with blonde hair that stood up from his head in all directions called out, "Give her to me! I've bales of hay for her to heft, and all the straw she can stack."

Leeinn gestured towards the man, "Hopeful Tiny, allow me to introduce Dragon Stablemaster Dooreg." The Stablemaster caught Tiny's eye, giving her a broad wink as he flexed his own massive bicep. The spectators loved his showmanship. They cheered as he sat back down, then returned their attention to the Hopeful still waiting for an answer from the father before her. Dehlawnay had calmly watched the entire exchange.

When everyone had settled, his partner touched his shoulder, "So? What do you say?" Dehlawnay bugled, and Tiny gave an obvious sigh of relief. Tancer cheered loudest of everyone, and his wife gave him an adoring look. Their obvious affection for each other made the people watching love them all the more. Dehlawnay and Faydrah cleared the center space for Cloudhoof and Randoi.

The stallion's rider gave Tiny a friendly wave, "Hello again! Well done so far. Ready for the final stretch?" Tiny set her jaw, and nodded. Randoi nodded approvingly. "What will you do if you are refused?"

"I will leave Del Abbey. I will cause no harm upon my leaving, nor harm the Abbey or its folk by my actions in the future."

Satisfied, Randoi turned to his mount, "Well then, how 'bout it Cloudhoof?" Everyone watched the winged horse with bated breath. Tiny held out her hand as she had done back at the stables, and the stallion politely nosed her fingers. As though he could not quite restrain himself, he dropped his head, and the crowd could barely contain itself as Tiny spent a good few moments patting and scratching the stallion behind the ears. When his rider gave a loud, "*Ahem*," Cloudhoof seemed to recall his surroundings. He stepped back to stand beside Randoi, and Tiny waited, as did the entire hall.

The stallion gave a loud whinny, actually nodding his head up and down! Tiny looked like she might faint, but Tancer crowed and leapt up towards the ceiling, clicking his heels and clapping his hands.

And that was it, Tiny was Accepted! Leeinn had readied her pillow with a second pendant, and held it out to Tiny just as she had for Tancer. At first, all Tiny could do was stare at the pin, as though afraid this was all a dream, to be banished at a touch.

"Take it, sister." Tiny's eyes went wide at Leeinn's words, but they seemed to break the spell. Tiny took the offering and pinned it to her robe.

The crowd turned to look at Rumaru, who had stood up from his seat, "Everyone, I am pleased to introduce you to Accepted Tancer, and Accepted Tiny. Welcome to you both!" The hall rang with the loudest applause yet. Tiny and Tancer hugged and wept joyous tears. Both dragons and the winged stallion bugled, just as pleased with the outcome as the people around them. Rumaru held up his hands, and the hall quieted. "Thank you, everyone, for joining us for this momentous occasion. Let us take one last moment as we near the ceremony's end to honor the Trinity." The three humans stood beside their mounts, beaming with pride. Leeinn, Tiny, Tancer, and the rest of the hall bowed to the farmer, the father, and the stallion. The Trinity, in turn, dropped their heads until their noses nearly touched the floor. The Del Doors opened, and the Trinity left the hall in the same order in which they had entered. When the Trinity doors were closed for the final time that evening, Rumaru spoke. "My thanks. A celebratory supper is available in the Dining Hall. The dining will be followed by dancing, then short sets from those who wish to share their talents. Please see Accepted Julip if you wish to add your name to the list of performers." The lights came back up, and the people began to slowly file out the large main doors. Leeinn went to her father's side.

"I think that went well," he whispered into her ear as he took her arm.

"I think so too," she answered.

Chapter 7

Stallion Feather Ceremony

After breakfast, Shail decided to join his grandmother on a
tour of the town to see the stalls that had been put up to sell
homemade wares. There were jars of jams and jellies, pans
of every kind of pie, pots filled to their brims with
simmering soups and stews, and a wide selection of fresh
fruits, vegetables, mushrooms, and cheeses. With food,
there must be drink, and there was no lack of variety there
either. There were country-brewed beers and cellar-aged
sherries, cordials, and wines for the adults, and chilled
punches and ice pops for the children. Women displayed
their delicate lacework and elegantly embroidered shawls
and scarves alongside sturdily woven baskets and rugs of
varying sizes, shapes, and colors, while the men proudly
offered their simple carvings, mostly inspired by nature,
and tools for farming and easy repair work. One or two of
the wealthier merchants offered unique items from faraway
lands; soft fabrics of silk and satin, incense with sweet and
spicy aromas, and all manner of trinkets and jewelry made
from foreign materials like light bamboo and dense

dragontimber. One stall sold nothing but furs, feathers, bones, and teeth from creatures of land, sky, and sea; the owner was so bedecked in his own merchandise that Shail wondered how he could move. Gran bought several small gifts for members of the family, including a cherrywood ring for Lisasin that emitted a tiny glow of light when the wearer twisted the top to the right, a two-in-one shaving and boot-blackening kit for Wengsper, "*I hope I'm in town to see his face if he ever mixes up the two*," she had cackled, a thin box of cigars she tucked inside a belt pocket, and a small toy dragon Shail had begged for that flapped its wings and roared when a person pressed a hidden button on its back.

"Shail! Hey, Shail!" Shail turned with a smile to greet his best friend, Tumatan. She and Shail had been born in the same summer, and had shared every feather ceremony since their birth. Despite the fact they were the same age, Tumatan was half a head taller than Shail. Her long legs and short dark hair usually made her look as much a boy as he did. He was startled to see today was different; she was wearing a white dress with wildflower embellishments along the hem, her hair looked freshly washed and combed, and a matching ribbon was tied around her temples. Shail could not help but notice the frock was more than a little faded; he suspected it had belonged to an older sister until she had outgrown it. It would likely belong to Tumatan until it could be passed to the next youngest daughter in her family.

"You look …. nice," he said awkwardly, not sure if he was supposed to comment on her attire.

Tumatan sighed, "My mother made me wear this silly old thing in exchange for some pocket money." She peered down at the dress as though it had done her a personal insult. "I should have held out for more. It doesn't even have any pockets!"

Shail snickered, "I just figured she hid all your pants."

Tumatan rolled her eyes and sniffed dismissively, "I'd just steal a pair off one of my brothers if she did. My ankles would show if I stole Syman's, but Justyn's would fit me better than they would him, now."

Shail groaned enviously, "ANOTHER growth spurt!"

Tumatan nodded, adding with amusement, "Mother said the same thing!"

Shail grumbled, "S'not fair."

His friend gestured around at the surrounding stalls, "Have you found anything good yet?" Shail showed her the toy dragon Gran Rox had gotten him, and she was appropriately impressed by its realistic roar.

"You?"

She shook her head, "Not yet, but I've only been here a short while.

83

Gran chatted with those watching the produce stands as Shail and Tumatan eagerly searched each merchant's offerings.

"Your tomatoes look even bigger than last years! My daughter would probably appreciate a few. Throw in a couple carrots too. And that watermelon on the end."

"Sure thing. This enough?"

"I think so, thanks. How much?

"For you, two coppers."

"Well! You ever have something fall off, I'll sew it back on for free!" She laughed when her friend gave her a *look* and muttered something about, "*the strange humor of healers*".

While his friend was looking at a small silver spyglass she'd picked up from among a table's collection of odds and ends, Shail stepped close to Gran and whispered, "Can I ask Tumatan to our house for lunch?". When she nodded her approval of the idea, he returned to his friend's side. "Thinking of buying that?"

"Maybe. Might come in handy. Look." She handed it to Shail. It was lighter than he expected. It looked similar to the one his uncle carried on his belt, which could be collapsed for ease of transport, but this one was fully extended as Shail used it to look out upon the Itoba River.

"Wow!" he exclaimed. He could actually make out individual sailors in the rigging of a ship he could barely see without the use of the spyglass. He handed it back to her. "Nothing would get by you with that."

She nodded and waved to get the stall keeper's attention. "Excuse me, how much are you asking for this?" The portly man she had addressed was garbed in a rich burgundy shirt, his belly slightly overhanging the waistline of his dark blue pants.

He regarded her critically, noticing the threadbare condition of her dress. "You've a good eye." He chuckled. "A little joke. It's called a unioculus, means *one eye*. I got that in the City. Something special, it is. Made from a metal called tytainiem. Exceptionally strong, can handle the roughest handling, and it won't rust. Course, being the trader I am, I bought it for a silver from a man who was selling them for five." Tumatan's brows formed a crease as she frowned.

She pulled open a purple pouch, loosened the pull string that secured it, and pulled out five small coins. "This is all I have sir."

The man looked at her palm, and shook his head regretfully, "Sorry miss, I couldn't be letting it go for only a handful of coppers. I'd need to at least break even." Tumatan sighed, returned her coins to her purse, and looked at the unioculus for a long moment before putting it back on the table. Gran had watched the exchange without

85

comment up to this point, but now stepped forward, holding out a coin held pinched between her thumb and forefinger. She handed it to the man, who took it with a slight bow, and Tumatan gasped as Gran picked up the spyglass and handed it out to her.

"I haven't given you a Feather Day gift yet. I think this will suit."

Tumatan's eyes welled with tears. "Oh no, I couldn't! That's much too expensive!"

"If it was just some bauble you'd probably lose before winter, I'd agree. But you've a good head on your shoulders, and that's a practical tool. I can respect someone who wants to be prepared for anything." Tumatan blushed and stammered as Gran pushed the unioculus into her hands.

She looked at Shail imploringly, but he just shrugged, "Want to come to our house for lunch?" His friend just nodded dumbly, too overcome to speak.

All three took turns using the unioculus on the way to Shail's house. "You can see the mayor's house! And the church steeple!"

Gran took over, "I think I see your uncle on the dock. I recognize his swagger. Has a friend with him. Do you know her Shail?"

Shail looked where Gran had pointed, "I can't tell, even with the glass."

"Nonsense, I can see halfway down her shirt from here. Ahh, I should have known, Marshawleene."

"She's nice to me," offered Shail.

Gran sniffed, "She's nice to *everybody*."

When it was Tumatan's turn again, she collapsed her unioculus into its closed, disc-like shape, "Hey, look! It's a magnifying glass too!"

"Any tool that can be used for multiple purposes is superior, if you ask me," Gran remarked.

"And you could start a fire with the lens, if it was sunny and you didn't have any matches," Shail added.

Tumatan looked at her new acquisition in wonder. "I never thought about it being useful for anything more than seeing far away things close up. Thank you, ma'am, I'll take good care of this.

They ate the midday meal on the same tables they had used for breakfast. Shail filled, and then cleaned, his plate, washing it all down with a cup of his mother's famous summer punch. Gran Rox sampled a little bit of everything, drinking tankards of tea, mugs of mead, and beakers of beer. Tumatan shyly showed her new spyglass to Wengsper, blushing prettily when he complimented her on it, and her dress.

After lunch, the adults sat around talking, lazily fanning themselves in the afternoon heat, while the children ran about playing tag and other such games. Shail had initially felt obligated to remain beside Gran, but was soon tempted into a spirited game of "catch the colt" among his many cousins and Tumatan, who was faster than all of them. When they were all winded from the chase, they sprawled on the grass and panted as they looked at the clouds, calling out shapes to one another. Tumatan shared her spyglass with everyone participating in the sky watching.

"See that one, there! Looks like a jumping rabbit!"

"Yes, I see it! Although, it could also be a charging bull. The ears could be horns, see? And that one to the left of it looks like a clover."

"I think it looks like a really comfy chair, with big, poofy arms!"

"The wind's blowing that one so it looks like a dragon opening its mouth!"

"No it doesn't, it looks like a fish going after a hook."

"It's a dragon you dummy!"

"You're the dummy!" A mild scuffle broke out between the arguing brothers, the winner sitting upon the loser until he agreed that the cloud in question did, in fact, look like a dragon opening its mouth, and the winner was ever so clever to have seen it, while the loser was the father of all dummies. Everyone enjoyed each other's company while the sun made slow progress from east to west.

When it was two hand-spans above the horizon, Tumatan said goodbye to Shail and his family, leaving to go home and change for the Stallion Feather ceremony. Her spyglass had been extremely popular amongst Shail's cousins, and she had generously agreed to leave it for them to use for stargazing after the ceremony. When Shail had asked if she was sure she wanted to be parted from it so soon after receiving it, she had shrugged and said, "I'm used to sharing. Besides, I'll be too tired to use it tonight, and I can get it back anytime." Shail had thanked her, waving to her as she ran down the road, then followed her example, climbing the stairs to his room to pull on an off-white robe that fell just above his ankles; all those expecting feathers would wear similar raiment. The collar had four thick bands of blue, brown, beige, and brimstone.

Shail and all of his attending family members made their way to the town's largest building. It was a multi-storied, multi-purposed structure, used for any event that needed a lot of space, such as town meetings, weddings, and communal ceremonies like the one that was about to commence. The outside had been lavishly decorated with colored lanterns that bobbed gently in the warm evening breeze. Shail waved to several friends he could see milling about with their own families, the followed his mother and Gran Rox as they filed through the front doors of the hall.

Shail bid his family a quick goodbye at the entrance, then went to stand with the other feather recipients on a slightly raised, square platform, while they went to sit among the many rows of spectators. He was pleased to note his mother seated in the front row, as were all the adults who also had children participating in the ceremony. Shail could see Tumatan's father, a large, broad man with permanent laughter lines around his mouth, leaning back in his chair to chat with someone seated behind him.

The lights flickered, and a loud voice called out, "Ladies and gentlemen, if you would please take your seats, we are ready to begin!" The town's mayor, a jaunty man in a saffron-and-seafoam-striped waistcoat and top hat, strode down the aisle leading to the stage, holding up his hands and waving them to attract the hall's attention. Everyone hushed to watch him perform. "Thank you, thank you all! Welcome to the summer festival's finale, the Stallion Feather Ceremony! We have many eager participants with us this evening, so, without further ado, on with the show!" There was a smatter of excited applause, and a wolf whistle or two. The mayor winked roguishly, "I see some of you started celebrating a little early.

A slightly slurred voice shot back, "We haven't shhtopped shhelebrating shhince yeshhterday!" This rejoinder was met with tolerant laughter.

The mayor rolled his eyes good-naturedly, and after a few, "*Yes, yes, alright my jolly gents, moving on*," began to call the name of each person gaining a feather, beginning with the youngest, and working his way to the oldest. After half an hour or so, it was Shail's turn. "Shail Touls, please step forward to claim your feather." Lisasin stood up from her seat, walked up the center isle to the stage, climbed the shallow steps, and met her son center stage. She presented Shail with a single stallion rut feather; the most colorful and highly prized pinion produced by winged horses. She beamed with pride as Shail accepted it with solemn dignity. He would add it to the other three he had at home, attained at the ages of one, five, and ten, alongside his nine, plain by comparison, mare feathers for the ages of less importance. His family cheered from their seats, and Shail's face broke into a wide smile as he triumphantly waved his three-foot-long prize over his head. Everyone in the hall erupted into gales of laughter and a round of applause. Shail and his mother took a quick bow, and he used the opportunity to quickly curl the cuffs and hem of his robe to reveal a prismatic lining. He returned to his standing place, Lisasin retraced her steps to her seat, and the next child was called for their turn in the limelight.

It was Tumatan! Her father Tasyn had taken the spot recently held by Lisasin, and offered his daughter a faux stallion rut feather fashioned from cloth. Their family was not as well off as Shail's, and Tumatan had six siblings, with an even mix of brothers and sisters. Tumatan did not seem to care; she took the feather gratefully,

91

hugging it to her chest in a way she could not have done with a real feather. Her family dominated the left side of the hall, and their boisterous approval prevailed for several minutes before the mayor could restore order. She laughed and waved to all of them, then bent over to roll up the edges of her robe just as Shail had done. Her father gave her a great bear hug before returning to his seat. When she returned to stand beside Shail they crossed their feathers like swords. They were children no longer, but young adults!

Once the ceremony was complete, Shail returned home with his family. Now came the feasting's finale, and his mother had spared no expense to make it special for Shail. All his favorite dishes were there, including lemon lotus! He ate until he felt he would burst. When the food was finished, and the tables cleared, it was time for presents. Gran gifted him her favorite knife, which had a dragon engraved on one side of the handle, and a winged stallion on the other. Uncle Wengsper gave him a red pouch filled with tinder and matches; he knew how much his nephew loved campfires. His mother had gone last, giving him the traditional Stallion Ceremony head band worn especially by those turning thirteen, woven from four thick cords the same colors as the collar of his ceremonial robe; the part centered over his forehead bore a stylized stallion with raised wings.

After his fifth jaw-cracking yawn, Gran suggested they both get some sleep, "I have both our tickets already;

we'll be taking the same ship that brought me here. I'd like to leave first thing, if we can manage to get away that early."

Shail had tracked down the last cousin to have Tumatan's unioculus, then put it, his new firestarter pouch, knife, headband, and a book he planned to read on the trip into his bag, making a mental note to ask Gran to make a detour in the morning on their way to the docks to say goodbye to his friend, and return her spyglass.

Chapter 8

One More Hopeful

The dining hall rang with song and music. Tiny and Tancer were the guests of honor, seated to the right of Rumaru, while Leeinn sat in her usual spot on her father's left. Now that she was Accepted, Tiny's appetite had returned in spades. She had cleaned three plates already, and was making headway into her fourth. Not to be outdone, Tancer had eaten enough for two men twice his size. There was a constant stream of well-wishers past the Abbot's table. At first, the pair would pause their feasting to greet and thank each person that came before them, but had given up and now simply nodded and smiled without stopping.

Gira was once again seated beside Leeinn. She was nearly breathless with excitement as she recounted her experience, "When I first saw the farmer, I felt so sorry for the poor thing. Imagine being a dragon, and not being able to fly! And then the father entered the hall, and he was so majestic! But best of all was the winged stallion! Never in my life had I ever seen such a beautiful animal! Are they all like that, or do you just choose the best for the ceremonies?"

When Gira paused long enough that Leeinn could get a word in edgewise, she responded, "They all look fairly similar, though Cloudhoof does have especially brilliant feathers. His rider cleans and oils his mount more than any other I know of."

Gira's eyes glittered, "So any winged horse rider could claim a mount as pretty as Cloudhoof?"

Leeinn considered how to answer this question. "I suppose, though the colts are typically selected more for temperament than for appearance."

Gira did not seem to hear Leeinn as she continued dreamily, "Imagine flying into the City with your own winged stallion. You could land in any square you wished, and every eye would be upon you from the moment you landed until you took off again. My sisters would turn positively green if I could do that."

"To be partnered with one of our winged horses, you would have to go through the same ceremony as last night. If accepted, you would then have to complete the two-year training program. It's no small task to become partnered to winged horse or dragon."

Gira looked almost petulant. "If that man with Cloudhoof can do it, who's to say I couldn't do the same? Maybe even better!"

Leeinn sighed, already regretting the track the conversation had taken. "I'm not saying you couldn't, I'm just saying it would be difficult. And even if you were partnered to a winged horse, which could just as likely be a mare as a stallion, you would be so busy with training and patrols that trips to the City would be out of the question."

Gira looked crestfallen. "You mean an Accepted rider never gets a holiday?"

Leeinn shook her head, "A rider can take time for rest, but they can't just fly off without informing the Stablemaster where they are going, and for how long. I can't see either master allowing someone to go to the City just for sight-seeing. It's a long ways off, and it can be a dangerous trip."

Gira looked curious at this. "What could be dangerous to a creature as large as a horse that can fly?"

"Bad weather, accidents, and sometimes bandits looking for an easy target on the long stretches between the abbey and the City. All could pose problems for a rider, possibly even lethal ones."

"There are a lot more restrictions to being a rider than I thought. Still," Gira looked dreamy once more, "A winged stallion that would carry me wherever I wished." Leeinn kept her face neutral and focused on the plate before her. They ate in silence for a few minutes before Gira asked, "What does a person have to do to become Hopeful?"

Leeinn wondered when her new friend would work around to asking this question. "It is customary to ask the acting Abbot or Abbess for their permission to stand before the Trinity."

Gira looked intrigued. "Does he ask a person questions? Are there answers to study?"

Leeinn shrugged, "Not that I know of, but I did not go through the normal process."

Gira nodded. "That's right, you were judged by the Trinity as a child. The youngest to ever be Accepted, right?"

"Mmhmm. The usual age for standing before the Trinity is twenty. There have been exceptions, like myself, and a few other special cases."

"Then I could become Hopeful after all! I turned fifteen this past winter, so I'm closer to sixteen now."

Gira suddenly eyed Rumaru, and Leeinn had a sinking feeling in her stomach. "Tonight is for Tiny and Tancer. The soonest my father would consider a new Hopeful is tomorrow."

She was relieved when Gira sighed and said, "I suppose that makes sense." Leeinn made a mental note to forewarn her father of the forthcoming petition.

The night grew late, and people began to leave the dining hall in search of their beds. After Gira had gone,

Leeinn laid a hand on her father's arm. "I'm ready to turn in. Will you walk with me to my room?" Rumaru scooted his chair back, bidding those around them a good night. Tiny and Tancer both stood at the same time, bowing respectfully to their new Abbot. Leeinn took up his arm, and they strolled slowly together through the quiet hallways.

"Your friend seems quite taken with our abbey," Rumaru remarked.

Leeinn huffed a laugh. "So you managed to catch our conversation. And?"

"I see no reason the young woman could not spend a trial period here. Perhaps some first-hand experience would give her a deeper understanding of the life she *thinks* she wants." Leeinn, "*hmm'd*". Her father chuckled. "I'll speak with her mother at breakfast and see what sort of agreement we can reach. Speaking of reaching something, here we are. Good night gosling."

"Goodnight father."

The next morning, Leeinn found Tiny and Tancer sharing a table with Gira. For a moment, she was not sure if she should intrude on the trio, but her doubt was quickly dispelled when Tiny caught sight of her and waved.

Leeinn smiled and moved to sit next to Gira. "Good morning," she said to each in turn. The trio returned her greeting in chorus. "I see you're making friends."

Gira beamed at Tiny and Tancer. "Yes, and we have been having a wonderful time talking about being Hopeful and becoming Accepted." Tiny and Tancer shared an amused look between them, and Leeinn wondered how much of the *"conversation"* they had contributed. "After our talk last night, I suppose you won't be surprised to hear I'm interested in becoming Hopeful myself. Do you think the Abbot would give me his blessing?" Leeinn hesitated, trying to think of how to best to answer without revealing that she and her father had already spoken about Gira's aspirations.

Gira noticed the pause, and her face took on a hurt expression. "You don't think he would."

Leeinn tried desperately to salvage the situation, "That's not it at all, really."

Gira's face flushed, and though she lifted her chin in challenge, her bottom lip began to quiver slightly. "Well then, what is it? Is there something wrong with me? Why not just say so? You said yourself there's no test. What's different between Tiny, Tancer, and me, that they should become Hopeful while I cannot?" Leeinn knew she was making an awful muddle of things. In anguish, she turned to their two tablemates. Her new brother looked simply bemused, but the change that had come over her sister sent a second, stronger stab of distress through her. Tiny's face had gone still and blank as a mask, and her eyes became flinty. Gira had proven hot-tempered, but Tiny's anger was all the more terrible for its coldness.

Tiny said in a low voice with no inflection, "Let's go ask him."

Gira looked startled, "Right now?" she squeaked, "But I ....," she faltered.

Tiny raised an eyebrow, "It's your life. Whatever you decide you want for yourself, I'll do what I can to help."

"Count me in," said Tancer. "The way I see it, you have two options." Gira gave Tancer her full attention. "Ask Father Rumaru for permission to become Hopeful ... or don't."

Gira let out her breath in a whoosh of exasperation, "That's it? That's your advice? Do it, or don't?"

Tancer grinned impudently, "Pretty much." Gira scowled, but Tancer did not seem in the least put-out. "So? What's it going to be?"

She shot a look over at the Abbot's table. "Maybe now isn't the best time. He's talking with my mother. I wouldn't want to interrupt."

Tiny looked at her shrewdly, "Do you think you mother will disapprove?"

Gira knotted her fingers together, "I'm my mother's heir, so I've had to undertake training to take her place when she eventually steps down from being the head of our family's trading business." Gira made a frustrated sound. "But I don't want to be a merchant! I hate keeping track of figures, the numbers get all mixed around when I'm the one doing the tallying. My younger sister Challi is the one with the head for columns and receipts. I'm hopeless."

"If you really think you'd be unhappy, why not ask your mother to take up your sister instead?"

Gira sighed. "That's not how things are done."

Tiny slapped her hand down flat on the table, making Gira jump. "If becoming Hopeful is something you want for yourself, don't let anybody stop you. Family can be wrong, and trying to change yourself to make them happy is a game you will always lose. Believe me," she glanced at Tancer, "I know better than most." He leaned his shoulder against her, but did not add anything.

Gira looked between them with surprise, "Did your families not approve of your match? You seem so happy together."

The pair exchanged a look, "Tiny's family, her parents especially, could not accept that their daughter did not want the life they had planned for her."

Tiny gave a small grunt, and Leeinn suspected his explanation had been a huge understatement. "I could never be myself, until I met Tancer. Now, I never want to be anybody else."

Tancer smiled at her in approval, "And I wouldn't change a thing about you, love." Gira looked dewy-eyed.

Tiny seemed to collect herself. "But we were talking about you. If you're afraid of facing your mother alone, we can go with you."

Gira looked indignant for a moment. "I'm not *afraid*." She squared her shoulders. "Alright, let's go."

Leeinn followed Gira, Tiny, and Tancer as they approached the Abbot's table. They stopped a respectful distance away, standing quietly as they waited to be noticed. When Gira's mother did, she looked surprised, "Gira. We were just talking about you."

Gira's confidence faltered. "Me?" she squeaked.

Her mother nodded, "Yes. The Abbot was suggesting you remain here at the abbey for a few weeks, to better learn its history and operations. I admit, such knowledge would likely serve you well when you become the head trader of our family."

Gira looked stricken, "O ….. Oh. Yes." For once, she seemed at a loss for words.

Tiny stepped up close behind Gira. "We're here with you, whatever you decide," she whispered.

Still eyeing her mother, Gira stammered, "Well, mother, the thing is, after watching the Hopeful Ceremony last night, and seeing how wonderful the abbey is, I was thinking of, well, there might be a chance that ... I .... might be allowed to become Hopeful?"

"*WHAT!?*" exclaimed Gira's mother. Leeinn saw her father stifle a sigh. She winced as, despite her best efforts, she saw they had ruined his subtle plan to slowly acclimate Gira's mother to the idea of her daughter being at the abbey. "Excuse my errant child Abbot Rumaru. She is young, and has not yet learned her place." Gira flinched at the reprimand in her mother's tone.

"And what if she doesn't like her place," asked Tancer quietly but firmly.

"I'll thank you to stay out of matters that don't concern you."

Before any more angry words were exchanged, Rumaru held up his hand, "Gira, would you take a walk with me please? The orchards are particularly lovely this time of day." Gira's mother looked as though she were about to protest, then held her tongue. Gira looked between the two.

"Well, answer girl!"

Gira jumped as her mother snapped at her. "Yes sir, of course sir."

Rumaru wiped his mouth and hands on his napkin. "We will speak later Nassine. Please, be easy."

The trader's voice was cool as she responded, "As you say, Abbot."

Rumaru and Gira left the dining hall, she glancing back nervously over her shoulder several times. Her mother stared after them both, her eyes and mouth gone flat. By unspoken agreement, Leeinn, Tiny, and Tancer made a swift retreat before Gira's mother turned her disapproval upon them. They returned to their table.

"Well, that could have gone better," muttered Tancer. Both Leeinn and Tiny murmured in agreement.

Chapter 9

Cookie Soup

Shail was awakened by a hand insistently shaking his shoulder. He rapidly blinked his eyes, trying to bring them into focus. His window was still dark around the edges of the curtains, and it took him a moment to recognize his grandmother's silhouette in the dim light of the campfire-shaped glow glyph he kept on a low shelf by his bedside. It flickered in a fair imitation of fading embers, but with a touch of Shail's finger, it was stoked back to full, flaming brightness, bathing the room in ruby light.

He yawned, pushing back his blanket as he sat up. "Gran? What are you doing in my room? Why did you wake me up? It's not even light out yet."

Gran halted his questions by pressing a single finger firmly against his lips while shaking her head. When she answered, her voice was pitched so low, Shail barely caught her words, "Not now. Get dressed. Hurry. We're leaving."

Shail felt utterly bewildered, and his fatigue fogged mind could not seem to make sense of her words, "Leaving? Now? Why? It's still nighttime, and I'm tired. And what about breakfast?"

Gran gripped him by the shoulder and shook him once, sharply enough to wake him fully. A hint of sternness entered her tone, though her voice grew no louder, "I will explain everything, Shail. Later, I promise. Just do I as say now, please." She let him go, stepping back and looking at him to see if he would argue with her.

He didn't, instead rushing to pull his pajamas off and change into the clothes he had worn the previous day. He grabbed his pack off the floor. Barely thinking about what he was doing, Shail swiped his glyph, snuffing it out as though it had been a real fire doused with a bucket of cold water. He stuffed it into his pack, securing the flap with a single, scratched silver buckle before slipping his arms through the straps. After he had finished tying his bootlaces, Shail went to find Gran, who had left the room when he had begun to change. He found her a moment later in her room, tucking what looked like a folded piece of paper under the clock Shail had painstakingly dusted a week before, balancing with one hand on the mantle. The pose made her look almost childish; a small girl stretching towards a jar of sweets.

"I'm ready Gran."

She dropped her heels to the floor, then turned to Shail and nodded, "Good. We'll each take one of my cases, like when I arrived." So saying, she took up hers, and Shail obediently grabbed the other. Gran motioned for Shail to precede her out of her room, and down the stairs. When they reached the bottom floor, Shail looked around, but no one else seemed to be awake. The ticking of a large grandfather clock echoed in the empty room. It was hard to believe the house had been filled with people only a handful of hours ago. Gran Rox didn't stop, but headed straight for the front door.

Shail was shocked when she opened it and began to walk out without looking back, "Where's mother? And Uncle Wengsper? Aren't they going to tell us goodbye before we go?"

Gran stopped, her back to him. She was still for a few moments, then turned and walked slowly back to stand before Shail. She put her free hand gently on his shoulder. She seemed to choose her words with care, "Your mother is still asleep. We don't have time to wake her. I've left a note explaining that we've gone."

Shail, more confused than ever, pulled away from his grandmother. "Don't have time? What do you mean? Why don't we have time?"

Gran shook her head, frowning. "We don't have time for questions either. You're just going to have to trust me. Do you trust me, grandson mine?"

107

Shail blinked. Of course he trusted his grandmother, she had never given him a reason not to. Still, this was all very strange. He suddenly noticed Gran Rox looked even more tired than he felt. Cheeks that had always been rosy with robust health were now pale and pinched; her mouth, laughing and smiling when she was not busy eating, was a thin line; but it was her eyes that shocked him the most. They were red-rimmed and sunken, with dark circles beneath, as though she had not slept in days. And when Shail stared into them, they looked uncertain, which was nearly as big a shock as her bizarre behavior; Gran always knew what to do.

That decided him more than anything else. "Yes ma'am, I'm sorry. I'll do as you say." Gran Rox sighed, her face sagging with obvious relief. She gave him a brief, one arm hug, then once again headed outside. Shail followed close behind, and it was he who gently closed the door behind them. He tried not to think about how he would not see anyone he knew other than Tabirc and Gran for a at least a few weeks. '*I'm too old to be afraid of leaving home*,' he thought himself. As his house faded into the night behind him, he swallowed hard, then quickened his pace to catch up with Gran Rox, trying very hard to convince himself he was also too old to be afraid of the dark.

Gran Rox led Shail swiftly through the summer night. Shail could hear a few sleepy crickets in the thickets that bordered the country lane between town and the docks, and in the distance, an owl's call grew first louder, then softer, as it winged its way home. Shail stumbled once or twice, hampered by his pack on his back, and Gran's bag in his hand, but each time managed to catch himself before falling.

Their walk to the docks seemed to cover double the distance of their day route, and the familiar path seemed strange in the pale light of the sinking moon. The brine of the river, a sharp contrast to the scents of dew-laden grass and night blooming jasmine, made Shail look up in search of ship's lights. Each craft tied to a pier had at least two lit beacons; blue on the bow, and scarlet on the stern. Those with rich owners also had small colored lanterns bobbing from their rigging. A sailor standing at the rail of the *Setting Sun* spotted them coming, and ran to meet them, one foot planted firmly on the dock, the other on packed earth, while in his hand he carried a fist-sized, golden glowing glyph ball hanging from a round handle. Shail though it made him look like a giant firefly coming to court them.

"Is it time then? We leaving?"

Gran Rox continued past him, heading for the *Setting Sun*, and the deckhand fell in beside her, taking the bag from her hand. "Yes. How soon can we cast off?"

"Soon as you and the lad are aboard ma'am. Only have the two mooring ropes to undo, then we can head down river."

"*Down* river?" Shail thought he must have misheard the man over the noise of their steps on the gangplank, which sounded particularly loud in the quiet of pre-dawn. Shail had gone with Gran to visit Tabirc before, and knew his grandmother's friend lived in a small village far in land. Down river would take them *away* from where they wanted to go, which made no sense at all. "Gran? Did he say *down* river?"

She spoke to him over her shoulder, "Just a little detour. Tabirc is going to meet us in in a town called Myrliot. I have a surprise for you, but you have to wait until we see him. Can you trust me for that long?" Shail nodded, thinking that it was a bit late not to, since the moment their feet had hit the deck, he had heard twin splashes fore and aft as the mooring lines were loosed, and he could feel the ship beginning to move away from the dock. The sailor that had met them handed the glow glyph to Gran, then left them to lend a hand in getting the ship underway.

Shail said, "I just wish I could have said goodbye to mother, and Uncle Wengsper."

Gran's face suddenly softened. "I'm sorry Shail, I didn't plan for things to go this way. I made you a promise to explain, and I'll keep it. Just wait until we meet up with Tabirc, please."

Shail felt that was asking a bit much, but he was suddenly too weary to care, "Is there some place I can go back to sleep? I'm really tired."

Gran led him to a set of small, but serviceable quarters they would be sharing. She tucked both her bags under the bottom bunk and hugged Shail before saying she needed to speak with the captain, leaving him to settle in. Shail slung his pack into a corner, curled up on the top bunk, and was soon snoring softly.

When he woke for the second time that day, Shail was not sure how much time had passed. Sunlight now poured in through the single porthole, and a cursory glance around the room showed Gran was still out. Shail decided to try and find her. He left their cabin, going back the way he thought they had come, intending to question the first person he found.

The corridor he was in led to a deck that appeared sandwiched between the twin blue lines of water and sky. He could see a safety railing running all along the ship's edges. He was intrigued by the view beyond, and walked over to put his hands and chin on the smooth wooden balustrade. The speed of their passage created a pleasantly cool wind that blew past Shail's ears. The Itoba River was wide, and they were currently situated near its center, far from either shore. Shail could barely make out the distant green bank as it slid by; this part of the river was lined mostly with forest, interspersed with large country estates, until the next port. Gulls like the ones from his hometown, ospreys, pelicans, loons, and other water birds were in great abundance, and all together made quite the raucous ruckus. The hot sun shone brilliantly on the water. The light dazzled Shail's eyes, and the smell of salt permeated the air. If not for the mysterious way in which they had departed, Shail would have felt thrilled to be here. As it was, his stomach grumbled, reminding him he had not had any breakfast, and judging by the sun's position, it was after lunchtime. That reminded him of his original plan to track down Gran.

Turning from the railing, he spotted a deckhand, recognizing him as the same man who had met them at the dock earlier that morning. "Excuse me, sir! Would you please tell me where they serve food on this ship?"

The sailor looked over at Shail, grinning at the question. "I remember when I was your age, I was always hungry too." Shail tried to look dignified, but his growling stomach gave him away. The sailor guffawed, and motioned for Shail to follow him. "This way, lad. We'll find you some tuck, and maybe Cookie will take pity on me too."

Shail fell in beside him, having to take two strides for every one of his long-legged escort's. "My name is Shail, sir. Thank you for helping me."

His guide chortled again. His brown eyes were full of good humor as he gave Shail a whack on the back that nearly winded him. "Name's Teegan, and you can lay off the 'sir'. Save it for the captain and mate."

Shail nodded politely. "Do you know my grandmother si... Teegan? Her name is Rox."

Teegan nodded. "Oh yes, I met her when she first boarded, back in Puqcrown. Nice lady, treats everyone nearly as politely as you." He gave Shail a wink to show he was teasing, and Shail decided he liked the cheerful man.

They reached the galley, and sure enough, there was his grandmother. She was leaning against a counter eating something out of a bowl, while a short man with a smudged shirtfront waved a dripping ladle, splattering the area with small spots of soup.

"And then he says to me, '*that's no dragon, that my wife!*' True story ... Oh, hello Teegan. Need something?"

Teegan doffed his cap and nodded respectfully. "Aye sir, I've brought the lady's grandson, per his request." Shail gave a small bow, and nearly fell forward as the ship dipped. Teegan grabbed Shail by the back of his shirt, saving him from a tumble. Shail sheepishly thanked him, and the ship's chef brought them each a bowl filled to the brim with something that smelled delicious, with a spoon and chunk of warm, dark bread inside.

"Get that in your bellies boys, it's an old family recipe. It'll put hair on your chest, and a spring in your step."

Gran paused with her spoon halfway to her mouth. "I certainly hope that was hyperbole just now, or I'll be borrowing your razor." Shail left off blowing across his bowl to snicker. Teegan had no such reservations, greedily gulping his portion, and smacking his lips after each slurp.

"No need to fret, 'tis only men it affects so. For beautiful ladies, such as yourself, it just makes you even more radiant than you already are, difficult as that is to imagine." Shail focused on his food and pretended not to see the broad wink the cook gave his grandmother. Gran Rox cackled, and even Teegan paused to chuckle.

They lapsed into a companionable silence for a short time, listening as Cookie whistled while he worked. Having wiped out the inside of his bowl with his bread, Teegan cast a hopeful eye at the soup pot still sitting on a simmering stove. Cookie reached out his hand. "That should hold you 'til supper. Off with you now." Teegan meekly complied, and Shail waved to him as he left. He sat and ate, listening to his grandmother talk with 'Cookie', for that was the only name the man seemed to have.

"I hear you two will be with us 'til the coast. I have a brother with a small pleasure boat, if you and the lad have any interest in fishing."

114

Gran shook her head. "That's a kind offer, but we won't be staying any longer than it takes to meet up with an old friend of mine." Cookie raised a curious eyebrow at that, but Gran said no more.

He sighed, then grinned roguishly. "Well, if you promise to make the *Setting Sun* your permanent mode of river travel, I can at least make sure you're never hungry."

Shail nearly choked, "That might be a more difficult promise to keep than you realize sir."

Gran Rox gave him a wicked grin, "Too late now, the offer's been made. And I accept! You keep the food coming, my good man!" The last statement she directed at Cookie, holding out her empty bowl and giving it a meaningful shake.

He made a low bow, "As you wish, oh cook's dream and delight." He seemed very pleased to have been asked for seconds, and laughed all the louder when Gran insisted on having another three slices of bread to go with it. He raised a questioning eye at Shail, who had stopped eating as the rolling of the ship stalled his appetite. He was just beginning to feel ill when Cookie gave him a knowing look. "I know the green tint of sailing sickness when I see it. I'll whip up something that should set you right." He turned to pull a few different ingredients from off shelves that lined the walls, and out of cabinets along the floor.

Gran looked on with interest. "I've my own recipes for such remedies. I'm curious what you use in yours."

115

Cookie talked as he added each item a to a clean mug. "Bit of ginger root, squeeze of lemon, a pinch of ash, but the thing that makes my brew special is …," Cookie unstoppered a vial shaped like a long feather, and allowed a single golden drop to drip from its tapered opening. "Del nectar. All's you need is a slurp, and you're better than new."

Gran's eyes widened appreciatively. "Genuine dragon egg lotus nectar. Cookie, how in all the many heavens did you get your hands on real del gold?"

Cookie looked smug. "I was thirty-seven seasons at the time; too old to be young, too young to be old."

Shail wondered at that, thirty-seven sounded plenty old to him, but Gran Rox crowed merrily. "Thirty-seven, *old*? Why, if I were thirty-seven again, not one of you young jacks could keep up with me!"

"I've no doubt, beautiful lady," Cookie sighed admiringly. Shail cleared his throat, and Cookie jumped ever so slightly, as though he had forgotten Shail was still in the room. "Anyway, there I was, in the City. I tell you, any tales you heard were true, and then some. 'Tis the most wonderous place, where a man can get anything for the right price." Cookie lifted the feather vial. "Including this, a rare fluid rendered from flowers grown far away from here. Powerful stuff. Here lad, bottoms up." Shail took the cup, giving it an experimental sniff. His stomach was truly unhappy now, and the thought of eating or drinking *anything* made him want to search for a bucket.

"Del nectar is not to be wasted, grandson mine. Down the hatch, as I believe the nautical types say." Shail obeyed, taking in a mouthful of the cup's contents. To his surprise, it was delicious. As soon as he swallowed the first mouthful, the churning in his gut began to calm. He drained the rest of the liquid, catching the final drops on his tongue. "Better?"

"Yes ma'am. Thank you sir, I feel much better."

Cookie winked at him. "At your service, lad. Don't mention it."

Shail looked to Gran. "Now that we're on our way, can you give me hint about my surprise?"

"Oh, I love surprises. Go on then, give us a hint marm. Bet I can figure out what it is."

Gran looked at them both with exasperation. "No hints! The point of a surprise is to *be* surprised."

Shail and Cookie exchanged a look full of long-suffering commiseration. "Sorry lad, I tried."

Shail sighed. "In that case, may I be excused? I want to see the rest of the *Setting Sun.*"

Gran nodded, making a shooing motion with her hand. "Stay out of the crew's way. Come find me for dinner."

"Yes ma'am. Goodbye sir, thanks again." Cookie waved before turning back to his cutting board.

As Shail left the room, he could hear sounds of chopping as Cookie spoke to Gran, "That reminds me of another story. There was this one time …."

Chapter 10

Abbey Life

Leeinn, Tiny, and Tancer finished their meal and piled all their used plates, cups, and cutlery in the center of the table for the servers to take back for washing. When Leeinn asked Tiny and Tancer their plans for the day, they looked at each other, then back to her, both shrugging in unison.

Tancer said, "I wouldn't say no to a nap."

"But you just woke up," laughed Leeinn.

"Eating is hard work. So is digesting, and both are best done in peace." Tancer leaned back slightly and rested both hands across his stomach, closing his eyes as though he meant to fall asleep right then and there.

Tiny rolled her eyes in mock exasperation, but she could not quite keep the edges of her mouth from twitching upwards. "At our ceremony, one of the Stablemasters said he would take us on if we became Accepted. I thought maybe we could find him, see if he was serious."

Tancer's eyes popped open as he groaned. "Our first day, and you already want to start working? There will be plenty of time for that. A lifetime, in fact." He rested his elbows on the table. "If a nap is not an option, then I'd like to see more of this place, now that it will be our home."

"Alright," Tiny conceded. "That's not a bad idea, even though I think we would impress the Stablemaster if we sought him out first."

Leeinn said, "Why not do both? I can take you on a tour of the abbey that ends at the dragon stable. Master Dooreg will likely be somewhere about the place, and if not, someone should be able to point us in the right direction."

Tancer nodded, "Sounds like a good compromise. Where would you suggest we start?"

Leeinn considered, "My father and Gira will probably be in the orchards for a while, so I'd suggest saving that area for later. Let's see. On the grounds there's the abbey pond, the fruit fields, vegetable gardens, and greenhouses. Inside there's the infirmary, the library, the kitchens, and larders. There's an entire floor under the abbey for cellars, storage, and safe rooms. You'll be stationed at the watchtower soon enough, so we can skip that for now. There's the abbey school. You'll be taking general lessons there that will teach you our history and lore, as well as instruct you on basic abbey operations."

"I knew this place was large, but you make it sound like the City itself!"

"Del Abbey needs all those things to support the people who live here. We're able to make or grow just about everything we need. I haven't even mentioned any of our many halls. If you are interested, there's the music hall and art hall. If you lean more towards practical skills, there's the blacksmith hall, the potter's hall, the weaver's hall ...."

Tiny's eyebrows had climbed nearly to her hairline, "If you have all that, what could you possibly not do for yourselves?"

"The land claimed by the abbey is poor in metals and stone. We also cannot make large quantities of glass. You'll have noticed at mealtimes that our cups and plates and bowls are mostly kiln-hardened earthenware. To obtain the supplies we need to make or repair our tools, buildings, windows and the like, the abbey has trading contracts with merchant families, like Gira's. In return, they are provided with the abbey's bounty of food, flowers, and feathers."

Tancer looked at Tiny. "Did any particular place in that long list strike your fancy?"

Tiny's gaze wandered upwards as she gave the choice some thought. "I wouldn't mind seeing the view from the ramparts. There were times on the way here when all I could see was road ahead, road behind, and trees to either side. And it's the highest we'll get without wings or the watchtower."

When Tancer nodded in agreement, Leeinn smiled, "Walltops it is, and I can show you one of my favorite places in the abbey."

Leeinn led her friends through halls filled with activity. People greeted one another, carried on conversations by the walls, out of the way of foot traffic, and there was an industrious squad wiping down surfaces, sweeping floors, and making note of anything in need of repair. "If you want, we can request you both be assigned to the same work squad as me. Your team works on an assigned chore to keep the abbey clean and running, and the chore changes day to day, so you get a chance to learn how to do everything. I like gathering from the berry bushes best, and my father loves the kitchens."

Tiny and Tancer both looked surprised. "Even the Father Abbot is expected to work?"

"Of course. It's his job to lead the abbey. How would he be a good leader if he didn't work like everybody else?"

Tancer reached up to play punch Tiny's shoulder, "What'd I tell you? This place is perfect!"

Tiny pursed her lips, "No place is perfect, but things that seem too good to be true often are. Not," she quickly said to Leeinn, "that I'm not grateful to be here." She winced, "I meant no offense."

Leeinn waved the apology away. "Even good places can be scary when you're first getting to know them. I think in time you'll see that the abbey is what it seems."

Tancer said, "I, for one, have no doubts. Unless you're hiding something nasty in the dungeons?"

Leeinn could not help but laugh. "No dungeons in Del Abbey, the dragons wouldn't tolerate it."

Tiny looked curious, "What do you mean, wouldn't tolerate it?"

"The dragons are very sensitive to negative energy. Winged horses too. They could not live anywhere that was filled with discontent. That's the most popular theory on why the Trinity rejects some Hopefuls. They are able to sense something inside a person that would pose a threat to the abbey."

"You mean it really was the dragons and stallion judging us? I sort of though their riders gave them a secret sign, depending on whether the Abbot wanted a person to become Accepted."

Leeinn blinked a few times, shocked at the suggestion of such subterfuge. "No …. No, I know that's not the case. I've seen people everybody thought was sure to be accepted, be refused. Even some of the children born and raised here are refused when they come of age."

Tiny looked sad. "A perfect place that throws people out of the only home they've ever known." Tancer winced at the dejected tone in his wife's voice.

Leeinn gave her a comforting touch on the arm, "It is sad when a person is refused, but no one is just *thrown out*. When the child of an Accepted reaches fifteen of their season, they go away from the abbey for three months. Sometimes it's to stay with a working family, like Gira's, or to apprentice in one of the guilds in the City. And they are given a chit that will allow them to draw emergency funds from the abbey's credit line at any bank. This time allows each person to see a bit of the world, so they can better judge if abbey life suits them. Some choose to stay in the City, rather than returning to become Hopeful. My father had a sister that willingly chose to leave the abbey when her husband was refused, even though *she* had been Accepted. I think they still exchange letters sometimes, but I've never met her."

"You didn't go stay with her when you turned fifteen? Or have you not gone yet?"

"Since I became Accepted as a toddler, I was allowed to skip the usual process. I've never been farther than the del water meadows."

Tiny gave her a guarded glance, "I'm not sure they did you any favors."

Leeinn shrugged, "My father asked if I was interested. I told him I didn't see the point. What could be better than Del Abbey?"

"What indeed? Now, about those walltops ….." Tancer took several steps towards the abbey wall, looking back at Leeinn and Tiny like a dog begging for a walk.

His wife snorted and rolled her eyes towards Leeinn, "Probably not a good sign when *that one* is keeping *us* on track." Leeinn laughed.

"I heard that!"

"You were meant to, dear. Now come along." Tancer pretended to sniff in a snooty manner, but almost immediately took up Tiny's hand as they walked to the wall.

"Do either of you mind stairs?" They both shook their hands, so Leeinn pointed to the wall corner closest to them. "Then up we go." They climbed all three flights, and none were out of breath for more than a minute or two when they arrived at the top. "It would take too long to complete a full circuit of the ramparts. We'll visit the spot I told you about. It has the best view of the del water meadows, and we'll probably see some dragons and winged horses." Tiny's eyes grew bright upon hearing this. Tancer spotted her excitement and grinned.

Leeinn led them to said spot, shaded by a slanted tile roof that also gave protection from the frequent

125

rainstorms. She watched their faces as Tiny and Tancer gazed for the first time upon the water meadows behind the abbey. From their vantage point, they had an unobstructed view of the wet westland. Both of the new Accepted *ooh*ed and *ahh*ed appreciatively, pointing out different features to each other.

"Look at the size of that dragontree! You could built a whole house with just the timber you'd get from its trunk alone, and a roof from all its branches!"

"Forget the trees, Tancer; look at the tree line!"

Tancer gasped. "Are those .... Winged horse foals?"

"Yes! Oh, aren't they darling? And so fast! They can't be more than a few months old, I can't even make out any feathers from here, but they'd leave you or me eating their dust!" An indignant cry came from one of the runners. "Oh, he didn't like that! The other bit too hard, I expect."

An answering low rumble, like rolling thunder, came from beyond their line of sight. A moment later, a male dragon became visible as he walked out from the shade of the trees. When he arrived on scene, all activity stilled. The colt who had cried ran up to stand between the father's front legs. The dragon gave it a quick lick along its back, then settled into a comfortable laying position, his wings held half-open and moving slightly. With evident glee, all the foals rushed upon him. Some pranced prettily upon their back legs in front of him, while others leapt back and forth over the length of his tail. Another favorite game seemed to be "dash under father's wings", which were high enough to clear their heads as they started, but the drooping edges forced them to duck their heads and push past, the canvas of his wings trailing along their backs.

"He's so gentle with them," murmured Tiny. "Ouch, that one just accidently kicked him in the eye while he was nosing the one next to it. He's big enough to eat them in two bites, and not a sign of temper."

"Foal sitting is his main job. The winged horses that can fly cover quite a bit of distance every day, leaving those that can't fly in the care of the fathers."

Tiny searched the surrounding area with her eyes. "I only see the one."

"They are surprisingly hard to see, when they're not out in the open, like that one. A mild disturbance like that would not warrant the attention of more than one father, but you can be assured they are close enough to reach the foals quickly."

"What do they do when they're not watching the foals?"

"Eat, sleep, clean themselves, check on the farmers. A father is naturally compelled to protect winged horse foals. Nothing else seems to hold their attention for long."

"So they don't hunt? But if they don't eat meat, what else could such large creatures live on?"

"It's not that they don't eat meat, most dragons are actually rather fond of fish. They eat closed dragon egg lotus, and dels that have had their nectar drained by a winged horse. And they keep their home clean by eating all the feathers shed by the winged horses. Otherwise we'd all be ankle deep in fluff."

Tancer pulled a face. "Feathers sound like an acquired taste."

"From other animals, maybe. Our treasure's sheddings have always tasted sweet to me."

"*You* eat the feathers too?"

"Oh yes, my father is famous for his feather pudding."

Tancer shook his head. "Even I didn't know that. Will those foals down there get their feathers soon?"

Leeinn nodded. "That group is about six months old. Winged horses grow their first set of feathers after a few months, and they fly by the end of their first year. If they are partnered with a rider, their ground time is vital for bonding and training. Once an animal is bigger than you and can fly away, it's all but impossible to force them to do anything they don't want to."

Tancer looked thoughtful. "I wonder if that's where non-winged horses came from. Foals that couldn't fly, but figured out how to survive despite the handicap."

Tiny smiled at him fondly, "If you don't fit in, make your own family out of misfits, is that it?"

"Worked well enough for us," he said as he gave his wife a wink.

She snorted, turning her attention back to the dragon. He seemed to be enjoying the attention being lavished upon him by his adoring treasure. The foals climbed upon his back and leapt off, and frisked around his body; there was no end to their play. "I could watch them all day," murmured Tiny.

"Only if they serve lunch up here," teased Tancer. The trio's good humor was doused a moment later by a voice they all recognized from breakfast.

"If you are not busy, Accepted, may I have a word?" Her words may have been phrased as a question, but it was clear that Gira's mother intended to speak with them, whether they wish it or no.

"Trader Nassine!" Leeinn bowed swiftly. "Of course! How may we serve ma'am?" Tiny and Tancer had copied her respectful gesture, and now stood looking decidedly uncomfortable.

"I would like to discuss my daughter. In particular, where she got the idea of becoming Hopeful."

"Tancer and I were eating breakfast this morning, and Gira sought us out. She was already interested in becoming Hopeful, we just answered her questions."

Gira's mother looked unconvinced, "Indeed? Well, be that as it may, the fact is, she is established as my heir, and has been in training since she reached thirteen winters. She does not need friends filing her heads with flights of fancy. I am sure Father Rumaru will agree with me, and set Gira straight."

Leeinn shot Tiny and Tancer a warning glance before replying, "I am sure my father will know what is best. Is there anything else, Trader Nassine?" When Gira's mother merely scowled at them, Leeinn tugged on the sleeves of her companions, pulling them towards the stairs, "In that case, we should be going. Good day ma'am." Leeinn thought she heard the woman give an irritated huff, but did not stop walking until they had reached the bottom of the stairs. Only then did all three give a sigh of relief.

"Well, she's …. intense," offered Tancer.

"Certainly used to getting her own way. I wonder what Father Rumaru will have to say. Do you think …"

"Leeinn? Hey, Leeinn!" They turned to see a pair of small girls running towards them. They skid to halt, then shouted as one, "The Abbot wants to see you!"

"See me? Just me?"

"Didn't say! He's still in the orchard, want us to show you where?" Leeinn nodded.

"Yes, please. You two can come with us," she said to Tiny and Tancer.

"Lead on!"

Chapter 11

The Raven's Roost

Shail left Gran and Cookie to go exploring. The *Setting Sun* was the largest ship Shail had ever been on. She was a handsome craft; her hull was made primarily of dragontimber, the hardiest of woods, which meant this vessel would easily outlive Shail *and* any children he might sire. Her sails were as Gran had described them. It looked like someone had cut a giant orange in half, then painted long streaks of juice out from it. She had three tall masts, and Shail wondered what it must look like from way up there. He imagined himself clinging to their tops, his head among the clouds, the wind streaming past his ears, as he swayed gently with the ship's movement on the water. It would be so peaceful, so utterly easy, above it all.

"Whatcha lookin at?"

Shail jumped at the voice that had spoken right next to his ear, "What?"

"I said, whatcha lookin at? S'nuthin up there but Polkstone in the raven's roost, and he's nuthin to stare at." The person speaking to Shail was a girl even smaller than he was, though the way she carried herself made her age difficult to guess. Her skin was nearly the same shade as the ship, and she had shaved both sides of her head so that only a strip of long hair remained, like a winged horse's mane. She wore clothing similar to Teegan's, a beige baggy shirt and tan trousers with patched elbows and knees, the ends of both getting a bit ragged; and her feet were bare. She stared intently at Shail's face, clearly expecting an answer from him.

"Oh …. Uh, nothing. That is, I was looking at the platform at the top of the mast. Did you call it a raven's roost?" When she nodded, he added, "Have you ever been up there?"

"Course, part of my duties"

"Duties?"

"S'right."

"Then, you're part of the crew?"

She looked at him like he might be a bit dim, "Why's would I have duties if'n I weren't crew?"

"I … suppose that's a good point." Fumbling for a way to recover, Shail asked, "What is your name?"

"Moyrah Magwynz," she said, and stuck out her hand.

Shail took it, surprised by the callouses on her palms. "I'm Shail Touls."

After a firmer handshake than he had expected from such a small girl, she took a step back and eyed him up and down. "Heard you and your gran was the reason we left port before sunup."

"I guess so, though I don't know why we had to leave so early."

Moyrah scratched the buzzed section of her scalp. "Captain wouldn't have agreed if there weren't a good reason. 'spect that's all we need to know."

"You know the Captain well?"

Moyrah grinned, her white teeth contrasting pleasantly with her dark skin. "Could say that. On board, I call him Captain. But on shore leave, he's my dah."

"You mean you get to sail with your father on his ship, as part of his crew? How old are you?" Shail winced at the directness of his blurted question.

Moyrah did not seem to take offense. "This winter will be my thirteenth."

"But how are you allowed to work when your still a child?"

Now Moyrah bristled. "Watch it, you! Passenger or no, I'll biff anybody says I'm not worth my salt."

Shail held up his hands placatingly. "I'm sorry, that came out wrong. I just thought, well, that a person wasn't given any kind of responsibility before their thirteenth stallion feather ceremony."

Moyrah sniffed dismissively, in a way that suddenly reminded Shail of Tumatan. "Shows what you know. Maybe it's that way on land, but I've been on the *Setting Sun* since I was ten winters. And let me tell you, that first season aboard, I didn't think I was gonna make it! You haven't been cold 'til you've been soaked to the skin with sea spray during a coastal squall in the middle of snow season. See this?" Moyrah turned around and pulled up her shirt so that Shail could see her lower back, where a pale, puckered scar almost looked like the hilt of a sword, with her spine its blade. "Got that in a real bad storm. Waves were tall as the *Setting Sun* herself, wind howled so you couldn't hear yourself think, and raining so hard you couldn't keep your eyes open. I got thrown against the guardrail, stunned me so's I couldn't move even to save myself. Lucky for me that Teegan saw what had happened, and risked his skin to save mine." She ran a forefinger from the left side of her scar to the right. "Not so lucky was the fact that Teegan had lost the sheath for his belt knife in a card game the week before. Got me good when he grabbed me." She dropped her shirt and turned back to face Shail.

135

"He was more upset 'bout it than I was. Doc patched me up, and then made me scrub all my blood off his floor."

"And you father kept you on board, even after almost losing you?"

"*Captain* don't play favorites," said Moyrah, stressing the title. "He wouldn't have a crew if he set every sailor ashore what almost went over."

They moved to stand by the railing as three burly men, and one woman nearly as large, passed them carrying buckets full of water. Shail sniffed, and was surprised to catch a hint of orange. He pointed after them. "What are they doing?"

"They're on scrub duty today. They fill those buckets with cleanser, carry them to whatever section of the ship they're scrubbing, shine the place up, dump the dirty water over, rinse and repeat."

"Is it some sort of punishment?"

"Naw, just something that has to be done every day, so the ship stays clean, and we don't get bugs."

"Oy, Moy!" A man called out as he approached them. Shail wondered if he was the captain, for he was dressed in a fine dark blue shirt tucked into loose black trousers.

Moyrah entire demeanor changed. Her back straightened, and her eyes became focused and alert. "Sir?"

136

"You feed Klanio?"

"Yes sir, he wouldn't let me forget sir!"

"Brush him?'

"Aye sir, 'til there wasn't a loose hair in his coat, and his whiskers curled, sir."

"Good job. Already found the other sprat on board, no surprise there. Shail was it?" This last bit was directed at Shail.

"Yes sir."

"Known your gran for a few years now. Good woman. Sensible."

Under her breath, Moyrah said, "Cookie certainly thinks so." Shail struggled to keep his face straight.

The man gave her a level look, then his own face broke into an amused smile. "He could do worse." He stuck his hand out to Shail, just as Moyrah had done. "Name's Ferlbas, I'm First Mate on the *Setting Sun.* Come find me if you need anything while you're with us. Or," he hooked a thumb towards Moyrah, "ask her. She knows this ship and its workings nearly as good as myself."

Moyrah squared her shoulders in a confident way and smirked at Shail, "She'll be mine someday."

Ferlbas' expression was one of stern, but tolerant affection, "*That* is no guarantee. Likely, but not for sure. Best not forget that."

Moyrah deflated slightly. "Aye sir."

Ferlbas relented. "What are you two up to?"

Moyrah looked at Shail. "I think the solander wanted to see the raven's roost. He was staring at it when I found him."

Shail looked at her curiously. "Solander?"

"Solid lander. Someone who spends their days on earth, not water," explained Ferlbas. "And not all together a complimentary title," he added with a disapproving look at Moyrah.

She had the grace to look embarrassed. "Didn't mean nuthin by it, just what he is." When Shail smiled and shrugged, Moyrah brightened. "With your permission sir, I don't mind finishing out Polkstone's roost shift, and I can take Shail with me."

Ferlbas looked at Shail. "I don't think Rox would be against it, so long as you wear a safety line. Up to you lad."

"Yes! Absolutely!"

Ferlbas laughed at Shail's enthusiasm. "Alright then, tell Polkstone I said he can take the rest of his watch off. That should please him no end."

"Aye sir! C'mon!" Moyrah pulled on Shail's sleeve.

"Goodbye Mr. Ferlbas. Thank you sir!"

Ferlbas waved to Shail and Moyrah, then turned to
address a sailor who appeared to be acting out a funny story
for the benefit of his handsome crewmate, who held a rag
loosely in his hand and was laughing appreciatively.
"Shodvic! Lougrun! Who taught you to scrub a deck? I can
see from here you've missed a spot a league long!" Shail
was amused to see both men jump, then return to their task
with a loud, "Yes sir, sorry sir!"

Moyrah led Shail to the main mast, and he craned
his head back to stare up at the roost. It suddenly looked a
lot higher than Shail had thought. He felt his stomach
tighten a bit at the prospect of climbing all the way to the
top. Moyrah seemed to notice his nervousness. To Shail's
surprise, instead of teasing him she said, "Roost used to
scare me stupid, 'til I got used to it. But trust me, it's worth
it, once you're up there." She reached out and unhooked a
clip secured to a rope that ran up the mast. "This here's the
safety line. You hook it to your belt, so if'n you slip, you
just dangle, 'stead of droppin." She held the clip out to
Shail. He lifted his shirt and secured the clasp around the
width of his belt. Moyrah reached out to give the rope an
experimental tug, and Shail felt himself pulled forward
slightly. "Looks good. Ready to climb?"

Shail steeled himself. "Yes, let's go!"

"You first, I'll follow."

Moyrah stood to the side of the mast, and Shail began to ascend. It was fairly easy, there were rungs all along the length of the mast for hands and feet. Shail was no stranger to climbing trees at home, but a tree didn't sway like a mast. With every roll and toss of the waves, Shail felt the ship dance under him. He mostly kept his eyes on the spot of wood directly in front of him, but now he risked a glance upward. The raven's roost still seemed awfully far away.

Just as he was about to turn his gaze in the other direction, he heard Moyrah yell up to him. "Don't look down! Keep going!" She reached a hand up to give Shail a light slap on his calf. Feeling as though he had little other choice in the matter, Shail resumed climbing.

Foot by foot, up they went. Shail's arms were beginning to ache. Each inch was now hard-won. The wind felt stronger this far up, almost feeling as though it were trying to peel Sail from the mast with prying, grasping fingers. Shail hooked his arm over a rung so that it was nestled between his arm and his body. He tried to catch his breath.

"Gonna make it, solander?" Moyrah's mocking tone let Shail know she expected him to fail, not being a sailor like she was. Well, he'd show her! Gritting his teeth, Shail reached his hand up to grip the next rung. The raven's roost was just above him, the small opening that was the only entrance and exit a spot of blue amidst the brown of the wooden platform.

140

And suddenly Shail was gripped at the wrist by a strong hand! "Whatthe? Who're you?"

"Uhh …. Shail?"

"Shove over Polkstone," Shail heard Moyrah shout from below his feet. "Mate says we're to take the rest of your watch." Polkstone's face went from suspicious to gracious in an instant. He hauled Shail up without another word. Shail moved as far to the side of the roost as he could so that Moyrah could join them.

It was a tight squeeze with all three, but Polkstone showed no interest in lingering. "Mate says it's alright, s'all I need to know." Before Shail could bid him goodbye, Polkstone had dropped through the opening, and was out of sight.

"Really had to twist his arm, huh," Moyrah said with a grin. Shail gave a shaky laugh, not entirely recovered from his climb. "Well, you made it solander. What do you think?"

Shail lifted his gaze. "Oh, wow. Oh, *wow*!" Shail could not believe his eyes. Standing on the river's edge was one thing, this was something else! He twisted his head to look in the other direction. Water and sky, in every direction.

He grinned at Moyrah, and she slapped him on the back. "Nuthin' better than this! Calm seas, strong winds, and your head higher than everyone else's." She nodded sagely. "'Course it's different when you're stuck in a squall."

Shail imagined what that would be like, and swallowed as his belly tightened. "Have you ever been up here during a storm," he asked.

Moyrah shook her head. "Only the most experienced run the rigging in bad weather, 'less there's an emergency. One of the captain's jobs is to make sure there aren't any emergencies. And our captain's the best there is." Moyrah stated this with utter certainty, and Shail saw no reason to argue.

They stood for a time, just looking at the river. Waves with white crests curled like fine lace upon shifting blue satin. Moyrah pointed to a small flock of gulls passing close by. Shail followed them with his eyes as they glided effortlessly less than three feet away. His attention was caught by two of the birds who had suddenly stopped their circling to drop like stones. Without thinking, Shail put both hands on the edge of the raven's roost, and peered over the edge.

He immediately regretted having done so. If the climb had seemed long on the way up, now they seemed impossibly high. He couldn't even make out the features of the individual sailors on deck, they were all mere moving specks. Shail felt himself go rigid. His grip on the railing tightened until his knuckled showed white. Shail felt his vision going black around the edges, and a roaring that was not the wind filled his ears.

"Hey? You alright?" Shail heard Moyrah speak, but he could not make himself turn to look at her. "You can go back down now, if you want. I've got to stay here 'til I'm relieved."

Shail finally managed to tear his gaze away from the scene below to stare at Moyrah in horror, "Down? How do we get down?"

"Same way we came up. Climb."

Shail's gaze darted to the opening, and he gulped, backing as far away from it as the small space allowed, "I c-c-c-can't!" Shail hated the way his voice stammered with terror.

Moyrah considered, "Well, there is one other way."

"How?!" Shail was willing to consider any possibility.

"See where your safety line connects to the mast? If you drop down below the roost, the line will lower you slowly to the deck."

Shail had taken a tentative step towards the opening, but now leapt back, glaring at Moyrah wildly. "*Drop*?! That's better than climbing?"

Moyrah shrugged, "Up to you." Shail whimpered softly. Moyrah looked at him, and sighed. "Alright, I'll help you." She reached over and gripped Shail around the wrist, just as Polkstone had done. Then, in one fluid motion, she pulled Shail towards the roost's opening. She turned him to face her, then shoved so he fell backward.

And straight down!

Chapter 12

Back to School

Leeinn, Tiny, and Tancer were led from the stairs at the west wall through Del Abbey, towards the orchard. Their enthusiastic guides held hands as they ran, with twin tails streaming behind them each time they dashed from one waiting spot to the next, casting impatient looks back at their lagging followers.

Leeinn pointed, "That's the abbey pond. It's a good place for swimming. Brother Altimer will tell you the lake is also good for fishing, but he's the only human with any consistent luck. The dragons are capable enough, when they bother themselves."

Tiny said, "Tancer likes to fish. He'll probably want the chance to prove Brother Altimer right."

Tancer considered, "Hmm, maybe, but I know you wouldn't like any kind of water related job. Why not keep looking for something we'd both enjoy doing?"

Leeinn cocked her head at Tiny, "Do you not like water?"

Tiny shrugged with embarrassment, "I can't swim," she admitted. "I grew up in a place where there wasn't a lot of water higher than a person's hips."

Leeinn brightened, "Oh, if that's all, Brother Altimer is also a wonderful swimming instructor."

Tiny looked hesitant, but intrigued, "Well ….. if he wouldn't mind …"

Tancer lightly punched Tiny's shoulder, "Besides, you're tall enough to just wade through most places. More like skipping than swimming."

Tiny scowled and swiped at her husband, "Unlike you, who has to charter a sailing craft when trying to cross a puddle." They locked eyes for a moment, and then burst into laughter. Seeing Leeinn's mystified expression, Tiny said, "Sorry, don't mind us. We make a habit of teasing each other."

Tancer nodded in exasperation, "*Everyone* back home seemed to think we had somehow overlooked the fact that I am shorter than my wife, and needed to be told. Over, and over, and over. I didn't mind so much, but Tiny hated it."

Tiny gave a sad smile, "It just seemed like everyone was telling us we were a bad match."

Tancer gave a snort, "Like I'd have stop chasing the most wonderful woman in the world just because she was taller than me."

Tiny's Lodvidian-dark skin made it difficult to tell if she blushed, but the shy way she cast her eyes downward made Leeinn suspect that is she were from Heylother, she'd have been red as a tomato. "Tancer was the one to figure out that if we were the ones making the joke, it made it lessened the appeal for other people to poke at us. It felt strange at first, but now it really can be fun."

"Exactly. And I wouldn't give up a single inch of her, she's like my own little farmer."

Tiny gave Tancer a pained look, then rolled her eyes, and looked to Leeinn for help, "Maybe one day you'll be lucky enough to have a husband that compares you to a really big lizard." All three laughed.

"Would you come *on*!" The trio jumped as they realized they had begun to trail even further behind their guides. Properly chastened, they quickened their pace to catch up with the girls.

They approached a line of fragrant trees. "This is the edge of the orchards. We have a line of trees for just about every fruit you could want. There's peaches, plums, and pomegranates; apples, apricots, avocados, and olives; cherries, lemons, limes, figs, oranges, grapefruit, bananas …."

"Alright, we get it, nobody here is in danger of contracting scurvy," laughed Tancer. Leeinn grinned at him.

"You said you liked picking from the berry bushes best," said Tiny. "Where are they?"

"On the other side of the pond, beside the beehives" answered Leeinn. "We've quite the selection there too. Strawberries, blueberries, blackberries, raspberries, cranberries, elderberries, dragonberries, delberries, …."

Tancer muttered loud enough to be easily overheard, "Catberries, dogberries, duckberries, rabbitberries, ravenberries *youch.*" Tiny had reached over and flicked the tip of Tancer's ear.

Leeinn continued as though nothing had happened, "And each can be made into a wine. There are cellars beneath the abbey that are kept cool for just such spirits." They had passed several rows of trees by now, and the air was sweet with all of their scents.

"It's like the street of perfumes in the City," exclaimed Tiny.

"The what," asked Leeinn curiously.

"The street of perfumes. It's a section of the City where all the best scent sellers showcase their wares. It's like a candyshop for your nose!"

148

Tancer sniffed appreciatively. "It's enough to give a man an appetite!"

"It should be lunch time soon, we can head back to the dining hall after we speak with my father. Oh, there he is now, and Gira's still with him."

Rumaru was seated comfortably among the gnarled roots of an ancient apple tree, its low hanging limbs heavily laden with rich red fruit. Gira was picking apples with one hand and dropping them into a basket cradled against her body with her other arm. Her face looked shiny with sweat, but she seemed in good spirits, for she smiled and sang.

"This apple is just perfect, I picked it just for you,

It's full of summer sunshine, and sweeter than sundew,

You shall have the left side, and I will bite the right,

'Til our lips meet in the middle, and we kiss all through the night!"

Rumaru was smiling and tapping his foot to Gira's tune. As they drew near, the two girls ran breathlessly up to him. "We've brought Leeinn Father Abbot!"

He turned his nearly closed eyes upon them. "Wonderful, thank you. Go to the kitchens and tell Sister Ikotyl I said you could have an early dessert. I think I heard her say something about peach tarts …." Both girls squealed and tore away from the orchard.

149

Gira smiled, "You're all here!"

Leeinn nodded towards her father, "Yes, Father said he wanted to see me, and I didn't think he would mind if Tiny and Tancer came with me." A hint of doubt crept into her voice. "I hope that's alright with you father."

She sighed with relief when he nodded. "Yes, I see no harm in them being here, although I suppose it really should be up to Gira." He leaned his head in her direction. "Did you want to tell them?"

Gira beamed at all three, "The abbot and I had a good, long talk, and he's going to speak with my mother about my staying here for a few weeks, taking on work just like an Accepted."

Tancer shared a look with Tiny, "Not that I don't have faith in your powers of persuasion sir, but I'm not sure Gira's mother can *be* persuaded to do anything she doesn't want to."

Gira looked at him sharply, "You only met her this morning. I know she was a bit short, but I don't see how you can make that kind of judgement from just one conversation."

"Well," Tancer hedged. "We've had two conversations, actually, although I'm not sure either time really counts as a conversation, since it was mostly her talking and us trying to escape." Rumaru laughed, and

Leeinn filled he and Gira in on the encounter they had had with Nassine.

Gira's smile faltered, "Did she really say she thought Father Rumaru would agree with her?" She turned beseeching eyes on the Abbot. "Sir, do you still intend to speak to her on my behalf?"

Rumaru nodded easily, "I will speak with her, though I can make no promises that she will listen. But your mother and I have worked together many years now, I think she will at least consider my council. If she does, whatever happens after will be up to you." He cocked his head to the side. "I think it would be a good idea if all of you attended the abbey school together. Leeinn can show you where it is."

The trio looked to Leeinn, and she smiled, "Of course father, I can show them right now, if you don't need us for anything else."

Rumaru stood and stretched, "I think I'll go see Sister Ikotyl too. I love peach tarts!" Leeinn stepped close to give him a quick kiss on his cheek, then all four bid him goodbye. He kindly took the apple basket from Gira and slowly strolled off in the direction of the dining hall, which was conveniently connected by enclosed corridors to the kitchens.

Leeinn said, "I'll show you the school, and introduce you to Brother Septibbs. You'll like him, he's a very talented teacher."

They walked between the rows of orchard trees, the sun nearly directly overhead now. "I'll be glad to go inside," Tancer said as he pulled at the collar of his shirt. "Getting a bit too warm for my liking."

Tiny smacked her lips. "And maybe get something cold to drink, I'm thirsty."

"Oh, that does sound good," Gira chimed in. She pulled a white lace handkerchief from a hidden fold in her skirt, and used it to wipe the sweat off her forehead.

They approached the main abbey building, and entered through the simple, unadorned doors, thrown wide during the day. A constant stream of people flowed both in and out.

Back inside, Gira said. "That's much better!"

"The school is this way," pointed Leeinn down a hallway that ran towards the back of the abbey. "At least, the room where they teach new Accepted and the children of the abbey is this way. Specialized training for individual tasks is normally done hands-on. Do any of you have a particular talent you'd like to pursue?"

Tancer looked at Tiny, "What about your painting? Bet you could do something like those doors the Trinity used to enter Hopeful Hall."

"You paint?" Gira seemed delighted. "How wonderful! I'm something on an artist myself, though I prefer the pencil over the brush. And of course my mother made all of my sisters and I take sewing and embroidery lessons. *So you can sew your own clothes, and then make them beautiful,"* she said, in a very good imitation of Nassine. "What about your mother Leeinn? Or has it always been just your father?" Tiny and Tancer shot Gira a quick look, then glanced back quickly to Leeinn to see if she had been upset by the personal question.

Leeinn nodded, smiling to show she had not taken offense, "Yes, to the second bit I mean. He found me when I was barely old enough to walk, and raised me as his daughter."

Gira's eyes went wide. "Found you! Where? How? What happened to your real parents?"

Leeinn twitched slightly, "My father *is* my real parent, and I wouldn't trade him for anyone else."

Gira looked abashed, "I'm sorry, I didn't mean that as it sounded. I just don't understand how someone loses a *child* way out here, and not at least *ask* the abbey residents about it. Wouldn't that make the most sense? Those that live here would know the country well, and there'd be more than enough for a search party."

Leeinn shrugged, "I really don't know. My father told me he found me playing at the edge of the del water meadows, and brought me back to the abbey. He wasn't

153

abbot at the time, so only I called him father then." She gestured back to the hallway. "We should probably be on our way."

The three followed her back into the corridor. Tiny asked, "How long will we be taking less lessons at the school?"

"Until you know the material. Brother Septibbs has a general exam he gives to students when he thinks they're ready to graduate."

Gira looked worried, "I thought you said there wasn't any test!"

"To become Accepted no. To pass Brother Septibbs abbey courses, yes." Leeinn smiled comfortingly at Gira. "Don't worry, I'll help you to study. I know all his usual questions." Gira looked at her gratefully.

Tancer raised an eyebrow, "What if we don't pass his test? Do we get kicked out?" Tiny looked alarmed at the prospect.

Leeinn hurried to reassure them, "No, no, you just retake the lessons until you pass. And here we are."

Leeinn paused outside a closed door. She rapped on it lightly with her knuckles, and waited for the, *'come in'* before opening the door. "Good morning Brother Septibbs. I've brought you some new students."

A jolly looking man looked up from a book he'd been reading, marking his place on the page with a single finger, "Welcome! I recognize our new Accepteds, but who is this?"

Gira curtsied, "I'm Gira. The Father Abbot said I could take lessons with Tiny and Tancer, and maybe become Hopeful someday."

Brother Septibbs smiled broadly at her, "Another Hopeful, so soon? My, my, but these are exciting times. Very well, come back the morning after your introductory week is over, I'll have your course materials made up by then."

Tancer raised a single, questioning finger in the air, "Sir? Does it have to be morning? I find the afternoon more conducive to scholarly pursuits …."

Chapter 13

A Long Drop, and a Sudden Stop

Shail dropped like a stone! And then jerked to a stop! He dangled limply for a moment, then began to struggle wildly. Why had he stopped falling? The memory of attaching a safety line to his belt came rushing back to him, and he almost wept with relief. He gripped the rope with both hands, hugging it close. He clung there with eyes closed, then choked back a scream as he started to drop again, albeit much slower this time.

"Hang tight solander, you'll have your feet on solid deck soon." Shail opened his eyes to see Moyrah staring down at him from the raven's roost.

A wave of anger washed over him, and Shail temporarily forgot his fear, "You pushed me!" You …. You …." Shail couldn't think of anything rotten enough to call her, and spluttered himself into silence.

"Had to, you was seized up with the wobblies." Moyrah had to raise her voice to shout this last parting shot, for Shail was nearly at the bottom of the mast. The line stopped holding his weight when he reached the deck, and for a few moments Shail simply stood with his palms flat against the wood, breathing deeply. He was not hurt, and he was down from the roost. That was all that mattered. "Better?"

Shail yelped in surprise. While he had been busy calming himself, Moyrah had apparently shimmied down to stand beside him. Shail felt like kicking her, but managed to restrain himself, "You could have warned me," he said stiffly.

Moyrah shook her head, "Woulda' made it worse." She seemed irritatingly unrepentant. "Anyhow, you're down, and I got to finish my watch." So saying, she scurried back up the mast and was back in the roost before Shail had time to unclip the safety line from his belt. Freed, he took a few wobbly steps towards the railing.

He could not tell how long he hung there, staring at the water, but eventually he felt a light hand on his shoulder, "Shail? Are you alright? Feeling sick again?"

Shail looked up into Gran's concerned face. He flung his arms around her, infinitely glad to see her, "No, not sick, just had a mean trick played on me." Shail told Gran Rox all that had happened since he had left her with Cookie. She listened without interrupting, her face grave when Shail got to the part about being pushed from the roost. "And then the line lowered me to the deck, and you found me here. *She*," he flavored the single word with an abundance of nuance, "came down for a minute, then went back up."

Gran's gaze sought the roost, "Did Moyrah laugh, after she pushed you?" Shail thought about it, and then had to admit that she had not. "You said she pushed you as a mean trick. I should think she would have laughed at her success in scaring you, if that was her motive." When Shail looked at Gran with indignation, she titled her head to the side. "Think it through, grandson mine."

"Well …. Even if it *wasn't* a trick, she should have warned me. Or something!" Shail was almost as angry with Gran for seeming to take Moyrah's side as he'd been about being pushed.

Gran raised an eyebrow. "And how often do upset people listen to reason? You remember when your cousin fell out of that tree in your front yard and broke his arm?"

Shail nodded reluctantly. "You tried to set his arm in a sling, but he wouldn't hold still, no matter how much you told him moving wouldn't help."

"That's right, he even took a swing at me with his good arm. But I knew it was just the pain of his injury, and the shock of the fall that had muddled his wits."

"He called you … well, a bad name I won't repeat."

Gran actually laughed, "He called me a pushy, grey-haired bitch. Right on all counts, I think." She laughed

158

again at Shail's look of shock. "Oh I was called that, and worse, when I worked as a healer. You learn not to take such things personal. More often than not, when all the fuss is over, the person is likely to be embarrassed at their behavior and ask for forgiveness."

"Did Dyllap?"

Gran grinned. "He apologized for trying to hit me but said he would never take back honest words." Shail felt that he had himself back under control and stood away from the railing. "Want to take a walk?"

Shail nodded at Gran's suggestion. "Anywhere but the roost! I'll never go up there again."

Gran had started to walk away from their standing point, but drew up sharp at Shail's statement, "And why not?"

Shail was surprised by the question, "Well ….. because I fell."

"And was caught by the safety line."

Shail couldn't argue with that, "It's too high up."

"You didn't think so when you went up the first time. How was it while you were up there? Before Moyrah .. *ah* … helped you down."

Shail snorted at her phrasing, "It was ….. well, I guess it wasn't bad, before I fell. Everything looked so different. And it felt …. I don't know. Free, but lonely."

159

"Sounds like being a healer," murmured Gran. When Shail looked at her, a crease in his brow, she explained. "The knowledge and experience we gain through healing helps give us a unique perspective, but it also stands us apart."

Shail looked at his hands, "What are you trying to tell me?"

Gran looked thoughtful, "What do you think I'm trying to tell you?" Typical Gran, answering a question with a question.

"I don't ….. that sometimes we need help facing our fears?" Gran looked at him. "And sometimes our friends help us, even when we don't want them to." He groaned. "Does that mean I have to *thank* Moyrah?"

Gran guffawed, "Maybe not so much as that. Recognize she did the best she could, under the circumstances. Growing up on a ship probably makes you more practical minded, and less worried about social niceties. No free time on the brine, fish or cut bait, all those nautical phrases your uncle likes to show off."

Shail smiled at the memory, then felt a knot form in his throat, "I won't see him for a long time."

Gran coughed out a laugh, "You haven't lived long enough to know what a long time is. I expect you'll be so busy shadowing Master Conlun that time will fly by. And

Tabirc will enjoy having another bachelor to waste his time with."

Shail brightened at the thought of time with Tabirc, "I can impress him with my new firestarter pouch! I wonder if we can have a campfire every day ...."

"You'll have to speak to him about that, though I doubt he'll deny you. He never was good at saying no to a child's request."

"Hey!" Shail felt indignation flare within him. "I am *not* a child."

"Then you'll be going back up to the raven's roost tomorrow?"

Shail deflated, "Tomorrow? Do I have to?"

Gran shook her head, "No, you don't *have* to. But you'll have to live with the fear if you don't."

Shail shrugged uncomfortably, "Not like I'd be spending a lot of time doing that sort of thing off the *Setting Sun*."

"Maybe, maybe not. You never know what life will throw at you. My life didn't turn out anything like what I *expected*."

Shail looked at her in surprise, "Really? How did you think it would be different?"

Gran sighed, "Oh, I was like every young woman where I grew up. I thought I'd grow old with my family, mainly my husband and my brother, and we'd all be surrounded by our children and grandchildren as we worked together to cultivate our pools of flowers." She smiled wistfully. "Or at least I would work. Those two would likely sneak off to nap, or cause mischief. I never had to wonder where Wengsper got his inclination for trouble."

Gran did not often speak of her early life, Shail he dared to pry, "If that's what you wanted... what happened?"

Gran Rox would not meet his gaze, instead staring out over the water, "Time has a way of … changing things. People too." She did not seem inclined to elaborate, so Shail dropped the subject. He started to walk away, but her softly spoken question made him stop. "Would it make a difference if I went with you?" He turned around to stare at her. She jerked her chin up towards the raven's roost. "Tomorrow, I'll ask Moyrah to take us both up. I wouldn't mind adding another perspective to my life." Shail shifted from one foot to the other. "Think about it." He nodded without comment. "Have you seen the rest of the ship, or did you spend all your time in the roost?"

"I wasn't gone *that* long."

Gran chuckled, and Shail walked beside her as she guided the rest of his tour. Passengers were not allowed to go everywhere on the ship, but those areas that were off limits were generally places that did not have anything interesting anyway. Gran introduced Shail to the woman manning the wheel, responsible for keeping them on course, and the ship's medic Patch, another man like Cookie who seemed to have a profession in place of his name. They were all respectful to Gran Rox, and welcoming to Shail. For his part, Shail was quickly becoming enamored of the sailing life, which seemed far more exciting than the day-to-day monotony of land life.

When he told Gran as much, she answered, "Why not combine both interests and become ship's healer, like Patch? Good money, fresh air. Cramped quarters by our solander standards, and the quality of the cuisine depends on the cook. Still ..."

"How long do you have to work on a ship to change from a solander to a sailor?"

"That's a question for Moyrah. Her watch should be just about over, sun's going down." Gran nodded towards the western horizon. "I won't pretend to be an expert, but I've traveled on this particular ship enough to be familiar with her routines. Roost duty is usually done in four hour shifts, I assume to keep the watchers alert." Shail did not want to think about being in the roost for that long.

Shail realized they had wandered back towards the scene of his afternoon embarrassment. Shooting an accusatory look at Gran, Shail stopped where he was. Gran leaned her shoulder against the mast, and for a moment all

163

Shail could see was Uncle Wengsper at the docks, in exactly the same position against a piling.

"Whatcha doin?" Shail jumped as, once again, Moyrah materialized as if by magic. She noticed Gran. "Evening ma'am."

Gran Rox nodded back to her, "Evening. I hear you and my grandson took a turn in the roost."

Moyrah gave Shail an amused smile, "S'right, and he tested out the safety line." Shail glared at her, feeling his cheeks burn with a blush.

"And how many times have *you* been booted out of the roost?" Gran asked.

Moyrah laughed, "I had to use the line first dozen times or so I had roost watch."

Shail looked at her in surprise, "You didn't tell me that!"

She shrugged, "You didn't ask. Does it matter?"

Shail mimicked her shrugging motion, "No, it doesn't *matter*, but it might have made me feel better to know."

Moyrah looked at him strangely, then addressed Gran, "Do all boys think like him, or is he just weird?"

Shail made a sound of outrage, and Gran's chuckle became a full-blown cackle, "He's still a bit sore over the safety line."

Moyrah peered at Shail, "S'at right?"

Shail looked at her cooly, "I didn't think it was funny."

To his surprise, Moyrah looked contrite, "Didn't do it to be funny mate, but really, it was the fastest way to get you down. Take it from me, the longer you stay up there, standing still, just thinking about it, the worse the wobblies get."

Moyrah stared at Shail with such a miserable look on her face, he was at last convinced of her sincerity, "Alright, I believe you." She sighed in relief. "What were you doing before you snuck up on me?"

"Wasn't sneaking, you weren't paying 'ttention." She looked at Shail, then Gran. "Cookie wanted me to tell you that supper would be soon, and he made you two plates himself."

At the mention of food, Gran jerked away from the mast, "Why didn't you say so?! Last one there is a rotten dragon egg!" After a shared glance, Shail and Moyrah took off in hot pursuit.

Supper was as tasty as lunch. Cookie had baked fresh loaves of bowl-shaped bread, which he'd filled with a delicious fish and vegetable chowder. Gran ate both her bowls in quick succession. She leaned backed in her seat, looking drowsy. Shail had been engrossed listening to Moyrah's stories about her time on the *Setting Sun*.

"And then the searpent tried to *court* our figurehead!"

Shail laughed, "It what?"

Moyrah held her fork upright, and then began waggling it side to side, "Came right up out of the water, and started dancing. The males have this bright orange spot under their chins. When they're trying to impress a lady searpent, they turn their noses up so's she can see that spot. Then they start a sort of croon, and it wobbles a bit. Looks a bit silly to me, but I suppose that 'cas I'm not a searpent."

"So, it kind of looks like your ship's sails?"

Moyrah's eyes grew wide, and then she laughed, "Never thought of it that way, but yes, actually."

"What did the searpent do when your figurehead didn't respond?"

"Sank back into the water. Looked sad, for a searpent."

"I wonder if it's the same face my uncle makes when his lady friends aren't impressed with his uniform."

Gran had appeared to be napping by this point, but Shail's comment made her snort. She opened one eye, "I will give you any amount of lemon lotus you want if you tell your uncle he looks like a lovesick searpent the next time he's making eyes at a lost cause."

"Deal!" To Moyrah Shail said, "How many do you think I should ask for?"

She considered, "Lucky thirteen sounds about right, so long as you don't eat them all at once."

Gran rolled her eyes, "And I suppose offering seven would spoil the deal, being a sign of ill omen."

Moyrah nodded emphatically, "Don't even joke about that ma'am! Just mentioning the Seven Sorrows is bad luck!" Moyrah crossed the first two fingers on both her hands, squeezed her eyes, and intoned, "Thirteen Joys, hear my words, save me and mine from the Seven Sorrows. For this I offer my last drop and crust." So saying, Moyrah solemnly offered the last mouthful of her soup bowl to the ship's parrot, who gobbled it greedily, then tongued the last bit of Moyrah's drink that she'd poured into her palm. "Birds are one of the thirteen joys you know."

Shail rolled his eyes, "Of course, *everyone* knows that. So are cats, which is another reason to keep Klonio, other than his hunting skills."

"Ha! He hasn't caught so much as a cold in years! Captain keeps the ship too clean for vermin to be a problem."

"I guess that's why your parrot is still alive?"

"Naw, Peatea had rank on Klonio. If'n he tried anything, she'd pluck his whiskers!" The parrot cried, "*reet, reet*" at the mention of her name, as if to clarify, "I rank above *all* of you too!"

Chapter 14

Tal

Leeinn, Gira, Tiny, and Tancer helped to clean up the simple repast Brother Septibb had laid out for them. Four piled plates sat next to four cups stacked one within the other, the topmost holding four forks. Every piece was made from polished dragontimber. Gira had been astonished to see so much of the precious wood used for such ordinary cutlery, and told Brother Septibb as much.

He had smiled broadly, "These have belonged to the abbey school long before any of us were born, and I dare say generations from now people will still be using them. Wonderful stuff, and the abbey has access to all the dragontimber it wants, being so close to the del water meadows."

Tancer peered at the plates curiously, "Does dragontimber only grow near dels?" Brother Septibb cast an eye towards Leeinn.

She stood, clasped her hands over her abdomen, and recited in a slight sing-song cadence,

"If dragontimber you would grow, step one gather seeds to sow,

Step two, find water made clean by del,

you'll know it by sight, and taste, and smell.

Then bury your seeds, and leave them to grow,

By season's end, you'll have something to show."

She gave her audience a grin and added, "One of the many teaching poems Brother Septibb insists we all memorize."

Septibb smiled at Leeinn's comment, "I know it may seem silly, but you never know what knowledge you'll need. Best to have as much as you can."

Gira looked intrigued, "So, knowledge is like money?"

Brother Septibb considered, "Not a bad analogy, though I would consider an uneducated soul to be poor, no matter how heavy their purse." He stood, and his four pupils did likewise.

"Thank you for the meal sir," Tiny said respectfully.

"It was a good first course. You did say we'd be going to the dining hall after we saw the school." Tancer looked at Leeinn with eyebrows raised hopefully.

"Most people would consider what we just ate to be an entire meal in and of itself," Tiny said.

As if on cue, Tancer's stomach growled, "See, told you so." When their laughter had subsided, they bid Brother Septibb goodbye, promising to return the next day to begin their lessons in earnest.

Tancer's efforts finally convinced the group to attend lunch in the dining hall, with Tancer in the lead, chiding them along. "Come along ladies, don't want the food to get cold!"

"You're as bad as the girls from this morning," accused Tiny.

Gira nearly fell over laughing as Tancer cocked out a hip, placing his hand upon it, and made a motion as though sweeping back hair, "I may be bad, but I make it look good!" He pouted his lips and fluttered his eyelashes.

"I'd say you look more like a duck with double eye infections," quipped Tiny.

"*Ignore* her, she's always been jealous that I'm the better-looking half."

"More like the better-looking quarter," Tiny said as she peered pointedly down her nose. "I'll admit, of the two of us, you're the better-looking *man*." For some reason her

171

comment seemed particularly funny to Tancer, for his face flushed red as he belly-laughed while slapping his thighs.

Gira shot Leeinn an amused look tinged with exasperation, "Do *you* have any idea why that was so funny?"

Leeinn could only shrug, "Must be a couples thing." Tancer's merriment was infectious, and before long all had tears in their eyes as they held aching sides. They each tried to shush the others, before dissolving into further giggles themselves.

"Gira, there you are!" Gira went stiff as a board upon hearing her mother's voice. The four turned reluctantly to face Nassine. None were prepared when she said, "I've spoken with Father Rumaru, and he and I agreed to let you stay."

"*What*?!" gasp Gira. "*You ... he .... I can stay?!*"

Tancer's expression made it clear he was as dumbfounded as Gira, "That's …. great! That's great! Really great. Really!"

"So speaks the poet ….," Tiny could not seem to help remarking. Tancer stuck out the tip of his tongue, but said nothing. "Still, that is great to hear. I'm glad you'll be staying with us."

Gira looked almost too stunned to respond, "What? Oh, yes. Thank you."

Nassine sniffed, "I thought you'd be pleased."

"Oh, I am! I'm just …. surprised."

"Well, Father Rumaru can be quite persuasive when he tries, and he agreed to my condition, so I really could not refuse him."

"Condition? What condition?"

"Only that you be attended by a female retainer while you are here, as chaperone"

"*Chaperone?!* I'll be staying at Del Abbey! Why in the world do you think I need a chaperone?"

Nassine narrowed her eyes, "Because it is unacceptable for the heir of one of the most prestigious merchant families in Jukyon to be left alone for so long. And I *suggest* you consider that I am being generous in this matter. My mother would never have agreed to such a request, if I'd dared ask in the first place."

While Gira could only fume in silence, Tancer asked, "Having somebody you know stay with you can't be anything but a help, can it?" Nassine seemed surprised to hear someone she'd so recently been at odds with now arguing in her favor. "It is a person she knows, right?"

"Yes, one of the retainers we brought with us has volunteered to stay. She's fairly new to our household, but she's done good work so far, and no one else was immediately suitable."

Despite herself, Gira look interested, "But who is it?"

"Tal."

Gira brightened, "Oh, well then, that's alright. She always washes and brushes my hair so gently, and she knows all the most fashionable braids!"

"Yes, well," Nassine actually smiled, "She was serving me while I spoke to Father Rumaru. I was naturally holding out against the idea, until she said she'd be willing to stay with you. Between her and Father Rumaru, I found it difficult to argue." Nassine pierced Leeinn, Tiny, and Tancer each with a separate look. "That being said, I expect her other *friends* to see my daughter comes to no harm whilst she is away from her *family*."

They all nodded together, "Yes ma'am!"

Nassine looked at Gira, and her face softened. "I'm only trying to do what's best for you."

"I know, thank you mother."

Tancer said, "Don't worry Miss-Gira's-Mother, we'll stick as close to her as two wings on the same dragon!" Nassine merely raised an eyebrow.

Tiny pushed her way in front of Tancer, "Being here will be new for all three of us. I'm sure we'll all benefit from Leeinn's help."

Recognizing her cue, Leeinn nodded quickly, "I'll teach them everything I know about the abbey!"

Nassine nodded, if a bit stiffly, "Good. I've sent Tal to move both your things to the room you two will share. Leeinn, if you'll show her the way, your father called it the *'gois'* room."

"Yes ma'am, I know the rooms he means. We were going to the dining hall, but I can show Gira where she'll be staying first."

The realization that she would actually be staying seemed to penetrate Gira's consciousness, "My rooms? My rooms! I'm staying!" She clapped her hands and twirled in a circle. Nassine seemed pleased with her daughter's reaction.

"Or, just a thought, we could go to the dining room first, and then see Gira's rooms. I mean, she's going to have them for a while, and lunch is only served once a day …" Four pairs of female eyes made Tancer hastily back pedal, "But we just ate, so really, why go to the dining hall? Just because it has all the delicious food a man could want, free for the taking …" He trailed off with a sigh.

"I'll just ask Tal to bring us some lunch to my rooms."

"*Gira!*" Gira jumped guiltily. "Tal has already moved your luggage, which I will remind you numbered more than all your sister's combined."

Gira winced, "I couldn't decide what to take and what to leave! What if I'd only brought my green dress with the gold fringes, but everyone else was wearing wisteria purple? You remember how that was all people wore last season!"

Nassine twitched irritably, "Do *not* ask the woman for more, at least today. She's done you a kindness. Better that you should be thankful."

Gira lowered her eyes, "Of course, I'm sorry."

Nassine waved her hand in a dismissive gesture, "I've things to tend, off with you." Needing no second bidding, the group all but ran, Leeinn leading, and the other three close behind. Nassine shook her head, but walked off more jauntily than usual.

When they had left Gira's mother behind, they slowed their pace back to a walk. Having caught her breath, Gira asked, "Why is it called the gois room?"

"Because it's for 'guests of indeterminate stay'." Leeinn's explanation was met with three groans.

"You're kidding?"

"What, so I'm a guest who doesn't know when to leave?" Gira seemed hurt.

"No, no, nothing like that! They're just the rooms for people who might stay for a short time, like a few days, or as long as a few weeks, though a person is generally expected to either makes plans to leave, or ask to become Hopeful, by the time the moon is in the same phase as when they arrived."

Gira sniffed, "Sounds like a good way to get squatters. Mother says to '*shift such people swiftly*'."

"That might be a problem if we were closer to the City, but Del Abbey's distance makes only the most determined likely to seek us out."

"I'll say! I thought I'd be riding in our family's travel carriage 'til the leaves dropped! Mother said it would take a week, but I thought she must be exaggerating."

Tiny said, "Must have been nice. Traveling by carriage I mean. Tancer and I were sometimes able to trade our labor for a spot on a crowded caravan wagon, but a good portion of the trip we made on foot."

Gira looked horrified, "On *foot*?! How long did it take you to get here?"

Tancer waved nonchalantly, "Oh, about a month. Wasn't too bad. Country was pretty, road was good in all weathers."

Tiny teased, "The only thing that worried Tancer was the state and quality of our provisions."

"Too few, and too plain, to satisfy a man of my standards."

177

"Maybe you should set your standards closer to your stature?"

Tancer clapped his hands, *"Oooooouch!* Good one, love!" Tiny looked pleased with his praise.

Leeinn shook her head, "You two are the strangest couple I have ever met."

"Oh believe me, Tiny only gets stranger the longer you know her."

"Ha, ha, ha," Tiny said while rolling her eyes. "Mine was much better."

When they reached Gira's room Tiny asked, "Should we knock?"

Gira placed her hand upon the doorknob, turning it and her head to say over her shoulder, "It's my room, I shouldn't have to knock."

"Your *shared* rooms," Tiny stressed.

"Tal won't mind, I'm one of her special favorites. When she's not with mother, she's usually with me." So saying, Gira pushed the door open. Her three friends shrugged at one another, then followed her in. It was a pleasant, glyph-lit chamber, lightly furnished with a small table and four low stools that had been whimsically crafted to look like giant mushrooms. The stone walls and floor had been cushioned with soft rugs and wall hangings in complimentary colors. At the back of the room were three

178

doors; just like the school's cutlery, they were made of dragontimber, with small dragon egg lotus shaped knobs set in their centers.

Leeinn pointed them out to her friends, "The center door leads to the bathing room, and the others lead to bedrooms."

Gira looked around critically, "Bit small for two people. This isn't even as big as my bedroom at home, and I have *it* all to myself. Why can't Tal stay with the other servants?"

"Because we don't *have* servants. Everyone, save the Craftmasters and those that serve them, follows a rotating work schedule. I was going to ask my group leader if Tiny and Tancer could join our team, I see no reason not to ask for you to be placed with us as well."

Gira stopped short, "A *work* team? I thought I'd be spending my time here learning about the abbey!"

At Gira's outburst, the door on the right opened, and a woman with pale skin and red hair stepped out, "Gira? I thought I heard your voice. Is everything all right?" She looked around at Leeinn, Tiny, and Tancer, then dropped into a simple curtsey, low enough that the hem of her simple brown skirt brushed the floor. "Fair day, master and mistresses." All three nodded back.

Leeinn answered, "Fair day to you. Tal, is it?"

"Yes, mistress."

"You don't have to call me that. My name is Leeinn." Tiny and Tancer each introduced themselves, echoing Leeinn's assurance that Tal was free to use their given names. Tal repeated her curtsey for each introduction.

When they were done, Tal turned back to Gira, "Is there something I can do for you, mistress? You sounded angry a moment ago."

Gira shot an accusing look at Leeinn, "I thought this was going to be an educational stay, but now I've found out I'll be expected to sweep and scrub and who knows what else."

Tancer tried to reason with her, "It's nothing Tiny and I won't be expected to do, and working all together will make everything go quick and easy."

Tiny said quietly, "Or, you could always go home with your family. Tell your mother you changed your mind."

That got Gira's attention. "I couldn't do that! I'd never hear the end of it!"

"Perhaps my mistress could be excused from work duties?"

Leeinn was firm, "Only those too sick or injured to work are excused. If you stay, you work."

"But I'm the heir of one of the most prestigious merchant families in Jukyon," protested Gira, her words an echo of her mother's.

Leeinn said, "I thought you wanted to become Hopeful? You can't be both."

Gira deflated, "But, but I'm not Hopeful. Not yet anyway."

Tancer offered gently, "Better to start practicing now, see if you even still want to become Hopeful."

"I will be with you mistress, I can help you with your work."

Leeinn said, "We can *all* help each other. That's the point of a team. Sounds like I'll be bringing my group leader *four* new recruits."

Chapter 15

Nothing but Practice

Shail slept soundly, rocked softly as the ship made her way smoothly towards the sea. He woke with a wide yawn, hearing the cabin's door open and close. Gran entered with a steaming mug in her hand. Shail sniffed, catching the pleasant scent of coffee.

"Morning, grandson mine." After Shail nodded a sleepy hello to her, Gran Rox said, "I've spoken with the captain. He says we should reach Myrliot by midday. I, for one, will appreciate a room that doesn't tilt and toss with every wave." Shail left her blowing across the top of her cup as he washed and dressed. He had to pull Tumatan's unioculous out to reach his clothes, placing it on Gran's bunk. He was about to put it back when Gran said, "Moyrah is waiting for us." Shail was confused for a moment, then felt his stomach sink.

He tried playing dumb, "Is she? What for?" Gran raised a single eyebrow to let Shail know she was not the least bit fooled. "Can't I eat breakfast first?"

"I should think a full stomach would be a hindrance in this case. As it happens, I asked Cookie to make us a basket, which Moyrah should have no trouble carrying up for us. The sooner you climb, the sooner you eat. I don't think Tumatan would mind if we used that." Shail stifled a gulp, putting the collapsed unioculus into a trouser pocket.

He followed reluctantly after Gran until they reached the main mast. Moyrah was sitting cross-legged on the deck, a woven wicker basket beside her, and a pair of dice in front of her. She collected them both in her left hand as they approached, offering Shail a smile, "Mornin mate! It's a good day for the roost. Water's flat as glass, and wind's gentle as a whisper."

Gran Rox had begun to perform a few stretching exercises. Once she was limbered, she peered up at the roost, "I assume there's someone already stationed there?"

Moyrah nodded, "Aye, Tinkerpin, though he knows to expect us. I sent Peatea a'loft with a change-of-duty band." She seemed pleased with herself for having had the foresight to send the ship's parrot.

"What's a change-of-duty band?" Shail was beginning to think of sailor speech as a foreign language.

"Hold on, I'll see if she'll come down. I'll give the signal to let her know it's not urgent, and if she feels like it, she'll respond."

183

"Why wouldn't she?"

Moyrah grinned, "She might want to stay in the roost, she loves it up there. Might even be taking a nap. She doesn't need a reason, beyond not wanting to."

"I thought she was trained?"

"Oh, she is! And if I or any of the crew made the emergency signal, she'd be down faster than a falling stone. Let's see if she's in the mood to answer." Moyrah pursed her lips and gave a loud, cheerful whistle. All three humans paused, waiting. Shail counted five heartbeats before Moyrah sighed and shrugged. "Guess not. Oh well, I can show you the band once we're in the roost."

At this reminder, Shail felt the urge to step away from the mast, "I never said I was going back up! I still don't see why I should. It's not *that* great."

Gran nodded in agreement, "And no one will make you. But I'm going up, regardless."

Shail stared at her in surprise, "But I thought the only reason you were going up was because of me?"

Gran shrugged, "I'd like to see Ms. Peatea's band. It sounds similar to the system my healer's school sometimes employed. I remember the birds being smarter than many of the students." Gran smiled at the memory. "There was one fellow, palest Isrenth I've ever met, who didn't mind other people's blood, but the sight of his own would make him pass out."

Moyrah laughed appreciatively, but Shail considered quietly before asking, "How does fainting at the sight of his own blood affect his abilities as a healer?"

"Remember Dyllap?" When Moyrah looked questioningly at Shail, he answered, "My cousin, who broke his arm by falling out of a tree. And wasn't very happy when Gran tried to set it."

"*That* is putting it lightly. Now what if one of his swings managed to hit me, and I started bleeding everywhere from a broken nose or busted lip?"

Understanding dawned on Shail, "If you'd been like that Isrenthian, the situation would have gone from one patient and one healer to two patients and no healers."

Gran nodded approvingly, "Got it in one."

"How did the man get over his problem?"

"He didn't. He tried, but eventually decided to quit healing for baking. Had his own shop, last time I saw him in the City."

Moyrah assessed Shail. "Good to have options I guess."

"I am *not* becoming a baker!" Shail was incensed. "I'll show you! Give me that safety clip!" Shail was so focused on his anger he did not stop to think about what he was doing.

"That's the spirit!" Moyrah was glad to assist, handing Shail the clip, which he snatched from her hand. After she secured it, Moyrah stepped out of the way. Shail grit his teeth, and began to climb.

He made sure to keep his eyes on the mast, and control his breathing as he ascended. Surprisingly, he seemed to reach the roost faster than he had the first time. A helping hand dropped down to snag his wrist, and just as before, Shail felt himself lifted effortlessly up.

"Ahh, so you're the one's Peatea brought me word of." At the sound of her name, a sleepy, "*reet*?" came from a sheltered section of the roost. "Sorry sweetpea, didn't mean to disturb you." To Shail he said, "Just you, or is there more?"

"Two more, my grandmother and Moyrah."

"I'll just be taking the safety line down to her then." So saying, and without waiting for permission, Tinkerpin unclipped Shail from the line, attached it to his own belt, and left the roost. Shail was momentarily tempted to watch him descend, then thought better of it. He moved away from the opening to give Gran room, hooking his arm over the side of the safety rail. He closed his eyes, waiting for her.

It wasn't long before he heard her voice. "Ahoy up there? Can you give me a hand?"

"Uh …. Are you sure you need one?" Shail was all too aware that he did not have a safety line. If he fell, his second time in the roost would be his last.

He watched as first one, then both of Gran Rox's hands reached out to grab the platform, hauling herself up. "*Phew!* That was a workout. You made it look easy." She waved down through the opening, then moved to stand beside Shail. She pointed towards the distant shore. "I recognize that building, we're nearing our destination. Another two, maybe three hours, I should guess."

Moyrah said, "Hmph, hour and half, tops. Captain suggested we stay up here while we dock, so's you can get an eyefull of Myrliot."

Gran managed to maintain her composure, but Shail nearly jumped out of his skin at Moyrah's sudden appearance, "Stop doing that!"

Moyrah looked confused, "Stop doing what?"

"Getting so close without announcing yourself."

"You knew I was coming up here after you." Moyrah seemed to think this all the explanation that was necessary.

"Don't harass her, grandson mine. She brought the basket of *food!*"

Moyrah grinned at Gran Rox, "Cookie told me to tell you he filled it with the best in the larder."

187

"I could learn to become very fond of that man," Gran remarked.

"Would suit him fine, I'm thinking." Shail cleared his throat, feeling embarrassed. "Got sumthin in your gullet mate? Here." Moyrah squat beside the basket, and pulled out a glass bottle with a tapered top that glistened with condensation. "This here is Cookie's personal brew. Have a swig."

Shail took the offered bottle, giving the open end an experimental sniff, "Smells nice, like strawberries and lemons." He took a small sip. "Tastes nice too."

He offered the bottle to Gran Rox. She accepted it, and took a long pull, "*Mmmm* veeerrrrry nice. If he every decides to sell this, I'd be a loyal customer." Gran hooked the basket towards herself, fingering through the contents. "More loaves of that black bread from last night. What's this? A Gieftari speckled cheese! And look at the size of these grapes, they're nearly as long as my thumb!" Shail shook his head at Gran Rox's excited list. Pulling a knife from the basket, Gran cut the bread into thick slices, which she then stuffed with a generous wedge of cheese. She handed Shail and Moyrah one for each hand, then made four for herself. They chewed in companionable silence, passing the bottle of berry juice around. They made short work of the basket's contents, and when it was empty, Moyrah set it aside. Belly full, Gran Rox stared out upon the water with a contented look on her face. "What a view!" Shail watched as she swiveled her head to look all around them. "Next best thing to riding a dragon."

Moyrah was impressed, "*You've* ridden a dragon?!"

"They're handy for getting to someone who is hurt or sick in a remote place, and I was always light enough to be able to ride tandem on the bigger beasts. I partnered with the man we're to meet in Myrliot more often than not, that's how we grew so close."

The *Setting Sun* had left the central current. With the shore growing ever closer, Moyrah pointed out landmarks, "That burnt section there is what's left over from when lightening struck a big pine 'bout two months back. Lucky it was rainin so hard, or a lot more mighta burned."

Gran looked to Shail, "Where's that unioculus?" Shail retrieved the object, extending it to its full length.

"A long eye!" Moyrah enthused. "Never seen a solander with one of those. Captain has one o'course." Shail put the smaller end of the spyglass to his eye, then trained the other end at the shore. The unioculous brought everything into clear focus, as though he were standing amongst the greenery. When he'd looked his fill, he passed the unioculous to Gran. She took it, and after a few minutes, gave it to Moyrah. She took it eagerly. "This is a nice one you got here, not a scratch. Captain's is nice too, but he had it from his dah, and he from his, so it's got some wear and tear." She enjoyed herself, narrating what she saw

189

as she scanned the horizon. "Looks like the *Salty Harpy* is bound for the same port as us. I know the ship's boy on'er, had to bust his nose the first time I met'em."

Shail stared at her in startlement, "You broke someone's nose after just meeting him? Why?"

Moyrah tossed her head, "'Cause he thought being bigger than me meant he could treat me how he liked."

Gran chuckled. "Let me guess, big boy?" When Moyrah nodded, Gran said, "I find the booger hook effective against such fools."

Moyrah brayed with laughter, "The *what?!*"

Shail rolled his eyes, "A more appropriate name would be DND, for double nostril domination. But it's not an official maneuver. I asked."

"Official or not, it's saved me more than once!" Gran looked at Moyrah. "Punching the nose of a seasoned brawler won't do you much good, but," she held up her hand, with all but the first two fingers curled in towards her palm, "no one can argue convincingly when you've got their nose." Gran mimed thrusting her two fingers upwards, then crooked them and pulled the arm towards her body.

Moyrah's eyes shone, "I'll hafta remember that one!" Shail groaned.

Gran said, "You may have that bit of self-defense in return for the meal. Thank you for bringing up the basket, I don't think Shail or I could have managed it."

Shail felt stung, "I could have! If I'd wanted to ….."

"'Course you could mate," Moyrah was quick to reassure him. "Nuthin to it but practice." Shail felt mollified, and missed the amused look Gran shot at Moyrah. "Look, there's Myrliot!" Shail followed with his eyes to where Moyrah pointed. "Take a peep." She passed the unioculous to Shail. Through it, Shail saw the town they were swiftly approaching. It looked similar to his hometown, with multiple long piers connected to a large floating dock in front of a line of warehouses. Beyond those were store fronts, and at the farthest reaches Shail saw large, dignified manors.

"It looks like home." Shail felt his throat constrict.

"Looks like port to me. The *Setting Sun* is home, wherever she is. Seems strange to want to stay in one place all the time." Moyrah glanced at Shail worriedly. "But to each his own, that's what the Captain always says."

"You really think a lot of your father," Shail said with envy.

"'Course. Don't you of your dah?"

Shail shrugged, looking away from her. "I never knew my father. He died before I was born."

"*Oh,*" Moyrah said quietly. "Sorry mate." Gran put a comforting hand on Shail's shoulder, and swallowed hard. Moyrah seemed to reach a decision, "Have you met the Captain?" When Shail shook his head, she said, "You got to before you leave the *Setting Sun.*"

Perplexed by her sudden vehemence, Shail nodded, "If you say so. But why?"

"You'll like him." Moyrah refused to elaborate. "Oh, I almost forgot. Hey, Peatea. C'mere." Moyrah held a coaxing finger out to the parrot, who had opened her eyes upon hearing her name. She lowered her head, butting it against Moyrah's finger. Moyrah gave her a good scritch, and was rewarded with a bird upon her hand. "This here's the band I told you about." Shail and Gran Rox focused on Peatea's leg, which had a thin coil of green. Almost as if she were showing it off, Peatea stretched the leg out to the side for a long moment, the switched to the other leg, before finally settling with a full body feather shake.

The *Setting Sun* came within hailing distance of a pier, and Moyrah transferred the bird to her shoulder. Their arrival had been noted, and two dockhands were ready and waiting to catch mooring ropes. When the ship was secured, Moyrah looked at Shail, "Gonna need another push to get down solander?"

Shail glared at her with all the dignity he could muster, "*No,* thank you."

192

"Age before beauty," Gran said as she held her hand out for the safety line. Moyrah politely handed it to her. "See you in a minute!" With a wink to them both, Gran dropped to sit with her legs dangling through the roost's opening, then scoot forward until the rope caught her weight and began to lower her down to the deck. Shail wanted to watch, but could not bring himself to do so.

Moyrah had no such compunctions, and kneeled at the edge of the roost's opening, staring downwards, "She's down! Your turn." The safety line made its way back to the roost. Moyrah held it out to Shail. He took it, hooking it to his belt. He held the line in his hand, staring at it as he listened to his heartbeat grow louder in his ears. He felt a gently touch on his shoulder, "Nothing but practice mate." Shail looked down into Moyrah eyes. "Done it once already, time to make it twice." She grinned, "Honest, most solanders who sail with us don't get to see the roost, so you and your gran are something special."

Bolstered by her encouraging words, Shail squared his shoulders, "I'm ready." He did as Gran had done, sitting down and then scooting close to the edge. When his legs were free to swing, Shail forced himself to look down. The knuckles on his hands turned white as he gripped the edge of the roost.

"You can do this," whispered Moyrah.

"I can do this," Shail whispered to himself. He moved his hands to the safety line. He looked at Moyrah. "See you in a minute!" He dropped.

Chapter 16

Settling In

Tal proved to be a demure woman, rarely speaking unless spoken to, and always answering in a low, somewhat raspy voice. Leeinn's attempts to learn more about her were only quasi-successful, for Tal was very good at deflecting personal questions. She asked Gira's servant, "You sound a little hoarse, is your throat sore?"

"No mistress, thank you. I caught a very bad case of the chills as a child, and it permanently altered my voice. It doesn't hurt."

"Call me Leeinn, please. Trader Nassine told us you haven't been with Gira's family long."

"Only a few months."

"What did you do before?"

"Similar work to what I have now."

"What made you take up with Gira's family?"

"It is an honor to work in such an esteemed household."

"Why did you volunteer to stay with Gira?"

"It seemed the simplest solution to my mistress' problem."

Gira shook her head impatiently, "Why do you care what a *servant* does? You never asked *me* all these questions.".

Leeinn fought a twitch of irritation, but decided it was not worth starting an argument, "You've seen your rooms, are we ready to visit the dining hall?" Tancer looked up hopefully at this suggestion. "Are you hungry Tal?" When she nodded, Leeinn said, "Join us, we were on our way to get food when Trader Nassine found us and told us about the change of plans."

"I haven't finished moving all of Mistress Gira's things …."

"We can help you with whatever is left," offered Tiny.

Tal seemed surprised at this offer. "That's very kind of you."

Tiny gave Tal a friendly smile. "It sounds like we're all going to be working together while you and Gira stay at the abbey. Tancer and I are always ready to lend a helping hand."

Tancer nodded his agreement, "Especially if the help is *after* a meal."

The group left the gois rooms, and made their way to the dining hall. Lunch was nearly over by the time they arrived, but there was still plenty for everyone. All five were quick to thank the men and woman who cheerfully waited upon them. The servers seemed to find Tancer's gluttony amusing, for they took great pains to bring entire dishes just for him.

"Here you are Brother, a pan of mashed potatoes with Sister Alkanet's gravy."

"And wash it down with this pitcher of fresh strawberry lemonade!" Tancer accepted all that was offered with a giant grin. By contrast, Tal ate sparingly, and drank only water. When Leeinn assured her she was welcome to eat all she wished, Tal insisted the meager portions she had accepted were more than enough. They talked amongst themselves while Tancer finished cleaning his many plates.

When he finished, Tancer looked decidedly sleepy, "That was a good lunch. I think I'm ready for a nap."

"Really? I was thinking of finding my team leader, see if she's willing to take all of you on." Neither Tancer, nor Gira, seemed particularly thrilled by this idea.

Tiny delicately pinched Tancer's ear between her thumb and forefinger, "Time we earned our keep." She stood, pulling Tancer up with her.

He plastered a fixed smile upon his face, while making his eyes bulge comically large, "Of course, dear, anything you say dear. Just don't take my poor ear off. I may need to wear glasses someday."

They left the dining hall, Leeinn guiding them expertly through Del Abbey. "The library is down that hall. It's always open, so people can read or study whenever they want. The infirmary is that door over there. If any of you have an interest in medicine, they are always glad for extra help." They stopped as they reached the open doors of their destination. "And this is the main staging area for daily operations."

They entered a room noisy with conversation and movement. A woman called out, "Is team four done cleaning Hopeful Hall?"

"Yes," a man answered, "they checked back in a few minutes ago. Where do you want team twelve?"

"Have them report to the kitchens. The visiting families are due to leave the day after tomorrow, so the abbot is throwing a final feast to send them off. They'll need all the help they can get."

"Yes sir." Leeinn waved a hand to get the Charge's attention.

"Oh, Leeinn. Good afternoon. You've got a crowd with you."

"Yes, I was looking for Rustylah, to see if my friends could join our work team."

"She'll be pleased, with Yoika being out on maternity, and Jokinson still on light duty for his sprained ankle." She checked the clipboard he held in her hand. "Looks like your favorite. Your team is on berry bush detail."

Leeinn wriggled with pleasure, "Thanks Zamch, we'll go there now!"

The berry bushes were near the northern abbey wall, by the beehives. Each berry type had its own long, neat row. There was a mixture of people along the lines, each gathering their harvest into a basket clipped to their hip.

A woman stood at the front, shouting instructions, interspersed with encouragement, "Toman, leave off that bush, you left the whole side of that last one unharvested! Tammin, good work, that's your third basket, take a break. Himonan, what have I said about eating the berries?"

"Don't eat'em 'til they're washed?"

"That's right. No sense in making more work for the infirmary." She noticed Leeinn and the four following her. "Afternoon all. Need something?

199

"I have some new workers for you, if you'll have them."

The team lead eyed them all critically, then smiled gratefully. "Looks like a decent bunch. Grab some baskets, and start filling them." They nodded their understanding, and joined their teammates among the bushes.

They spent the rest of the afternoon going up and down the rows, laughing and singing snatches of songs to ease the work. Another team seemed devoted to toting the full baskets from the fields to the kitchen's storerooms. A couple of children with buckets of water walked among the workers, offering the contents to each in turn. Everyone they approached gratefully accepted, drinking down gulps of the cool liquid, some splashing their face and hands. After a couple hours, the team lead clapped her hands to get everyone's attention. "Good work! The kitchens should be pleased at all you've managed to gather, should make quite a few pies."

The pile of baskets was much reduced, with the last being carried away as Tancer smacked his hands clean, "A job well done I'd say. Now, how about a snack?" Three women groaned. "It should be nearing dinner time, right?"

Gira's eye lit, "Maybe there'll be dishes made with the berries we picked!"

"So they'll taste extra sweet, because Tiny handled them herself."

Tiny ducked her head in embarrassment, while Gira looked on with envy, "I hope I find someone someday that talks about me the way Tancer talks about you."

Tiny looked at her husband with fondness, "Omal aid you in your search. I think I was lucky. Am lucky."

Tancer winked at his wife, "I'm the lucky one, love. Imagine a low-born man like me having a wife like you!"

Gira looked surprised, "Oh, is *that* why your families didn't approve of the match?"

Tancer nodded, "My family digs ditches."

Tiny was quick to defend her husband, "Roads would flood anytime it rained without ditches. I don't see why that job should be any less important than someone who sits in an office all day." Tiny ran a hand through her braids, making them click together. It was obviously a self-soothing gesture.

Gira tried to act nonchalant, "Love can't be denied. I had an aunt, the family doesn't like to talk about her. She was supposed to inherit, but she wanted to marry the second son of a shoreman. He didn't even have his own boat! My grandparents were frightfully angry. Threw her out, then took up my mother as heir." Gira shook her head sadly. "I never saw Auntie Fehau after that. I hear she went to live with her husband's family."

Tiny said quietly, "I hope she's happy."

201

Gira roused herself from her memories, "As do I! She was always funny, my aunt. I think that's what brought her to her husband's attention. A silly joke."

"Do you know it?"

"Know what?"

"The joke?"

Gira looked pained, "Yes, but it's not very good."

Tancer looked interested, "Now I have to hear it."

Gira took a deep breath, "Why did the dragon cross the road?"

Tancer looked expectant, "I don't know. Why?"

Gira looked at her audience with a deadpan expression, "To get to the other side."

When nothing else seemed to be forthcoming, Leeinn asked, "Is that it?"

Gira nodded, "That's it. I told you it wasn't very good."

"She was right."

"I guess love makes things funnier?"

"Sounds about right. Tancer may love to eat, but anytime he cooks the food comes out funny."

"*Ha, ha, ha*, very droll, dear wife."

"Did you just call me a troll?"

"Never, you aren't *nearly* green enough."

Tal said, "I still need to move the mistress' things …"

"Right, let's lend a hand with the luggage, then go for dinner!" There were no strong objections to his plan.

As the Charge had said, Del Abbey was throwing a last feast to bid farewell to the Hopeful Ceremony visitors. Leeinn and Gira said goodbye to Tiny and Tancer, with Tal keeping near Gira's elbow. Husband and wife went to find seats among the Accepted, and were soon swallowed up by the crowd.

Trader Nassine was sitting next to Rumaru, having her glass refilled by a passing pitcher-bearer. She returned her daughter's nod of acknowledgement, but when she spoke, it was to Leeinn, "Your abbey has outdone itself. It even rivals the City for splendor."

Leeinn said, "Thank you, Trader Nassine."

"Should you ever decide to go Abroad, my family and I would be happy to host you."

"Again, thank you, but I don't think I'll ever leave Del Abbey."

"And I never thought my heir would want to become Hopeful. Always keep your options open, that's our family motto."

"And I'm sure my daughter appreciates the sentiment of your offer." Leeinn felt glad of her father's saving remark.

Nassine picked up her glass, swirling its contents before taking a sip, "Your father also assured me that you will attend my daughter, in addition to Tal."

"I believe what I said was that my daughter has a tradition of befriending the newly Accepted, and potential Hopefuls, so Gira should have no trouble fitting in."

"Yes, well, I was paraphrasing."

"Of course." Rumaru smiled, nodding understandingly.

"She's already introduced me to our team lead. I helped pick berries before dinner."

Nassine looked mildly impressed, "Really? Put you to work already? Well, I suppose that shouldn't surprise me. For an abbey, this place is run tighter than most businesses." Leeinn was not sure she cared for the comparison, but chose to keep quiet. Gira's mother would leave tomorrow, Leeinn could tolerate her until then.

"You are too generous," said Rumaru. "We are a fortunate people. I am glad we were able to share our bounty with good friends." Trader Nassine preened under the compliment. Leeinn was impressed by her father's diplomacy. Small wonder he was Father Abbot of Del Abbey!

Dinner and dessert were done, and people made their goodnights. "Can you find your way back to your rooms?" asked Leeinn.

Gira looked doubtful, "I'm not sure I could find them again. Tal?"

Tal shook her head, "I should hate to lead you astray mistress. This place is so large, I fear finding our way could be difficult."

"Then I'll show you both the way!"

When they got to their quarters, Gira dropped into a chair, "I'm glad you were with us! I was lost as soon as we left the dining hall. It feels like it's been a long day." Tal looked tired too, but made no complaint.

"I'm glad I could help. I hope you sleep well. I'll come to get you in the morning, take you to breakfast."

Gira winced, "How, uh, *early* should we expect you?"

Leeinn stifled a smile, "Oh, an hour past sunrise, I should think."

Gira's face took on a miserable mien, "Really, as early as that? I'm not certain I'll be hungry quite so soon after the feast we just had." Tal ducked her face to the side, but Leeinn thought she caught a smile on her face.

"I suppose I can make it *two* hours past sunrise, if you really want to sleep that late."

"This is the first place I've heard two hours past sunrise called *late*."

"Tancer would probably agree with you. I guess it wouldn't hurt to let you sleep in a little, until you're used to being here."

Gira's face became serious, "No, come get me on time. If I'm going to become Hopeful, I need to prove I'm worthy."

Leeinn felt her estimation of Gira rise, "As you wish, but try not to worry about *'being worthy'*. Just be yourself." Tal shot Leeinn a surprised look, but was quick to drop her gaze. Leeinn ventured, "Tal, did you have any interest in becoming Hopeful?"

Tal's eyes widened, and she paled slightly, "I, uh, that is …."

Leeinn had yet to see the woman so flustered, "You don't have to, I just wondered if maybe that was one of the reasons you volunteered to stay with Gira."

Gira did not look as though she cared for the idea, "But what if she were to be Accepted, and I refused? What would I tell people?"

Leeinn huffed in exasperation, "You didn't even *consider* that might be why she wanted to stay?"

Gira flushed, "No," she said softly, "I'm sorry, that was selfish, wasn't it?" Gira turned to Tal. "If you want to become Hopeful too, then of course I'll help you, just have you've been so helpful to me."

Tal looked uncomfortable, "It is my duty to serve you mistress, you owe me nothing."

Leeinn said, "Think about it, we can talk again after you've experienced abbey life for yourself."

And with that, Leeinn withdrew for the night.

Chapter 17

The Last of the *Setting Sun*

Shail dropped! But this time, he knew what to expect. The safety line took his weight as soon as he was clear of the roost. Shail fought the urge to shut his eyes, forcing himself to focus on the flowing river. "Looking good solander!" Shail glanced up and saw Moyrah grinning down at him, her hair hanging over one shoulder. He gave her a shaky smile, while maintaining his tight grip on the line. Sooner than expected, Shail stood with his feet flat against the deck.

"There you are, well done grandson mine!" Gran Rox beamed at Shail.

"I …. I did it. I did it!" Shail was elated.

"Never doubted you," said Gran. "And here comes Moyrah." Gran helped Shail unclip the safety line from his belt, and both stepped away from the mast.

When Moyrah joined them, her smile was so wide that Shail could have counted every one of her teeth. "Now you've two visits to the roost under your belt. Keep this up, and you'll be a sailor in no time."

Shail felt a little embarrassed. "Thank you. For everything."

Moyrah cocked her head, "Everything?"

"For helping Gran and me to the roost, and bringing up the food, and not teasing me about not wanting to go up there …."

Moyrah waved her hand dismissively, "Oh, that. Nothing I wouldn't do for any shipmate."

"But I'm not your shipmate. I'm a solander, remember."

Moyrah's eyebrows made a shallow *v* as she considered, "Hmm, you got a point there." Then she brightened, "But I know how's to fix that." She dug into a pocket, and drew out the pair of dice she'd been toying while waiting for Shail and Gran Rox. "Here. Every proper sailor has a pair of these."

She handed them to Shail, who took them carefully, "Are you sure?"

"Sure I'm sure. I got more, and this way, you got something to remember the *Setting Sun*."

Shail suddenly felt shy, and nearly stuttered as he said, "Thank you. I don't think I'll forget it, or you, anytime soon." He looked at the dice nestled in his palm. They were made out of some sort of stone, mostly a shade

209

of seashell interspersed with silver stripes. He showed them to Gran.

"Very nice. Thank you Moyrah."

Shail put his new dice into his pocket, feeling their slight weight against his thigh, "Should we get our things Gran?"

"'Long as you promise not to leave without meeting the Captain!" Moyrah seemed determined to have her way.

"But I already know the Captain," said Gran in confusion.

Moyrah said, "But *he* don't."

Gran glanced at Shail, "Is that important?"

"Yes."

Gran shrugged, "If you say so. Want to take us to him now?"

Moyrah jerked her chin towards the ship's helm, "Should try there first." She led Gran and Shail to the ship's wheel, where a tall, strongly built man was standing with his back to the dock, eyeing his crew as they reefed the *Setting Sun's* sails. "Captain?"

The man Moyrah addressed looked towards the three approaching him, "Hello. Did you get an eyeful of Myrliot?"

"Aye sir! We were in the roost these last few hours sir." Moyrah gestured to Shail. "Thought you should meet my shipmate, Shail."

The captain held his hand out for Shail to shake. "Any shipmate of Moy's a mate o'mine. Names Cohaff." Shail's hand was dwarfed by Cohaff's. "Now that we're here, you'll be leaving us?"

Gran nodded affably, "Soon as we get our gear."

Cohaff nodded, "Well then, Amik and Omal watch over you. You're welcome back on the *Setting Sun*, anytime."

Gran said, "Thank you for the safe and swift trip."

Cohaff bowed slightly, "It is a pleasure with passengers such as yourselves." His tone was merry as he added, "And the food seems to improve dramatically when you are onboard."

"See that you keep your cook, and I'll book passage often as I can."

"Done!" Gran took a turn shaking Cohaff's hand.

Moyrah inserted a muttered, "Captain? A word?"

"Hmm?" She motioned him a few steps away from Shail and Gran. He followed her, and when she deemed they were far enough away, they held a whispered conference. As it happened, the wind was blowing in such a way that Shail was still able to catch most of what they

211

said. However, that did him little good, for they spoke in a language he did not recognize.

"*Ehe t'neseodo evaha a hada.*"

The captain rubbed it chin, "*Tahata oso?*"

"*S'ehe werce wono. Ylimafa, uoyo duluoco yasa.*"

Captain Cohaff barked a laugh, "*Danaa uoyo ginitanawa mihi saa a rehotorbo?*"

"What do you think that's all about?" he asked Gran.

Gran was studiously watching the water, "Quiet now, grandson mine, and maybe I can tell you." Shail felt his eyes grow large.

"*You* can understand what they're saying?"

"I speak a smattering of Haryomo. Enough to get by."

"Where did you learn to ..." Gran shushed Shail with a warning glance. Shail obediently shushed.

"*Tii duluowo ebe daba tono oto evaha a hada.*"

"*Woho duluowo uoyo wonko?*"

Moyrah gave him a pleading look, "*I epoho I revene wonko! Er'uoyo ehete tesebe hada erehete sii!*" Captain Cohaff made an audible sniff, and Shail saw him blink a few times very fast. Sensing she had nearly won, Moyrah pressed her advantage, "Shail *sii werece, ehe severesede oto evaha a doogo hada, emasa saa ydobaynaa.*" If the sound of his name was not a giveaway that they were discussing him, the way Captain Cohaff cut his eyes towards him, and then quickly away, all but confirmed Shail's suspicion. Was Moyrah telling the captain about the roost?

The captain said, "*Uoyo erusu s'tahata tahawa ehe satanawa? Ehe tihigimi revene eese suu niaga.*"

"*Tubu fii ehe diasa seye?*" Moyrah answered. A low rumble from deep in his chest was the captain's only comment. Moyrah smiled, and all but danced back to Shail and Gran Rox. "Got a question for you," she said to Shail.

"Oh?"

"You want a dah?"

"What?"

"You can share mine, if you want." Her follow-up statement seemed to make as little sense as her first.

"Share? You want to share your father with me?" When she nodded, Shail could only blurt, "*Why?!*" That was apparently *not* the response Moyrah had expected.

She actually looked a little hurt, "Because you said you've never had one." An idea seemed to occur on her, for she was quick to add, "And the captain's a good enough dah, having one more son won't make any difference."

213

"How many brothers do you have?"

"Five." Gran chuckled at Shail's impressed look.

"And how many sisters?"

Cohaff said, "Moyrah is my only daughter."

Shail was suddenly vibrating with excitement. "Did you hear that Gran? Moyrah's family is like the one in my favorite book!"

Gran nodded, rubbing her chin thoughtfully, "The Six Sons And the Seven Sorrows? Hmm, you're right. Which would make you …."

"Erryk, The last Son!"

"Didn't he turn out to be a prince?"

"Yes, the only trueborn son of King Dutchee. The Seven Sorrows would have conquered all of Mousar if not for Prince Erryk." Shail grew quiet, "But we know who my father was, and he was no king."

"No," Gran murmured, "But a good man, none-the-less." Shail struggled with himself. Would it be right to accept Moyrah's offer, or would it be disrespectful to the father he had never met?

"Do you think he would mind?" he asked worriedly.

Gran shook her head, "No, I don't think he would have had a problem with anything that made you happy."

Shail considered his feelings, "What about Tabirc? Would it hurt Tabirc's feelings?"

"I would answer the same. If you're happy, he'd be happy for you."

The last of his worries laid to rest, Shail nodded to Moyrah. "Then, yes. Uh, sister?"

"Maybe if we ever meet on land. On the Setting Sun, it's just *shipmate*." Shail felt strangely pleased at Moyrah's clarification.

Captain Cohaff had been silent as he watched the exchange, but now stepped forward. He put a calloused hand onto Shail's shoulder, "Welcome to the crew, and the family, son."

"Thank you sir," Shail could barely get the words past the throb in his throat.

Moyrah seemed fit to burst, "Told you you'd want to meet'em!" Laughter broke out amongst the new family.

"Captain, there's a man on the dock, says he's looking for our passengers."

Gran grew tense, "Did he give a name?"

"Yes ma'am, said it was Tabirc."

Gran visibly relaxed, "Alright, Shail, sounds like it time for us to go."

Shail felt almost dizzy with dismay, "But, do we have to leave, right now?"

He felt Captain Cohaff gently squeeze his shoulder, "Tide waits for no man." Shail looked up into soft brown eyes. "No matter where you go, you're crew."

Moyrah touched Shail's elbow, echoing their father, "No matter where you go, you're crew." Shail nodded, but could not speak.

Gran said, "Thank you Captain."

"Shall I have one of my men bring your things, so you and the lad can meet up with your friend?"

"Yes, thank you."

"When should we expect you back?"

"In the morning."

"The *morning?!*" Shail could barely believe his ears. "But I thought you said there was a surprise."

"Which you will get once we're off the *Setting Sun.*"

Moyrah tried to bolster Shail's spirits, "I'll want to hear what the surprise was, next time we meet."

"But who knows when that will be," whispered Shail.

"Wind and waves, shipmate. Trust them, and they'll take you where you need to go."

"Though not always where you want," commented Gran in a somber voice. "Still, Tabirc is waiting." She began to walk slowly towards the gangplank that connected the *Setting Sun* to the Myrliot dock. "Tomorrow morning Captain. *Early.*"

Cohaff gave her a crisp salute, "We'll be ready and waiting." He gave Shail one last smile, then turned his attention back to his ship.

"Good luck!" said Moyrah, who followed after her captain. Shail watched them both go, a storm of emotions warring within him.

He and Gran both looked landward as they heard a familiar voice. "Ahoy you two!"

There was naked relief on Gran's face as she answered, "Ahoy yourself! Been waiting long?"

Shail recognized Tabirc's rough, smiling face, "No more than half an hour or so. Shail! Have a good Stallion Feather Ceremony?"

Shail's sadness could not withstand Tabirc's genuine enthusiasm, "The best! Uncle Wengsper gave me a firestarter pouch."

"That'll come in handy. Feel like having a couple campfires?"

"You may have to twist his arm," laughed Gran. "Is everything ready?"

Tabirc sobered slightly, "Everything. Give the word, and we'll fly."

"Then let's not waste time. Soon as they bring our bags, we'll follow you."

Shail's ears had perked upon hearing the word *fly*. "Is he talking about my surprise?"

Gran shot Tabirc a look, "Yes, and that's the only hint you get!"

Teegan brought their things and gave them both a farewell salute.. With Tabirc's help, they made their way through Myrliot, which looked as much like Shail's hometown up close as it had from the roost. He almost expected to see his mother walking down to meet them. But of course, they had left her far behind. Shail did not have time to dwell on this thought as Tabirc lead them up, down, and across streets, until Shail could not have said which way the docks were. "Are we getting close?" Gran asked. Tabirc nodded. "Then I will thank you to close your eyes from here," she said to Shail. She held an arm out for him. "I'll make sure you don't trip." She refused to budge until Shail obeyed her. They continued walking for a few minutes, then Shail felt Gran stop. "Here we are. Keep your eyes closed!" Shail squeezed his lids tighter.

"I'll bring them 'round," said Tabirc. Shail heard his footsteps recede.

He waited impatiently beside Gran, shifting from foot to foot, "Can I look now?"

A moment passed.

"Yes, you can look now."

Shail opened his eyes, and gasped!

Chapter 18

Dragon Stables

Leeinn went to the gois rooms after a long dawn stroll around the abbey walltops. When she knocked on the door, Tal took mere moments to answer, stepping to the side and closing the door behind Leeinn..

"Good morning Tal. Is Gira up?"

Tal shook her head, "Not yet. Should I wake her?"

"I'm up," mumbled Gira as she stumbled out of her bedroom, her eyes barely open.

Leeinn greeted her, "Good morning Gira! Sleep well?"

Gira nodded, then yawned, "Bed isn't as soft, or as big, as I'm used to, but I managed." Leeinn pretended to stifle her own yawn to mask her smile, "That's good. Do you want breakfast?"

"I can bring you a plate if you'd prefer to eat here, mistress," Tal offered.

Gira seemed to consider, saw Leeinn, and slowly shook her head, "No, I can be ready in just a few minutes." She scurried off to the bathing room.

Leeinn tried making small talk with Tal while they waited. "You were already up, I hope you slept well too."

"Yes, I'm just used to rising early."

"Is it necessary for your work?

"Some things are easier to get done before the official business of the day."

"Like what?"

"Preparing food for my mistress to break her fast, laying out fresh under garments, bringing in fresh flowers to scent the room, things of that sort."

"It sounds like a lot."

"I'm compensated well enough."

They turned as the door to the bathing room opened, and Gira popped her head around, "Tal, have you seen my face cream? I need it for the circles under my eyes."

"I think it's in your travel case mistress. The gray one." Tal left Leeinn to assist Gira. They returned a short time later, Gira in a pale green dress with golden dragon egg lotus along the hem and neckline, and stallion feather patterns running down both sleeves.

She twirled in front of Leeinn, "Do you like it? I had it made just for our trip here. I was going to wear it last night, but mother said it wouldn't be appropriate to take attention away from the Hopefuls, so I'm going to wear it today."

"It's very nice, but are you sure you want to work in it?"

Gira looked at Leeinn's brown habit, belted at her waist with a braided cord. She pinched her dress between her fingers, feeling the delicate cloth, "I didn't think about that."

"Maybe save it for later. I don't know what chore our team will be assigned today, and I'd hate for it to be ruined."

"Very well," Gira said, a bit sulkily. She went back to her room, and emerged a short time later. Leeinn was gratified to see she was wearing a sensible blouse and skirt. "Will this do?"

"I should think so."

"Good, then let's go to the dining hall. I'm famished!"

"Of course. Tal, are you ready to go?" When Tal nodded, the three women made their way towards the Dining Hall. Leeinn made conversation, "Your family is leaving tomorrow. I hope you two won't be homesick."

"I've never been away from my family for more the a few days." Gira seemed to waver. "But I won't be alone, not really. Tal will be staying with me, and I have you, and Tiny, and Tancer. And all the other Accepted have been just as nice."

Tal dipped her head when Gira mentioned her name, "I will do all I can do ensure your stay is pleasant, mistress."

"And I'll do all I can to make sure *both* your stays are pleasant," said Leeinn.

It was no surprise to see Tiny sitting with Tancer, but to Leeinn's amusement, Cloudhoof's rider was also among them. Their table was just large enough to sit all six, so the three late comers grabbed bench.

Randoi greeted them warmly, "Good morning ladies. A better morning for us, now that you're here."

Tiny feigned insult, "What am I, chopped dragon liver?"

Randoi winked at her, "No, just taken."

Tancer pulled his wife closer, and Leeinn thought she caught a hint of challenge behind his pretend protectiveness, "And don't you forget it Bright Eyes."

Randoi laughed merrily at the epithet, "That's better than most nicknames around here, I think I'll add it to my list."

Leeinn could not help but tease her friend, "You might convince Lorelia, but I want to be there when you try to talk Rena into calling you anything but silly."

"You leave my sister to me, when I turn on the charm, not even she can resist."

"I can believe that," Gira said, fluttering her eyes. "You're more handsome than all my brothers combined."

"That's why they paired me with Cloudhoof, I'm too pretty for a mare."

"That is *not* how it works," Leeinn said with mild exasperation, casting a glance at Gira. "And not everyone here knows you're joking."

Randoi looked properly chastised, "Sorry, I didn't mean to confuse anyone."

"Not at all, it was quite funny!" Gira was proving to be a bit of a flirt. Leeinn suddenly better understood Trader Nassine wanting her daughter chaperoned.

Randoi said, "Now that you're all here, I can tell you the good news. Master Dooreg heard from Ramch that all of you joined the same work team, so he pulled a favor and had you assigned to his stable today. Wanted to try your paces, so to speak."

224

Tiny leapt up from her seat as though she had been scalded, "*Really?!* Why didn't you say so? When is he expecting us?"

Tancer looked faint, "Not before we finish breakfast, I'm sure."

"Grab a couple rolls to go!"

Tancer sighed, then smiled as hooked his arm through Tiny's, "Alright, I can see you won't be happy 'til we go. Onward to dragons!"

Randoi raised a questioning eyebrow at Leeinn, "Do you want to lead, or shall I?"

"I think you can handle it."

Randoi made an elegant bow, "Your confidence gives me wings as sure as Cloudhoof's."

"Are you sure he won't mind you going to the dragon stables?"

Gira's curiosity couldn't resist such rich bait, "Why would he mind? I though dragons and winged horses got along. Needed each other, even."

Randoi nodded, "It's not so much about them not getting along, as that some mounts of either species can be a bit jealous over their partners. The scent of the dragon stable might make Cloudhoof worry I had a wandering eye. And it's not unheard of for humans to switch from one species to the other."

Gira's eyes grew wide, "I'm trying to imagine a jealous dragon, and I don't think I like it!"

Randoi was quick to reassure her, "Oh, it would never go any further than a bit of noise. Creatures with wings can't afford even minor injuries, so they settle their arguments by performance."

"What about the farmers? They're bigger than the other dragon types, and the winged horses."

Leeinn said, "True. It's their size, and claws, that grant them the last word on most things. Not that they use the advantage very often."

Gira looked relieved, "That's good to know!"

Tiny asked, "But if a farmer wanted a human partner, that'd be that?"

Randoi scratched an eyebrow, "The only other creature that might argue is another farmer."

Gira asked, "And what if the human did not want to partner the farmer?"

"They seem to have a knack for knowing who would make a good companion. I've never seen a person turn down a farmer that showed real interest in them. Ahh, here we are." Randoi stood with his back to the dragon stable, one hand held over his head. "I'll let you take it from here Leeinn, no reason to give Cloudhoof a reason to sulk. He gets enough sugar cubes as it is!" He waved goodbye to all of them, then left for his own stable. Leeinn felt like a father dragon guiding a nervous group of foal fledglings.

Before they'd made it more than a few feet into the building, a voice called out to them, "Ahh, excellent! You're just in time." Master Dooreg had to put down an armload of sweet grass to greet them, dusting his hands against each other. "Your team is spreading new bedding in the stalls. Here, take this bit, and start on that one over there. Leeinn can show you how it's done."

Tiny was quickest to answer, "*Yes sir!*"

Master Dooreg boomed a laugh, "That's what I like to hear! If you need anything, or have any questions, don't hesitate to ask anyone in the stable, myself included." Gira appeared slightly overwhelmed by the big man, and tried unsuccessfully to hide behind Leeinn. Master Dooreg didn't miss a thing, and lowered his voice, as though speaking to a frightened animal. "You'd be the Trader's daughter?"

"Ye-yes," Gira squeaked.

"Hard workers, traders. I'm glad to have you here."

"O-oh, uh, thank you." Master Dooreg winked at Leeinn, and she smiled back.

Tiny pointed to the sweetgrass at Master Dooreg's feet, "May I take that for you sir?"

"If you think you can handle it. It's actually two bales bound together. Most people only take one at a time, but I," he flexed a massive bicep, "like to work up a sweat."

Without further comment, Tiny bent and lifted the sweetgrass with ease, "I'll just take it to that stall, thank you sir."

She suited actions to words, Tancer following behind with a smug expression. "Tiny is no light weight, she's always been stronger than me."

Tiny dropped her burden in the middle of the stall Master Dooreg had directed them to, "It's nothing, really. I pick things up, and put them down."

Gira said, "Well I would have needed Tal *and* Leeinn's help to carry all that."

All four looked to Leeinn. She gestured towards the floor, "We sweep the old grass out twice a week, and replace it with fresh so the dragons have a nice nest to sleep in."

Gira said, "Oh good, I was afraid we'd have to clean it *every* day."

Tancer said, "I would have thought such large animals would need their stalls cleaned more often than that."

Gira was quick to agree, "I know our head groom makes the stableboys change out our horses litter every day."

"Dragons don't foul their sleeping areas. Those who work in the winged horse stable have to do like your stableboys."

"Sounds like a lot more work," said Tancer. "I think I'd rather stick with the dragons."

Gira crossed her arms firmly, "Not me. Winged horses are much better."

Tiny said, "Maybe we can ask to be assigned to the other stables tomorrow?" Gira looked at Leeinn hopefully.

Leeinn hedged, "I'll ask Master Wyntrin." That seemed to satisfy Gira for the moment.

The six busied themselves gathering thick handfuls of sweet grass, and walking over every inch of the stall, making sure there was an even layer of bedding.

Tancer paid particular attention to the dragon's water source, "I've never seen a bucket on the *outside* of a stall door. Is that the food bin is against the far wall?"

Gira said, "Goodness, either must be as deep as my arm!"

"Dragons eat a lot."

Gira shuddered, "And you're *sure* they don't eat any meat but fish?"

Leeinn considered, "I suppose if you weren't familiar with a beast, it would make sense to be cautious." She shifted her feet upon the soft surface under her feet. "But I've known these dragons all my life, and I've never seen them act aggressive."

"I hope we can become as familiar with them as you," Tiny said fervently. "I think we've done all we can in this stall. Should we see if any others need attention?"

Gira put a hand to her lower back as she arched backwards in a stretch, "Can we take a break first?"

Tal was immediately by her side, "Shall I found a place for you to sit mistress? Maybe I can find some water for you too."

Gira almost looked like to would accept the offer, but seemed to think better of it after looking around the group and realizing no one else was complaining. "Thank you Tal, but I don't want to slow everybody down. If no one else is ready for a rest, I can wait."

Leeinn tried to think what her father would say, "I don't see why we couldn't sit for a few minutes."

They left the stall, leaving the wide sliding door open for when its occupant returned. Gira managed not to groan when they were directed to another stall, pasting a smile on her face that looked more grimace than grin. But with her friends to share the work, their chores were done soon enough. Freed, they returned to the Dining Hall for lunch, much to Tancer's delight.

Chapter 19

Goodbye Gran

Shail felt all the air leave his lungs as he breathed out a single word, "*Dragons.*" Tabirc stood before him and Gran Rox, holding a leading line in each hand. They were attached to the most beautiful, golden-brown beasts Shail had ever seen.

"Surprise, grandson mine! Was it worth the wait?"

"*Yes!*" Gran and Tabirc laughed at Shail's delight. "Where did you get them?"

Gran winked, "Called in a favor or two."

"Can I touch them?"

Tabirc held out the leading line in his left hand, "You'll have to, if you're to be my wingmate."

Shail could not believe his ears. "*Wingmate? Me?* We're *flying* to my assignment?!"

"Sure are. This one is your mount, she's called Stendow. Other one is mine, named Lowkrist." Shail was charmed when both dragons chirruped softly upon hearing their names. It reminded him of answering roll call at school. Tabirc tilted his head towards them, "I think they said, *'Nice to meet you'.*"

Shail took Stendow's lead in both hands, just as he had the safety line on the *Setting Sun*. She dropped her snout to sniff delicately at his head. Shail felt his hair being pulled up gently by her indrawn breath, and wondered if his face would crack from his smile. "It's nice to meet you too! Can we fly now?"

Gran *hurumphed*, "Oh sure, first it was, *'Gran, you can't leave tomorrow'*, but now it's, *'Thanks Gran, bye!'.*"

Tabirc chimed in, "Don't forget he's also getting an upgrade in traveling companion. Getting to spend time with yours truly, *and* ride dragons. Sorry, but nobody can beat that."

Shail had stopped listening to Gran and Tabirc's teasing to focus on his mount. He tentatively reached out to touch her nose. She accepted his caress, and Shail was surprised to find her scales warm to his hand. He had thought a dragon would feel cool, like a lizard. Stendow felt like she had been basking in direct sunlight.

Lowkrist let out a polite cough, and Tabirc reached over to pat her. "You're a good dragon too, aren't you?"

Lowkrist rumbled in a way that sounded suspiciously like a person saying, "*Mmhmm.*"

Gran said, "They're a fine pair friend, well done."

"I tried them out myself while I waited for you two. Both have been well trained, and they're able to maintain speed for long stretches. Perfect for our needs."

Shail felt a moment's puzzlement. "Why do we need fast dragons?"

Tabirc glanced towards Gran Rox, and Shail saw her shake her head very slightly. Tabirc was still smiling, but Shail thought it looked more forced than before, "Quicker we get home, sooner you can rest up for your assignment. Riding dragons is like riding any beast. First day is fun, second and third day you'll be feeling all the muscles you don't normally use."

Shail had nearly forgotten the reason he was going to stay with Tabirc. "When do I meet Master Conlun?"

"You get one day to recoop, then you're to attend him during his working hours, as well as be available in an emergency."

"Just like a real apprentice healer," Gran added. "I've known Conlun a long time, and he's a good teacher. I think you'll enjoy your time with him." Gran stared at Shail for a moment, then asked Tabirc, "*Could* you leave now?"

He considered, "I'll need to grab my gear, and the tack for the dragons."

Gran pressed, "That won't take long. You could cover some ground before it gets dark."

"Wait, *what*?" Shail whipped his head around to stare at Gran. "I didn't mean we should leave now! I thought we were going to see you off tomorrow. I thought I'd get one more chance to see M… the *Setting Sun*."

"It would mean an earlier start for me too. I'm sure Captain Cohaff would be able to leave tonight if I asked."

"But we had an early start, when we left home in the middle of the night."

Gran said, "Less time you waste here, more time you'll have to learn." Shail was not convinced.

Tabirc handed the leading line he still held in his right hand to Gran, "You two stay here with the dragons, and I'll get everything we need, and some hands to carry it all." Gran took the line, and Lowkrist merely blinked as she was handed off to a stranger. She and Stendow regarded the three humans before them, and Shail wondered what it must be like, to be so big, but to defer to smaller creatures.

Gran said, "Sounds good, see you soon." Tabirc waved to Shail, and was soon lost from sight. "He should be back soon, Tabirc can be quick when he wants."

"You're not telling me something," Shail said stubbornly.

Gran sighed, and the sound seemed loud in the quiet courtyard behind a large building Shail assumed was a dragon stable. "I've been thinking of your mother, and what I'm going to say to her the next time I see her. She's going to be angry with me for leaving like we did."

"But you left a note."

"Which I doubt did much to make her feel better, after waking up to find you gone. But it was the best I could do at the time." Gran Rox looked at Shail, but her face was inscrutable. "When I come to pick you up from your assignment, we will sit down and have a long talk, grandson mine. But like Captain Cohaff said, the tide waits for no one, and you should focus on what's ahead of you. The next few weeks are likely to be very busy, not to mention the next few days, which I will remind you will be spent riding the winds." Her last statement was enough to distract Shail from his reservations. He and Tabirc were going to ride *dragons*!

"You said you've ridden before, is there anything I need to know?"

"I was usually just baggage, so I'll leave your education to Tabirc. All you'll really need to do is enjoy the ride. You had a taste of height in the roost, but this will be a whole new level." Shail looked up at Stendow, his stomach fluttering at the thought of being up higher than the roost.

But he was no coward, and he certainly wasn't going to waste this singular opportunity. "Listen to Tabirc, and you shouldn't have anything to worry about."

"So we're flying all the way back to his village?"

"The dragons will drop you two off, then make their own way back here. They have a wonderful sense of direction, and most are trained to *'go home'* without a rider if need be." Shail was impressed. He and Gran made small talk while they waited for Tabirc to return, mostly about the dragons in front of them. Gran compared them to mounts she'd been on in the past. "I'm sure Tabirc has mentioned Indregas. She was one of my favorites too, though she was smaller than both these beauties."

Tabirc was true to his word; it was not long before he and another boy twice as big as Shail came around the corner, each carrying a thin saddle upon their shoulders, with bags hanging front and back so that Shail could barely tell what color shirts they were wearing. They dropped their burdens by the dragon's front feet, and Tabirc asked his assistant to saddle Lowkrist while he made his goodbyes. "This is everything. When the dragons are loaded up, we'll secure Shail and go." Shail eagerly watched the stableboy, trying to visualize *himself* performing the preparations. It did not seem much harder than saddling a horse, other than having to account for the wings. Loops and straps were made snug to Lowkrist's body, without impending her movement. "Watch this Shail, it's one of the first commands we teach both riders and mounts." He nodded to

Gran, who still held Lowkrist's lead line, "A trained dragon will only obey the person holding their reins, and you have to say their name before the command."

Gran said, "Lowkrist, saddle check!" Upon hearing the order, Lowkrist began to vigorously shake like a wet dog.

One strap proved looser than the others, but was quickly tightened by Tabirc. "One more time."

"Lokrist, saddle check."

This time, everything was flight ready. "Looks good. Now I'll load up your dragon." Tabirc managed to saddle Stendow even quicker than the stableboy had done Lowkrist, and he quietly explained what he was doing as he fixed each point. "And then you pull here, until it's tight enough to be flush against the skin, but you can still get your fingers underneath. My teacher always used to say, *'Make the saddle snug, not tight, and your dragon will fly comfortable day or night'.*" Shail wished he could get out his quill and parchment, everything Tabirc was showing him was important, and Shail always did better taking notes, and studying after, than remembering things the first time. Well, he'd have all of the time between now and when they got to Tabirc's village to ask questions. And the questions wouldn't really stop then, only their topic would change. From dragons to healing, what a strange way to end the summer. "Now you try."

Shail cleared his throat, "*Stendow*, saddle check. Please."

She obliged, and Shail saw the stableboy smile at him. "Proper respect! The Master will be happy to hear his dragons are in good hands."

When they luggage was loaded, it was finally time to say goodbye to Gran Rox. She held her arms out to Shail, and he hugged her as hard as she hugged him, keeping Stendow's reins firmly clutched in one hand. "You're going to do great, grandson mine. I can't wait to hear all about your assignment when I come to get you in three months' time."

"Have a good trip back. Tell mother and uncle that I miss them."

"I will."

Tabirc said, "You did pretty good with your first command. Ready for your second?" Shail nodded, hoping that Tabirc could not see how nervous he was. "Then ask your lovely skylady to *kneel down*."

Shail said, "Stendow, *kneel down* please." Stendow gracefully lowered her left leg until it lay on the ground, while keeping the other three bent just enough to accommodate the movement.

"Keep the reins in one hand while you climb. See the toe holds? Use them, and the saddle strap, to get to her back. I'll give you a boost."

With Tabirc's help, Shail was able to scramble up the scaled incline until he could hook a leg over and settle into the saddle. He looked down at Tabirc, then over at Gran. "I'm really on a dragon!"

Gran looked up at him, her face tender. "So you are."

Tabirc tapped Stendow's shoulder to get Shail's attention. "Here, put these on." He handed Shail a pair of clear-lensed goggles. "They'll protect your eyes while you ride." When Shail had complied Tabirc said, "Last part is the safety straps." Shail followed Tabirc's instructions until he was secured to the saddle at several points from the waist down. "She could fly upside down, or you could be unconcious, and you'd stick to her like a burr."

Shail gulped, "*Uhh*, neither of those things are likely to happen, right?"

"I hope not. Sleeping in the saddle doesn't *sit* well with me."

Shail giggled at Gran's groan. "Less puns, more flying. Off with you two!"

Tabirc said, "Shail, third command! *Stand ready*."

"Stendow, *stand ready* please!" Shail's mount stood.

When Tabirc was mounted and secured, he said, "We'll give two different commands now. You first. *Follow wingmate.*"

"Stendow, *follow wingmate.*" She looked at Lowkrist expectantly. Shail felt her muscles tense under his legs.

"Good, now secure the reins on the saddle hook, you won't be needing them." Tabirc waved to Gran, "Be seeing you."

She lifted a hand to him, "Clear skies and fair winds." She met Shail's eyes one last time.

Tabirc said, "Lowkrist, *fly!*"

And she did! A moment after she had leapt skyward, Stendow followed. Shail was immensely glad of the safety straps, for the sudden jerk would certainly have unseated him otherwise. He tried to yell, and felt his voice choked off as his teeth clicked together. Both dragons beat their wings hard to gain altitude. They were soon above the treetops, but Tabirc showed no signs of evening out. After what seemed like a long time, Shail saw Lowkrist's body straighten, and her wingbeats slowed to a steady rhythm. Stendow copied her wingmate, flying a little behind on Lowkrist's left side. It felt very strange, because to Shail it seemed as though he and his dragon were staying still, while everything else moved past them. He decided to risk

241

a peek down. The world had become a patchwork of green and brown. While they were still fairly close to Myrliot, Shail could see estates that looked like dollhouses, with people no bigger than ants. Focusing closer, Shail could see the delicate pattern on each of Stendow's individual scales. Most were bigger than his whole hand, overlapping one another to form the perfect natural armor. His added weight did not seem to bother her in the slightest. Lowkrist flew just as easily with Tabirc, and Shail let himself simply enjoy the experience. This was better than any surprise he could have imagined!

Chapter 20

The Farmers in the Dels

Gira held her palm out, "My hand hurts, I think I'm getting a blister. What do you think?"

Tal inspected the area with a look of mild concern. "That spot is rather red. Perhaps you should consider wearing gloves while you work?"

"But nobody else wears gloves!"

Leeinn interjected, "The infirmary has a salve for damaged skin. Your hand would be better by tomorrow if you used some of it."

"Really? Then I would certainly like to try it, thank you."

"Would you like to go now?"

Tiny said, "Why don't we visit the infirmary, and when Gira has her salve, we can all share each other's company until dinner?"

Tancer stood up from his bench, "Sounds good to me. I think I can remember how to get there, we passed close by it on our way to the school."

Leeinn motioned for Tancer to take the lead, "By all means, you can be the father, and I'll be one of your foals."

Tancer managed to find the infirmary with only one wrong turn, gently corrected by Leeinn. He pretended to bluster, "I knew that wasn't the right corridor, I was just making sure *you* were paying attention."

Tiny said in an undertone, "If we keep following him, we're going to end up in the City."

"What was that? Did you say something love?"

Tiny answered in a normal voice, "You're doing a great job, and you're so pretty." Gira snickered in a most unladylike manner.

Tancer said, "I choose to believe you, for the sake of our marriage."

"Like when *I* believed *you* when *you* said you knew the way to Del Abbey?"

Gira looked properly scandalized, "Oh Tancer, you didn't!"

"I had it from a very reliable source that the road we followed ended at Del Abbey. So as long as we followed it, we knew we would find what we were looking for."

Tiny's rolled her eyes, "And what if you're source was wrong, and we ended up in the middle of nowhere, footsore and empty-bellied?"

"My source wouldn't do that to me!"

"The source you can't name, because *it's a secret.*"

"I should think my unwillingness to name names would make me more attractive. Proof that I'm one of the few you can trust to not kiss and tell."

Tiny quipped, "What a shame you didn't go in for spywork. Sounds like you really missed your calling."

"And leave you stuck with some snitching stableboy. Never!"

Tiny made a speculative face, "But a stableboy *would* be helpful with impressing Master Dooreg. Just think of all the insider tips you could give me."

"I can give you plenty of advice about drainage. May not seem like much now, but you just try keeping your streets dry without a decent system of ditches."

Leeinn interrupted their banter, "Here we are, the infirmary." The door in front of them swung open.

Gira looked impressed, "You have self-opening doors! I've seen them in the City."

"There are glyphs in the floor that respond to a combination of *detect motion* and weight."

Tal said in a low voice, "That was clever of them. I would probably have just set it to detect life."

Gira titled her head, "What's the difference." Leeinn gestured encouragingly to Tal.

Tal said, "Detect life is too broad, that would have the door opening for every mouse and moth that passed close enough to activate the glyph. But if the glyph responds to motion *and* additional weight in this area, it has a good chance of opening for an actual person, or maybe a cart or stretcher they were trying to take into the infirmary."

Gira stared at Tal, "I never would have thought of that."

A polite voice said, "If you're not going to enter the infirmary, please step away so the door can close."

Leeinn walked through the door, stopping a respectful distance from a man with a thick mane of hair to match his black scrubs, "Sorry Pael, we are here for some of the soothing skin salve. Gira's hand are a little sore from all the hard work she's put in." Gira flashed a pleased smile at Leeinn upon hearing the explanation.

Pael said, "Easy enough." He turned from them and walked to a tidy desk. "We had enough people asking for it on regular basis that we always keep some in here." He brought back the salve, and Gira stepped forward to take the tube. She turned it around a few times in her hands. "The cap will pop off if you pull while applying pressure. And you only need a little, put it on your injury, then rub it in until the area is dry. I can also wrap the area if you would like the extra protection."

"I'm sure once I use this my hand will be good as new." Gira poured a generous amount onto both palms, then rubbed them gently against each other until the salve had been absorbed into to her skin. "Look! Its better already!"

Pael said, "Typically the only scars you see on Accepted were gotten before they came here. Anyone injured here have good odds of recovering without a mark."

Tancer said, "There was a brother that came to congratulate us the night we were accepted. He had an eyepatch, but I caught a glimpse of the sunken skin beneath when he scratched an itch."

"You're probably talking about Brother Murtok. He was captured by a bandit clan that likes to stalk the miles between the abbey and the City. He managed to break free, but not before they'd beaten him bloody. By the time he made it here, our healers could only do so much. When you see him again, ask him to tell you his escape story. He's a decent tale weaver, and he's always looking for a fresh audience."

Tiny said, "I'm surprised that's a story he'd want to tell."

Pael said, "He's one of the toughest people I've ever met. One of the kindest too, strange as that may seem." A pair of women entered the infirmary. "I'm sorry, but if that's it, I should tend to my next patient."

Leeinn said, "That's all we needed, thank you."

Gira looked at her companions, "Now what?"

Five pairs of eyes went to Leeinn. "Well, if no one has any objections, why don't I introduce you to the farmers? There's always a few in the water meadows during the day, and they're used to visitors. One of the most frequent requests the abbey receives is for a chance to collect dels among the farmers. Some say the dragon egg lotus meadows are the best part of our abbey."

Gira clapped her hands, "I think visiting the farmers is a good idea."

Tancer shrugged, "Sounds good to me. Tiny?"

She nodded, "I'd like the chance to learn more about them."

They approached the gates nearest to the del water meadows. A smiling Sister old enough to be their grandmother sat in an elevated chair to the side of the doors. She greeted Leeinn and her group, "Good day all! Going out?"

Leeinn said, "I'm showing them the farmers." She gestured to the woman, "This is Timalia. She's acting as gate guardian, a job you'll likely be given yourselves once you've settled."

Tiny tensed, "I've never heard that people couldn't leave the abbey without permission."

Timalia said, "Oh I don't stop anyone from leaving. The gate guardian just keeps a tally of everyone who goes out, so we know if anyone goes missing." Timalia raised a quill pen over parchment, "Leeinn I have you. Returning by nightfall?"

"Yes ma'am." Timalia scribbled something, then handed Leeinn a palm-sized, bright pink disc pieced with a pull string to make it snug against a wrist.

Leeinn held it out for the group's benefit. "Before you go out, you have to tell the gate guardian your name, when you will return, and the person on duty will give you a hereiam. If you don't come back at the time you said you would, search parties can be sent out to find you. And if you ever need help quick, just press your hereiam three times, and it will send the alarm to the abbey."

Timalia pointed her quill at Gira, "Name and return time please."

"Gira, before dark with Leeinn."

"Very good. Next?" When she had taken down all their names Timalia said, "Thank you, I have everything I need. Everyone have their hereiam? Then have a good time."

A mixed chorus of, "Thanks" and, "Thank you Timalia!", and they were out the gates.

From the back of the abbey, their path was a fairly straight stretch. Leeinn indicated in front and behind them, "Another chore our team will be assigned at some point is sweeping this road. Sometimes the farmers track things in from their time in the meadows. Speaking of female dragons, you're in luck, because that one there is Grognareian. She's the oldest dragon at the abbey." When Leeinn said the farmer's name, Grognarian rumbled as she turned to the group approaching her, peering down at them from her great height. She blinked calm blue eyes and flexed her giant claws. "Good evening Grognareian! I have some friends I want you to meet." The farmer splashed her way out of the pool she'd been standing in. Leeinn beckoned her friends, who had taken a collective step back, and bunched closer together, "You don't have anything to fear from Grognareian. I've known her my whole life, and she's the sweetest dragon I've ever met. She would have

250

been at Tiny and Tancer's Hopeful Ceremony, but the morning of she felt like being in her meadows, so her substitute took up the farmer's role."

Gira screwed her up face in concentration, "Deiga, wasn't it?"

Leeinn said, "That's right! Speak of the dragon." The group now had *two* farmers looking at them, Deiga walking forward until she stood level with Grognareian. Both were a pleasant green color, the only difference being that Grognareian was markedly darker, like pine needles, while the second farmer was a lighter lime. "Good evening Deiga! I hope you'll meet my friends too." The dragons tucked their long front claws between their back legs, folding down neatly into a half-seated position. Leeinn held up a hand, "These are my friends: Gira, Tal, Tiny, and Tancer." Grognareian gave her focus over to Tiny, and practically knocked the tall woman off her feet while '*asking*' for attention.

Gira shot a charming smile up at Deiga, "Hello. Want to be friends?" She held out a hand, and Deiga allowed Gira to stroke her nose.

Tancer joked, "Are you sure you want a winged stallion? You seem to get a long with farmers just fine."

Gira withdrew her hand quickly, "Don't even joke about that. Farmers can't fly, and they're so plain! Definitely not for me!" Grognarian's attention had switched to Gira upon hearing the girl's scolding tone, and

251

she blew noisily out of her nose. "Eck, and now I need another bath!"

Tancer snickered, "Be glad she's not like dragons from the old tales that could breathe fire, or you'd be singed as well as snotted."

Leeinn shook her head, "I wonder where in the world they ever got that idea. Dragons, breathing fire? Next you'll be telling me that their treasure is gold and gems instead of winged horses."

Tiny said, "If not singed, then maybe satined?"

"Bet raw dragon silk looks about the same as what's in Gira's hair."

"*My hair!?* We have to go back, *now!*"

Chapter 21

Flying

Shail wished Moyrah and Tumatan could see him now! He and Tabirc had kept up their pace for nearly two hours, and Shail felt invincible, high above it all, as though he, Tabirc, and their mounts were the only living things in the world. No wonder Tabirc had been a professional rider, flying was wonderful! Shail watched the world beyond Stendow's shoulder slowly darken as night approached.

Shail heard Tabirc yell, "*Lowkrist, land!*" Shail could not make out any discernible difference in where they were compared to the stretch of miles they had covered, but Lowkrist evidently saw Tabirc's goal. She twitched her head back towards Stendow, letting out a barking growl. Shail heard Stendow respond, and could swear he could almost understand them. '*This way*', and '*On your tail*. He held tight to the saddle hook as Tabirc landed in a hole in the tree cover. Shail felt Stendow's wings fold over him as they snapped to her body. Shail's stomach made a bid for freedom as they dropped, but Shail managed to clamp his jaws hard enough to keep everything down. Stendow's landing was surprisingly gentle for a mount her size as she used the muscles in her legs to cushion their drop.

"And here we are," crowed Tabirc. "And I for one could use a break." He dismounted Lowkrist alone, but Shail needed a lot of help getting down. He was fumble-fingered as he tried to undo his safety straps, and could barely move his legs enough to swing to one side, and would have fallen if Tabirc had not caught him.

"Ow ow ow, my legs won't straighten out."

Tabirc gripped the inside of Shail's upper arm, "Don't worry, we'll walk the kinks out, and I have something to put in our drinks that will help. Except for the test rides with these two, that was the longest I've been on a dragon in years." Tabirc helped Shail gingerly walk around the clearing they'd landed in, a quiet pine-lined area with a chuckling stream passing through. While Shail and Tabirc walked, Lowkrist and Stendow snuck to the stream for a slurp.

"I need to grab those two before they drink too much. My first flying instructor used to say, '*More wet, less wing*'. Can you stand by yourself?" Shail nodded, and Tabirc left him to herd the dragons away from the water. "You two know better than to drink without permission." Both dragons looked like naughty children caught with their hands in the cookie jar. Tabirc yelled back over his shoulder to Shail, "Keep walking, when you've worked yourself loose, I could use a hand with these two."

Those words galvanized Shail. He awkwardly shambled until he could walk normally again. "What can I do Tabirc?"

"Take their reins." Shail did so, and Tabirc gave his attention to his mount and soon had Lowkrist in nothing but scales. He dropped the saddle next to a spot Shail could now see had recently served as a firepit. A chance to use his uncle's gift! "Are you up to a lesson, or do you need to rest?"

"No! I mean yes! I mean, I'd love to learn."

Tabirc laughed as he walked over to Stendow, "Then watch as I do this." Shail was attentive while Tabirc showed him how to unsaddle his mount. There were so many straps! Tabirc's hands moved expertly as he divested the dragon of tack and luggage. "And that's it. Easier to take it off then put it on."

Shail said, "I'd like to try doing it myself tomorrow."

"We can definitely make that happen. Here, carry it over there, and set it next to mine." While Shail obeyed ,Tabirc opened one of his bags and handed Shail a brush with stiff bristles on one side, and soft bristles on the other. "Give your saddle a good once over with the stiff side of this. Soft side is for your dragon." Tabirc brought a second brush out of the bag, then began giving his own saddle a once over. When they were done Tabirc said, "Now the dragons."

"We have to brush their *entire* body?"

"Course, got to make sure nothing needs tending."

"But we did nothing but take off, fly, and land here. Why would anything need tending?"

"It's for safety. A loose scale, a sore spot where the saddle rubbed, a strained muscle, there are lots of little things that are easy to miss. Start at the front, and work your way back." Lowkrist lowered her head as Tabirc walked over to her with brush in hand. "Be gentle, their face and wings are sensitive, the rest not so much." Using the soft side of his brush, Tabirc delicately stroked Lowkrist's snout. It looked much the same as when Shail had seen horses curried.

Stendow nudged Shail's arm, and he realized that he'd been so engrossed watching Tabirc, he had not been paying attention to his dragon. "Sorry Stendow." Shail held out a hand, and Stendow gently put her chin in his palm. With the other hand, Shail brushed as Tabirc had demonstrated. He was able to direct Stendow's head position so he could reach every inch. He was gentle when he went over her closed eyes, nostrils, and ear holes.

"Touch her leg, and then ask her to *extend*."

Shail said, "Stendow, extend please," and touched her front leg. She did so, and Shail worked from her shoulder down. When he got to the end of her leg, he saw that her claws were long and curved, but blunt as a badgers. "Is Lowkrist the dominant dragon because her claws are bigger than Stendow's?"

"No, she's just older. Dragons aren't hunters, and they don't like fighting, so claw size doesn't really matter."

"If dragons don't fight, how do they settle a disagreement?"

"They dance."

"*What?!*"

"They dance. It's a common alternative for animals with wings who can't afford even a small injury."

"How does a dragon a dance?"

"They can be graceful when they want to. Lots of leaping up high as they can, wing flapping, head bobbing, that sort of thing." Tabirc had finished with Lowkrist, and went to their luggage to start making camp. Shail was still brushing Stendow when Tabirc had finished laying out glow glyphs and pitching their spacious sleeping tent.

"You got *all* that done while I only brushed Stendow."

"Nothing but practice."

257

Tabirc's comment instantly reminded Shail of Moyrah. "I have a friend who says the same thing."

"They must be pretty smart."

"Oh she is! Moyrah showed me the stars while we sailing to Myrliot, and she knew all the constellations, the way they changed from season to season, and all the phases of the moon too."

"She must be a good sailor, to know all that."

"She said I was her shipmate."

"After just a couple days on board? You must have impressed her."

"I went to the roost twice."

"That's two more times than I've ever been in a roost."

Shail felt particularly pleased with the knowledge that he had done something Tabirc had not. "I wouldn't have gone a second time, but Gran went with me." Shail had finally finished brushing Stendow, and without work to occupy his mind, the mention of Gran brought back the memory of their recent leave taking. "She made us leave early, and gave good reasons for why we had to, but I don't think she told me the *real* reason."

Tabirc looked uncomfortable, "Rox usually knows what she's doing, even if the rest of us can't make sense of what she does."

"But she must have told you *something*."

"Which she will tell you when it suits her. I'll respect her judgement, and I suggest you do the same. Now, where's that pouch you were telling me about. I have some wood stacked, I just need someone to light it for me."

Shail sprang to his pack and brought out his firestarter pouch "I have it here!" Shail stuffed some kindling between the gaps under the wood Tabirc had stacked, and struck a match alight before putting the box back in his pouch. Wisps of smoke began to curl up, and within a couple minutes, they had a cheerful campfire.

Tabirc said, "Looks like your pouch is a success."

Shail beamed with pride. "I'll have to thank uncle Wengsper when I get home."

"I think I'll join you on the return journey. I haven't seen Wengsper in a while, or had your mother's cooking."

Shail couldn't believe his ears, "Really?! That'd be great!"

Tabirc said, "Let's eat some supper, then go to bed. We have a long day of flying tomorrow. Can you fill this with water at the stream?" Shail took the pail, and soon returned with it full of water. "Thanks. I brought some travel pies, one should be enough for the two of us." Tabirc had brought one of the larger pieces of luggage to the fire's side. Shail saw several wooden boxes held within the leather shell. Tabirc took out the top-most box, and when he opened it, Shail could see that it contained a pastry fat with whatever it had been stuffed with. "This one is a veggie, and I have a fruit one for dessert." Tabirc placed the pie over the fire.

"What do the dragons get to eat?"

"I'll show you while the pie bakes." Lowkrist and Stendow had used the time since their brushing to lie down and get comfortable. They watched Tabirc expectantly. He dragged over a bag as long as his arm. He undid the drawstring, and stuck his arm inside. When he drew it back out, he held it out to Shail, "This is what they eat." In his hand he held what looked like a yellow pellet, save that it was as long as Shail's foot. "A dragon gets three of these a day. Here, take one and feed it to Stendow while I give this one to Lowkrist." Both dragons flicked out their tongues, snapping them back into their mouths with a pellet stuck to each one.

"That's really all they get to eat? And they can't drink water? That doesn't seem fair."

"Those tablets were made from special ingredients, chiefly del nectar. They have all the energy a dragon would need, though they'd need more if the work was hard. And dragons like ours don't need a lot of water. Look, they're bedding down to sleep. We should eat, and do the same."

The travel pies proved delicious, and Tabirc put some powder in both their drinks that soon took the ache from Shail's legs. When they entered their tent, it was more than big enough to accommodate them both. Tabirc said, "I laid out our bedding. That's you near the back, and this one by the door is mine."

Shail looked at the odd configuration, "But wouldn't it make more sense to have them lying side by side? If I have to get up in the night I'll have to step over you."

"I want to know if you leave the tent, whatever the reason."

"I am *thirteen* now."

Tabirc smiled, "I seem to remember you saying that firestarter pouch was a *thirteenth* feather day present."

"I brought my fishing kit too."

"Excellent news, because I have a few more stories you'll be interested to hear." They changed into their night clothes, and Shail crawled into his bedroll. "I'll be back in just a minute, I want to check on the dragons one last time."

"You didn't tie them to anything."

"Don't need to, they know to stay with us."

"What if they lost us?"

"They'd return to their home stable."

"Always?"

"Well, you do hear stories of dragons coming across a prime patch and deciding to make it their own. Or running into a winged horse herd. The most well-trained dragon would be sorely tempted by such an encounter. Be right back." Shail watched Tabirc leave the tent, and heard his soft footsteps on the grass outside. Shail was already half asleep when Tabirc returned. He saw Tabirc's hand move against his leg. '*Must have been a bug,*' Shail thought. Tabirc secured the tent flap, and as he turned to his own bed roll, Shail looked at the leg Tabirc had just brushed. Strapped to the outside of Tabirc's thigh was a foot long leather sheathe, out of which peeked a blade with a worn wooden grip. That was odd. Why would Tabirc have a knife?"

"What's that?"

Tabirc followed Shail's pointed finger, "This is Shaylah. We been together all my flying days, saved my life a time or two."

"But why would you need that to check on the dragons?"

"Better to have it, and not need it, then need it and not have it."

"I guess you might have to worry about animals that hunt at night."

Tabirc snorted, "Not with two dragons nearby." Shail was about to respond when Tabirc said, "Time for sleep. I'll see you in the morning."

Shail closed his eyes, too tired to argue, "Goodnight."

Chapter 22

The Family Pool

Tiny and Tancer choose to remain with the farmers, so
Leeinn left Gira and Tal in the gois rooms, and then
wandered in search of her father. Where could he be?! The
kitchens were a good bet, so she headed there first. She was
greeted upon her arrival by the Chief Cook. When she
asked him if he'd seen her father, he pointed to the
appropriate table. She thanked him, and went to Rumaru.
Her father was using a roller on dough, placing the finished
flat pieces upon a buttered tray. She sidled up to him, and
he stopped his work to tilt his head towards her.

"Hello wind chime. Where are your friends?"

"I think Tiny and Tancer wanted some time to
themselves, and Gira is washing her hair after Grognarian
... uh, *reacted* to her tone."

Rumaru chortled, "You introduced her to
Grogonareian, that was good thinking."

"And Deiga."

"Well, you rarely find one without the other."

"Deiga at least seemed to like her."

"And what about you?"

"She's a bit fussy, and spoiled, but overall I think she's a good person."

Rumaru chuckled, "As you seem to believe of everyone. I've always admired your ability to see the best in people. Let's not forget her maidservant. I was having trouble convincing Nassine until Tal spoke up."

"I asked her if she had thought about becoming Hopeful, but she didn't give a definite answer."

"Another two Hopefuls, so soon! Our abbey is truly blessed."

"I'm even less sure about Tal than I am of Gira. She's very good at deflecting questions."

"Perhaps that is a necessary talent for a good servant. Her job is to be of service to others, not bring attention to herself."

"I don't think I'd like such a life."

"Then let us be glad you are Accepted, and will live out your days in a place where such concerns will never be yours."

"Will you join me in our pool before dinner? I'd like the chance to reflect and balance."

"Of course, lead the way."

"As if you need me to!"

"I'll admit that even were I lost, I would only have to follow the scent of your lotus to find your pool."

"*Our* pool."

"Well, I help as I can."

Leeinn said, "And our flowers would not grow as well as they do without you."

"I am happy to help my daughter however I may. *Hmmm*, my nose tells me it's this way." Rumaru's sense of smell led him as surely as Leeinn's sight, and they were soon at their pool's door. They entered the enclosed room, Leeinn leaving her father to open the sky lights. He might not need such niceties, but she and the dels appreciated the extra illumination. The flowers seemed to swell as the bright light hit them, though none would open without a winged horse's breath. Leeinn and her father removed their socks and shoes, and curled their pants legs to wade knee deep, gently pushing their way between the lotus. Each delicate blossom bobbed upon the disturbed surface, rocking gently like an egg trying to hatch. Most were the usual mottled white and grey, but there were a few varieties, courtesy of Leeinn's experimentation, that had petals of a brighter color. She had managed to perfect a blue del, a red del, and a green del, and was close to a yellow del. The nectar within the special dels took on the shade of the petals, seeming to possess different properties, depending upon the color. This small pool represented two years of Leeinn's dedicated work, and she planned to spend the rest of her life caring for the flowers that grew within.

"I gathered all that were ready for the Hopeful Ceremony. I think we should leave what's left to grow a bit."

"You know best duckling." Leeinn splashed water at her father while making quacking sounds. "Dearheart, I don't think ducklings say *quack*. I think it's more of a *peep peep*."

Relaxed and happy once more, they left the pool, using a pair of towels to dry off their legs and feet. Leeinn perched on the edge of a square, open window that looked out upon the abbey's inner grounds, bare heels braced against the smooth stone wall, while Rumaru calmly poured tea he'd brewed for them both from a kettle they kept in the pool room. His movements had been precise, exact; Leeinn had always envied his self-control. Once filled, he brought both cups with him to join her at the window. Leeinn watched her father's face as he slowly inhaled the curling steam wafting up from his drink. When he spoke, Leeinn was glad they were so close, or she would not have been able to hear his words. "I've been thinking about the day you were accepted. You know our traditions dictate only those chosen by the Trinity, and our children, too young to be judged, be allowed to live here. It is every parent's fear that the Trinity will refuse their child, and they will be sent from our walls forever. I've always wondered what I would have done if you had been refused. I was nearing forty, and it had not been long since I'd found you. It would have made more sense to send you to a willing patron family, rather than my taking a toddler and leaving the abbey to start over somewhere else. You sneaking on stage, and the Trinity accepting you before I could catch you, was one of the best things to ever happen to me, second only to finding you in the first place."

Leeinn nodded, she'd heard the story of her acceptance many times, "I can't imagine what my life would have been like, living somewhere else, without you." Leeinn felt moved by Rumaru's tender tone. She sat her cup down on the window's sill and gently hugged him, pressing her face into the side of his chest, breathing in his familiar, comforting scent.

He held her under an arm, resting his chin upon her head. Leeinn felt his jaw move as he spoke, "I don't see why Tal couldn't be judged alongside Gira."

"Gira did say she was worried about being refused while Tal became Accepted."

"I suppose from her point of view that would be most embarrassing."

"And more than a little selfish."

"Not everyone can be as generous as you. When I spoke with Gira in the orchard, I told her about you, and how special you are. She said she'd be honored, not to mention lucky, to learn anything you'd care to teach her about our abbey, and our ways."

Leeinn suddenly felt ashamed of her statement about Gira being selfish, "I wasn't being a very good friend just now. Gira works hard, and deserves better."

"I'm sure she would be happy to hear you say that." The kettle emptied, Rumaru said, "I think I'll go back to that tree in the orchard, take a nap before dinner."

"Another reason for you to get along with Tancer."

"I appreciate a man who appreciates his sleep. See you later."

"Have a good nap father."

Leeinn figured she should search for her friends at the del meadows first. If they had returned while Leeinn had been with her father, Tamalia might know where they had gone next. When she drew within sight of the back abbey gates, she saw that Tamalia had been replaced by a man a few years older than Leeinn; a fairly new Accepted himself, having only been judged by the Trinity the winter before. "Hello Haller."

"Ahh, Leeinn. What can I do for you? I see on my list that you already went out and came back today. Going out again?"

"No, but I'm looking for two of the people I went out with, Tiny and Tancer. I thought they might still be seeing the del meadows."

Haller glanced down at the sheet before him, "They haven't signed back in."

"Then I'll see if I can find them. We'll have to start back soon to make it back by nightfall."

"I've got you down, here's your hereiam."

"Thanks, see you soon." Leeinn passed through the back gates for the second time that day. She didn't see either Accepted on the road, and figured they must be at the farthest edge that ran right up against the water meadows. She increased her pace to a slow jog, clutching her hereiam in her hand, then broke into a mile-eating trot. Leeinn loved to run, and was glad for the opportunity to get rid of more energy before having to settle for the night. She heard voices coming from a short distance in front of her, and knew she was close. She soon saw two people, recognizing the shapes of her friends. They were looking out over the water meadows, which were spread out to the west and covered with closed dragon egg lotus. Leeinn called out to get their attention, "Hello?"

Tiny waved, "Welcome back. Everything good now?"

"Yes, Tal was helping Gira when I left them."

"Weren't you wearing socks when you left?"

270

"Oh, I took them off while I tended my pool with my father. It seemed like too much trouble to put them back on."

Tancer said, "Heard that a good amount of the dels at our Hopeful Ceremony were from your pool."

Tiny said, "I didn't know that. Thank you Leeinn, they were more beautiful than I ever thought a flower could be." Her expression shifted to one of concern, "So you have no more dels for another Hopeful Ceremony?"

"Not right now, but dels grow quickly, so I should have a new harvest in a few weeks."

"Oh good, I know Gira would be disappointed otherwise."

Leeinn sighed in relief, "Dinner should be soon, we should head back. It's the final feast before the visiting families leave."

Tancer jumped, "You hear that! Move it ladies, this man is hungry!"

Chapter 23

Made for Flying

Movement outside the tent pulled Shail from sleep. He was greeted by the sight of Tabirc stirring about the camp, and the mixed scents of pine and breakfast pie. When Tabirc saw Shail poke his head out, he gave a wave from beside the rekindled campfire, and set aside a cup and platter, both filled with steaming contents.

"Eat up, we've got a long way to go today." Shail dug into his food, grateful for Tabirc's forethought in bringing such easy to make meals. This one tasted like dough mixed with eggs, bacon, potatoes, and a light gravy. "You finish up, I'll feed our skyladies."

"Can I feed Stendow, please? I owe her for carrying me."

Tabirc gave Shail a pleased nod, "Proper respect indeed. If healing people doesn't work out for you, you'd be valued in a stable. Could even be a dragon doctor. Pays well, and you'd get to be around beauties like these all the time." Tabirc finished the contents of his cup and set it aside for packing. "When you're done eating, give Stendow her morning meal pellet and brush. I'm going to collect our gear and stow the tent."

Shail polished off his plate, then took up his brush from the night before. Stendow chirruped sweetly as he gently went over her face, which had scales no bigger than Shail's thumbnail. "Stendow, extend please." She held out each leg in turn, and Shail was covered in a sheen of sweat by the time she was done.

"Good job, I see you remember the command I taught you yesterday. And look at her shine!" The meager morning light that had managed to peak through the narrow break in the trees glittered off his mount's scales.

"Do you want me to do Lowkrist too?"

"Yes, thank you. I want to give the area a once-over to make sure we didn't leave more signs that we were here."

"My nature teacher taught us about leaving little to no trace of your presence so as not to disturb the wildlife that make your temporary camp their permanent home."

"Ye …. Yes, that's true. You brush Lowkrist, I won't be long." Tabirc began a slow circuit of the circular rest area while Shail focused on the task before him. When he got to Lowkrist's tail, Shail thought his arms might fall off. And they hadn't even started their flight yet! Shail stifled a groan at the thought of having to pull himself into the saddle. He consoled himself by thinking, *'At least I don't have to actually hold on, the safety straps will do that for me.'*. Shail looked around for Tabirc, spotting him as he put bridle and saddle on Stendow. Shail almost protested, for he had wanted to start practicing his skills, but his arms felt rubbery enough he decided it was probably better that Tabirc do it, this morning anyway. Shail promised himself he would insist on unloading Stendow when they stopped for the evening. For now, he watched Tabirc, who made the task seem easier than it was. Only years of practice would give a man's hands the muscle memory he would need to perform the job as quickly as Tabirc.

"You're so good at that, I'm surprised you quit being a rider."

"Being good at something doesn't necessarily mean it's something you want to do. You're good at script, why not become a copyist instead of a healer?"

"I see your point."

"There has been a part of me that's missed riding the wind, and I've enjoyed the short time I've had with our dragons. But I'm just not cut out for it anymore."

"You could still work in a stable."

"My back would not thank me for that."

"With all your experience, maybe you could be a supervisor."

"And listen to stablehands complain all day? *'Tabirc sir, I can't work today, my hands are blistered.' 'Well then, put on some gloves.' 'I could, but also, I need to leave early.' 'Oh, why is that' 'My grandfather died.' 'Your granddad is remarkable! That would be the third time he's done that' 'Err, did I say grandfather? I meant grandmother.' 'That's makes more sense, she's only died once.'"* Shail laughed until he could hardly catch his breath. Tabirc pulled a final strap tight, "Alright, take up her reins. Do you remember the command to have her check the fit?"

Shail said, "Stendow, saddle shake please!" His mount shook vigorously, and the saddle remained perfectly in place.

Tabirc said, "Looks good. I'll get the luggage loaded while you keep her standing still." He did so, making sure the weight was evenly distributed on both sides. "Alright, she's done. Do you want to stand holding her and Lowkrist's lines, or do you want to get in the saddle now?"

"I want to be in the saddle!"

Tabirc laughed, "I thought you might. Give her the signal."

"Stendow, kneel down please."

"Up you go," Tabirc said, giving Shail a boost. After Shail was settled, Tabirc soon had him secured with the safety straps. Within minutes Tabirc had done the same for Lowkrist and himself. He nodded at Shail, who had put his protective goggles on and hitched Stendow's reins to the saddle hook.

"Stendow, follow wingmate." She gave a whistle in acknowledgement.

Tabirc said, "Lowkrist, fly!" Once more his mount bunched all four of her legs, then sprang upwards, beating her wings hard. Stendow was right behind her, throwing Shail back and then forward. In mere moments they were above the treetops, and still climbing. When their dragons eventually evened out, they switched to a glide; moving their wings only to maintain their positions, but otherwise allowing the wind to carry them onwards. Shail was glad Tabirc had given him eye protection, or they would be streaming too much to see anything. Dragonback was definitely different from the roost, and Shail was enjoying looking first over one of Stendow's shoulders, than the other. Shail held himself flat to Stendow's neck, imagining that *he* was the dragon, and her wings were his. How wonderful it must be to be able to fly like this all the time. Shail wondered how disappointed Gran would be if he decided to become a dragon rider instead of a Travealer.

One hour turned into two, then three. Despite that, Shail's enthusiasm for flying remained as high as their altitude, although he wished that Tabirc would land more often so they could stretch their legs. Neither Stendow nor Lowkrist showed signs of slowing, living up to Tabirc's assessment. The scenery beneath them continued to resemble a green sea, the tops of the trees rustling so they moved like water. Riding with his nose nearly against Stendow's neck, the prevailing scent was dragon, which Shail found to be both pleasant and exotic, similar to cinnamon. He could definitely see himself partnered to a dragon permanently. Thoughts of being a Travealer seemed dull by comparison. People were normal, boring. But dragons? They were special, unique, and their riders shared some of that by proximity. Still, Gran had spent her life helping people, so it must be worth doing. Of course it was worth doing, helping people always was. But, flying … Shail had never felt so comfortable, like this was where he was supposed to be. Gran had chosen her surprise well. Tabirc looked back over his shoulder, locking eyes with Shail. Shail smiled broadly, holding a thumb up to show he was ok. Tabirc returned the grin, then turned back to Lowkrist. She began to beat her wings rhythmically, increasing her speed from the glide she'd been maintaining up until now. Shail dug his feet into the treads of the saddle, gripping the pommel. At least the motion was easy to match. Shail soon had the timing, moving his body with Stendow instead of against.

They flew for another hour before Tabirc showed signs of searching for a landing space. "Lowkrist, land!" Shail knew what to expect this time. The feeling of Stendow's wings folding over him reminded him of his mother's hug. Tabirc was a little slower getting down this time, moving nearly as stiffly as Shail. After they were both back on solid ground, Tabirc showed Shail how to unsaddle a dragon step by step. They spent a second night much like the first. Shail was especially glad for the powder Tabirc added to their drinks, sure he would not be able to move at all without it's help. They and their mounts settled down for the night.

By the next day they had reached Tabirc's village. They caused a bit of a stir, landing on the outskirts but drawing more than a few spectators; and not just children, every age could be counted among the welcomers. They waved and yelled in excited greeting, eyeing Shail with curiosity and envy. Tabirc waved and laughed at the small crowd, dropping down from the saddle and landing in a bow. His audience applauded in appreciation. Tabirc went to help Shail, loosening the safety straps and catching Shail under the arm as he dropped to the ground. Shail wished he could have dismounted with as much flare as Tabirc, but settled for the fact that most of the village had seen him arrive on a dragon. Tabirc soon had both mounts unsaddled and divested of their luggage. He and Shail brushed their dragons, then fed them their meal pellet. Tabirc gave them the *stay* command, and they curled around each other to go to sleep.

Willing hands took up the baggage, and made their way to Tabirc's house. It was a neat little hut, just the right size for two people, but did not have nearly enough room to accommodate all of Tabirc's neighbors. He thanked them all for the help, promising to stop by the Apple Barrel later for drinks and stories. A couple of boys around Shail's age had introduced themselves, wanting to hear about his ride with Tabirc. Shail felt a little shy from all the attention, but conducted himself well, modestly explaining that he had been as much baggage as rider. That did not seem to lessen his standing; if anything, it earned him a greater reputation that he would have had as a braggart. Shail was glad when Tabirc finally closed the door, all the excitement had left him drained. He even refused Tabirc's offer of a meal, wanting only to crawl into bed and sleep. Tabirc had laid a pallet out for Shail in the hut's single bedroom, which Shail gladly dropped into after quickly downing more of the soreness powder. Relaxed and relieved of pain, Shail was shortly asleep.

Tabirc was up and dressed by the time Shail got up the next morning. He seemed to be in a good mood despite the fact Shail could see through a window that it was pouring rain outside. The fare was not in pie form this time, so Shail was free to choose among the fruits, fried potatos, fresh bread, bacon, and eggs. Shail's stomach let out a

279

growl, and he gave into his hunger. Tabirc seemed to have a similar appetite, and between them they ate all the laid-out food. Full, Shail's thoughts went to the dragons. "Will Stendow and Lowkrist be ok in the rain?"

"Rain doesn't usually bother dragons, they like water whatever form it's in. If they wanted to, they could take shelter in the tress."

"Will they have to leave for their stable today?"

"No. Flying in the rain is different than just being in the rain, and dragons do *not* care for a soggy flight. They can use the day to rest before they go back. I have enough meal pellets to last another day or two."

"Can I meet Master Conlun today?"

"If you'd like. Want to go now?"

Shail nodded, and he and Tabirc cleaned up before leaving. Tabirc grabbed a rainshade from a closet, holding it between them so that it's convex top covered them both as they made their way to the building that was used as the village's infirmary. They saw few people out and about, most keeping inside while the weather was wet.

When they arrived and walked through the door, they were greeted by one of the strangest looking persons Shail had ever seen. If he could have stood up straight he would have been as tall as Tabirc, but his crooked spine made him bend sideways so that his white-haired head was not much higher than Shail's. He adjusted his blue tunic before holding out a hand to Tabirc and saying, "Welcome back." He shifted his gaze to Shail, "Is this my new apprentice?"

Shail bowed nervously, "Yessir, I'm Shail."

"Heard a lot about you from Tabirc and Rox. Normally I wouldn't have agreed to take on someone so young, but I could hardly refuse such glowing referrals. Are you here to start, or did you need a day to recover from your flight here?"

"I wouldn't mind starting now, if you don't mind."

"Not at all, I respect a hard work ethic."

Tabirc said, "I'll leave you two to it then. If I'm not at home when you get done for the day, check the inn. I promised to stop by the Apple Barrel and might lose track of time."

After bidding Tabirc goodbye, Master Conlun began with a tour of the facilities, showing Shail where things were stored, the area for mixing medication, and the cleaning sink. He provided Shail with a pair of healers gloves, thin enough to allow for tactile sensation, but tough to protect against all bodily fluids, not to mention ripping or wear from washing, and a blue apprentice sash to wear over his shirt.

"Keep those on you at all times, a healer never knows when they'll be needed."

"Yessir."

"I think you can call me just Conlun when we don't have any patients. Do you prefer to be called Shail?"

"Yes, thank you."

"Would you mind if I asked you a few questions? I'd like to get a feel for your education so far."

"Of course, ask me anything."

"What is the normal resting heart rate of an adult?"

"Sixty to eighty beats a minute."

"Very good. Breaths?

"Twelve to twenty."

"How would you stop bleeding from the nose?"

"Have the patient pinch the bridge of their nose and lean forward until it clots."

"And if that did not work?"

"Replace the pinching fingers with a cold pack, and add another to the back of the neck."

"And if they are bleeding from somewhere else?"

"Elevate the bleeding point above the heart and apply pressure. If the bleeding is severe, you can also apply a tighttie."

The questions continued, and Shail was happy to be able to answer all of them. Master Conlun seemed equally pleased, "I've had assistants twice as old without the knowledge base you already have. I think we're going to get on just fine." He looked at the clock hanging over the doorframe. "I have a couple patient appointments, you'll start by acting as my assistant and observing."

Shail said, "Yessir, of course."

The door opened, admitting a young mother with a babe asleep in her arms. She spoke quietly so as not to wake her child, "I'm sorry Master Healer, he won't go to sleep unless I hold him."

Conlun answered just as softly, "Not at all, please have a seat. This is my new apprentice Shail. He's going to be studying with me for a few months." Shail bobbed his head but said nothing. Master Conlun continued, "This is Mrs. Majowl. She tripped last week and sprained her ankle. She's back today for a follow-up assessment." He gently untied her sandal, revealing a slightly swollen ankle wrapped in a supportive cloth. "Have you been staying off it as much as possible?"

Mrs. Majowl answered, "Yes, which hasn't been easy while trying to take care of this little one."

"I can imagine. How does it do bearing weight?" Shail watched and listened avidly as Master Conlun performed his physical assessment before rewrapping the injured ankle.

"Another light week I think. Shail, put a cold pack on while I make up a draft."

'I'm doing it, I'm actually helping a master just like an apprentice," Shail thought. He had helped Gran for years, but this felt more real. Mrs. Majowl thanked Shail and Master Conlun, and when she left, Shail felt buoyant enough to fly without Stendow.

Chapter 24

Challi and Constellations

Leeinn and her group of friends walked the path back to the abbey's rear gate.

Tancer said, "They let us a lot closer to their dels than I expected. I never realized they were so tall! The flowers I mean. I'd only ever seen the real ones after they'd bloomed."

They passed through the back abbey gates, returning their hereiams to Haller. "Good to see you found you friends Leeinn. What did you all think of the meadows?"

"They were beautiful!"

Haller beamed at Tiny, "I've always thought so. Meet any farmers?"

"Two! Grognareian and Deiga."

"Pair of sweeties, you lucked out."

Tiny asked, "How many farmers are there?"

Haller answered, "Right now? I think twenty-six. That sound right Leeinn?

Leeinn nodded, and Tancer let out a whistle, "Twenty-six! Where in Albael do you hide them all?! And how do you keep them all fed?"

Haller answered again, "They tend to take care of themselves. They can eat a del whole, and sometimes they go for fish or vegetation. Only the fathers and flyers make a habit of staying in the stable, the farmers prefer their meadows, which extend over many miles."

Tiny said, "I can understand that. The meadows are something else."

Tancer quipped, "A little lacking in common fare for hardworking Accepted like yours truly."

"That's alright, you're lacking in lots of common ways. Sense for example."

"Well missy, you married this dummy, so what does that make you?"

"Charitable."

"*HA!*"

Tiny tugged the bottom of her shirt, eyeing it critically, "I wouldn't mind freshening up before the farewell feast."

Leeinn asked, "Meet you at the Dining Hall?"

"My two favorite words," Tancer said dreamily, "Dining. Hall."

It was agreed, and Leeinn went back to her alone. She washed, then picked out her best habit, which was the color of dark chocolate, and softer than rabbit fur, with a braided beige belt to secure it around her waist. With matching sandals on her feet, Leeinn made her way to dinner. She wasn't alone, the hallways were full of people streaming in the same direction. She greeted, and was greeted by, many fellow Accepted, dressed equally fine for the final feast. For the last time, Nassine sat next to Rumaru in a ruby red robe, and Gira next to Leeinn, wearing the pale green dress with golden dragon egg lotus along the hem and neckline, and stallion feather patterns running down both sleeves. Her hair had been brushed with oil and left loose, it shone in the bright lights of the Dining Hall. Leeinn could see sparkling earrings when Gira moved her head, which she seemed to be doing a lot. Tal waited over her mistress's left shoulder in a demur gown of toffee that complimented her red hair.

When Gira noticed Leeinn, she gave a little gasp, "What a lovely robe!" She gently rubbed the fabric between her fingers, "What is it made from? I've never felt anything so soft, and I have an eiderdown shawl!"

287

"You're close actually, it *is* down, but from winged foals." The sound of Nassine's laughter distracted Gira, and Leeinn used the opportunity to sip some water.

When she gave her attention back to Leeinn, Gira smiled radiantly. "I'm glad you thought of saving my dress for something special."

"It would have been a shame to ruin it in the stables."

"Now I just have to make sure I don't dribble any of my drink on it."

Leeinn felt a Tiny-like mischief come over her, "You could eat and drink only those dishes that wouldn't stain the cloth."

"That's a good idea too! You really are smart."

"No, I didn't mean …"

"What?"

"Nevermind. Water?"

"Yes please! That certainly won't stain." Leeinn wished Tancer was sitting with them, he'd been hiccupping with humor by now. The dishes were swapped out so that appetizer was replaced by entrée, and entrée by dessert. "Is this your father's feather pudding?"

"It is! Do you like it?"

"Very much! It's sweeter than I expected something made from feathers would be."

"Even I don't know his secret recipe."

Rumaru leaned forward, turned his head towards Gira with both robin's egg blue eyes open wider than usual, and winked! "My pudding is the real reason they made me abbot. If anyone learns my secrets, I'll be dropped back down to abbey duster faster than you can say, '*Trumpet Vine Valley*'."

Gira looked a little shocked, "Surely that's not true sir! I don't know anyone who would make a better abbot than you!"

Rumaru laughed, "Thank you! What a kind thing to say. But I was only joking."

Gira flushed as red as her mother's robe, "Of course you were. I'm stupid."

Rumaru's face took on a more serious mien, "You must not say such things. You are not stupid. Your mother would not have a stupid heir."

"*That* I would not." Leeinn had never felt more charitable towards Trader Nassine than at that moment. She watched Gira relax under the double assurance from Father and mother.

"When you've finished your meal, Challi and Shealah are looking for you. Last I saw they were sitting …

yes, there they are." Almost as if she could sense her mother's regard, Gira's sister stopped midsentence, bringing her eyes up from the abbey brother in front of her to glance at the abbot's table.

Gira stood, then curtseyed to Rumaru. "Then may I please be excused?"

"Of course apple basket." Gira cut startled eyes towards Leeinn.

"Congratulations, you've reached pet name status."

"But, apple basket?"

Leeinn hazarded a guess, "Probably because that's what you were doing when you and he walked in the orchards."

Gira's eyes widened in sudden remembrance, "And I sang *Apples Are Best When Shared*!

"Off with you Gira, I have things to say to the Father Abbot."

"Right, off we go. Goodbye mother!"

Tal kept close as they approached Gira's sister and another woman Leeinn assumed was Shealah. Challi gave Gira a brilliant smile, "Evening. Who's this?"

"This is Leeinn, Leeinn, this is my sister Challi, and her chosen Shealah. Mother said you were looking for me."

290

Challi nodded, "Yes, Shealah here wanted you to sniff out a good spot for starspotting."

Gira gave Leeinn a beseeching look, "Is there something special you could show us?"

"I know just the place …"

As it turned out, Leeinn's favorite spot was also good for star gazing. She pointed out some of her favorites, "Look there, near the horizon! The Guiding Star is so bright tonight!"

Shealah seemed particularly enthusiastic, "I see it! And directly up from are the Twinkling Triplets."

Challi seemed amused at her chosen's knowledge, "It's like Leeinn knew how to charm you."

Gira linked arms with Shealah, "Ignore her, she should have been a Vercoh."

Challi gestured to Shealah, "I thought you said I was an Eirez?"

"You are, but you do have very strong overtones of Vercoh."

Leeinn looked intrigued, "I've heard of the Star Signs. I remember being a Cahnsir."

Gira said, "A water sign! No wonder your pool grows such beautiful dels."

291

"What sign are you?"

"I'm a Leyho."

Shealah looked down at Gira's dress, "I should have guessed."

Gira did a little twirl, laughing at herself. "Guilty as charged." She gestured to Tal, "What about you?"

Tal shrugged, "I'm afraid I don't know."

That admission drew Gira and Shealah's full attention. "When were you born?"

"Late spring, just before summer."

Gira whispered to Shealah, "Jimanai?"

"Sounds right."

"Suits her too."

A few more whispered words, and the two girls pronounced, "Jimanai."

Tal curtseyed, "Thank you mistresses, I will remember."

Challi was getting impatient, "Stars are stars. It's silly to think they have anything to do with people."

Shealah gave Gira a pained look, "Eirez, what are you going to do?"

Gira nodded sympathetically, "Endure, that's all you can do."

Challi crossed her arms, "Oh I like that. *Endure.* Like I've been *enduring* this silly conversation?"

"Of course, and thank you." Shealah shot a quick wink to Gira, who bit a finger to stifle her giggles.

Leeinn offered, "It's getting late, shall we go down?"

"You all go, I want to stay up here with Shealah for a while." Challi's chosen snuggled under her arm.

Gira sighed, "Another happy couple."

Leeinn said, "Good night then. Gira, Tal, shall I show you to your rooms?"

"I want to try finding them myself!"

Gira's self-assurance was found to be somewhat wanting, but with the help of her friend and servant, she managed to make it back to her rooms with only a few wrong turns. Leeinn promised to come get them both for breakfast in the morning. Gira's family was scheduled to leave after the meal. Once gone, Leeinn intended to see that she and Gira joined their work team as soon as possible, to help keep her friend's spirits up. She briefly worried that Tiny and Tancer might have taken offense at her and Gira's sudden disappearance, then considered their personalities,

293

and realized she had little cause for concern. If anything, Tancer had probably enjoyed the opportunity to eat that much later ….

Chapter 25

Healing Ain't Easy

Shail's concentration was broken by a loud, angry voice. "Are you even listening to me?" Shail prayed for patience, while assuming a pleasant demeanor. All healers learned to wear this face; Shail had watched Master Conlun weather the most quarrelsome patient without altering his mask by so much as a muscle twitch. Shail tried to think how his master would manage Shail's current frustration, resisting the urge to glance at his mentor over his patient's head. Master Conlun currently sat upon a three-legged stool by the front facing window, appearing to gaze idly out between the drawn curtains, tapping a quiet staccato upon the head of his cane with his nimble fingers. Shail recognized the pretense, although he wasn't sure if his patient realized Master Conlun was anything but politely bored. Master Conlun's right ear was directed towards the other two occupants of the room, and Shail was certain the man missed nothing of the conversation being held, for the moment, without him. He had started letting Shail handle the easiest patients; easiest being in relation to their complaint, not their temperament. The Masterhealer would feign a backache, ask Shail to take over, and sit nearby to observe, and advise when needed.

Shail felt the impulse to snap back at his current patient, an impatient, portly man of fifty-two winters by the name of Elkgnere, "If *you* had listened to *us*, we wouldn't be having this conversation *again*". Instead, Shail replied, "Yes, I'm listening. You were telling me that you're having trouble breathing again, right?"

Messir Elkgnere gave a gimlet glare, obviously unconvinced of Shail's sincerity. "You said if I took that draft you sent me home with, and started exercising more, this wouldn't keep happening. Well, I've taken it every day for a week, and started walking every evening, and I still can't sleep lying down without feeling like I'm suffocating."

Shail surreptitiously dropped his gaze to peer at his patient's legs. As he suspected, both ankles were swollen to the point his patient had had to unlace his boots just to get them on. "That's excellent that you're walking every evening. How long would you say your walk takes you?"

Messir Elkgnere shrugged, "I walk from my house to the center of town and back". Shail thought the term "town" might be over-generous, but decided now was not the time for semantics. He did, however, struggle for just a moment on how to respond to his patient's assurance he was getting exercise by walking two dozen paces, which was the approximate distance between Messir Elkgnere's

296

front door and the post that marked the center of this "town".

"Well, sir, it's less about the distance, and more about keeping your body moving for longer than usual." Shail frowned, "You said you've taken your medicine every day. I believe Master Conlun told you to take it twice a day, with the rising and setting of the sun?" Shail went to a ledger open on a counter, close to the table where a shirtless Messir Elkgnere sat with arms crossed. Shail ran his finger through the notes he'd written, confirming the last recommended dosage. "That would definitely explain why you're not showing much improvement."

Messir Elkgnere's face had been steadily reddening since Shail first began his exam, the flush had extended partially down his neck as he spat, "And how am I supposed to get any sleep when it makes me run to the necessary every hour of the night? Bad enough during the day! Sometimes I skip it until lunch, just so I can get through the morning's chores!"

Shail grit his teeth, bracing himself for the inevitable reaction to his next question. "Master Conlun also recommended you take less liquid in your diet. How has that been going?" Shail knew quite well how it had been going. Judging by his patient's ankles, or lack thereof, it had been going as well as this appointment.

Messir Elkgnere's look became shifty, "Well, so far as that goes, much easier said than done. A man gets a thirst, you know?" Then his eyes went sly. "Or maybe you don't. Know what a *man* needs, I mean. Not yet anyway." Master Conlun shifted his seat, making a noise in his throat that could have been construed as warning, and Messir Elkgnere pinched his lips until they turned white.

Shail strove for calm. "So, you have not had less to drink? Master Conlun was quite clear how too much fluid would worsen your complaints".

"I drink as I need to! I'm not going to live my life thirsty because you healers can't fix a simple problem!"

"But if you followed the master's instructions, you *would* feel better," Shail replied tersely, cursing his loss of composure even as he watched Messir Elkgnere swell with indignation at Shail's tone. If Shail made a mistake, he knew to own and learn from it, but being assigned blame for the results of someone else's stupid stubbornness wasn't something Shail thought he'd ever get used to. They stared at each other in silence for a few breaths; Messir Elkgnere scowling, and Shail striving for his "healer" face, with only moderate success. "Perhaps it would help if we reviewed Master Conlun's instructions, and his reasoning for them?" Messir Elkgnere sniffed irritably, but before he could object, Shail interrupted, "Let me get the consult stones. You remember them from your last appointment, right?" Shail had been present and knew without asking, but Master Conlun had overseen that visit, with Shail acting as an assistant and observer. "They'll be useful for visual demonstration."

Shail walked to the room's largest cabinet and opened the topmost drawer. He drew out a box a bit bigger than both of his outstretched hands laid side by side and brought it back to a table next to his patient, placing it down gently, unlatching the front catch that secured it, and lifting the lid. The box held multiple palm-sized stones lying within their own separate, molded beds. Shail took one out that looked like a squat hourglass, with the bottom half being twice as wide as the top. Shail placed the base against Messir Elkgnere's bared chest, just over his heart, and the smaller top turned from bone white to an angry orange. "This is one of our Consult stones, as you've seen before. It's been enchanted to detect abnormalities inside the body. The stone's top will change its color depending on the condition of an organ. In this case, it shows that your heart is under considerable stress." Shail removed the stone from his patient's chest, patted it onto a cloth that was soaked in a cleansing solution, lifted his own shirt, and placed the it against his own chest. The stone had returned to its original pale color when Shail had taken it away from Messir Elkgnere's chest; as it lay against Shail's skin, the top became a pleasant green, like spring leaves. "You see", Shail indicated, "when it assesses an organ, and finds it healthy, it turns this shade of green to signal everything is functioning properly". Messir Elkgnere did not seem impressed, he had seen the Consult stones used nearly every time he came for an appointment. Shail lowered the stone and his shirt, cleaned the stone a second time, and then on impulse, handed the stone to Messir Elkgnere.

299

"Here, sir, try it for yourself. It doesn't take any training to use, only to interpret the resulting color and treat accordingly. Touch it to any part of your body, and I will tell you what the reading means". Messir Elkgnere took the stone, and with a dubious air pressed it to the inside of his left wrist. The stone's top turned bruise purple. "That color typically means a combination of inflammation and agitation of the area. Have you injured that wrist lately?"

Messir Elkgnere handed the stone back to Shail, almost tossing it, and shot back, "What, your fancy stone didn't tell you my wrist's been giving me trouble all season?" The man glared at his own limb as though it were a recalcitrant employee who had been shirking his duties.

"That explains some of his bad temper", thought Shail, willing to excuse the man's antagonistic behavior, now that he knew one of its underlying causes was chronic joint pain. Patiently, Shail explained, "I'm afraid these stones aren't that sophisticated. This stone only alerts me to the abnormality, it can't discern the symptom's cause. And the recommended treatment would change depending on whether this was an injury that could be expected to heal on its own with a healer's support, or something that would require maintenance going forward. These stones are just a tool, it requires the trained questioning from a healer to accurately diagnose and treat an issue."

Messir Elkgnere seemed to consider this, before reluctantly answering, "It's been hard to keep my shop's tally book straight, I can't use my quill for longer than a

300

quarter of the hourglass without my wrist stiffening up on me, and I have to stop and rest it." Messir Elkgnere subconsciously rolled his wrist as he described what sounded to Shail like the ordinary stiffening most people got in their joints as they aged into their winter years, particularly ones that were hard used, like a shop keeper's writing wrist. Fifty wasn't old, but his patient's staunch refusal to follow his healer's educated advice would see the man infirm before his time.

Shail spoke to Master Conlun, "Application of the heat stone, sir?"

"An excellent idea."

Shail said to Messir Elkgnere, "I have something that can help with that." Shail cleansed the consult stone one last time before returning it to its box, and the box to the cabinet. Shail then retrieved another box, but from the third drawer. This one was smaller, holding only three stones in a row, all round, but different colors. The one on the left was red, the middle blue, and the right a fresh egg white. Shail set the box on the table recently vacated, drawing out the red stone with his left hand, and motioning with his right for Messir Elkgnere's wrist.

"What is that for?" Messir Elkgnere peered at this new stone suspiciously, not offering his limb.

Shail tried to smile encouragingly, "This is a heat stone. It should help your wrist to feel better, if you'll allow me, please?" The man finally stuck out his arm, none-too

301

politely. Shail took heart at the small victory, gently grasping his patient's forearm. He slowly and evenly passed the stone completely around the joint. The stone glowed, then became palpably warm. After five full, slow circuits, Shail released his patient, inquiring, "How is that? Better?"

Messir Elkgnere gave the joint an experimental roll, and looked surprised, then pleased for the first time since his arrival. He twisted his wrist left, then right, back and forth, while admitting, "Actually, yes, it does seem improved." Grudgingly he added, "My thanks. I didn't think to mention it before, silly thing for a busy man to complain about. Still, one less annoyance is a blessing".

Shail took the thanks, however unenthusiastic, and brought the conversation back to the man's initial complaint. "I'll get you a list of exercises you can perform at home to improve your wrist's flexibility. The heat stone can help alleviate the symptoms, but the best long-term results come from a combination of treatment methods." Shail pointed to Messir Elkgnere's chest. "We don't have anything that will cure the weakness of your heart. Just like with your wrist, your best chance of living symptom free is to follow Master Conlun's instructions. We can't force you to do as we ask, but you will continue to suffer if you don't. It is as simple as that". A light chime sounded, and Shail handed Messir Elkgnere his shirt. "That's all the time we have for today sir." Messir Elkgnere grumbled something that was lost in the folds of the shirt he pulled on, and he left without further thanks or farewell. As the man walked away, Shail couldn't help pulling a face at his back, feeling a little better for the childish response.

He heard Master Conlun chuckle, "Always fun, that one."

"Yes sir, a barrel of giggles." Shail took the cloth that he'd soaked in cleansing solution and gave everything Messir Elkgnere had touched a thorough wipe down. That was the procedure after every patient, regardless of their complaint. Since his patient was plagued mostly by pig-headedness, it was the work of a moment. Finished, Shail requested to spend the remaining time before the next patient arrived outside the Healer's building. Stepping into the sheltered entrance, he looked out upon the villa-, *town*, Shail corrected himself. It consisted of fifteen single-family homes, most with attics above, and basements below. Shail enjoyed the fresh air until he saw the next patient approaching. Waving to her, he stepped to the side, holding the door open so she could precede him. "Good afternoon Mrs. Jespers. How are you today?"

The young woman gave him a shy smile. "Good day Healer Shail, I am well. And you?" Shail closed the door and gestured for Mrs. Jespers to sit on the low table recently occupied by Messir Elkgnere. She obeyed, and spent a few moments exchanging pleasantries with Master Conlun before coming to the reason for the appointment.

He asked, "I assume you're here for the usual?" She nodded, blushing slightly as she pressed both hands to her flat belly. Once a week, every week that Shail had been in residence, Mrs. Jespers made an appointment, always with the same request. Master Conlun nodded, and Shail retrieved the box from the first drawer of the cabinet. The Masterhealer selected a stone in a crescent shape. While he did this, Mrs. Jespers exposed the lower expanse of her belly. Master Conlun pressed the semi-circle stone to her skin, and all three looked at it expectantly. Five heartbeats, ten, fifteen. The stone stayed its mist gray color. Shail watched his mentor meet his patient's tearful gaze, shaking his head sadly. "I'm sorry. You are not pregnant at this time." He made a show of handing the stone to Shail to clean, to allow their patient a moment to compose herself. They knew from experience any other attempt to console her would just make her uncomfortable. Shail heard the rustling that indicated she'd pulled her clothing straight. When they turned back, her face was pale but dry.

Their ritual nearly complete, she spoke her final, familiar phrase, "Thank you, Healer. May I see you next week?".

Master Conlun gave a shallow bow, "Of course, Mrs. Jespers. Same time?" She nodded, bid him goodbye, and Shail held the door for her to exit, watching her as she walked home. Shail cleansed the workspace, then checked the roster.

The next appointment wasn't just for one patient, but three. A mother was bringing her two daughters with the sniffles, and a young son with reoccurring nosebleeds. Shail used the consult stone on both girl's faces, but when it did not turn the yellow that would have indicated infection, Master Conlun soothed their mother by concluding her children's symptoms were most likely no more than seasonal allergies. He gave their mother a lotion to use on her daughter's noses after they blew them clear. The boy was even easier to diagnose. While his mother had tearfully related how her son's nose had mysteriously begun to bleed several times a day, Shail observed the lad's attempts to scratch a brain itch through his nostrils, first one, then the other.

Straining to control his amusement, Shail directed the mother's attention to her son. "I think I see the problem, ma'am." The boy's mother gave a horrified gasp, alternating between apologizing profusely to Master Conlun for wasting his time, and scolding her son. She packed up her family, and all four bid Shail goodbye as they left.

The last appointment for the day was for a young hunter with a broken arm Shail had helped Master Conlun to splint and swathe. He'd been told to return every third day so Shail could track the healing process. Unfortunately, like Messir Elkgnere, the hunter took his healer's concerns for granted, and hadn't showed up to any of his appointments after the first. Nor had he followed his aftercare instructions, specifically to rest his arm until the splint was removed in a month's time. Shail had seen him the day after his first missed appointment, breaking firewood outside his house. Shail had run to him and remonstrated with the man.

The hunter had easily shaken Shail off with a curt, "Chores won't wait, leave off boy". That had stung Shail's pride, but Master Conlun had called him back, having heard Shail's shouts.

"You can't help people who don't want helping", his master had said philosophically.

Today was no exception; the time for the hunter's appointment came, and went, and Shail spent the time staring out the building's front facing window. When it became obvious the hunter wasn't coming, Shail helped to close up for the day. He would still be expected to respond to an emergency, but was otherwise considered off duty.

Master Conlun waved Shail off, "Tell Tabirc I said hello. See you tomorrow."

"Good evening master."

Chapter 26

Goodbye Mother

Leeinn woke at her usual time, washing, dressing, and picking up Gira and Tal before heading to the dining hall for breakfast. Gira seemed subdued, but Leeinn was not sure if that was solely because her family would be leaving soon, or if the early hour was catching up with her late sleeping friend. Gira's hair had been braided back from her face, which had been dusted with cosmetics so you could not tell if she was pale or just powdered.

They did not have to wait long at the dining hall before their group was completed with the arrival of Tiny and Tancer, the latter looking as sleepy as Gira. He yawned his way through a cup of coffee, looking marginally more awake when it was settled in his belly.

Tiny said, "What's the plan for today?"

"Well," Leeinn answered, casting a glance at Gira, "We'll say goodbye to the visiting families after breakfast. After that ..... we'll see what everyone else feels up to."

Tiny caught on to what Leeinn didn't say, "Sounds good. We did what I wanted to do at the stables, I think it's only fair to let someone else choose today."

Tancer was quick to add his two cents, "In that case my suggestion is we stay here. All day. That way, we have seats for every meal."

Tiny pulled her husband towards her, fixing her hand over his mouth to silence him, "What would you like to do Gira? Tal?"

Gira shrugged, "I don't feel like moving much, but I'll work if everyone else want to."

Tancer managed to mumble through his wife's fingers, "Everyone else does *not* want to."

Leeinn offered, "Why don't I show you the meditation glades? They're a good place to just sit and *be*."

Gira looked grateful, "They sound lovely."

They finished up their meal and left the dining hall, making for the main gates. There was much hustle and bustle as the visiting families prepared to leave. Leeinn watched Gira search the area with her eyes, before settling on the knot of people that was her family. Trader Nassine was giving last minute orders to her retainers while Challi and Shealah made silly faces at her back. Gira giggled at their antics.

Her mother noticed their arrival, and bid those waiting upon her to see to their tasks. "Gira, I'm glad you're here. I have some final instructions for you and Tal."

"*O ... oh*, really?"

Nassine nodded dismissively to Leeinn, Tiny, and Tancer, "I must borrow my daughter for a moment."

Tancer all but fled, "You heard the lady!" Leeinn could hardly blame her brother, and was close on his retreating heels. Tiny was able to keep up with their quick strides by lengthening her own.

Leeinn said, "I'm going to find my father."

Tiny said, "I think we'll just stand over there." She and Tancer moved to a spot where they could watch the proceedings without being in anyone's way.

Leeinn found her father by the gates, smiling at a pair of trader family children before him. He handed them each a small, wrapped candy, and they fled laughing while holding their prizes high over their heads. He greeted her, "Hello dew drop."

"Hello father."

"How's your friend?"

"Nervous, I think."

"She's doing a brave thing."

"I've offered to show her the meditation glades after her family leaves."

"A quiet place will be good today, but tomorrow I want all of team Leeinn on work duty."

"Yes father."

"I think it's just about time."

"Shall I get everyone's attention for you?"

"I think I can manage. I've always been a first class waver you know."

Leeinn rolled her eyes good naturedly, "Wave away then."

Without changing the rest of his demeanor in the slightest, Rumaru lifted his left arm. At once, all activity ceased, eyes snapping to the upraised hand. The sound of silence stretched her father's smile even wider than before. "Shall we get started?" A rustle of agreement met the abbot's question. "Very good. Our servers will now walk among you, anyone who wishes to participate may take a cup."

On cue, Accepted carried platters covered with cups made from real del petals. In the center of each was a large pearl of del nectar. Each person took a cup, then lifted it in toast. "We wish a swift and easy passage for those passing through our gates." A murmur of voices repeated the phrase. Rumaru tilted his cup until the nectar rolled out onto his tongue, swallowed, then popped the cup into his mouth, chewing with evident enjoyment.

The offering made and accepted, those leaving filed out of the gates. They entered their assigned carriages, hanging out the open windows to wave back at those staying. Leeinn excused herself, and went to find Gira. She was standing on the threshold looking torn. Leeinn linked her arm through Gira's, "I'm glad you're staying."

Tancer did the same with Gira's other arm, "Me too! The more newbies there are, the less silly I'll look."

"Don't count on that dear."

"Hush you, I'm being *supportive*."

"Watch yourself Gira, or he may attach."

"You make me sound like a leech."

"But a *cute* leech."

"I'm not sure that helps."

The drivers gave their charges the go ahead, and the families were off. "Goodbye mother! Goodbye Challi, and Shealah!" Gira did her best to wave goodbye with both arms entangled with her friends.

Tiny said, "You'll have to introduce us to your sister when she comes back."

Gira looked confused, "When she comes back?"

"For your Hopeful Ceremony," Tiny clarified

"Of course, I almost forgot about that."

"They'll all come back for that, wouldn't they?"

Gira nodded confidently, "They would. All of them."

"It's wonderful you have such a supportive family."

Gira's voice developed a hitch, "A family that's gone now …"

Leeinn consoled her friend, "Gone back to the City. Not *gone* gone."

They watched the carriages slowly move away from the abbey. When they had gone beyond a curve in the road, those watching began to disperse. Tancer breathed a sigh of relief, "Now things can get back to normal."

"You've been Accepted for less than a week. How do you know what normal looks like here?"

"That's what I'm hoping to find out."

Leeinn asked, "Shall we go to the glades now?"

Gira said, "I think that's a good idea. I could use some quiet time."

The glades were in an older section of the abbey, farther away from the general goings-on. The atmosphere quieted the spirit. When Tancer spoke, it was in a hushed voice, "I've never even heard of the glades before."

Leeinn answered, "They're usually reserved for Accepted. They're a special place any brother or sister can go to when they're minds are troubled."

Gira suddenly looked worried, "But *I'm* not Accepted! Neither is Tal."

Leeinn reassured her, "Don't worry, you're with us. If three Accepted say they want you in their group, no one is going to say anything as long as we follow the rules."

"What are the rules?"

"The glades are a sanctuary. There can be absolutely no aggression, any disagreements have to be taken elsewhere. Conversation is allowed, but we must keep our voices low, to be respectful of anyone else enjoying the area."

Tiny said, "Sound like easy rules."

Gira said, "But you'll warn me if there's a rule I don't know about, right? I don't want to get in trouble the minute my mother leaves."

Leeinn smiled, "Of course, but you really don't need to worry so much. It's a place to rest and relax."

They approached a line of high bushes with a break in the middle wide enough for two people to easily pass each other. The walked through single file, Leeinn first, and

Tiny brought up the rear. Once on the other side there was plenty of room for the group to bunch back together.

Gira said, "*Oooooh*, it's so beautiful!" And it was. The glades were encompassed by the abbey wall along the back, and around the other three sides by hedges. The area sheltered within was shadowed by the tress that had been planted all throughout the glades. Footpaths allowed visitors to stroll about as they wished, with many benches for those wishing to sit. Set into the ground were numerous shallow pools, home to del koi that swam lazily about their liquid world. Gira's spirits seemed restored, "Look, that one wants attention. Hello fat fishy! Do you like scritches?" The koi in question, over twelve inches long, lifted its white chin out of the water. Gira laughingly scratched it with a single fingernail. "It's fins are so bright, just like a winged stallion!"

Leeinn said, "These kind of koi can only survive in del cleansed water. They eat the flower too, which may have something to do with the vibrancy of their scales."

"If I *do* become Accepted, I want to work here!"

Tiny said, "I may not like water, but I could definitely see myself working here. The pools aren't even knee deep on Tancer." Tancer stuck his tongue out at his wife, resulting in a quickly hushed bout of giggling, each one shushing the others as they tried vainly to control their own merriment.

"Leeinn? Is that you?" A round-faced Brother with glasses the same color as his abundant black hair waved to Leeinn and her group.

"Hello Tehrani. No surprise finding you here. Everyone, this is my brother Tehrani. He's a poet, so he's always here for the peace and quiet."

"And for inspiration. Beauty evokes beauty."

Gira sighed, "So very true."

Tal addressed her mistress, "While we stay at the abbey, I don't see why you couldn't be assigned here, like Tiny and Tancer will likely be to one of the stables."

Gira fluttered her eyes at Tehrani, "Then we'd get to spend lots of time together. You could show me the glades, maybe even read me some of your poetry."

"I'd like that."

Tal said, "We should definitely get you some gloves if you're going to have your hands in water all day."

"Al …. All day?" Gira's face said the thought of working in the glades suddenly did not seem quite as appealing.

Tiny hid a smile behind her hand, pretending to brush her braids back from her face. "At the very least, we can ask for a trial period, to see if the work suits."

Gira's gaze strayed to her friendly koi, who was holding his chin out for more scritches. She couldn't seem to resist the creature's charms, actually sitting on the ground so to be able to reach it all the better. "You'd like it if I worked here, huh Lucky?"

Tehrani seemed delighted, "Lucky? Is that his name?"

"His? You're sure it's a he?"

"With colors like that, he's got to be male. The females aren't as pretty, they don't have to be."

"Why not?"

"They're a lot like the winged horses. And female fish are much bigger than the males."

"You know a lot about the koi, don't you?"

Tehrani smiled, "Of course, they're some of my best audiences."

"Well this one seems lucky to me, so Lucky I shall call him."

"Appropriate. Water cleansed by dels must make for sweet living."

Tancer pretended to boggle his eyes, "So they're *all* Lucky?"

Tiny joked, "Makes it easy to call them for a meal."

Leeinn added, "Which they're always ready for, gluttonous things."

Tiny said, "You're spirit animal Tancer."

Tancer flashed a smile that was probably meant to be seductive, but ended up looking quite silly, "Right you are. Both of us have a noble appetite, and are gorgeous to boot."

"Gorgeous?"

"You're right, not strong enough. *Hmm*. Mind numbingly gorgeous? Spirit soothing spectacular? Fair beyond compare!"

Groans were his only answer.

Chapter 27

AhhB Inn

Tabirc's face broke into a huge grin as Shail came home, "Hey, how was your shift?"

"Two words. Messire. Elkgnere."

"*Oh* …. So how soon will you be leaving?"

Shail laughed, "If I start walking now I should be home by my next Stallion Feather Ceremony."

"You could try yelling really loud for our dragons to come back."

Tabirc's words reminded Shail of Lowkrist and Stendow's leaving. The second day in Tabirc's village had dawned fine and pleasant, the storm having rained itself out. There were still a few stray clouds, but they were white and fluffy instead of grey and heavy. Shail had been delighted to find both dragons wrapped together, taking turns washing each other's faces with their long tongues. "They really do like each other!"

"Wingmates are often bonded, 'specially if they've flown some difficult missions."

"Gran says the same about the healers she worked with."

"And she worked with some *real* dragons."

"So you worked with fake ones?" Tabirc barked a laugh, attaining the attention of their mounts. They peered down at their riders, looking expectant. Shail has insisted on accompanying Tabirc for each of their meal pills, determined not to miss a single chance to be with them. They in turn had become rather sweet on Shail, excitement and pleasure written plain on their highly expressive faces. They became animated upon seeing who it was. Shail called out, "Good morning skyladies!" He had taken Tabirc's habit to heart, and now called them nothing else.

"Will you look at those two? Sight of you and they're like puppies." Tabirc got a sudden gleam in his eye, "Puppies with their mah, or *paw*." Shail pretended to be sick, holding his head and stomach while moaning pitifully. Lowkrist and Stendow made chuckling sounds. "Seriously though, you've a way with the beasts I've seen some handlers never achieve."

Shail shrugged modestly, "I just treat them nicely, like I'd want to be treated if I were a dragon."

Tabirc tussled Shail's hair, "Is that all? Well then, what would Shail the dragon want now?"

319

Shail sighed, "To go home."

"Let's give them one last good rubdown as a thank you."

Tabirc let Shail clean Stendow by himself, though he finished Lowkrist in half the time. Stendow reveled in Shail's attention, her eyes fluttering as he carefully went over her brow ridge, and then down her long, broad nose. Shail loved the way she trilled with pleasure, letting him know he was doing a good job. Stendow gently bopped Shail under the chin with her nose, a sign of affection, as far as he could tell. They were each given the last of the meal pellets, then it was time for them to leave.

"Can they really find their way back without us? What if they get lost?"

"Animals with wings tend to have a good sense of direction. Have to, considering the large area a flying creature can cover. I promise you, they've both kept an eye on the land we passed, and will follow the same path home, more or less. With yesterday's rest, they should be as fresh as hatchlings. Let's get them saddled, all the riding equipment goes back with them." When both dragons were kitted out, and all was secured properly, Tabirc said, "We say our goodbyes now. Then I teach you one last command."

Shail reached out to scratch under Stendow's jaw hinge. "Thanks for everything. Have a safe trip home!" In return, Stendow folded her wings forward, crossing them over Shail's head in an approximation of a hug.

When she finally withdrew them, Tabirc said, "Tell her to *follow wingmate.*"

"Stendow, follow wingmate!" At once the dragons were alert, Lowkrist looking to the sky.

Tabirc backed away from where they stood, motioning for Shail to do the same. Clear of the area, Tabirc said, "Now, tell them to *go home.*"

Shail took a deep breath, "Lowkrist, Stendow, *go home!*" The next instant Shail had to shield his eyes as the wind from their wings blew dust and dirt out from where they had stood. They were soon mere dark specks against the blue, and then Shail could not see them at all. He sighed, "I wish they could have stayed a little longer."

"I know, but they'd have gotten hungry, and not had the benefit of a meal pellet to speed them on their way."

Shail felt guilty for his selfish thought, "I wouldn't want that. I'm just going to miss them."

Tabirc pulled Shail under his arm. "And they'll probably miss you to. Your skylady was quite enamored with you."

"Lowkrist looked like she liked you."

"She tolerated me well enough, but I didn't win her heart like you did with yours. I think if you ever find that dragon again, and want a partner, she'd be willing to have you."

Shail felt his heart pick up at the thought. *Him*, a dragon rider. Lots of people dreamed of doing such a job, but what were the odds Shail would ever be among their number? "I'll doubt I'll ever see her again, but who knows?"

Shail shook himself back to the present, asking the ritual question, even though he already knew Tabirc's answer, "What do you want to do for supper?"

"Apple Barrel?"

"You always say that."

"We can eat at home, if you're cooking."

"I can make us something."

"Besides a blackberry jam and peanutspread sandwich?"

Shail blushed, "Gran says it has all the basic things a body needs."

"But maybe not everything a body could *want*."

Shail relented, "Alright, the AhhB it is."

If you couldn't immediately spot a stranger among the few dozen regulars, you could always mark an outsider who regularly called the Apple Barrel by its proper name. Shail had thought the inn was called the "abbey", the first few times he'd heard the name. Tabirc offered, "Tell you what, we'll grab some supplies from Maqbern to make a picnic, and go out to the lake tomorrow."

"That sounds great! Are you going to tell stories too?"

"Well, if you insist ..."

"I want to hear about when you were training to become a rider."

"Looking to pick up some tips?"

"Maybe"

"Here's one: don't fall off your dragon."

"They have to teach people that?"

"If there's a rule, it's because something happened."

They heard someone call out, "Hey, there he is! Tabirc! The hunters found a downed dragon, no sign of the handler. They think it's hurt, but it won't let them get close. You were a handler, right? What should we do?"

Tabirc shook his head, "There aren't any regular flight paths anywhere near here."

The speaker shrugged, "We had that storm. Maybe it got blown off course, lost its handler, and has been wandering since. I don't know, but the hunter's swear it's a dragon."

Tabirc seemed to consider, then made his decision. "Give me a quarter of an hourglass. I'll pack up what I'll need for a couple days in the woods and have one of the hunters take me to their dragon. Can't make any plans past that, just have to see what we find, and go from there." The speaker nodded and ran off, presumably to find the hunters and tell them the plan.

Shail trailed after Tabirc as he broke into a quick jog towards his house. "Do you really think they made a mistake, and they found something other than a dragon," he asked.

Tabirc didn't slow his pace, answering over his shoulder, "If I knew, I wouldn't be going. Not sure what we'll do with a dragon even if we find one."

Shail looked surprised, "Return it to whoever owns it, I should think?"

Tabirc countered, "And if it isn't obvious who it belongs to? This town couldn't keep a dragon nearby, there aren't any winged horses here, nor could they afford to buy enough to feed a dragon for long."

Shail hadn't considered that, but he was now, with a growing sense of unease. "Well, then, I suppose you would take it to the closest place that has dragons and leave it to them what to do with it."

Tabirc had reached his house, and Shail followed him through the front door. Tabirc fetched a traveler's pack from a hook, and began to stuff it with warm clothes, his tinder kit, and other such items he'd need in the woods. As he worked, Tabirc commented, "Could be an opportunity for a lad to claim a dragon for himself. Could do a lot of things with a loyal partner. Scout work, carrying messages where the speed of the delivery counts as much as the contents of the missive, a clever person could make their fortune with a dragon." Shail went still, not sure what his uncle was getting at.

When Tabirc seemed to expect an answer, Shail said reluctantly, "If you couldn't find the dragon's original owner, I suppose you could take it to a judge and have the beast granted to you as salvaged goods."

Tabirc seemed to choose his next words carefully, "Maybe you should come with us? We might find the dragon's handler, and they might need a healer."

Shail considered, "I'd have to have Master Conlun's permission."

Tabirc nodded quickly, "Of course! Why not run and ask him now? I can find the hunter and get the whole story until you're ready to go." Shail was touched by his uncle's earnest desire for Shail to join the expedition. Shail nodded, and left Tabirc's house at a run.

When Shail found Master Conlun, he related the events between panting breaths, ending with his request to accompany Tabirc and the hunters. Master Conlun looked surprised, "I can understand Tabirc wanting to go, having been a handler himself, but I'm not sure an apprentice Travealer can lend much to this endeavor." At Shail's crestfallen look, Master Conlun seemed to regret his words. "But it is a rare opportunity for a young man. I know I would have jumped at such a chance, when I was your age." He nodded, and said, "You may take three days, but make sure you are back by the fourth, whether you find the dragon or not."

Shail had nearly leapt for joy, but contained himself to a quick, "Thank you Master, I will!" Shail sprinted back to Tabirc's house, arriving winded but grinning as he greeted his friend with a, "I can go! I must be back in four days, but otherwise I'm at your disposal. What should we do now?"

Tabirc whooped, grabbing his pack and motioning Shail out the door. When they were both outside, Tabirc locked up, and took the lead as they walked towards the general store. They spent a few minutes there as Tabirc barked out his order over Messir Elkgnere's complaint that the store was closed, for it was his shop. Tabirc ignored the man's attempts to dismiss him, repeating his list in rising volume until Messir Elkgnere deflated, throwing all the items in a traveler's pack that had seen better days, before shoving the pack into Shail's arms, and ordering them both out. Having gotten what he wanted, Tabirc called back thanks as he and Shail headed for the Apple Barrel.

"That's where the hunters are bound to be, if I know them."

Tabirc's guess proved correct, the bar hosted two men holding the room's occupants spell bound as they recounted their find. The hunter that had been speaking paused as he saw Tabirc and Shail enter. He waved to Tabirc, and Shail was surprised when the hunter granted him a respectful nod. Shail returned the gesture, striving for every inch next to Tabirc, who had Shail beat for breadth and height. One of the hunters addressed Tabirc, "I take it you two heard about the dragon?"

"Heard you found something anyway. Might be worth looking."

The hunter looked mildly offended, "Hard to mistake a dragon for anything else Tabirc."

Tabirc assumed a look of tolerant amusement, "I'd better hear this story from the beginning."

The audience gave a collective complaint, but the hunter merely scowled. "It won't hurt you lot to hear it from the start twice, and you heard Tabirc, he needs to hear the whole of it". This appeal was met with mutinous grumbling, but the crowd eventually subsided back into attentive silence. Two seats were made available to Tabirc

327

and Shail at a table that supplied an unobstructed view of the hunter.

When everyone was settled, the hunter drew breath, and began. "We were out in the East Woods, looking for anything that was wounded or killed in that roof rattler we had a few days back, me and the Osler twins. Lots of downed trees, and past the Crooked Cricklet, one of the twins, never could tell'em apart myself, but he says, "*You hear that?*" So, we listened, and sure enough, there was a sound like the grandah of all bulls trying to push its way through the wood. We tried creeping close enough to get a look at whatever was making the racket. I saw the beast and thought it best to fetch you."

Shail glanced from the hunter to Tabirc. Tabirc's face was thoughtful, but otherwise betrayed no emotion that Shail could see. "I suppose it's possible that a dragon messenger could have been blown off course by storm winds, maybe even downed if the handler was foolish enough to try to fly through it. Did the dragon look injured?"

The hunter shrugged, "We didn't get that close. It was having trouble navigating around all the downed trees, kept its wings against its body, so couldn't get a good look at them." The hunter took a draft from his mug. He wiped his mouth with his sleeve, then raised an eyebrow at Tabirc. "You looking to see the beast yourself? I can take you to the spot I seen it. Prove to you I ain't crazy."

Tabirc gave a roguish grin. "Never said you was mad. Stupid, maybe," and Tabirc strode over and gave the hunter a good-natured punch on the shoulder.

The hunter grinned, "Don't have to be smart to know a dragon when I see one, Handler, even if it is funny looking. You'll be wanting to bond it yourself, get back into the saddle as it were?"

Tabirc shook his head, "Not me, I'm retired. I had all the fun a'wing I could stand. But if it *is* a dragon, it probably belongs to the Guild, and they'll pay handsome for its return. Seems like it *might* be worth my time to verify your assessment."

The hunter narrowed his eyes at Tabirc. "Worth your time? We'll see, Handler."

Tabirc said, "Shail's coming too, in case we need a healer."

The hunter eyed Shail, who tried to sit as tall and straight as he could, "If'n you say so Tabirc. He gonna be an apprentice handler too?

Stung by the man speaking as if he were not there, Shail said, "A person can't have too many skills." That brought a round of laughter from the onlookers.

A voice called out from the audience, "Need any more help Tabirc?"

"A guide and a healer, what more could I ask for?"

Chapter 28

Yes

When Tancer mentioned that it was just about lunch o'clock, they agreed to return to the dining hall. The glades seemed to have done Gira good, for by the time they left, she was back to her gregarious self.

She bounced alongside Leeinn as they walked, "I think I really will ask to become Hopeful."

Tiny, who was sedately strolling at the back asked, "What about you Tal?"

Tal interlaced fingers with short, half-moon nails flat against her stomach, "I don't think Mistress Gira would like that."

Gira stopped her bouncing to look back at Tal, "Nonsense! If you want to become Hopeful, then we can go together, just like Tiny and Tancer."

Surprise colored Tal's voice, "*Well* ...."

"Don't you think you'd be happy here?

"Yes, but …"

"And they can just as easily take two Hopeful as one, right?"

Leeinn nodded, "Easier, because then we only need the one ceremony."

"So you see? Oh please say you'll go with me Tal!"

Tal seemed to be weakening, "But would your mother approve?"

"Of course she would! Then she'd know I'd always have someone here to serve me."

Tancer said gently, "Except, if Tal became Accepted, she wouldn't be your servant anymore."

Gira blushed to her roots, "That was a stupid thing to say, I'm sorry."

Tal pat Gira on the arm, "I would still do my best to serve you, if I were granted the honor of becoming Accepted."

"Does that mean you'll be Hopeful with me?"

Tal seemed to realize she'd lost, "Yes mistress, if it would truly please you."

"You hear that! Tal and I are going to become Hopeful together! Do you think tonight is a good time to ask the Father Abbot about it?"

331

Tancer had been admiring the abbey, but chimed in, "And your family should still be relatively close, so it won't be long before they get back."

Gira turned beseeching eyes upon Leeinn, "Could I have some buds for my hair, like your father wore in his for the last ceremony?"

"Of course."

"And I've heard that del blossoms last for a long time, so I could wear them over and over." Gira twirled in a circle with happiness. "I'll have to have a new gown made, but I can go to the tailors here. I'm sure they're very good dress makers."

Tancer looked confused, "But you have that other dress you said you had made special for your trip here? Why do you need a new one?"

"Because I already wore that one silly. I can't wear the same dress twice for such an important occasion."

"Oh."

"Tell him Tiny."

"I've never been much of a dress person, *no pockets*, so just one is enough for me."

"And she looks wonderful when she wears it!"

Tiny tried for sarcasm, but it was plain she was pleased, "How do I look when I'm wearing pants?"

332

"Still wonderful, of course."

Gira exclaimed, "He's right, you really are very pretty. Especially your hair beads!"

Tiny said shyly, "Tancer gave me most of them."

Tancer winked, "One, I actually made myself."

"Did you really? Which one?"

Tiny pulled forward a braid with a white bead twined near the top, shiny from a long history of loving attention, "He found out I really like opals, bought one, and had a bead maker show him how to carve it."

"I gave it to her when I asked her to marry me."

Gira gushed, "That's so romantic! No wonder she said yes!"

"I'd like to think she'd have said yes without it, but I'll admit, it probably won my case."

Lunch was a simple affair, a hearty potato soup with bread and the diners choice of teas and lemonades. After lunch, Gira wanted to find Rumaru.

Leeinn considered, "He's probably taking a nap in the orchard."

Gira looked disappointed, "We shouldn't wake him if he's sleeping."

"He'll know when we're close by and wake up on his own."

Tancer asked, "How does he do that? Being blind doesn't seem to slow him down at all."

"The way he tells it, he was quite helpless when he first lost his sight. But with training and practice, he eventually became as he is now."

"But how did he become blind in the first place?"

"He hit his head when he was twenty, knocked him out for over a day. When he woke up, he was blind."

Gira looked stricken, "How awful."

Their arrival at the orchard was marked by those gathering fruit from the trees. Many greeted Leeinn, wanting to know who her friends were. After many introductions, Leeinn managed to find out that her father was indeed in his favorite napping spot.

Gira needed reassuring, "But if he's asleep, we won't wake him, right? I don't want him to be annoyed when I ask to become Hopeful."

"My father is slow to anger, and quick to forgive."

"Better not to need forgiving. Tal, are you going to ask him at the same time?"

Tal nodded, a strand of red hair sticking to her face now that they were back out in the heat of the day, "No reason to bother the Father Abbot twice."

Leeinn gave an amused sigh, "Once you get to know him better you'll see that you don't have to worry about *bothering him*, or *annoying him*. My father loves being abbot, and loves helping everyone under his care."

Tiny pointed to the base of a tree, "Is that him there?" Having been pointed out, Rumaru was easy to see sitting nestled in a curvature of roots, his arms and legs pulled inside his hazel habit, so his head was the only part of his body that was visible.

Leeinn motioned for her friends to stop where they were, "Watch this." They were still a good distance away, at least ten feet, when Leeinn whispered, *"Hello father. Having a good nap?"*

Rumaru had appeared asleep, but smiled upon hearing his daughter's voice, "Lunch was delicious, but it made me rather drowsy."

Leeinn giggled as they closed the distance, "You need a reason to sleep like Tancer needs a reason to eat."

Her father laughed at Tancer's grunt of indignation, "You mustn't deny a man his simple pleasures, sugar cube." Rumaru sat up and stretched, "Did you want just my company, or is there something I can do for you?"

Gira was quick to answer, "I have a question I'd like to ask you Father Abbot. Tal too."

"I see. Well, ask away, and I'll do my best to answer."

"With your permission sir, I'd like to become Hopeful."

"Really? Your family hasn't even been gone a day."

"I was already thinking of asking, and then Leeinn took us to the glades with the del koi, and I made friends with one, and I just knew there wasn't any point in waiting any longer."

"I see. And you, Tal?"

"The same Father Abbot, I ask to become Hopeful."

"And your reason?"

"To support my mistress."

"*Hmm.*"

A shallow furrow formed between her brows, "Is that a wrong answer?"

"No, it is a generous answer. I wonder though, if it is the full answer."

"What do you mean?"

"If you were accepted, you would live here the rest of your days, unless you chose to leave. Is that really something you want?"

"Your abbey is beautiful sir."

Rumaru gave her a wry smile, "So I remember. And you've barely scratched her surface."

"And your people are so kind."

Rumaru's eyes were completely closed by the fullness of his grin, "None kinder than my daughter. She's been that way since the day I found her," he boasted with obvious pride.

Tal murmured, "This place is like a fairytale. Dragons, winged horses, and magical flowers. Even you, sir, have lived a charmed life here. A blind man who found an orphaned child, became a single father, and then eventually Father Abbot of Del Abbey."

Rumaru leaned back against the tree trunk, his hands resting on his cane, "It didn't feel like a fairytale at the time. When I was your age, I could see. It never occurred to me, just as it has likely never occurred to you, that a time might come when that would not be the case."

Tiny spoke quietly, "Leeinn told us you were blinded in an accident."

"True. Soon after I became Accepted, I had my fall. Nothing our healers tried ever worked."

Gira looked as though she wanted to pat Rumaru on the arm in sympathy, but didn't quite dare, "How terrible. What did you do?

"For a long time I thought it was the end of everything. How could I not, when everyone around me thought the same?"

"But they made you abbot?"

"Not for another twenty years. Then, I was just a young man, angry with the world for having damned me so." The group held their breath, hanging upon every word. "What can a blind man do? Nothing important, nothing special. Just try not to be nuisance. Or so I thought."

Tal seemed as enthralled as the rest, "But what happened to change your mind?"

"The abbess at the time put out a special request to the City Guild, and they sent me a teacher."

"A teacher?"

"Yes, and blind herself. It was she who taught me how to see without my eyes. My teacher was eventually accepted herself, one of the oldest to ever do so. You'll meet her at some point. She doesn't like crowds, so she mostly hides until things calm down."

Tiny said, "Your abbess was a clever woman."

"I have tried to follow her example."

"How long did it take for the others to take you seriously?"

"It was a slow process. Teaching myself to believe I could do things took some time, more so with others. I don't think I convinced everyone until I found Leeinn and adopted her as my daughter. Keeping up with a toddler meant I had to learn fast, so I was able to make friends with many of the mothers at Del Abbey, a bunch I'd never had much to do with before my accident."

Tancer said, "So she made you a father twice over."

Rumaru laughed heartily, "So she did, for I doubt I'd ever been made abbot without her.

Gira gently reminded, "Umm, Father Abbot, about us becoming Hopeful?"

"Yes."

"Can we?"

"I've already answered; *yes*. To both of you."

Chapter 29

Tracker

Shail followed close behind Tabirc as they trailed behind their guide. It was pleasant in the woods, the towering trees still had all their leaves, though more than one had begun to change into its fall finery, providing ample shade from the sun. Small insects buzzed about Shail's face, and he swat at the them first with one hand, then the other. Shail could hardly contain his excitement. They were going to find a *dragon*. Ever since Stendow had left, Shail had felt strangely lonely, as though the brief time with the dragon had satisfied a need he didn't even know he had.

"How much farther Rafger?" Tabirc asked.

"We're nearly to the spot me and the Osler twins last seen it."

Shail studied the area around them, trying to spot signs of a large animal having been through. Here and there Shail had to hop over a shallow puddle, though his two companions were able to stretch their stride to avoid stepping in the water. The pack Shail carried was heavy, but not so much as to slow him down. It held his share of the provisions, a sleeping sack, a basic healer's kit, his firestarter pouch from Uncle Wengsper, and Tumatan's unioculus. He made another mental note to return it to her as soon as he got back home. And what stories he'd have to tell! Not just riding a hired dragon, but finding a lost one! What were the odds? The hunter said, "We should spread our search out from here, we can cover three directions if we split up."

Tabirc shook his head, "Don't you know, you *never* split the party? We stick together."

Grumble grumble grumble, "As you say, *Handler*." The emphasis he put on the title was a clear indication that if they were dealing with anything but a dragon, Rafger would have argued. "Which way d'you wanna look first?"

"Let me look at the tracks, see which way it was headed last. Then, we follow." The trail wasn't hard to find, all the greenery was slicked into a muddy trough. "That's not good, she's dragging her tail."

Shail peered at the track curiously, "How can you tell?"

Rafger spat contemptuously, "Cuz ifn it weren't, there'd only be foot marks, not this sludge."

Shail winced, "Oh."

Tabirc had had enough, "Rafger, if I suddenly went unconscious, what would you do?"

"I'd … get a healer?"

Tabirc nodded, "And what would you do while you waited for the healer to arrive?

Rafger shrugged, "I dunno, give you water?"

Tabirc flicked his eyes to Shail, "What would you do?"

"I'd also call for a healer, but in the meantime, I wouldn't give you any water, because you'd choke. I would turn you onto your side, that's called the recovery position, with your arm supporting your head."

Tabirc raised his eyebrow at Rafger, "So he knows what to do for a healer, and you know how to read tracks because you're a hunter." Rafger got the hint, and while he did not apologize, he also did not make any more flippant comments at Shail's expense. Tabirc stopped so suddenly Shail nearly ran into his back, "Wait, what's that?"

"Probably the dragon," whispered the hunter.

"Why would it be coming *back* the way it's gone? If this turns out to be a joke …"

"It's not!"

Shail said, "I hear it too. But why would a dragon be trying to push through the trees instead of flying over them?'

"Best guess, she's too injured to fly, so she's trying to make it home on foot. Which is another problem. She may not let us close if she's alone and hurt."

"What'll we do if she doesn't let us near her?"

"Send a distress call with the mayor's longcomm. I'll send you back with Rafger so you don't get in trouble with Master Conlun, and I'll stay out here and keep an eye on her until they send someone." Rafger started to draw his bow and an arrow. "And what do you intend to do with that?"

"Just in case."

"Just in case nothing. We don't shoot dragons. Put those away."

Rafger did as he was told, though not without some more grousing, "And what are we supposed to do if it attacks us?"

"Dragons are rarely aggressive. So long as we give her the space she needs, she's no threat to any of us."

Rafger sniffed, "After you Handler." Tabirc took the lead, with Shail now walking between him and Rafger. Shail suddenly caught movement up ahead. Whatever it was, it was *big*.

Tabirc gave a whistle, then sang out, "Skylady, are you there?" An inquisitive chirp and louder rustling were his answer. "Sounds like a dragon."

Shail saw a flash of color, "Uhh, Tabirc? Are all dragons brown?"

"Most of them, 'cept the females, they're green."

"What about red?"

"I know of only one breed of red dragon, but I've never seen one. Not even sure the stories I heard were true."

"Then I'm not sure what we're looking for *is* a dragon. Look!" Shail pointed, and a random ray of light shone on scarlet scales.

Tabirc frowned, "Odd place to find a TD."

"A what?" Shail asked.

Growing concern tinged Tabirc's tone, "The red dragons I was talking about, they're called trackers, because they're better than a bloodhound." Further discussion was halted as the dragon in question increased its pace towards them. "You two keep out of sight. Let me see what I can do." Rafger dropped back behind a tree. Shail picked his own hiding spot, one that gave him a good view of Tabirc. The dragon was close now, Shail could make out the head as it ducked under low hanging branches. One thing became obvious; it was, in fact, a red dragon. She was the same size as their mounts had been, but there the resemblance ended. Stendow and Lowkrist had been well muscled beasts, but this dragon was whipcord thin. The length of her spine and the edges of each wing had a row of black spines. Her face was narrow, where Stendow's had been broad, and the end of her tail had two smaller flight flaps. Tabirc had been right, she was dragging it, and stumbling as she walked. Shail felt an immediate pity for the dangerously beautiful creature. She wasn't meant to walk on the ground, but wing effortlessly through the air. She sniffed, then turned avid eyes on Shail's hiding spot. She gave an excited, high-pitched roar, and Tabirc yelled, "Shail, I think she's here for you!"

"Me? Why?"

"*GO!*" Startled as Shail was by the command, the urgency in Tabirc's voice convinced him to obey the strange order. Tabirc placed himself in front of the approaching dragon, "Here now beauty, you don't want the boy. Let me check your hurts, huh?" The red dragon ignored Tabirc. Rafger had nocked an arrow, aiming it at the dragon's head. "Shail, get going!" Shail scrambled away from his hiding spot, heading back the way they had come. The dragon whipped her head to follow his progress, pushing past Tabirc as he tried vainly to ward her off. Shail heard the twang of a bowstring, followed by a curse as Rafger's arrow failed to pierce the dragon's scaley hide. Shail felt the earth shiver as the dragon pursued him. Shail cut to the right, between two thorny bushes, tearing his shirt and arms in his frenzy. The scratches stung, but Shail did not dare stop. The dragon had swung about to chase after him, but thin as she was, she was still hampered by the close-set trees. Shail started running back towards where he thought Tabirc and Rafger were.

He saw little point in being quiet now, "*Tabirc! Where are you?*"

"Here! Over here lad!" Shail followed the voice until he saw Tabirc and Rafger running towards him. "Get behind me!" Shail dashed past Tabirc, then swung around to stand by his side. Rafger sighted, pulled back, and was just about to release when Shail shoved him hard, knocking him off balance, making him shoot his second shaft into the soft soil.

"What didjer do that for," he howled furiously.

"She hasn't hurt us."

Tabirc kept his eyes on the dragon, speaking out the side of his mouth, "She doesn't want to hurt us, she wants to steal you! Trackers have another name: retrievers."

"But she can't even fly herself, how could she possibly steal me?"

"You'd be surprised what a dragon is capable of. We need to get back to the village, now!"

"But won't that just lead her home?"

"Probably, but there we'll have help to convince her to leave."

While they held this quick conference, the tracker decided to take things into her own claws. Wings lifted as far away from her body as the space would allow, she lowered her head and *hissed*. Tabirc looked more startled than any of them, and Shail remembered Tabirc's insistence that dragons weren't aggressive. This one seemed determined to be the exception. She stalked forward, one long, lean leg at a time, shaking her half open wings.

Rafger hooked his bow over a shoulder and began running away, "I didn't sign up for this!"

"Coward!" Tabirc's insult fell on deaf ears. The dragon did not even deign to notice the other man's flight, being wholly focused on Shail. "Alright, here's what we do. I'll rush her, and you run as fast as you can back to the village. The way that Rafger was going."

"But I can't just leave you out here!"
"No choice. Ready?" Shail was about to say no, when Tabirc dashed forward, stopping just shy of the tracker's feet. This finally seemed to break her concentration. It was almost funny watching her draw up like Old Nan faced with a mouse. Tabirc tried a few feinting strikes, never actually making contact, but bellowing like a bull. The bluff might have worked had his opponent not been twice his height, and thrice his weight at least. She cuffed Tabirc

out of her way, throwing him bodily against a nearby trunk. Shail heard him give an *oof*, before collapsing at the base of the tree he'd been thrown against. When he made to move to rise, Shail felt his stomach grip in a spasm of pain. Tabirc was hurt, and it was Shail's fault!

"Leave him alone you great bully!" Shail flung himself over Tabirc's prostrate form, glaring up at the tracker with tears in his eyes. "We haven't hurt you, so just go away, please!" Shail felt like a rabbit under the hawk's gaze, terribly exposed and vulnerable without a protector. But Tabirc was injured, so it should be Shail doing the protecting! Shail looked wildly around for *anything* that might help. He spotted a dark hole at the bottom of a tree not five feet from where Tabirc lay. Tabirc had landed on his side, now Shail rolled him onto his back, wrapped his arms around the unconscious man's chest, and *pulled*. His uncle would usually have been too much for Shail to drag alone, but fear lent him strength. Shail took another step towards his goal, dragged Tabirc another foot, then peered fearfully up to see what the dragon had been doing while Shail was preoccupied. He was astonished to see that it had actually sat back on its haunches, its head drooping slightly. Shail realized the poor beast was not only hurt, but exhausted and probably starving. "Just let me help him first, and then I'll see what I can do for you, skylady." The tracker did a double blink, but made no other move. Another step, another foot. The hole was so close now! With all his might Shail staggered the last two feet. He let Tabirc's back-end slide in first, then tucked his legs and

348

arms. The hole was not as deep as Shail had thought, Tabirc's head stuck above the entrance like a strange mushroom. Better than nothing. Panting, Shail turned back to the tracker. "Thank you ... I don't know your name. In a flash Shail remembered what Tabirc had called her, "Teedee?" The red dragon gave no indication she'd understood Shail's words. "Here, let me see if I can clean you up a bit." Shail took out a canteen of water and an all-purpose cloth from his healer's kit. He soaked the fabric, then approached the tracker slowly. "See, I can clean your face with this. Wouldn't it be nice to have a clean face?" Shail kept his voice low and even, as he'd seen grooms do with feisty horses. What's more, it seemed to work. The red tracker lowered her head until it was level with Shail's shoulders. Up close, Shail could see that her eyes were not golden like Stendow's, but black as ebony, matching her spikes. He gently ran the moistened cloth the length of the tracker's snout. She blinked slowly, and gave a little sigh. Shail did the same to the other side, revealing a truly beautiful face. Every scale he could see was perfect, and she was not a solid color, but a range of reds, oranges, and yellows. "You're the prettiest dragon I've ever seen Teedee!" If the tracker could not understand his words, Shail's soothing voice communicated his desire to be friendly. She held still for his attention, closing her wings to her body again. "Are you thirsty Teedee?" Shail poured a palmful of water and held his hand out the dragon. She gave it a sniff, then licked his hand twice. "I'm sorry I don't have anything to feed you. Can you wait here while I check on Tabirc?"

As Shail took a step away from her, the tracker's eyes widened and she jerked herself back to wakefulness. Her prey was trying to escape! Like a mother cat with a reluctant kitten, she gripped Shail by the back of his shirt and hoisted him into the air. Shail yelled, "Hey, put me down! I have to help Tabirc." Ignoring his protests, the tracker did her best to turn around and started walking back the way she'd come. Shail wriggled and squirmed, and almost managed to get his shirt off, when the tracker dragon brought him into a small clearing in the woods. She transferred Shail from her mouth to her two front feet. She gave one last shake, then leapt for the sky. Shail would not have believed she could fly, given her poor condition, but evidently the tracker was made of sterner stuff than Shail had accounted for. This kind of flying was vastly different from riding in a saddle with safety straps. The only thing that kept him from falling to his death was the dragon who was kidnapping him! Shail had time to shout one last hopeless plea, "*Tabirc! Help!*"

Then, they were gone.

Chapter 30

Setting the Stage

Gira looked at Rumaru like he'd suddenly grown a second head and started speaking a foreign language. She turned to stare at her servant.

"Tal?"

"Yes mistress?"

"We're Hopeful?"

"Yes mistress."

Rumaru asked with amused confusion, "Isn't that what I just said?"

Gira leapt and clapped her hands, "We're Hopeful!" She grabbed Tal, drawing her into a dancing spin, "We're Hopeful! We're Hopeful!" Tal was flushed, and smiling, and it was a triumphant smile.

"I suggest you both start considering your answers for your ceremony."

"Yes Father Abbot," the Hopefuls answered in unison.

Leeinn said, "There's no time to waste. I should get back to my pool, see which dels I coax into blooming early."

Gira was most enthusiastic, "We can help you!"

Tiny reminded her, "I think she's talking about the pool that only she and her father tend."

"Oh."

Gira looked so disappointed Leeinn relented, "Many hands make for light work, and I couldn't ask for better helpers than you four."

Gira's frown turned upside down, flashing even white teeth, "We'll be ever so careful while we're in your pool, and follow your directions exactly. You'll see, you might even decide to take us on as *permanent* pool assistants."

Leeinn, Tal, Tiny, and Tancer strolled normally, with Gira circling the group like their own little moon. She seemed too excited to walk as they did. When they arrived, Tancer was kind enough to hold the door for his companions, closing it behind them. Leeinn warned them, "Everyone watch your eyes, it's about to get bright." Just as she'd done when she and her father had last visited, Leeinn opened the sunroof to let in brilliant beams of light. It flicked and flirted off the top of the still water, outlining each flower with dazzling brilliance. The temperature got noticeably warmer, but the cool pool kept it from being uncomfortable.

Gira's hands flew to her cheeks, "Oh Leeinn! What a wonderful place!"

Tiny had to agree, "It's like your own little meditation glade"

Gira peered eagerly into the water, "Are there fish here too?"

Leeinn shook her head, "I like to focus on my flowers; fish would be too much."

Tancer looked around, "What can we do to help?"

Leeinn pointed to a burlap bag, "Can you hand me that sack please?" After Tancer had done so, Leeinn loosened the drawstring and reached inside. When she drew her hand back out, she showed her friends what she held. "This is dried winged horse droppings. It does wonders for dels of any sort. If you take off your socks and shoes, and take double handfuls, you can walk all over the pool, letting it slowly sieve into the water.

Gira made a face, "*Eww*, you want us to handle *poop*?"

"It's been dried, so it doesn't smell. It's crumbly, like rich earth, see?" Leeinn demonstrated, and the material proved easy to shred with fingers alone. "I'm afraid I don't keep gloves here, since neither my father nor I use them. But I do have a rinse sink to wash our hands when we're done."

"Perhaps there is another task my mistress could perform," Tal suggested.

Tancer added, "Maybe something that doesn't involve actually getting *in* the water."

Tiny gave him an affectionate pat on the shoulder, "Thank you for the thought, but I'll be fine."

Leeinn considered for a moment, then brightened as she addressed Gira, "You can use the testing stone." She went to a neat little tabletop, turning back with a clear, foot long baton in her hand. "This one has been calibrated to the particulars of this pool. Walk about, and dip the end of the rod into the water wherever you want. It will turn colors depending on the properties at that point. You want it to turn blue."

"I can do that!" Gira reached out for the testing stone. "It's heavier than it looks." They all sat near the edge of the pool, pulling off socks and shoes, and rolling up pants, habits, and dresses until there were five sets of bare feet. All but Gira took double handfuls of the dried droppings, waded into the pool, and began to slowly sprinkle the material throughout the water. Gira wandered happily, dipping her testing stone every few steps until she reached the further side, then she started back. "Blue …. Blue …. Blue again, your pool is really healthy!"

"Thank you. I spend a lot of time here, my father too, when he has a spare moment. I love growing dels, and I'm getting really close to a yellow variant."

Tiny pointed at a row of red del, "You've got blood lotus here!"

Tancer pointed out another row, "These are green, and those are even bluer than the testing stone. How did you manage that?"

"Every so often a del would grow with more of one color on their petals than the others. I focused on growing the next generation from their seeds especially, and each time they would be a little more vividly colored than the last. It took nearly two years to get solids like those, for the longest time they were just swirls and splotches."

Tiny said, "That's impressive dedication."

Gira asked, "Are they just different colors, or do they do anything special?"

Leeinn preened with pride, "Nectar from the greens is better than any coffee, you'd fly though any chore! The red is good for almost any illness. You'd be back on your feet in no time. And the blue is good for concentration and clear thinking."

Tal pointed, "What about the yellow?"

"I haven't perfected the yellow yet, but the few times I've experimented, it seemed to give happy feelings."

"Like ale?" Tancer quipped.

"More like a great night's sleep, a fantastic breakfast, and getting to do your favorite thing with people you love."

Tiny said, "Oh, so like what we're doing now?"

"I know tending my pool is one of *my* favorite things, but I'm glad you like it too."

"It's really peaceful, and I get to work with friends."

"I think that del you're next to is ready to harvest now. Here, I'll show you how it's done." Leeinn pulled a pair of hand-length shears from a deep habit pocket. "You need something to cut the stem. I usually use these, but you can use anything sharp."

"Hear that Tiny, you can use your tongue." Leeinn heard a swat, and Tancer jumped slightly, then rubbed his backside gingerly.

Leeinn tilted the lotus to the side, "Once you cut it loose, you can lift the del out of the water. I have a couple baskets I usually carry them in over there." So saying, she snipped the stem, placed the shears back in her pocket, then lifted the flower with both hands. She handed it to Gira, who handled it as though it were made of glass. Leeinn giggled, "You don't have to be quite that careful, dels are fairly tough. You would have to be trying to break it to do any real harm. Even dropping them doesn't hurt them, they bounce."

Tiny whispered, "Like Tancer, when they dropped him on his head as a child."

"Very droll wife. Leeinn, do you have a del that stills a wagging tongue?"

Gira padded over to the carry baskets, carefully sitting her del inside. She winced when she turned around and noticed she'd left a trail of wet footprints behind her, "Sorry. Do you have a towel?"

"In the cupboard, there." Gira cleaned the tiled floor until it shone in the sunlight.

After a quarter of an hourglass, Leeinn called a halt, "That should be plenty. I'll leave the dome open so the flowers can get all the light they can before sunset. Between the two they should mature quickly."

With the job done, they all relaxed with tea, though Tiny and Tancer had to share a cup, since Leeinn only had four on hand. Neither minded, and a good time was had by all. Gira asked Leeinn, "Will your father send a dragon messenger to call my family back?"

"Probably a pair of winged mares, they tend to be faster since they weigh less."

Tiny smiled with memory, "I hope Tancer and I get assigned to the stable with Cloudhoof. That would be just perfect."

"Don't forget about the kitchens. Just think of being around all that lovely food, and having access to it before anyone else. We could be taste testers even!" Tancer's eyes were half closed with the thought of such largesse.

"I suppose we could alternate, one day at the stables, on day in the kitchens, if that's allowed."

Leeinn said, "Both always need help, and people wanting to work are always appreciated."

"And Tancer will need the exercise of the stables to offset his kitchen belly."

Gira asked, "Can we visit the tailor's hall? I want to see if they can make my dress by the time of the Hopeful Ceremony."

Leeinn laughed, "Of course. Let's go now."

They passed through long, lit hallways with Accepted going about their business to the sounds of happy living scented with lavender. The tailors were happy to provide Gira with a new gown, carefully taking her measurements while her friends chit chatted. She mused over the different materials: satins, silks, chiffons, cottons, linen, lace, all in a wide variety of colors. She dismissed some out of hand, like the wool, fleece, and flannel, as being far too warm for this time of year.

Gira held a swathe up to her arm, "I think this color suits me, don't you?"

"Oh yes," said the tailor, studying the cloth critically.

"Is that a tattoo?" Gira asked curiously. The tailor held up her hand, which had been marked with a small pair of shiny silver scissors, a threaded needle, and a bolt of blue fabric.

"It is! I got it when I joined the hall. I knew I belonged in this place, and wanted to get something to show everyone else my passion."

Gira inspected the ink, "So you had it done here at the abbey?"

"They have their own tattooing section in the artist hall, I can show you if you want."

Tal's eyebrows rose in alarm, "Perhaps you should wait until after the ceremony before getting anything permanent."

Gira stuck her lower lip out petulantly, "I could get a small koi fish, have it look like Lucky. I'd love to work in the glades or the stables. I haven't given up on my own stallion you know. I know, a winged del koi!"

"I really don't think your mother would approve mistress."

"But once I'm Accepted I'll fit right in!"

Leeinn moderated, "Perhaps you should sleep on the idea. There are still a few days until your ceremony."

"Oh, very well," Gira huffed. She held her hand out in front of her, studying its back as though picturing it with a fish.

The next few days were very busy. Upon her family's return, Gira's mother managed to restrain her temper in being called back so soon, even going so far as to give her daughter a brittle smile. "I suppose if the Father Abbot doesn't mind putting his abbey through a second ceremony, I should be glad we didn't have to turn around just as we got home." Challi and Sheala found it all great fun, thumping Gira on the back as they laughingly related the moment Trader Nassine had been asked to return. "You should have seen her face! She looked like she swallowed a whole puddle of tadpoles."

Gira made a face, "*Eck*, do you have to be so disgusting?"

Challi turned to Shealah, "Did she not?"

Tiny and Tancer cleared their throats, and Gira made the introductions. Shealah admired Tiny's braids, "Your beads are lovely."

"So she's been told," Tancer said smugly.

Challi laughed, "And I'm guessing you gave them all to her?"

"Most of them."

Tiny pulled a small dangling bird from behind her right ear, "My mother gave me this one. Our family crest is an eagle in flight, so she had this made for me."

Gira said, "That was nice of her. Maybe she'll get you one with a del now that you're accepted."

Tiny shook her head, "Don't see why she would, since they don't know."

"Aren't you going to tell them?"

"They cut me off after I married Tancer."

"That's awful!"

Tancer took Tiny's hand, kissing her knuckles, "Now I get her all to myself!"

Leeinn phrased her next question delicately, "If you didn't have family to go back to, what would you have done if you hadn't been accepted?"

Tiny answered, "Find work in the City I suppose. I'll admit, we didn't think much farther than just getting here."

Tancer said, "I heard that you get a decent going-away pack even if you're refused, so it seemed like a win-win. We'd either be accepted, or get a great story to tell *and* free food!"

Gira turned to Leeinn, "Would you help me practice? I want to speak well when it's my turn."

Tancer grinned, "Tiny can pretend to be a female dragon, and I'll be her partner!"

Tiny snorted, "More like a winged horse butt."

Tancer ignored her jibe, "Hopeful Gira, my name is Tancer, and this is my farmer Tiny. Isn't she cute? Why do you want to live to Del Abbey?"

"Because I could be happy here."

"You could be happy anywhere," Challi scoffed, "What's the abbey got that home doesn't?"

"Del koi, for one."

"Ask mother, and she'll buy you all the fish you want."

"It wouldn't be the same!"

"Still, you're going to need a better reason that that." Gira stuck her tongue out at her sister, not bothering to answer.

With her friends help, Leeinn was able to get two dozen dels ready for the ceremony, in addition to the buds she had promised for Gira's hair. The kitchen master grumbled a bit about the extra work, but didn't mind really. Within a week, everything was ready.

Chapter 31

Dragonnapped

Shail clung to the claws that held him. If she wanted, the red tracker could have dropped him to his death. She handled him delicately, as Shail imagined she would carry an egg. But then again, if she had an egg, she would be a true female, and thus unable to fly. His mind seemed foggy with random thoughts, the altitude and rush of wind stealing his wits. Shail had thought he loved flying, but he definitely did not care for this mode of transportation. He felt each wingbeat, the down stroke pushing him against the dragon's chest, the up making his stomach clench as he was forced against her life preserving talons. He tried calling out to her, beseeching her to land. She ignored him as though he were no more than living luggage.

Shail went from being afraid, to being angry, "TeeDee, *go back. Go back*, you hear me?" Whether she did, or didn't, the tracker dragon flew on all the same. An itch on his shoulder made Shail aware of his pack. He thought of all the things he had inside, trying to plan for when the dragon landed. If he could manage to escape his kidnapper, he'd have to figure out where he was, then how to get back home. Shail didn't have any money on him, but he was sure that once he explained what had happened, help would be forthcoming from the local people. That hope faded as the tracker took a course away from people, and towards miles and miles of trackless forest. Shail could do nothing but wait to see what would happened.

They flew for several hours, much longer than Shail would have guessed the dragon could manage, given her state. Finally she seemed to tire. The beat of her wings became uneven, and she lost altitude. She did not land, but made a controlled crash in a clearing, awkwardly running on her back legs while cradling Shail with her front. As soon as she released him, Shail tried to run, but *his* legs refused to obey him, asleep after all the time in the air. He stumbled and fell, and lay still. The tracker made an irritated grunt, gripped Shail by his ankle, and dragged him back to her side. She tucked him under a wing, then lay her head down in apparent exhaustion. Shail waited until her breathing slowed, indicating she was asleep, before making another escape attempt. He crawled, inch by inch, out from under her wing and then away from her. He did not stand until he was beyond the ring of trees. On his feet, he held his breath as the tracker gave a warble, before sinking back into a deep sleep. Shail did his best to leave quietly, choosing a direction at random.

365

He walked and walked, the scene around him changing little. Shail had never been in unfamiliar woods by himself, and every noise seemed to suggest danger. He could tell the sun was beginning its descent by the lengthening shadows. He found a tree that had been hollowed by fire, and decided to stop for the night. He could decide how to proceed in the morning; for now, he wanted nothing more than to sleep. Shail pulled his pack from his back, laying out the contents on the ground. Firepouch, unioculous, rations, water bag, fishing kit, although what good the last would do him in the woods, he couldn't imagine.. Shail did his best to clean out his chosen hollow, clearing the floor until only soft earth remained. He remembered his nature teacher telling them about smoking out a sleeping place, to rid it of bugs, and smoke might mask his own scent, but then disregarded the idea when he realized the smoke would serve as a beacon in an area empty of people. Shail repacked his bag, unrolled his sleeping sack within the hollow, crawled in, and tried to go to sleep with the rounded truck at his back. Tired as he was, he found it difficult. His world had been turned upside down. He did not know where he was, or why the tracker dragon had kidnapped him, or how to get back to Tabirc.

Tabirc! When Shail had seen him last, he'd been hurt, and their guide fled. Shail worried himself into a light doze. It seemed like only a short while before he was awakened by an angry roar. Shail sat up quickly, clutching his sleeping sack to his chest. So, his absence had finally been noticed. Should he stay put, and hope she didn't find

366

him, or make a run for it? It was full dark by now. The odds of hurting himself while trying to run away in the dark were higher than he liked. And he wasn't the only one at risk, the dragon might injure herself in chasing after him. Shail didn't think he could keep running away from her if she needed his help. He could hear her crashing through the trees, making an unholy racket as she trumpeted her frustration. Shail's stomach tightened as he realized the sounds were getting closer. He kicked off his sleeping sack, rolling it into a tight cylinder shape, and stowed it on top of his pack. The dragon definitely sounded as if she were moving in his direction. Shail sat down, hugged his pack to his chest, and waited.

Time seemed to pass strangely within the hollow. As Shail stared out into the darkness, listening to the dragon coming closer and closer, it felt as though he'd been hiding for days. A snuffling sound by the entrance to his hiding place marked her arrival. She whined pitifully, and Shail sighed in defeat. Drawing a steadying breath, he swung his pack to his back, and crawled out of the hollow. It was pitch black on the forest floor without a torch, so Shail had nothing but his ears to guide him. He was suddenly poked rather hard in the middle of his chest. He reached his hands up and felt a scaly snout. "Looks like you found me Teedee." The tracker grunted, then to Shail's surprise, she pushed him gently back into the hollow. Once he was inside, she curled herself at the entrance, effectively blocking him within. Shail felt reluctant admiration for the ingenuity of the beast. He laid back down in his sleeping sack, wondering what morning would bring.

The dragon's soft crooning wakened Shail. For a moment he forgot where he was, and what had happened, feeling as though he were waking from a strange dream. Blinking himself awake, he saw sunlight outline a large, red-scaled flank. Sack packed and on his back, he went to the leg and gave a gentle push. "Teedee? Are you awake?" The tracker uncurled herself from her sleeping ball, yawning hugely. She gave a full body shake, then *streeeetched.* Shail almost laughed at the sight, but then remembered that this animal was taking him somewhere he did not want to go.

When he stood in front of his sleeping tree, Teedee grumbled a warning, which Shail took to mean, *"Don't try that again."* She looked intrigued when Shail brought out a biscuit, some dried jerky, and his waterskin, accepting the half he offered her. Shail wondered if he was making a mistake, feeding his captor, but realized he didn't have the heart to starve the pretty creature. He wondered if he should try to groom her, as Tabirc has taught him to do with their departed mounts. He didn't have the appropriate tools, but he did have his own hairbrush. He wasn't sure how much good it would do. "Teedee, want a brush?" To his astonishment and delight, she lowered her head level to his chest, and waited. Shail brushed her as best he could with the what he had, and she seemed to appreciate the attention. He was just as careful with her eyes as he'd been with Stendow's, moving past them to her neck, then shoulder and front legs. Shail was beginning to tire by this time, but pushed on. He finished Teedee's back legs, then tail, all the way to the tip. Arms aching, he shook the dirt from his brush, packed it, and swung the pack to his back.

For her part, she waited until Shail was done before trying to herd him back between her front claws. Shail wished he had some means of fastening himself to her back, but without a safety strap, his best bet would be to let her carry him as she'd done so far. He crouched down, making himself small for her benefit. She grasped him as lightly as she'd done yesterday, flapped her wings a few times to limber up, and then leapt to the sky.

The second day of flying went much like the first. Teedee seemed intent on reaching their destination with all haste. Shail tried to keep track of their direction by noting the position of the sun. They were heading west, in-land, that much he could deduce. Beyond that, all he could see were the tops of trees. It was impossible to stretch out while in the dragon's grip, and Shail felt himself starting to cramp. He didn't think it would work, but he tried anyway, "Teedee! Can we take a break? *A break* Teedee?" Close as he was to her chest, he both heard and felt her grunt.

She began peering down at the land below them. After a few minutes, she saw an opening and circled once before dropping into it. Shail gripped her claws tightly, the wind blowing his hair back from his face. Teedee landed, releasing Shail to stumble as he tried to catch himself. He stretched his legs, wincing as the blood began circulating through the numbed bits. Teedee never took her eyes off him. Shail's stomach rumbling reminded him he'd had a very small breakfast, and that had been hours ago. Since he didn't know how much farther they had to fly, Shail wanted to ration his supplies as best he could. His lunch was the same as his breakfast, quickly shared, eaten, and leaving Shail wishing there was more. He felt wistful as he remembered Gran's favorite saying about wishes, "If wishes were fishes, we'd all be pescatarians."

Tabirc had heard her say this once, and laughing rebuked her, "I don't think that's how that saying goes."

Gran had shrugged with a grin, "Gets the point across." Teedee made an impatient noise, and Shail realized he'd been standing still, lost in his memories.

"I'm sorry Teedee. I'm ready to go. Though I wish you would take me back to Tabirc." Her willingness to oblige him did not stretch quite that far, but she continued to handle him with all the gentleness she could. Back in the air, Shail found he was not as afraid as he had been. He was beginning to trust Teedee to an extent, and that included not dropping him.

They flew on and on, and the sun followed its course through the sky. When it began its western descent,

Teedee found a spot to rest for the night. As though they had done this a thousand times, Shail brushed Teedee down, had his dinner, which he shared with the tracker, and both went to sleep, curled together this time.

Shail slept surprising well and woke to early morning bird song. He drew a deep breath in through his nose, relishing the scent of trees and earth. He stretched, waking Teedee. She did the same, then bumped Shail's chest hopefully. "You want another brushy brushy?" Shail laughed at her eager wriggle.

Shail was as good as his word, and when she was done, they were back in the air. Shail had become almost accustomed to the experience now. It was not long before Teedee seemed to know where she was, for she gave an excited bugle, and was answered by the sound of a horn. She turned into a tight spiral, angling to land amidst what Shail could see from the air a decently large grouping of tents, with people shading their eyes as they watched her approach.

When she landed, a boy that looked to be a few years older than Shail greeted them. He was blonde, muscled, and wearing a well-worn shirt and trousers that looked a lot like Tumatan's hand-me-downs. Teedee trilled as he caught her face in his hands, cooing over her, "You're back! Oh no, you're all banged up! Did you try flying in a storm again?" Teedee gently nuzzled his chest, making a purring noise. "Well, at least you got your target. Good girl!" He eyed Shail up and down, "Looks like you could do with a wash."

Shail tried to maintain his dignity, "I haven't had a lot of opportunity the past couple days.

The boy winced, "No, I expect not. Let me get Jogslen settled, then I'll see to you."

"Jogslen, it that her name?"

"Yup, and mine's S'ton. Heard your name was Shail.

Shail startled at his name being known to this stranger, "It is, but how did you know?"

"My father told me. Come on, he'll want to see you once you're cleaned up."

"Is he the one who sent Jogslen after me."

"Course."

S'ton seemed to think that answer enough, and Shail was suddenly aware that he was surrounded by people who may mean him harm. "But why?"

"Didn't say, not to me anyways. Ask him yourself."

Shail followed S'ton as he led Jogslen to what Shail assumed was her normal stable area. There was no permanent building, but someone had stretched a large skin over four long rods in the ground, making a covered area for the dragon to sleep. "Bet your both hungry."

Shail's stomach reminded him he'd had nothing but travel rations the last couple days, "I had some biscuits and jerky in my pack. Not nearly enough to fill a dragon, but it was better than nothing.

"Your shared your food with Jogslen? Even though she was nabbing you?"

"I can't be mad at her for doing what she's been trained to do. My uncle told me she was a tracker."

"How'd he know what a tracker is? Not a lot of people would have recognized her."

"He used to be a dragon handler, before he retired." Jogslen stretched gratefully under her protective shade, and S'ton went to a bag hanging from one of the support poles.

"Here ya go Jogs, you earned this." S'ton emptied the bag of its contents. Several large petals fell out, a rather drab grey color, but nearly as long as Shail's forearm. Jogslen rapidly dragged each petal into her mouth, barely pausing to chew before swallowing.

"What are those?"

"Dragon egg lotus. Bit old, but Jogslen don't mind. Should help with all the bumps and bruises too. Like magic, dels are."

"I had a drink with some del nectar when I was seasick on a ship."

S'ton looked impressed, "They gave you del nectar, just for being nauseous. You must come from a rich place."

"I think the man that gave it to me only did so because he likes my gran." Shail was seized by the realization that he was calmly speaking to one of his kidnappers. "She's got to be wondering where I am, if Tabirc managed to get home and send a message." In a small voice he added, "I want to go home."

S'ton nodded sympathetically, "Don't blame ya. Let's get you scrubbed, then I'll take you to my father. He can tell you what's what."

"Aren't you going to brush Jogslen?"

"After I'm done with you."

S'ton gave the tracker dragon one last pat on the nose, then began walking away, assuming Shail would follow. Shail saw no other option than to comply. After all, if he made a run for it, where would he go that that Jogslen couldn't track him down?

S'ton led Shail to a tent large enough to house half a dozen people. It was partitioned by a hanging flap, the half they entered looked to be living quarters. He pointed to a wash basin sitting in a stand beside a mirror. "Give yourself

374

a scrub with that." Shail used his hands to scoop water up onto his face. He noticed a cloth hanging nearby. He took off his shirt, dipped the cloth into the basin, and rubbed his body, particularly under his arms where he had sweat the most. He felt much refreshed, even if there hadn't been any soap. He had no option but to put his soiled shirt back on. S'ton had watched Shail while picking at a nail, clearly bored.

Shail turned to him when he was done. "Ready?" When Shail nodded, S'ton pointed to the partition. "Lemme check to see if he's free." He stuck his head around the flap, and after a moment said, "Sir, Jogslen's back, and she brought the target. Did you want to see him now?" Shail heard a muffled reply that must have been a yes, because S'ton gestured for him to go before him. Seeing little point in arguing, and with the hope that he'd get some answers, Shail obeyed.

The other half of the tent seemed to be some sort of command center. There was a large table in the center that dominated most of the space, covered with a map Shail guessed was of the surrounding area, with marks and small objects sitting on it. A short, broad man was studying the map. By his resemblance to S'ton, Shail guessed this must be his father. He looked up as Shail and S'ton entered, giving Shail an appraising glance. Shail waited, not sure how to begin.

When the man spoke, it was to his son, "The boy will be in your charge. See that he's taken care of, and stays out of the way until Seedruf arrives."

"Yessir."

At the word *boy*, Shail bristled. "I am thirteen summers. My name is Shail, and I want to know why you've kidnapped me!" With each word Shail's voice had risen, until he was shouting.

S'ton looked horrified, "You can't talk to the Chief like that."

The Chief barked a laugh, "You may not look like your grandfather, but you have his temper."

Shail went weak-kneed as he realized what must have happened, "I don't have a grandfather, sir, at least not one that's alive. You've stolen the wrong person!"

"No I didn't, you're the very image of your uncle."

"Wengsper? How do you know my uncle. What's he got to do with you kidnapping me?"

The Chief smiled, "Seems you don't know quite a bit. Well, my name is Omagroef, and we've plenty of time for talk, since you'll be staying with us from now on."

Chapter 32

Accepted and Yearling

Leeinn caught up with Tiny, Tancer, Gira, and Tal at the dining hall the morning of the second Hopeful Ceremony. They joined Leeinn in her pool, harvesting the very last of the mature dels. Gira was delighted when Leeinn shyly offered her a bunch of del buds. Tal accepted two buds for herself, thanking Leeinn for her generosity.

Gira held a flower up to her head, "What do you think, a crown along my forehead, or maybe in a braid down my back?"

"You have enough there to do both mistress. Like this." Tal nimbly threaded the lotus into Gira's hair, managing to make the work of moments look like something you'd get from the highest quality salon. Gira admired her reflection in the pool while her friends shared tolerant smiles.

Just as they were about to leave, Leeinn presented Tiny and Tancer with their own buds, "For all of your help." Tiny tried to refuse, saying no thanks were necessary, but Leeinn wouldn't take no for an answer, and Tancer politely accepted for them both.

Leeinn took the basket of dragon egg lotus to Hopeful Hall, dropped them off at the dais, and returned to her room to wash and change.

Shortly before the Hopeful Ceremony was due to start Leeinn went to the gois rooms to fetch her two friends for their big moment. She knocked, then let herself in and found Tal alone. She was wearing the two buds Leeinn had gifted her braided at each temple. Tal was pacing and wringing her hands, her face set in a worried frown.

When she spotted Leeinn, Tal rushed forward, "Have you seen Gira? She said she needed to take care of something, but wouldn't tell me what it was. Said she wanted it to be a surprise. I thought maybe it had something to do with her new dress, but I checked with the tailors, and they said she left the hall hours ago."

"We know she has to be at the ceremony."

"All the same, I should like to know where she is, and what she is doing. Her mother would not approve of her being left unattended."

"If you're ready, why don't we go to Hopeful Hall and see if she's there?"

The hall was still filling with people by the time they arrived. Tiny and Tancer were waiting for them near the front doors, both in brand new abbey habits with their acceptance pin proudly sitting over their heart, right beside their tiny lotus.

They found Gira standing amongst her family and a few well-wishers. She looked stunning, her dress covered her body from neck to ankle, with elbow-length sleeves. It was a radiant pearl color, and some enterprising seamstress had actually sewn faux dragon egg lotus seeds into the shapes of delicate del koi. Her left hand and forearm were bandaged, and Leeinn wondered how she'd been injured. Whatever the reason, Gira did not seem affected. Indeed, she hardly seemed to walk, but floated with pure joy.

Gira and Tal took their places on the Hopeful Dais, with Leeinn performing the same service for this ceremony as she had the last. She pressed the hidden switch in the Del doors, and the familiar unlocking noise that preceded their silent swing open signaled everyone to stand for the Trinity. Leeinn felt her stomach flutter as she watched Grognareian enter the hall. All three of the Trinity were different from Tiny and Tancer's ceremony. The father and winged stallion who followed Grognareian moved with quiet dignity, both looking old but able.

When the Trinity were standing in their places, Rumaru spoke from the abbot's chair, "Please be seated."

Once the hall had quieted, the lights dimmed and the starscape colored the tableau. "We have gathered here tonight to bear witness as two Hopefuls stand for judgement before the Trinity. Hopeful Tal Belaqwa, if you desire to join Del Abbey, step forward." Tal did so, dressed in an unadorned off-white robe that looked all the plainer compared to Gira's finery. Yet somehow, Tal shone without the need of bauble or trinket. She walked to the point of judgment, laced her hands before her, and waited.

The farmer and her partner did not keep her waiting. Grognareian gleamed green in the low light, clearly having been polished for the occasion. Her partner's sun-bleached hair had more than a few wisps of white, and her smile was matronly. "Hopeful Tal, my name is Majjie, and this is my partner Grognareian." Tal curtseyed before them. "Why do you wish to make Del Abbey your home?"

Tal took a breath, "To live the life I was meant for." That answer confused the audience, and was met with whispers. Leeinn was just as surprised, for Tal had chosen not to share her answers before the ceremony.

"I see. Grognareian?" The farmer peered at the Hopeful before her, lowering her head to get a better look. She folded her long claws under her belly, effectively halving her height, which was still considerable. She laid her flattened tail on the ground behind her, and almost looked like an old aunty sitting down to tea and a chat. Tal kept her eyes demurely on the floor before her. To everyone's great surprise, Grognarian began a soft song. It was a low, deep croon, occasionally punctuated by a higher note. Tal raised her face, seemingly spellbound by the singing dragon before her. After the second time Grognareian repeated her piece, Tal raised her husky voice as accompaniment. The hall was transfixed by the sight and sound of farmer and Hopeful. As the last notes fell away, Grognareian closed her eyes and gave a satisfied grunt. "The First says yes!"

An exuberant round of applause, and the farmer stood to her full height. She returned to her spot, and was replaced by the father. He was slightly smaller than Dehlawnay, wearing a turquoise ceremonial saddle. Both dragon and the man who partnered him were walnut brown, the large wings of the father patterned to mimic the spots and stripes on mare feathers. His partner was relatively young, appearing to barely be out of his twenties, but conducted himself with all the maturity of a man in his middling years. "Hopeful Tal, my name is Jambor, and this is my partner Timbatoo. What occupation would you seek here if you are accepted?"

"Someplace quiet would suit me best. The library, I think."

"A noble position. Timbatoo?" Hopeful and father made for quite a pretty picture, she with a respectfully bowed head, he with a twinkle in his eye that said he was having fun sharing the spotlight. He blew a teasing breath into Tal's face, making her blink rapidly in astonishment. Timbatoo made a sound that could only be laughter, and the hall joined him. The father placed his snout before the Hopeful at waist height, and waited. Tal reached out tentatively, as though she hardly believed her own daring. She placed her palm flat against Timbatoo's skin, held for a moment, then took her hand away, clasping it before her with a look of awe on her face. No one needed Jambor to translate the father's cheerful bugle, "The Second says yes." The father dipped his head in farewell, and made way for the winged horse.

The stallion's eyes were the darkest gold, like the sun sitting on the horizon at dusk, and his white hide gleamed like the stars on the ceiling above. His partner was a slight woman dressed in shirt and pants the same shade as her partner's blue feathers, with a stylized silver stallion rampant upon the breast. "Hopeful Tal, my name is Ristani, and this is my partner Kinokan. What will you do if you are refused?"

"I will leave Del Abbey. I will cause no harm upon my leaving, nor harm the Abbey or its folk by my actions in the future." Kinokan made a delicate cough, drawing all attention to himself. He swished his tail, then opened his magnificent wings, richer than any rainbow. Tal sank to a kneeling position. Kinokan knickered, playfully tapping Tal on the chin with his nose. He pranced backwards, clearly showing off. The crowd loved it, hooting their approval. When they had quieted, Kinokan stamped once, and Ristani said, "The Third says yes."

When the applause had died down enough to be heard, Rumaru said, "Hopeful Tal, be recognized as Accepted Tal." Tal closed her eyes, and silent tears began streaming down her face. Gira looked dew-eyed at the drama. Leeinn brought forth her ceremonial pillow. There was a hush until Tal took it, then wild applause. She rose, pinning her prize to her robe. She walked shakily back to her standing spot, her eyes unseeing, like a sleepwalkers.

A hush fell over the crowd, enthralled by the first act, and ready for the second. Rumaru spoke, "Hopeful Gira Sulnvoc, if you desire to join Del Abbey, step forward."

Gira was a moving jewel as she took the appropriate steps to the judgment point. When she stopped, she used her right hand to undo the bandages on her left. They fell away to the dais flooring, revealing a tattoo of a del koi with elegant wings, its head dominating the back of her hand, its fins wrapping around her wrist, and its body and tail flowing up her forearm. Leeinn quickly sought out Trader Nassine in the crowd, who's pale face had taken on a fixed smile. Hoping that Gira knew what she was doing, Leeinn returned her gaze to the Hopeful Dais. Gira seemed confident enough as she was met by the farmer and her partner at the judgement point.

"Hopeful Gira, my name is Majjie, and this is my partner Grognareian. Why do you wish to make Del Abbey your home?"

"This is the most beautiful place in the world, with the nicest people. I know I would be happy here. I don't think a person could be *un*happy here." She looked beseechingly up at Grognareian, who had been still through the verbal exchange. Gira reached out with her tattooed hand, and when Grognareian bent down to inspect it, the farmer shook her head, as though to rid herself of an annoying fly. She gave the barest growl of disapproval, flicking her gaze to her partner.

"Best not do that, dragons are very sensitive to the smell of blood." Gira flinched backwards, looking shocked. In that single moment her confidence seemed to shatter, leaving her a scared little girl in front of a crowd of strangers. Leeinn wanted to rush to her friend's side, but dared not interrupt the ceremony.

Gira explained, "I'm sorry, I didn't know! I got this as proof I want to live here."

Majjie patted her partner's should soothingly, "It's alright, isn't it Grog?" The farmer *hmmed,* clicked her claws together, then stood tall. She made eye contact with her partner, and they seemed to communicate without speaking. "Grognareian abstains."

A deathly silence followed. Then, a whisper from the crowd, "What does that mean?"

Rumaru raised his hand for order, "To abstain is to withhold judgement. Grognareian leaves the decision to the father and stallion."

384

Leeinn heard Gira give a sob, "I didn't know the tattoo would upset her! I just wanted to show my passion, like the tailor!"

Majjie tried to soothe her, "No reason to cry, just means neither yes nor no. Be strong, stand straight, make your family proud, no matter what happens." The kind words seemed to bolster Gira's spirit, for she drew back her shoulders and lifted her chin.

Grognareian was replaced by the father. "Hopeful Gira, my name is Jambor, and this is my partner Timbatoo. What occupation would you seek here if you are accepted?"

Gira's eyes went to her tattoo, "I'd like to tend the fish in the meditation glade. I made friends with one. I named him Lucky. My tattoo is of him."

Jambor smiled warmly, "Fish are good judges of character. What say you Timbatoo?" Gira kept her left hand pressed to her belly, covering it with her right. She almost cowered away from the dragon in front of her. The father shifted his weight from one foot to another, the flicked his wings upon his back. He gave a grunt, tilting his head one way, then the other. He turned, and walked back to his spot. Jambor's smile tightened, "Ahh, the Second also abstains."

A long, low moan of misery issued from Gira. Leeinn wanted desperately to help her friend, but could think of nothing to do.

"I'm sorry Hopeful Gira. I wish you luck with the stallion." Jambor took his place beside his father.

Everyone's eyes went to the winged horse. He was large, both broader and taller than Cloudhoof. He walked with his wings held wide, his peacock eye feathers making him look like a still larger creature with a rainbow mane stalking the helpless Hopeful. Gira was visibly trembling, biting her lip to keep it from quivering, her eyes shiny with unshed tears. The stallion stepped slowly, placing each foot solidly before raising the next. His hoofbeats echoed in the hushed hall.

When her partner stilled, his Accepted said, "Hopeful Gira, my name is Ristani, and this is my partner Kinokan. What will you do if you are refused?" Gira seemed unable to answer. "Hopeful Gira?"

"I will leave Del Abbey. I will cause no harm upon my leaving, nor harm the Abbey or its folk by my actions in the future."

"Very good. Kino?" Not a sound was heard, no one moved a muscle.

In a small voice, so low that it could not have been heard had it not be spoken into such complete silence, Gira said, "If I couldn't work in the glades, I would gladly be assigned to the stables. I had thought about trying to partner a stallion myself. That's why I asked them to put wings on my koi." A sympathetic murmur from the audience.

Kinokan lifted his head high, then stamped his front foot thrice.

"I'm sorry, Hopeful Gira, but Kinokan abstains."

"*No!*" Gira screamed. "But *why?!*"

Leeinn could bear it no longer, and rushed to grip her friend's hand, "You are not Refused, only made a Yearling."

"I'm what?"

Rumaru said, "Hopeful Gira, you are not accepted at this time. Should you wish to try again, you may do so one year and day from now. You may only be Hopeful twice, and your second judgement would stand for life."

Gira's shoulders sank, she dropped her face into her hands, and wept. An uncomfortable murmur went through the crowd, and Leeinn was suddenly sorry, not just for Gira, but for Tal as well. She had been accepted, but that fact was forgotten in the face of Gira's tragedy. When she looked, Tal's face was inscrutable. Leeinn suspected she was trying to be brave for her mistress' sake.

Leeinn whispered, "Come on Gira, stand up now, that's it. Show them you're the daughter of a trader family."

"But, but, but I'm not," Gira hiccuped, "Not Accepted."

"But neither are you Refused."

"I might as well be, my mother will never let me come back after embarrassing her like this. Oh Omal, my tattoo!"

With that horrible realization, Gira promptly fainted. Leeinn caught her as she fell, lowering her to a lying position. The next moment, Trader Nassine was beside her. She pulled a small bottle from a pocket, unstoppered it, and wafted it under Gira's nose. Her daughter cringed away from the potent scent, blinking her eyes open, and then recoiling from her mother. "Now, now, it's alright. Come on, on your feet."

Nassine and Leeinn helped Gira to stand, keeping hold of her arms to steady her. "I'm sorry mother, I didn't mean to disapp ..."

"Hush, we will talk later. For now, Tal deserves our support."

"Tal?" Gira's eyes sought out the new Accepted, and for a brief moment her face clouded with undisguised righteous envy. "But, how can they accept a servant, and not a trader's daughter?"

Nassine hissed a warning, "Enough Gira, I mean it. She was judged and accepted, you will respect her."

Gira's entire body seemed to droop, "Yes mother."

Tal had watched the exchange between mother and daughter, and when Nassine motioned her forward, she knelt at her mistress' feet just as she had for Timbatoo. In an echo of her words to Gira, Nassine said to Tal, "Stand up. You are a servant no longer. You are Accepted."

Tal did as she was bidden, and Gira's gaze flashed to her acceptance pin before dropping to the floor. "Congratulations Tal, you deserve to live here."

Tal took hold of Gira's tattooed hand, cupping it between both of hers, "I'm sorry you weren't accepted mistress. My father used to say that everything is a lesson, if only we can see it from the right angle." She folded her fingers under Gira's wrist, "Lucky here will make sure you never forget this day."

Chapter 33

Denied

Shail could make no sense of the Chief's words. Stay? Here? Shail couldn't stay here, he had to get back to Tabirc, and eventually home to his family. He wondered if his mother knew he was missing. S'ton pulled at Shail's sleeve, motioning towards the exit with his chin. The Chief had already gone back to perusing the map, his son and Shail apparently forgotten.

Shail fought the urge to obey. "Excuse me, but you haven't answered any of my questions. Who are you people, why did you send your tracker dragon after me? And I'm not staying here, I have to finish my apprenticeship with Master Conlun."

At Shail's outburst, S'ton grabbed him roughly by the shoulder, "Nobody speaks to Chief Omagroef like that. C'mon you, outside."

Shail was dragged from the tent, still shouting for all he was worth. "You can't keep me here! I want to go home. Tell Jogslen to take me back to Tabirc's village."

S'ton cuffed Shail over the head, momentarily stunning him. "What are you trying to do, get us both in trouble?" hissed S'ton.

"But," Shail began.

"But nothing. Chief brought you here and says you'll stay, so you might as well settle in."

"But," Shail tried again.

"How many butts you got? Ain't just the one enough?" So saying, he smacked Shail on the backside, laughing when Shail hopped a few steps, rubbing the injured area.

"Would you just listen?"

"No, *you* listen." S'ton wasn't much taller than Shail, but he was far more muscled, and he put the strain on his shirt to emphasize his point, "Your opinion don't matter, my opinion don't matter. The only opinion that matters is the Chief's. Got it?"

"No," Shail said sullenly, "I don't understand any of this." To Shail's horror, his eyes filled with tears, and he felt his lip begin to quiver.

S'ton softened, "Alright, alright, I can answer a few questions, if it'll keep you from blubbering."

"I'm not blubbering," Shail sniffed angrily. "I'm having a perfectly normal stress reaction to being kidnapped by people I've never met."

S'ton looked nonplussed, "You're having a what-now?"

Shail fought the urge to roll his eyes, *"Who are you?"*

S'ton puffed out his chest, "We're the Denied. You've met our chief, and me, and Jogslen."

Shail shook his head, "The Denied? What have you been denied?"

"There's a beautiful land with a stronghold that only allows certain people to live there. This camp is full of the people they kicked out, and their kin."

"But what does that have to do with me? I don't know about any stronghold."

"Dunno, but the Chief does. He might tell you his reasons, or he might not, as he sees fit."

"But when can I go home?" Shail almost wailed.

"From what the chief said, I'm guessing this *is* home, for the time being." Seeing Shail's bewildered expression, S'ton said, "Look, can't do nothing bout it now. You help me with Jogslen, and I'll see that you get a full plate before tucking in."

S'ton lead Shail back to the tracker. She was sleeping, and snoring softly. "Watch this," S'ton said mischievously. He tickled one of the dragon's nostrils. She twitched at his touch, but remained asleep. S'ton scratched the other nostril, causing Jogslen to flare her nares before sneezing. Now awake, her pupils dilated as she opened her eyes. When she recognized her handler, she woke fully, becoming alert. S'ton laughed, "There's my beauty. Sorry for running off without giving you your scrub down. I brought help to do it now." S'ton handed Shail a brush of such size it was obvious it was made for cleaning a large creature. "You want the front end or the back end," S'ton asked.

"Uhh, the front."

"Front includes the wings you know."

"I'm used to doing the whole dragon by myself, half won't be a problem." S'ton took his own brush and started on Jogslen's flank. Shail went to her face, and Jogslen lowered her head into his outstretched hand. Shail brushed her face, then her neck and shoulders. Jogslen extended her wings when Shail got to them, shivering slightly when he brushed over a sensitive patch of skin. The job took half the time with two pairs of hands, and Jogslen soon stood before them, gleaming red as any ruby, her hurts seeming to have melted away.

Their task complete, S'ton took Shail's brush and stored it with his own. S'ton rolled his shoulders, "Usually takes me an hour when I'm alone. Thanks for the help."

Shail did not want to be pleasant to his captor, but found he could not find it in himself to be contrary. "I'll admit, she's prettier than the mount I had on the way to Tabirc's village."

"Ahh, so you've been round dragons afore. Makes sense, targets she's brought in the past weren't near so useful."

"They probably didn't have a reason to be helpful, being kidnapped and all."

S'ton had the wherewithal to look embarrassed, "Suppose you're right. Look, for what it's worth, I am sorry it has to be this way."

"But *why* does it have to be this way? Why bring me here at all?"

"Told ya, I don't know."

"But what is this place?" Shail gestured around them, "You can't live here, there are no houses, just tents."

"Can't build anything permanent, one of the rules. So we don't get too comfortable and forget why we're here in the first place. Someday we're going back to the land that was stolen from us."

"How long have you been here?"

394

S'ton raised an eyebrow, "If you mean me, I was born here, been here all my life. If you mean the camp, it moves about as need be, but the Denied have been together for ages."

"Haven't you tried to go back to this other place?"

S'ton said defensively, "We're planning, gathering our strength."

"So the people that kicked you out are strong fighters?"

"Oh yeah, and they got lots of dragons that they've trained to attack people that don't belong."

Shail was shocked, "But Tabirc said dragons aren't aggressive."

"Told ya, these are greedy people. They make their dragons do bad things."

"Your father mentioned someone named Seedruf. Who is that?"

"One of the Chief's best soldiers. He was born in the promised land, but was chased out by a rival. You'll like him, he's tough but fair."

"What happens when he gets here?"

"The Chief will tell us what he thinks we need to know."

Shail could have pulled his hair with frustration, "But I've never heard of a Seedruf, what could I have to do with someone I've never heard of?"

"You're thinking too much. Let's get some sup, then I'll show you your bunk. You'll feel better after some sleep."

Shail's exhaustion from the last few perilous days hit him at all once, and suddenly he could barely keep on his feet. He must have wavered, because S'ton's expression became concerned, and he put a steadying hand on Shail's shoulder. When he'd straightened, S'ton handed Shail his pack, "C'mon, this way." They walked through the camp, S'ton pointing out various spots of interest as they went. "That's the supply cache. It's overseen by Quartermaster Dignaha. Down at that end is the where the horses are picketed. You did good with Jogslen, you any good with animals besides dragons?"

Shail felt a jolt go through him, "You have *winged* horses?"

"Naw, least, not yet. We don't have enough dels to keep a fortune. But when we get Home, we'll have so many winged horses we'll all have a mount of our own." This appeared to be a fervent wish, for S'ton's voice had gone wistful.

"But you already have Jogslen."

"Oh, she's not for riding. She does as she was bred for, goes out and brings back whatever the Chief wants. She's smart enough not to need a handler, and a rider would just be more weight for her to carry, once she got her target."

They'd approached a long olive-tinted tent and S'ton pushed though the entrance flap, holding it open for Shail. He let it drop when they were both inside, but it remained light enough to see due to several smoke holes in the tent's roof. There were cauldrons sitting over fire pits, all bubbling in way that reminded Shail of his kitchen at home. There were lots of people tending the pots, and even more at tables Shail could see were being used for chopping, mixing, and general preparation.

An older, greying woman stirring a soup with a long-handled ladle noticed their appearance, and smiled broadly, "Look what the dragon dragged in. Bet you boys are hungry."

S'ton returned the smile, "This is Shail. Shail, this is Nan."

Nan picked up two empty bowls off a nearby table and began filling them with her soup, "Get this in ya Shail, and be welcomed."

Shail felt his anger flare, and nearly knocked the bowl from her hand, "Be *welcomed*? You kidnapped me!"

397

Nan nodded knowingly, "Ahh, like that is it. Well, Omagroef has his reasons, and they're usually good ones. No sense starving yourself, come on." She waggled the bowl invitingly, causing the scent to waft over to Shail. Days of half rations made his mouth water at the delicious smell. Shail's resistance melted, he grabbed the bowl, and began spooning the still steaming contents into his mouth, sucking in air to cool the food as he chewed. S'ton took his bowl from Nan, emptying it nearly as quickly as Shail did his. "Seconds?" inquired Nan.

"Yes please," Shail said, politely holding out his bowl.

"Manners! This camp needs more of your sort. I've managed to teach S'ton his p's and q's, but the rest! You're going to be a welcome change my lad."

"Thank you ma'am."

Nan stroked Shail's cheek, "Omal, I thank you for this unlooked-for gift." Her touch reminded Shail so much of his mother that he began to cry. Nan *ahh*'d, released the ladle, and took Shail into her arms. "There now, you've had a hard few days. You'll see, this place isn't so bad, and I'm sure once Omagroef is done with you, he'll send you home. I'll even put in a word myself, next I see him." She squeezed Shail, then let him go. "I've dinner to get ready, off with you now."

Shail nodded his thanks, his throat too tight to answer. He turned reluctantly to S'ton, ready for ridicule.

The other boy was giving an undue amount of attention to his nails, seeming not to notice Shail's breakdown. Shail scrubbed his eyes with his sleeve, cleared his throat, and said, "Can you take me to my bunk now?"

S'ton waved goodbye to Nan, "'Course, this way."

S'ton led Shail back the way they'd come. "You can share my tent for now. We'll see if we can get you your own later. We can get you anything else you don't have in that pack, and refill what you do have."

"If you have so much already, why do you need to go back to that other place. You could just settle here."

"Because they have no right to deny us!" S'ton said vehemently. "There was plenty *there* too, enough for everyone, but they don't want to share. They want everything for themselves, and leave the rest of us to make do. It's not fair, but we're going to fix things."

Shail didn't like the sound of that, "Fix things *how*?"

S'ton's stopped in front of a tent roughly the size of the Chief's living quarters, "Sleep first, we'll talk more later."

Inside, Shail dropped his pack and laid out his sleeping sack across from S'ton's pallet. He kicked off his shoes, crawled into his bag, and was asleep moments after he closed his eyes.

A noise outside S'ton's tent pulled Shail back to consciousness. For a few foggy moments Shail could not remember where he was, and his heart began to race. He heard muffled voices, as though there were people nearby trying to be quiet. Shail kicked out of his sack, put on his shoes, and cautiously approached the entrance. He peered outside, then to the side where the noise was coming from. S'ton and two others were working nearby, putting up a small tent. One of the assistants noticed Shail and pointed him out to S'ton. S'ton turned and stood arms akimbo, "You're up earlier than I expected. Still, we're nearly done. See, told ya I'd getcha a tent of your own." Shail eyed the patched cloth, wondering if it would keep out the rain. "It's been used by a few other folk, but it's clean and nobody will mess with the things you keep inside."

"No, you just steal *people*." S'ton stiffened and Shail sighed, "I'm sorry, you're doing me a favor. Thank you for the tent."

"Not just a tent. Check inside." Shail did so, finding a wooden pallet like S'ton's to put his sleeping sack on, and a bucket of clean water with a few strips of linen hanging along the edge.

S'ton said, "Chief wanted to see you soon as you were up. Let's go." Shail was getting rather tired of having to do what the *Chief* wanted.

They returned to the first tent S'ton had shown Shail, using the other entrance, the one that led into what Shail had begun to think of as the war room. The Chief was just as he had been, concentrating on the map in front of him. They waited for him to notice their arrival, and Shail got a better look at the man. He'd cropped his blonde hair short, and had a well-trimmed beard and mustache. The shirt he wore strained with the breadth of his shoulders. Shail noticed that the Chief's hands were calloused, but the nails were whole and even. Clearly he was particular about his appearance. He turned grey eyes upon his son, "Report."

"Sir, the target has eaten and slept, and I got him a tent next to mine."

"*Hmm*, good. He give you any trouble?"

Shail interjected, "No, *he* did not. *He* is still waiting for answers."

S'ton winced, but the Chief laughed, "I think I can set a few things straight. But first, I have someone I want you to meet." He whistled, and a figure emerged from the living section of the tent. The Chief addressed him, "He's here, just as I promised."

Shail studied the newcomer. He was a head taller than the Chief, with dark red hair and green eyes. He stared at Shail, and then he suddenly looked sad. "You're right, he looks just like him."

401

The Chief grinned, "Maybe, but he's got your spirit."

The man held his hand out to Shail, "Forgive me, I should introduce myself. My name is Seedruf."

Shail reluctantly shook Seedruf's hand, "I'm Shail."

"I know. I know a lot about you actually. You just turned thirteen, and you're training to become a Travealer."

Shail dropped Seedruf's hand, stepping back in alarm, "How do you know all that?"

Seedruf's eyes went soft, "I've been looking for you for a long time."

Shail continued to back up, "Who are you?"

Seedruf spoke to the Chief, "What have you told him?"

"Nothing yet, I was waiting for you."

Seedruf took a deep breath, nodding as though suddenly nervous, "Good, good." He turned to Shail, "You probably have a lot of questions, and I can't wait to answer them all. So, as to the one you asked just now. Who am I?" He glanced down, then back up, meeting Shail's stare, "I'm your grandfather."

Chapter 34

Abroad

Leeinn helped Gira off the Hopeful Dais, where waiting hands were ready to receive her. They offered Gira water, which she took automatically, sipping to appease her soothers. Gira's mother was by her side, whispering encouragement. Leeinn was surprised to see the trader being so attentive, but then again, Gira was Nassine's heir. And heir she was likely to remain, now that she had not been accepted.

Leeinn looked around for Tal, finding her a short distance away, surrounded by the other menials to Gira's family. Leeinn supposed it must seem like a dream come true, to go from being an attendant to an Accepted. The servants would probably be telling this story for years to come.

Gira had subsided into silence, not even bothering to watch where she was going, allowing herself to be led like a child. Rumaru had left his seat to speak with Nassine, their heads close together as they murmured to each other.

When they had finished, he turned to Leeinn, "Would you help Gira back to her room?"

"Of course," Leeinn answered.

She gently took Gira's arm, pulling her away from the crowd around them. Gira followed without comment, seeming not to care or notice what went on around her. Leeinn led her friend out of Hopeful Hall, a space opening in front of them and then closing behind as they passed. Whispers, like wind through bare trees, followed in their wake.

Back in the gois room that was solely hers for the time being, Gira stared into the distance. Leeinn took the buds from her braided hair, coaxing her into her bedroom to change out of her dress and into a sleep shift. A knock at the door startled Leeinn, but Gira gave no indication she'd heard the sound. Leeinn left Gira siting on her bed to answer the door.

Tiny and Tancer were waiting outside. "How is she?" Tiny asked.

"Quiet, she hasn't spoken since we left the hall."

"Is there anything we can do?"

"Nothing I can think of. I can see if she wants to come out and sit with us for a bit, though she might just want to go to bed."

Tancer suggested, "Should we see if she wants to go to the feast? I know food always makes me feel better."

"I can ask, but I doubt she's feeling up to it."

"Then we'll meet you in the dining hall."

Leeinn waved her friends goodbye, returning to find Gira just as she'd left her. "Tiny and Tancer were here. They came to see if you wanted to go to the feast."

"Why?" Gira said brokenly, "So everyone can laugh at me."

"No one is going to laugh at you."

"But I was so sure I would be accepted. I must have looked ridiculous in that dress."

"You looked beautiful, everyone said so. And you weren't refused, remember?"

Gira's shoulders bowed inwards, "I might as well have been."

"Do you want to go to sleep? I know its early, but you might feel better after some rest."

"Feel better? Feel *better*?" Gira thumped her fists on her mattress, "I'll feel *better* when I'm away from this place!"

Leeinn tried to soothe the distraught girl, "I know this isn't how you thought things would turn out, but we have to trust the Trinity knows best."

405

"Easy for *you* to say, you're Accepted." At Leeinn's hurt expression Gira scrubbed at her face, "I'm sorry, you're only trying to help. I just feel so terrible. I'm never going to hear the end of this."

"It's not like you did anything wrong."

Gira threw up her hands, "Then why didn't the Trinity accept me?"

Leeinn could only shrug helplessly, "I don't know."

Gira's tone took on a suspicious lilt, "You would tell me if you did, right?"

Leeinn nodded vigorously, "Of course, I'd do anything I thought would help."

A new voice startled both girls, "I'm glad to hear that." They turned to watch as Trader Nassine entered the room, looking far more pleased than when Leeinn had seen her last. "I've been talking with the abbot about an interesting idea."

Leeinn did not like the predatory way Nassine was looking at her, "Oh?"

Nassine said, "It is common knowledge that because you were accepted so young, you have never been Abroad. You are now of the age when you would normally spend some time away from the abbey, to see a bit more of the world. Now that Tal will not be returning with us, Gira will need a companion. Why not return with us to the City?

You and Gira can keep each other company, and our household would be honored to have you."

Leeinn blinked in astonishment, "But, my father couldn't have agreed to that! I can't leave Del Abbey."

Nassine pressed her lips in irritation, "You certainly can, and while he did not give his approval, neither did he refuse. I think he wanted to talk with you about it before making a decision."

Gira looked hopefully at Leeinn, "It would only be for a little while, and I'd love to show you the City. Oh please, say you'll accept."

Leeinn felt torn, "But, I don't want to leave. This is my home."

Nassine argued, "And it will still be here when you get back. It's good for a young person to have new experiences. Who knows, you might meet the love of your life in the City."

"Ho .... How long would I be gone?"

"No more than a few months."

"*Months?!*" Leeinn broke into a cold sweat, "No, I'm sorry, I couldn't leave my dels for that long."

"Your father brought that up too. A simple enough problem. I know you had Tal help in your pool before the Hopeful Ceremony. She should be able to tend to your flowers, and if she has any issue, she can ask your father for help."

Gira touched Leeinn's arm, "I think you would enjoy staying with us. I promise I'll help you in any way I can."

Leeinn stalled, "I …. I have to speak with my father. Excuse me." Leeinn fled the gois rooms, refusing to look back as she all but ran away. She couldn't leave the abbey, it was ridiculous. Once she found her father, she'd make him see reason. He probably hadn't said no to keep from angering Nassine.

Rumaru wasn't in the kitchen, or the orchard, so Leeinn tried her pool. She could have cried with relief when she found him there, his walking stick by his side, sitting on the edge with his bare feet dangling in the water. He looked up as she opened and closed the door, smiling knowingly, "I wondered how long it would take you to find me. I thought this place would afford us some privacy to talk. I assume Nassine wasted no time and found you already?"

"She did, and she said .."

"That she wants you to spend your time abroad with her family."

"Yes! *And* she said you didn't tell her no when you heard her proposal."

Rumaru chuckled, ""Yes well, not many people tell Trader Nassine no."

"But you can't seriously be thinking of sending me away!"

Rumaru pat the empty spot beside him in invitation, "Let us consider the pros and cons. Your main concern is with leaving the abbey, yes?"

Leeinn sat beside her father, "You know I've never been farther than the del meadows." She placed her palms down flat, willing the stability of the ground into herself.

Rumaru tilted his head slightly to the side, "What happens if you put a plant in a pot?"

"What does that have to do with my leaving the abbey?" Leeinn asked crossly.

Rumaru tucked his hands into his sleeves, "Indulge me poppet."

Leeinn tried to slow her thoughts, "It would grow to fill the pot."

Rumaru nodded encouragingly, "And when it had filled the pot?"

"It would …. Stop growing?"

Rumaru smiled proudly, "Exactly. It might be more comfortable in the pot it grew up in, but it would never reach its full potential if it stayed put."

409

"But I'm already Accepted! I don't need to go Abroad, because there's no chance I'll have to leave."

"Why not think of it as a holiday? Getting to see new places, meet new people."

"Nothing could be better than Del Abbey."

"Then some time away would make you appreciate your home all the more."

In a small voice Leeinn asked, "You want me to leave?"

"No, of course not duckling. But Tal was very persuasive."

"Tal? What has she got to do with this?"

"It was her idea. Didn't Nassine mention that?"

"No, I thought it was her idea."

"She liked it well enough, once she'd heard it. Tal was concerned for Gira's wellbeing, and thought having a friend would help her through this difficult time."

"Gira has family and friends at home, she doesn't need me."

"Maybe, maybe not, but it would help strengthen the bonds between her family and the abbey to be able to boast they hosted you."

"So this is about making Nassine happy, because Gira wasn't accepted."

"That is part of it, but I really do think the experience would be good for you. I won't force you to go, but I want you to give it some real thought."

Leeinn could not believe her ears, "And was it Tal's idea to tend my pool while I'm gone?"

Rumaru looked surprised, "She did make that offer. She seems to want to be helpful."

"It's *our* pool."

"But didn't you have all your friends help you in it before the ceremony?"

Leeinn shrugged angrily, "That was different. I was with them."

"I'm sure Tal would follow any directions you left her. She seems a capable sort. Working for Nassine couldn't have been easy, but she managed to garner enough trust to be assigned to the family heir. Gira will likely miss her attention, having a guest to distract her would be a great help."

Leeinn stared into the water, picking out strands of her and Rumaru's hair without looking and braiding them together, "We've never been apart."

Rumaru laid an arm across her shoulders, "And I would miss you terribly. But I would know you'd be back, and have lots of stories to tell me about the City."

"But didn't you go there for your time Abroad?"

"I did. I'll admit, I was fortunate to have my sister and best friend with me, so it really was just like an adventure."

"I'll only know Gira."

"And her mother, and her sister, and her sister's chosen. They mentioned you showed them the wall top."

"Challi and Shealah, they like star signs."

"And you've always been able to make friends of the people who visit our abbey. No reason you can't do the same in the City." When she made no comment, Rumaru sighed, "Why don't we go to the feast. You do have a new sister to welcome."

"A meddling sister."

"Daughter," Rumaru said somewhat sharply, "She has been nothing but helpful, and she was accepted by the Trinity. She deserves better."

Leeinn ducked her head in embarrassment, pulling Rumaru's head down with her, "I'm sorry."

She untwined their plait, freeing her father, who stood and then helped Leeinn to her feet, "It's a big idea, and not one you'd ever thought you'd have to face. Try not to worry, and just enjoy the evening. We'll talk more about it tomorrow."

Leeinn could do nothing but bow to her father's wisdom, though she secretly wished she could have skipped the feast. Her stomach was far too tight for her to eat. Still, she knew her duty, and followed her father to the dining hall, taking their usual seats at the abbot's table. Nassine had given up her spot to Tal, who sat with hands in her lap, looking tired but serene. A line of people walked past her, offering congratulations. She accepted the accolades with aplomb, nodding her head slightly to each person and murmuring thanks. Leeinn had to admit, Tal looked every inch the Accepted.

From the next seat over Trader Nassine asked casually, "Have you had time to discuss my suggestion?"

Rumaru cleared his throat, "Briefly, yes. It is certainly an intriguing idea. But this has been a busy day, and some decisions are best slept on."

"You have my word that my household would treat your daughter like family." Nassine directed her attention to Leeinn, "You would want for nothing while you stayed with us. We would show you the highlights of the City, introduce you to the elite, and provide for every need you could have."

Leeinn fought the urge to fidget, "I'm not worried for myself, but my dels can be surprisingly delicate. Even following instructions, someone who isn't familiar with them could do irreversible damage."

"I'm sure your father would be able to correct any oversights. Really, I think you worry too much."

Tal interjected, "You've put years of work into your pool, it's natural you'd be protective of it. What if we spent all day there tomorrow, and I can take notes of all the things your flowers need. How much sun, and how often to spread the winged horse fertilizer, and a dozen things more I'm sure."

Leeinn could not see a way to refuse without causing offense, "I suppose it won't hurt to show you my routine. Not that I'm agreeing to go."

Tal smiled sweetly, "It must be a scary thought, leaving your home for the first time."

Leeinn stiffened, "I'm not afraid, I just don't see the point."

"The point," Nassine snapped, "Is to provide a show of faith. I didn't think Gira becoming Hopeful was a good idea, but you and your friends convinced her. I don't like seeing any of my family publicly embarrassed, bad for business."

Leeinn bit her tongue to keep herself from spitting, "*So you'll trot me out for your friends and hope they forget*

414

about Gira." Instead, she took a long sip of cold water, imagining the liquid dousing the embers of anger that burned in her chest. "Noone could have guessed the Trinity would not accept Gira."

"Perhaps not, but will you really cause her further discomfort by refusing? She thinks quite a lot of you. I can't imagine she'd react favorably to being rebuffed by the Trinity *and* you."

Leeinn hedged, "I …. I'll think about it." She doubted she'd be able to think of anything else until Gira's family left. *"Without me,"* Leeinn thought fervently.

Chapter 35

A Story

Shail stared at Seedruf in confusion. *My grandfather?*

Realization made Shail almost giddy, "You really have made a mistake sir. I have only one living grandparent."

Seedruf nodded, "I'm sure Gabani thinks I'm dead. I certainly thought *she* was for the longest time."

"Gabani? My grandmother's name is Rox."

Seedruf huffed a laugh, "Is that the name she took? *Tough as rocks*, that's what they always used to say about her. I guess I shouldn't be surprised." He searched Shail's face, "You look so much like her."

The Chief said, "He looks just like …"

"His grandmother, and my son," Seedruf said sharply.

The Chief conceded, "But his temperament is closer to yours. You should have heard him shout when he first arrived."

Seedruf grinned, "He's going to make us proud, once he's been trained."

Shail tried to reason with his captor, "But you said you know I'm already training to be a Travealer. Please, you have to send me home. Everyone must be so worried, and I need to finish my apprenticeship with Master Conlun."

Seedruf spoke to the Chief, "Have you explained nothing to him?"

"No, I thought he would take it better if it came from you."

Shail stomped his foot, "Stop talking about me like I'm not standing right here. I don't know what's going on, and I don't care. I think you have the wrong person, but either way you should not have stolen me like you did." Shail glared at Seedruf, "If you knew where I was, why didn't you come to me and explain things properly, instead of kidnapping me?"

Seedruf ran a hand through his short red hair, "It's not that simple."

"Or send me a letter! Anything but send a dragon. Tabirc was hurt!"

Seedruf held up his hands placatingly, "I know it looks bad, but I can explain." He addressed the Chief, "If you don't need me, I'd like to take my grandson somewhere we can discuss our family business privately."

The Chief waved a dismissive hand, "He's all yours."

Seedruf said to Shail, "Will you come to my tent?"

Shail crossed his arms, "Do I have a choice?"

Seedruf shrugged, "Honestly, no, you don't, but I would prefer to keep things civil. Which is why I am *asking* you to trust me, just for a little while."

Shail realized the Chief and S'ton were watching him, waiting to see what he would do. It occurred to him that he was alone in this camp, and if this man claiming to be his grandfather wanted him in his tent, he could drag Shail there, and no one would be likely to help him. Shail felt even smaller than he actually was, and wished there was some place he could run and hide.

"Fine," he offered sullenly. Seedruf took the win without comment, nodding to the Chief before turning to leave the tent. S'ton caught Shail's eyes as they left, and he gave an encouraging smile. Shail felt a bit better for having seen it, though he would not have admitted it out loud. Shail followed Seedruf through the camp to a tent nearly as large the Chief's. Seedruf politely held the flap so Shall could precede him, following after and drawing the

418

entrance closed with a thick string. The interior looked a lot like S'ton's tent. There was a padlocked trunk at the foot of Seedruf's bed, very much battered and scarred.

Seedruf pointed to a portable desk with a tri-legged stool, "How about you sit there, and I'll try to answer your questions." For his part, Seedruf dropped gracefully to the floor, sitting comfortably cross-legged as he waited to see what Shail would do. Seeing little choice but to obey, Shail mustered all the dignity he could as he sat rigidly in the offered chair. For a few moments they just stared at one another, Shail desperately trying to think of a way to convince this man he'd made a mistake. His story was outlandish.

"What makes you think I'm your grandson?"

"The family resemblance is difficult to ignore."

"Lots of people can look similar."

"Not *that* similar. You're the spitting image of my son."

"That makes even less sense. I never met my father, but I've seen pictures of him, and I don't look like him at all."

"I didn't say my son was your father."

"You're not even trying to explain, you're just saying cryptic things you know I won't understand. What's the point of my asking if that's how you answer?"

419

"I'm not handling this well." Seedruf stared down into his hands, "I've thought about our first meeting for a long time. I'll admit, I underestimated how angry you'd be."

"How did you think I would react to being kidnapped?"

Seedruf winced, "I guess in my mind I was bringing you home."

"I have a home, and this isn't it."

"Your home is a place you've probably never even heard of. Did Chief Omagroef tell you anything about our people?"

"He didn't, but S'ton told me you call yourselves the Denied, because you're not allowed in some promised land."

"S'ton can only tell you what he's heard himself, he's never been there. I have, I was born there, raised there. I should have grown old there with my wife and children. I was robbed of what was rightfully mine, and by extension so have you. Imagine, a paradise where you want for nothing. And the only reason we're here is because some fools take a dragon's opinion as seriously as the word of Amik."

"If you want to go back, that's your business. I just want to go to my home, with my family."

"You are *my* family, grandson."

"Do you have any proof of that?"

"Let me tell you a story. It might help clear up a few things." Seedruf took a deep breath, as though gathering his thoughts, "I was born in a special place to loving parents. I grew up with other children, making especially good friends with two in particular, your gran Gabani and her twin brother. We were thick as thieves, the three of us, and by the time we were your age, we knew that we'd stay together, no matter what. See, there's a ceremony each person has to go through, before they can call the special place their forever home. For those who are born in the special place, there is even a time each child spends someplace else, just in case they have to leave someday. We all spent our time in the city college closest to our home. I was always good at cooking, so I spent my time in the kitchen, while Gabani went into healing, like you.

"What did her brother study," Shail asked despite himself.

"That is not important to my story. He has only one role to play, and I am getting to that. We three turned twenty, and our friendship became a romance. On the eve of our judgement, we made a vow to see our childhood dream of remaining together come true." Seedruf swallowed hard, and his eyes closed in remembered pain. "We stood together, were judged together. They were

421

accepted. I was refused." Shail could see the muscles stand out in Seedruf's jaw as he clenched his teeth. "I was forced out, and I think I could have handled it if we'd stuck to our plan. The morning I was to leave, your grandmother met me at the gates, prepared to share my path, but her brother never showed." Seedruf looked past Shail, seeing the distant past as clearly as the present. "I couldn't believe he would betray me like that. After all his pretty words, his pledges, he was nothing but a coward and a traitor." Seedruf blinked his eyes rapidly, and Shail was astonished to see tears in the man's eyes, "I'll admit, things were dark for awhile after that. I wasn't happy in the city, so I drank more than I should have. It was a nice place to visit, but too big and loud for my liking. Gabani finished her training, and was scheduled for a journeyman's tour. I wasn't allowed to go with her, and those were the longest days of my life.

While she was away, I was approached by the Denied. They'd heard about my failure and wanted me to join their cause. They described a sweet and easy life, ours for the taking if we were bold. I thought they sounded a bit extreme, but their words helped to ease my wounded pride. I made no promises, but neither did I turn away their company.

Nothing could have prepared me for when your gran returned with a swelling belly. It had been three months since our parting, and she didn't know she was pregnant until after she'd left. I forgot all about the home that had thrown me away, and started making the place I was in ready for our child." Now Seedruf smiled, "Gabani gave birth to a beautiful little girl, and we named her Elissom. I never knew I could love anyone as much as I loved my daughter. The next thirteen years went by, and she grew up so fast.

Then, Gabani became pregnant again. We had lived comfortably enough when there was only three of us, but when we found out Gabani was carrying twins, things took a turn. She couldn't work the last two months of her pregnancy, and I didn't make enough to support a growing family. We had to resort to *charity*," Seedruf spat the word, "We who were born in plenty now struggled with poverty. I had all but forgotten our former life, but with people knocking on my door asking for money I didn't have, all the memories came back. Did you know, where I come from, everyone is given the basic necessities freely. It galled me to think of Gabani in patched clothes while her brother was given all he would ever need without even having to ask. I'd introduced her to a few of my Denied friends, but she never got on well with them. Said she wanted to live her life forward, not back.

The twins were born, and I now had a son in addition to two daughters. The boy we called Seedrufson, and the girl Lyonness. Gabini went back to work, and with Elissom able to help with the twins, we managed. It was not easy, but we managed.

The years went on, the twins turned five and Ellisom eighteen. She fell in love with a boy her age, and despite our cautions, she became pregnant. The father ran away, leaving her to raise the child alone. She did alright, at first, but she'd had her fill of babies with the twins. She and Gabani made arrangements for the child. I'm afraid I didn't pay much attention to the matter, for I was working long hours to help pay for decent schooling for all three of my children."

Shail leaned hard upon his knees, completely caught up in the tale, "But you can't think *I'm* that grandchild. My mother raised me, with my grandmother and uncle. It's a good story, but it doesn't add up."

"I did not say that *you* were that grandchild. I'm saying you have a half-sister somewhere. Gabani and Elissom never told me who they gave the child to, and without their knowledge, with so little to go on, I've all but given up hope of finding her. But I was there the day *you* were born. Your mother had found a good man, and she named you for him."

"She did say I was called Shail after my father …."

"I had already lost one grandchild, and I could barely stand the sight of my own son, so I was desperate to connect with you."

"Why didn't you get on with your son."

424

"Because the older he got, the more he grew to look like his uncle, my old friend. Every time I saw his face, it was like salt in an open wound, an active reminder of the worst day of my life. It did not matter that his name was Seedrufson, I could not stomach his company." Seedruf cleared his throat, "It was a mistake, one of many I hope to set right."

Seedruf continued, "Anyway, Elissom reached her majority the year the twins turned seven." He gave a harsh laugh, "They say seven is an unlucky number. Well, it certainly was for our family. Gabani and I quarreled often, about money, about our son and daughters, about our life. All of my children deserved the best, and I knew where the best was. I had told Elissom of our old home often enough, and had all but convinced her to ask for her own judgement ceremony. If she had been accepted, then she could have brought her brother, sister, and you with her, and in a few years, you could all have become Accepted. Elissom's siblings were Gabani and her brother all over again, and both of *them* had been accepted." Seedruf lowered his voice so Shail had to strain to hear him. "I went a bit mad with it all. I convinced myself that if my whole family was allowed to live in our homeland, they would have to let me join them, or at the very least give me a second chance to be accepted. But your namesake loved the city too much to settle into a quieter life, and your mother would not leave the father of her child."

"Nothing I could say would sway her, and eventually she turned to her mother for help. We argued, badly, and I lost my temper. I made threats I should not have, and scared your gran into running away with our children. There was only one place she would take them, back to her treacherous brother. With the Denied's help, I too made the journey home. I found my wife, just as I'd known I would. Gabani and her brother tried to make me see reason. I …. I hurt him, unforgivably. The people who lived there forced me out, *again*."

"I waited outside for my moment, I knew Elissom would try to go back to her husband in the city, and that your gran would want to keep the family together. I was right, but …" Seedruf went still, and Shail saw his face go pale as parchment, "I just wanted to talk, to get my family back. I don't know how things went so bad so quick. I managed to save Lyonness, though she was injured, but I thought Gabani, Elissom, and Seedrufson had been killed. I would have gone truly mad without Lyonness. I took her and formally joined the Denied. We've lived with them ever since."

"Until someone recognized Gran?"

"Her and her dragon handler partner Tabirc. They went carousing and got noticed by some of our agents who knew her from when we'd first moved to the city. They were quick to let me know, and I've never stopped looking since. From there, we set plans into motion to have you brought to us, with hopes of putting my family back together."

"Then why not approach Gran? Kidnapping me seems like a poor way to reunite."

"I tried!" Seedruf said emphatically. "She wouldn't speak to me. Said what she always said, that'd it been thirteen years and she wanted to leave the past in the past. She wouldn't even let me near you. I had no choice." Seedruf got up and paced the few steps across the tent, then back. "You're training to be a healer, right?" When Shail nodded, Seedruf said, "If we lived back home, you'd have the best teachers and all the resources you'd need to complete your training."

"I've *had* the best teacher in the world. Gran Rox."

"So you've had one apple when you could have had the whole bushel."

Shail sat back as though he'd been slapped, "That is certainly the worst way to look at it." He and Seedruf merely stared at each other, and Shail wondered if the man was disappointed in their first meeting. It certainly didn't seem to be going the way he'd planned. "So, what now?"

"For now, we'll stay with this Denied camp. I'm good friends with Omagroef, and he's promised us whatever we need."

"But when can I go home?"

427

"You only just found out your grandfather is alive, and you want to leave? If you do, I don't know when, or if, we'd ever see each other again."

"I'm sorry sir, but I don't think I'm your grandson. My mother's name is Lisasin, my uncle is Wengsper. I've never heard of any of the people in your story."

"What about the part of you being named for your father?"

"Lots of boys are named for their father, your own son included. It doesn't prove anything."

"Then how did I know your name to begin with?"

"There's got to be more than one Shail in the world."

Seedruf's shoulders drooped, "Alright, I can see you won't be so easily convinced. That's ok, we have all the time we need now."

"You can't keep me here, I'm going home."

"Now that the tracker has your scent, you are going nowhere unless I allow it."

"Then I'm your prisoner?"

Seedruf met Shail's gaze, "If that's what it takes to get my family back, yes."

Chapter 36

Decisions

Leeinn was just about done getting ready for the day when she heard a light knock at her door. Wondering if it was her father, she opened the door with a smile, and froze when she saw Tal.

"Uh, good morning"

Tal's mouth quirked upwards, "Good morning. I know you're an early bird, and I thought it'd be nice to let Gira sleep in today." She held up a bag hanging from her wrist, "I have everything I need to take notes on your pool. Did you want to go now, or visit the dining room first?"

"Let's eat first. We'll probably find Tiny and Tancer there too. They might be interested in joining us."

Tal brightened, "What a clever idea! Then you would have four people looking after your pool while you were gone." Leeinn hadn't thought of that angle, not liking the implications.

She decided not to make an issue of it, "Many hands make light work, as my father is fond of saying." Tal stepped to the side, and Leeinn joined her outside, closing the door behind her.

They walked to the dining hall while making small talk about the weather. They were among the first to breakfast. They'd each finished their plates and were drinking cups of chococafe when a sleepy-eyed Tancer followed a more chipper Tiny to their table.

Tiny greeted them, "Good morning. I don't see Gira with you?"

Tal replied, "We're letting her rest, she's never been a natural early riser."

"I can appreciate that," yawned Tancer. "Mornings are for sleeping, and breakfast should be after noon."

Tiny snorted, "Then what time would we have dinner?"

"After midnight, naturally," he retorted, filling his own plate.

Tiny gave him a playful shove, "Eating a major meal after midnight is not natural. Might be a sign of mental illness though."

Tancer leered comically, "Best not upset the crazies dear, lest you wake up with me snacking on your leg." He clicked his teeth together meaningfully, and the table broke into appreciative laughter.

Tiny asked, "Do we need to meet up with our work team today?"

"You're still in your grace period, so it's up to you. If you want to work, you go to the dispatch center, but I was hoping you'd both come with Tal and me to my pool."

"You still need more help, even after the ceremony?"

"Oh, that's right, you wouldn't have heard." Leeinn looked sideways at Tal, "It's been suggested I go Abroad with Gira's family. If I did, I would need someone to watch over my flowers while I was gone."

Tal nodded, "I've offered to take detailed notes of her instructions. Leeinn thought you two might like to join us."

Tiny and Tancer offered enthusiastic assistance, "Of course! You just tell us what needs doing, and we'll see it done."

Their support cheered her, and Leeinn felt her usual good spirits return. She stood from the table, "Should we get Gira?"

Tal nodded, "She's probably awake by now. Let's check in anyway."

They found Gira in the gois sitting area, wrapped in a fluffy robe. Her face fell when she saw all four friends together, "Everyone is already up and about? Tal, why didn't you wake me!"

"She's not your servant anymore," Tiny pointed out.

Gira flushed, "Well, you still could have gotten me up for breakfast."

Tal bobbed her head in apology, "I'm sorry, I thought you'd like to get up a little closer to your normal time. There was no reason to wake early today."

"Nevermind, give me ten minutes and I'll be ready." Truth be told, it was closer to twenty minutes before Gira emerged, but with Tancer providing comical entertainment, no one begrudged her the time. "What are we doing today?"

"Going to my pool to show all of you my daily del routine."

"So you've accepted my mother's offer!"

"No, not yet."

"Why else would we need to know how to take care of your flowers?"

Tiny said, "Even if we don't end up watching Leeinn's pool specifically, learning how to cultivate dragon egg lotus can only be advantageous in a place named for them."

Gira pressed her case, "I'm sure my mother meant what she said about showing you the best of times. I can introduce you to my city friends, and we can have fancy dinners every night."

Tancer perked up, "Better than the abbey feasts?"

Gira made a doubtful expression, "Maybe not that good, but still delicious."

He leaned forward eagerly, "If Leeinn doesn't want to go, can I?"

Gira made a face, "*Somehow* I don't think mother would be as pleased, thank you all the same."

The five friends made their way to Leeinn's pool. It was dark and quiet when they entered the room. Gira double stepped ahead of the group, "I remember you opening the skylight last time. Should I do that now?"

"Yes please. Just turn the handle." It became nearly as bright as though they were standing outside.

"Except for your solid color variations, your pool is rather empty," Tiny observed.

"It won't be for long. In the right conditions dels grow weed quick."

Tal took out a stiff-backed sheaf of paper, a horse quill pen, and looked expectantly at Leeinn, "I'm ready."

Leeinn pointed to the tabletop that held most of her tools, "Best to start with the testing stone."

Tal made a notation, "Do you test at the start of each day?"

"No, but I've been taking care of this pool for so long I can tell when something is off by the color, smell, or taste of the water. If you're taking care of a pool you're unfamiliar with, then it's a good idea to test the water daily."

"You said that stone has been calibrated for your pool. Is that also something that needs to be done daily?"

"It takes a practiced hand to inscribe stone with something that advanced. If you have any troubles, you have to take it back to the glyphsmith."

Gira pulled a small rock from a pocket, "I know the glyph for light! Here, look, I made my own glow." It was just possible to see a slight shimmer between her fingers as she cupped her creation.

Tiny looked at Gira's glyphlight with interest, "Where'd you learn to do that?"

"Oh it was a fad a year ago. The whole city was mad for basic glyphology, for a time you could barely tell night from day."

Leeinn said, "We have a lantern festival that's like that."

Gira's eyes became as bright as her glyphlight, "Oh that sounds lovely. When is it?"

"It marks the onset of autumn, when the days get dark early."

"Long after I'm gone," Gira said sadly.

There was an uncomfortable silence, then Tal said, "There's a harvest celebration in the city soon, maybe you and Leeinn could go to it."

"I have *not* said I'm going," Leeinn said shortly.

Tancer shrugged, "Don't see why you shouldn't. Free vacation, with someone else paying the bill, sounds like a good time."

At Leeinn's scowl Tiny elbowed her husband, "To each their own, and some people are homebodies."

Leeinn crossed her arms, "It's not like I'm ever bored here. There's always something going on, or a job to lend a hand with, and the meditation glades if I simply want peace and quiet." Leeinn could have bit her tongue for her flippant remark. Gira's tattoo drew all eyes like a lodestone.

Tiny cleared her throat, "I haven't seen a section of the abbey that *wasn't* beautiful."

"Including this place that you've been kind enough to share with us," Tal said smoothly. "May I try the testing stone?"

Leeinn gestured with one hand, "Be my guest."

Tal retrieved the testing stone, sat at the edge of the pool to remove socks and shoes, pulled the hem of her habit to knee height, and stepped into the water. "I just walk around?"

"I would test the four corners, and then the center." Tal made her way around the edge of the pool, dipping the testing stone where Leeinn had instructed.

"All blue." Tal exited, dripping but smiling. "I'll record todays results, then we can move on."

Leeinn produced a burlap bag, hefting it as though it were heavy, "This is actually something having all of you here will be good for. I'll show you how to plant del seeds, and then we can all take a section of the pool." In her other hand Leeinn held two hollow bamboo tubes nearly as long as her arm with a rounded cap on one end, and a sharpened bevel on the other. "I only have two soil punches, so I'll demonstrate, and then you four can take turns using them. There are a few different designs of punches. This is one of the simpler to use."

Leeinn's friends watched intently as she took out a palmful of the seeds before handing the bag to Gira. She waded into the water, chose her spot, and stabbed the punch into the soil at the bottom of the pool. She then twisted off the cap, and pulled out a rubber cylinder as long as the tube. "This keeps the water out until you've got your punch stuck where you want it. Then when you pull out the center, you have a tunnel to drop your seeds down to the soil." So saying, Leeinn palmed a few seeds into the opening. "Last thing is to use the center to push the air, and the seeds, down into the dirt. Then you can pull up your punch, and do it again at the next spot." Leeinn held up her tool, "Who wants to try first?"

Gira's hand shot up, "I do!" Leeinn climbed out of the pool and handed one punch to Gira, and the other to Tiny.

Tiny peered into the water, "How close to each other do the seeds need to be?"

"I usually put them about an arm length away from each other. That leaves them plenty of room to grow, so they won't crowd when they flower."

Tal wrote another line of instructions, "What do you do with your variations once they've bloomed?"

"I give them to the infirmary to make potions and tonics."

Gira said, "I remember a stall near the front gate selling flasks with liquids the same colors as your flowers! I bought a blue bottle for the next time my math tutor gives me a surprise test."

437

Tancer said, "I've never been a fan of math myself, not a lot of it called for in ditch digging other than, '*Make it this wide and this deep*'."

Tiny groused, "I had a math tutor too. Absolutely hated him. Wouldn't allow for rounding, every figure had to be exact."

Leeinn was sympathetic, "Brother Septibb isn't quite that strict, though the masters of craft can be."

Tancer crossed his arms, "Right, stick to the simple, that's my motto."

Tiny quipped, "Simple for the simple minded. *I* always did well on *my* math tests."

"That's why I married you! Brains *and* brawn."

"So what do you bring to the table?"

"Charm, wit, and a saucy sense of humor," Tancer said with a wink.

"Mmhmm, then tell a joke."

Tancer considered, then said, "*I used to run a dating service for chickens, but I was struggling to make hens meet.*" A chorus of groans met his answer. "No good? How about, '*I used to hate facial hair, but then it grew on me!*'"

Tiny rolled her eyes, "I said tell a joke, not *be* a joke."

"Beyond your ken. I understand, you just can't appreciate my humor."

"Is that what you were showing off?"

Tancer put his hands on his hips and leaned forward, "I have more."

Tiny pasted a rictus grin on her face, "Best save them for later. Too much of a good thing and all that."

Gira said, "I think you're funny."

Tancer beamed at her, "Thanks, but looks aren't everything."

Tiny and Gira chose their first spots, holding their soil punches like a spears, "How deep do we need to drive the end?"

Leeinn held up her hand, then curled all her fingers save for her thumb and index, holding them as far apart as she could, "About this much. The soil at the bottom is only a couple feet thick."

Tiny drove her soil punch down, "And now I pull out the center?"

Leeinn nodded encouragingly, "You got it."

Gira watched Tiny remove the rubber stopper, then jabbed downwards with her own punch. She suddenly started hopping on one foot, "Oww! I caught the side of my big toe!" A spot of growing red could be seen rising from

Gira's injury. Tiny was at her side in an instant, offering her arm for support. Gira took it and hobbled to the pool stairs. Leeinn had grabbed a clean rag from a cupboard and once Gira was sitting at the edge of the water she pressed the wound to stop the bleeding.

Gira covered her face, "How stupid can I be? Stabbing my own foot."

Leeinn gave Gira's shoulder a consoling pat, "It was an accident. You'll be more careful next time."

Gira sniffed, "Except there won't be a next time. Not for me." She grabbed Leeinn's hand, "Please come back with us! I want to show you I'm not really a screw up. I'm much better at home."

Leeinn heard the desperation in Gira's voice, and averted her gaze from Gira's pleading eyes, "I don't think you're a screw up."

Gira squeezed Leeinn's hand harder, "I'll be the perfect host. Anything you want, you have but to ask."

Leeinn looked around at their audience, "What do you think?"

Tancer said, "You know my vote."

"And mine," Tal answered.

Leeinn looked to Tiny, "And you?"

Tiny said, "I think you should make your own decisions. What do *you* want to do?"

"I don't want to leave my home." She heard Gira's quick indrawn breath, "But I also want to help my friend."

"Is that a yes?" Gira asked hopefully.

Leeinn nodded, "I guess that's yes."

Chapter 37

An Apprentice Abroad

Shale stared at Seedruf. Seedruf stared at Shail. A scratching at the tent's entrance flap broke their stalemate.

Seeduf said, "Enter."

S'ton ducked inside. "Chief wanted me to tell you he wants to talk when your through with the target."

"Shail. My name is Shail."

S'ton shrugged, "Yeah, ok. When you're done with Shail."

Surprisingly, Seedruf smiled, "Demanding respect, good for you."

Shail did not like the warmth such praise produced. "If that's what you think, then I demand you take me back to Tabirc."

Seedruf chuckled, "Nice try, but no. I think we'll keep you around."

Shail hadn't really believed such a tactic would work, but he still felt disappointed. "For how long?"

Seedruf ignored Shail's question, instead speaking to S'ton, ""I think we're done, for now. I'll go speak with the Chief."

S'ton jerked his chin towards Shail, "What about him?"

"Keep him company for me." Shail heard Seedruf's unsaid order, "*And keep an eye on him.*"

"Yessir." S'ton peered at Shail, "Want to see more of the camp?"

"I guess."

That seemed good enough for S'ton. He turned and left the tent, clearly intending for Shail to follow him. Shail gave Seedruf one last glance, then went outside. He had to squint for a few seconds while his eyes adjusted. S'ton said, "Let's go to the training field. Give you an idea of our strength."

They toured the camp, S'ton introducing Shail to people as they passed them. Shail's ears pricked as he caught the sound of louds thumps, occasionally accompanied by shout of pain. The training field was just that, an open area big enough for two Jogslens to stretch to their fullest. There were two parallel lines facing each other, mostly men, but with a few women as well. They each had a wooden sword, and were taking turns attacking

443

and defending. They seemed to be performing a known drill, for each combatant attacked the same way, and each defendant blocked with the same maneuver.

A grizzled grey-haired man stood at the head of the lines, bawling out pointers, "Watch your footwork Clemans! The wind could push you over with that stance. Bhelis, keep your guard up. Better!" S'ton and Shail stood on the sidelines watching the practice until they were spotted by the instructor. "S'ton! You and your friend there grab a practice blade. Might as well join as watch."

"Aye sir!" S'ton retrieved two blades from a wooden barrel full of them, handing one to Shail. He held his with ease, clearly having used the weapon many times before.

Shail held his awkwardly. "I've never fought with a sword before."

"Really? Never?"

"Not for real. I had play fights with my friends and cousins, but we usually just used sticks."

"Nothing playful bout combat," S'ton said with a worldly air.

""Nuff jawin, get to it!"

Both S'ton and Shail jumped slightly at the rebuke. S'ton dropped into a defensive stance, "Just you come at me then."

Shail left the point of his sword buried in the dirt, "Why?"

S'ton stood straighter, looking non-plussed, "Cause that's orders."

"And you always follow orders?"

"Good soldiers follow orders," S'ton said stubbornly. "Everyone knows that."

A sudden stinging blow got Shail's attention. While he'd been arguing with S'ton, the drill instructor had come up behind him, giving him a swat with the flat of yet another practice sword. "Thought I told you two to get to it. Well?"

S'ton answered smartly, "He's not been trained, sir."

"First time for everything." The man took up position besides Shail. "Do as I do." He held his weapon with one hand. "We'll start with a simple stab." So saying, the instructor thrust forward almost faster than Shail's eyes could follow. "Nobody likes having more holes than they was born with."

Shail made a half-hearted jab towards S'ton, wobbling slightly as he overextended. The instructor barked, "Watch me, then try it again," and then demonstrated the movement a second time, but slower. Shail noticed one of his more obvious mistakes. When the instructor had performed the maneuver with his right arm

445

while his right leg was positioned in front. Shail had the right arm, but the wrong foot. He placed his feet correctly, then tried the jab again. He felt the rightness of the motion, and gave the instructor a begrudging nod.

"Try this one." The man held the sword diagonal, motioning for S'ton to attack him. When S'ton tried his own jab, the man disarmed him with barely a flick of his wrist. "Again, quarter speed." S'ton picked up his sword and made a second, significantly slower attack. The instructor had dropped back into his defensive stance, and as S'ton's blade tip crossed his, he turned his sword in a clockwise circle. The instructor stepped back, "Your turn."

Shail mimicked the defense pose. He felt the drill instructor's hands push down on his shoulders, "Feet a touch wider, bend your knees a bit. There, see?" Shail could feel the difference. He locked eyes with S'ton, who raised an eyebrow in query. Shail nodded, and S'ton jabbed. Shail's movements were nowhere near as smooth as the instructor's, but he did manage to disarm S'ton. He felt a strange mixture of pride and disquiet. He didn't like the idea of using a sword against a real person, he might hurt them.

Something of his internal conflict must have shown on his face, for S'ton said, "We'll need to know how to fight if we're to take back our homeland. They won't just let us in you know."

"Have you tried asking nicely?"

S'ton scowled, "I don't think I like your tone."

"I'm serious. When was the last time someone tried talking to these people. You said the Denied are an old faction. Maybe the people who live there now are more open-minded. They might welcome you back. You don't know if you don't try."

S'ton's look became uncertain, "I guess I never thought of it that way."

Shail seized upon the admission, "So try my idea, and we can both go home."

Another whack from the instructor had Shail dancing on tiptoes, "Don't worry yourself about the Denied. Omagroef will tell us what needs doing, and then we'll do it. End of story."

S'ton looked relieved to be given such a straightforward answer, "Good soldiers follow orders." The instructor grunted, then motioned for the two boys to take up their practice positions. Shail wanted very much to throw the sword down, and jump on it for good measure, but knew such an action would likely earn him a dozen smacks.

He and S'ton spent the next quarter of an hour exchanging blows before a shrill scream was heard from farther down the line. Everyone ran to see what the matter was. Through a circle of arms and torsos Shail saw a young man holding a profusely bleeding hand. He was gripping

447

the injury by the wrist, staring at it and squealing like a stuck pig.

Shail did not stop to think, but pushed through the crowd, "Let me pass, please!" A space opened up for Shail, closing behind as he progressed. The injured fighter did not notice Shail's arrival until Shail took him by the elbow and said, "Hold your hand above you heart."

Startled, scared eyes look back into his, "Are you a healer?"

"I've had basic training, enough for something like this."

That seemed good enough for the fighter, for his thrust his inured hand under Shail's nose, "I'm bleeding!"

"*No kidding,*" thought Shail. Out loud he said, "Yes, you are. Hold your hand up above the level of your heart." Shail pushed gently at the man's elbow until he'd done as instructed, "Good, that's good. Now we need to apply pressure and bind your wound." Shail glanced around at the onlookers, "Does anyone have a clean cloth I can use?" A blushing woman stepped forward and offered a silken square handkerchief. Shail accepted it with thanks. He pressed the scrap of cloth where the blood seemed to be coming from. "This will do for the moment, but we should get you to your resident healer. They'll have something to clean your cut, and bandage it properly."

The fighter went white around the lips, "Will I need stitches?"

Shail hedged, "Maybe, though I was taught quickstick was just as effective. It depends on what your healer has in stock."

"Huh, well, that don't sound so bad. Not like getting sewed up like a pair of ripped trousers."

"Can you walk?"

A jeering voice from the crowd crowed, "It's his hand that's hurt, why wouldn't he be able to walk?"

Shail retorted, "Each person reacts differently to blood loss. If he is feeling dizzy or lightheaded, walking would be a bad idea. He'd probably hurt himself worse."

Three strong looking men stepped forward, "We can carry him for you healer."

Shail felt a minor thrill at being called *healer*. "Thank you for the offer, that is very kind." All three of Shail's new assistants shuffled their feet with embarrassment. Shail addressed his patient, "Sir? Do you want to walk or have your friends carry you?"

"I think I can manage. But maybe if just one went with us. To help me along if I need it." Shail nodded at the one who had spoken out, "Sir, would you accompany us please?"

"Course. Anything you need."

449

"At the moment what I need is a guide. I'm afraid I don't know my way around your camp."

"Easy enough. Follow me."

Shail kept a solicitous grip on the fighter's non-injured elbow. They weaved their way with Shail keeping up a low drone of encouragement. They approached one of the largest tents Shail had yet seen, twice as big as the cooking pavilion. This one had no openings in the ceiling, but had glyphlamps strung about the framework, making the inside nearly as bright as the outside. There was a double line of cots, mostly empty save for one bundled figure at the far end.

Shail's guide called out, "Healer Baker, Feninon's been hurt."

A man old enough to be Shail's father stood from his seat, "Put him here." Feninon sat himself upon the indicated cot. The healer had taken one look at Feninon's hand, then motioned to one of his apprentices, "Bring me a basin of cleanser and some bandages." When the supplies have been brought, the healer put on a pair of protective gloves. "Put your hand in the cleanser."

Feninon eyed the liquid suspiciously, "Will it sting?"

Shail gave S'ton a, *"This your army?"* look.

Whatever Healer Bakers feelings, he managed to keep his upbeat attitude, "It shouldn't, but even if it did, I'm sure a tough fellow like you could handle it without a whimper."

"Don't like stingy stuff," complained Feninon. Shail tried his luck, "A little pain now is better than infection later."

Healer Baker looked curiously at Shail, "Who are you?"

"My name is Shail."

"Had some healer training have you? Look a big young for that," Healer Baker observed.

"I'm only an honorary apprentice."

Feninon looked insulted, "You was giving me orders and you're not a real healer?"

His friend punched his shoulder, "He got your hand to stop bleeding, and helped you here. Show some gratitude."

While the two men argued, Healer Baker drew the fighter's injured hand into the basin. The clear cleanser took on a rosy hue, and when the hand was lifted out, it was as clean as if it'd been scrubbed. "There, much better. What happened anyway?"

"Likios was using a practice sword with rough edges."

451

"I shall have a word with your drill master about proper weapon maintenance." Healer Baker eyed the cut, "We'll have to do something to keep that closed while it heals." He turned the man's hand to the light, "See how the sides are splayed open? Won't heal properly like that."

Feninon jerked his chin towards Shail, "He said glue works just as well as stitches."

"Did he now?" Healer Baker said with a twinkle in his eye. "True enough, if that's what you'd prefer."

"I don't like stitches."

Healer Baker chuckled, "Most people don't. Alright, we'll do as our visiting healer suggests."

It was the work of a few moments for a pretty apprentice to bring the necessary supplies. She'd put on her own gloves, and held the skin together while Healer Baker applied the quickstick. When he was satisfied, he put a thick pad of gauze over the laceration, then swathed the entire hand. "Keep this on for two days, then come back for a checkup."

"Yes sir," answered Feninon. "Can I go now?"

"Yes, yes, off with you. But no practicing with that hand until it's healed."

Feninon groaned, "Deronas will probably make me sand down all the practice swords."

Healer Baker gave a wicked grin, "Well, you'll have to ask someone to give you a *hand*." Feninon was not amused, but the healer's joke got a chuckle from everyone else. Feninon mumbled a thank you and left the tent, his friend following behind after giving Shail and the healers a farewell nod.

When he'd gone, Healer Baker turned his attention to Shail and S'ton, "I know everyone with a head for healing in this camp, so where did you come from?"

S'ton replied, "Jogslen brought him back."

"Ahh," said Baker. "Most people she brings back aren't of a mind to be helpful."

Shail shifted uncomfortably, "Someone was hurt. I couldn't *not* help."

"Spoken like a true healer! Young you may be, but you definitely got the guts for the job." Healer Baker spoke to S'ton, "If you're father doesn't need him for anything else, let him know I'd like this young man as one of my apprentices while he's here."

Shail bowed slightly, "Thank you sir, but I won't be staying that long."

Healer Baker raised an eyebrow, "Oh, leaving us so soon?"

S'ton shook his head, "He's staying, just hasn't gotten used to the idea yet."

The healer gave Shail a sympathetic smile, "Well, we've time for talk once you're settled."

S'ton elbowed Shail, "I'll bring you back another time."

Healer Baker waved them off, "Thanks for the help. And if no one has said it yet, welcome to the Denied. We're a rough bunch, but from what I've seen you'll fit right in. Give my offer some thought."

Shail followed S'ton, feeling very confused.

Chapter 38

Fivefs

Leeinn's agreement to leave was out of mouth before she'd properly thought her words through, and she knew with a sinking sensation that she could not take them back.

Gira's response was almost enough to distract her. Forgetting her injured foot, she threw herself at Leeinn, hugging her fiercely. "You won't regret it, I promise! We are going to have such fun!"

Leeinn could have kicked herself, but the die had been cast. Now to deal with the results. "I never thought I would get a chance to see the City."

Tiny said, "It's a big place, much bigger than this abbey."

"And with more people than you've ever met in your life," added Tancer.

Leeinn felt another twinge of worry, "I don't like being crowded in a small space."

Gira rushed to reassure her, "The outdoor areas are all made for holding lots of people, and the buildings are so grand you could get lost in them! And I won't leave you while we're out, so you'll never be alone."

Tiny struck a fist into an open palm, "I just remembered one spot I know you would like. The Little Abbey!"

Tancer nodded, "Good idea love! A bit of home away from home."

Gira clapped her hands together, "I've been there a few times, I can show you around."

Leeinn looked between them, "But what *is* the Little Abbey?"

Tiny explained, "It's a section of the City modeled after Del Abbey. I think it was originally built by people who couldn't stay here, but wanted to live somewhere similar. So they built their own abbey, albeit a fraction of the size. That's where I saw the winged horses, though they only have four that I know of."

Leeinn was intrigued, "Do they have dragons?"

"Yes, but not like the ones here. They're called silkwyrms, and they only get about as big as a cat."

Tancer added, "The silkwyrms have other names that are sort of like the dragons here. I've heard people call the females silkbellies, and the males are skysilks."

Leeinn was surprised to feel a stir of anticipation, "That could be interesting."

Gira started edging towards the door, "Are we done here? Can we go?"

Tiny handed her punch to her husband, "We haven't switched off yet. Give it a try."

Tal and Tancer took their turns with the soil punches. No further injuries were obtained, and by the end all those who would be staying at the abbey were fairly proficient. Tal had taken half a dozen sheets of notes, all in clear, neat writing. They reseeded all of Leeinn's pool that was not dedicated to her variations. She showed them where to store the seed supply, and then put away her tools, agreeing with Tancer that hard work deserved lunch.

After the midday meal, Gira wanted to find her mother, "To tell her the wonderful news!" Questioning the family servants led them to a secluded patio where Nassine and Rumaru sat playing a game of fivefs. Leeinn's father knew her step and was smiling in their direction before they'd come to a stop a respectful distance away.

Nassine noticed the diversion of her opponents attention and took advantage, "Farmer to square thirty-seven. That puts your fortune under my sway!"

Rumaru raised his eyebrows, "Oh dear, that's not good."

Nassine sat back and crossed her arms smugly, "Not for you. Your move."

"Umm, mother?" Gira tried.

"Not now, I've almost got him."

"But Leeinn …"

Leeinn hushed Gira, for she had seen the crinkle her father always got at the corner of his eyes when he was being sneaky, "Let them finish." Gira subsided into an aggrieved silence. Rumaru stroked his chin meditatively, "I suppose I have no choice but to send my flyers to harvest your dragon egg lotus. Oh dear, what will you feed your new treasure?"

Nassine looked like she'd sucked a sourberry, "Very clever." She shifted her attention to their audience, "What are you all doing here?"

Gira bounced on her toes, "That's what I was trying to tell you! Leeinn has agreed to come back with us!"

Nassine's sour expression turned sunny, "I knew you'd see sense."

"I couldn't say no to Gira"

Nassine cast a proud eye over her daughter, "It's her trader blood. We always get what we want."

Gira looked embarrassed, "Leeinn is going as a friend to me, it has nothing to do with trade."

"Everything relates to trade. Sooner you learn that, the better your business will run." Gira gave Leeinn an apologetic side-eye.

Rumaru stretched, "Well now, I didn't expect this." He gestured to the game board, "Shall we call it a tie?"

Nassine gripped the abbot's hand in hers, "Deal." They held the pose for a moment, then broke into the kind of laughter you only have with old friends who know you well. When she'd sobered, she said to Leeinn, "With Tal staying, there's an empty spot in Gira's travel carriage. You'll be bunking with her, Challi, and Shealah."

Gira clapped like a happy child, "We can stay up and watch the stars!"

Rumaru gestured towards Leeinn, "If you're going to be stealing my daughter away, would you mind if I borrowed her for a bit?"

Nassine stood, "Not at all. I'll see to the arrangements on our end. Gira, you're with me."

The group broke up, and soon only Leeinn and her father remained in the courtyard. He had reset all the pieces to their starting positions, toying with the last with an unusual show of nervousness.

"Father?"

He set the piece down, "I'm worried you're going because *I* said you should, rather than because *you* want to."

"It wasn't just you. Everyone except Tiny thought it was a good idea."

Rumaru raised a surprised eyebrow, "And she didn't?"

"She said *my* opinion mattered more than hers."

Rumaru winced slightly at the implied rebuke, "Which is why I was worried. If you change your mind, I will tell Nassine, whatever her arguments. Do not feel as if you *have* to do this."

His support finally tilted the scale, "I want to go, really. I get along with Gira, and I can buy you presents while I'm in the City!"

Rumaru threw affectionate arms around her, "You're going to be having too much fun to think about me."

Leeinn squeezed him back, "I'll never *not* think about you, and wishing you were with me."

"I suppose if you *have* to bring me something back, I could use a new bottle of my favorite scent. The one I can only find at Batista's."

"How about I bring you *two*?"

"Such wealth, such luxury, such generosity! You've enough for the Twins twice over."

Leeinn asked quietly, as though afraid to be thought silly, "Do you think Amik and Omal will watch over me on my journey?"

"They watch over all Accepted, no matter where they may wander. So behave yourself!"

Leeinn giggled, "I can't get up to anything worse than you did when you went Abroad."

Rumaru looked mildly scandalized, "*Who told? Whatever you've heard was exaggerated!*"

"Really? So you didn't win pocket money with cards?"

"*Weeeellll* ..... things in the City are so expensive. And that was when I first found Batista's."

"Except you had a particular trick. What was it called?"

Rumaru stared off in another direction, feigning nonchalance, "I forget."

"The old switchamaru, I think they said."

Rumaru looked prim, "If I find out who *they* are, *they* will be on *Abbot's Report*."

Leeinn poked his middle with a finger, "So it's true?"

"Do you hear the dinner gong? It's later than I thought."

"No, I didn't."

Rumaru pulled her along, "Trust me, my hearing is much better than yours."

Leeinn allowed herself to be shepherded to the dining hall, where dinner was not yet being served yet. "We seem to be early."

"Huh, must have been the wind."

"The wind sounds like a gong?"

"It does when you're completely reformed and respectable father says it does."

They went ahead and took their usual seats, content to chat until the hall filled with other diners. "Have you thought about what to pack?"

Leeinn's eyebrows raised nearly to her hair line, "I hadn't thought about it! I've never *not* been at home."

"Of course there's one thing I know you'll take with you."

Leeinn cocked her head, "What?"

"Flappy!"

It was Leeinn's turn to blush, "I'm a little old to be taking a stuffy."

"But you've never slept without him!"

Leeinn looked around hurriedly to see if anyone had been sitting close enough to overhear their conversation, "Not so loud! Not everybody needs to know you know!"

Rumaru smiled mischievously, "Should I say something mortifying about myself to even the odds? *Hmm*, how about having to listen to scary stories during the day so I don't get nightmares?"

Leeinn considered, then shook her head, "Lots of people don't like scary stories. You'll have to do better than that!"

Rumaru tapped his cheek in thought, "I cry at the drop of a feather."

Leeinn shook her head, "Expressing emotion is not embarrassing. Come on, really try!"

"I've got it!" Rumaru pulled a folded, well-worn cloth from a pocket, "I always carry my favorite towel. It's like my own Flappy, except I take it everywhere."

"I guess a grown man with a security blanket is kind of embarrassing."

Rumaru shook the cloth meaningfully, "Security *towel*. It belonged to my mother. She made it herself as an art project. See, she sewed a del in the middle of it." He held the towel up by the two top corners, revealing a somewhat lopsided lotus at the center. "This is one of a kind, and reminds me of her." He motioned Leeinn closer, making as if to whisper in her ear, "It's also good for grabbing hot handles in the kitchen."

"Speaking of the kitchen, it looks like they're bringing us an early course." They shared out the salad and bread, Leeinn making a verbal list of things to take, each item considered and then approved or vetoed by her father.

Diners trickled in until the hall was full, and dinner began in earnest. Gira followed her mother to the abbot's table, flashing an infectious grin at Leeinn. Nassine for once also seemed in a good mood.

She peered at Rumaru over the brim of her cup, "Is your daughter any good at fivefs? I could use another partner once we leave."

"She's even better than me."

"So she'll be a challenge," Nassine laughed.

"I believe our last game was *tied*."

Nassine tossed her head, "Only because I was distracted at the last minute."

Leeinn turned away from her father and his friend's gentle bickering, focusing on Gira, "I've been talking with my father about what I should and shouldn't take. You've traveled more than I have, is there anything you would suggest?"

Gira shrugged, blowing on a spoon of hot soup before taking a cautious sip, "It's not quite the same, because anything you forget or miss we can get for you at home. I left my best wet hair brush behind, and couldn't find anyone here who sells them."

Leeinn sat back in her seat, "I don't even have a travel pack to put my things in. So many things to do!"

Chapter 39

Trust

Shail and S'ton left the healer's tent in silence. S'ton watched Shail from the corner of his eye, his face impassive, and Shail was too busy thinking to talk. He was sure helping Feninon had been the right thing to do, sure that Gran would have praised him, just as Healer Baker had done, but at the end of the day, he had helped an enemy. A man that wanted to make war on a people that may or may not deserve retribution. Either way, it was a situation Shail wanted no part in. Had he given the impression he approved of their cause by aiding one of their number? But what would it say about his instincts as a healer if he had refused? Shail did not know the answer to any of his questions.

S'ton broke into Shail's reverie, "That was impressive."

Shail was only half listening, "What?"

S'ton jerked his chin in the general direction of the training field, "Back there."

"I didn't do anything special."

S'ton pressed, "But there was a whole crowd of folk just standing around, with people lots older than you. Wasn't 'til you took command that anybody got something useful done."

"I've had training."

S'ton mulled over Shail's answer, then stuck out his hand, "Seems to me like you're a good friend to have. If I can help you while you're with us, just whistle."

Shail felt a little silly accepting, but the hearty shake he got in return convinced him he'd make the right choice. "I'll be honest with you, since you've been decent to me. I don't plan on staying here long. I have to get home."

S'ton freed his hand, scowling in irritation, "Not that again. You heard Seedruf. If you run off, they'll just send Jogslen to bring you back."

Shail pleaded, "But I have to let my family know I'm alive and well. Last they know I was kidnapped for no rhyme or reason."

S'ton resumed walking, "Chief says you should always keep your enemies guessing."

Shail matched his stride, "Am I an enemy? I thought I was supposed to join the Denied."

467

S'ton sniffed, "Once you've proven yourself, you *might* get that honor."

"Seedruf acted as though it's a done deal."

S'ton looked down his nose, "Your granddah ain't in charge."

Shail stopped in his tracks, feeling as though he'd been doused with cold water, "I don't know who that man is, but he's no family of mine."

S'ton raised an eyebrow, "You think he's lying?"

Shail shrugged, "I've no idea. Maybe what he says is true, but he's got the wrong person. Maybe when his family died he went mad and made up this story to cope. Have you met his daughter?"

"Which one? If you mean your mum, then no. If you mean Lyonness, I've known her long as I've been alive. She was my first sparring partner. Wicked quick with a blade that one."

Shail was stunned, "Do I look anything like her?"

"Not really, but then again, she's done her best to alter how she looks."

"Why?"

"She's never said outright, but I'd guess to lessen the similarity between her and her mother. Seedruf has a history of disliking his own son, just for looking like his

468

old friend. He could feel the same about a daughter that reminded him of his wife. Lyonness even dyes her hair red because Seedruf has red hair. Wants to make her dah happy. Be closer to him, yah know." S'ton stared into the distance, "You can understand that, can't ya? I know I can."

"My father died before I was born," Shail said automatically.

S'ton made an apologetic wave, "Sorry."

To ease the embarrassed tension, Shail offered, "I do have sort of an honorary father. The captain of the ship that my gran and I sailed on. He has five sons already, and I made friends with his daughter Moyrah. It was her idea, her father taking me on I mean."

"Easy as that? Sure she wasn't sizing you up for a ring?" Shail stared open mouthed with outrage. S'ton relented, "What's his name?"

Shail had to think for a moment, "Cohaff."

With a serious expression, S'ton said, "Well, Shail Cohaffson, are you hungry?"

"I … yes, a bit."

"Good, me too. And since Nan likes you, we'll both get double portions." At the mention of food, Shail's stomach gave out a growling noise.

He shared a sheepish smile with S'ton, "More than a bit, I guess."

S'ton gave Shail a friendly slap on the back, "This way."

S'ton was right, Nan was more than happy to stuff both boys with savory soup and soft bread, washed down with a sweet tea. Shail had not tasted such good food since the day of his Stallion Feather Ceremony. Memories flooded his senses, so that for a minute he was back home, surrounded by friends and family, in a familiar place. The next moment his elbow was jostled by an irritated cook's assistant, insisting he was in the way despite Shail having tucked himself into a far corner. Shail apologized out of habit, blinking away unshed tears. S'ton had been chatting with some kitchen help, heard Shail's voice, and turned upon the assistant haranguing Shail.

The angry man shuffled off, muttering darkly about the state of the world, leaving Shail to cast a thankful glance at S'ton, "I don't know what I did to annoy him so."

S'ton made a motion as if throwing something over his shoulder, "Robynt likes to be mad, pay him no mind."

"But he seemed so upset."

"If he weren't, he wouldn't know how to feel," S'ton quipped.

Shail shrugged doubtfully, "If you say so." Finished with their meal, they left the mess tent, S'ton picking his teeth. "Should we check on Jogslen?" Shail asked.

"If'n you want." S'ton lead the way through a sunset camp. "She's not some wilting flower you have to check on regular like. She's a flyer, and that means she's tough as it gets."

"And what does she get out of it?"

S'ton flexed an arm, "A devoted servant who tends to her needs before his own."

"But I thought you wanted a winged horse for a mount?"

"I do, and I'll get one, you wait and see."

Shail personally thought a dragon was better than any horse, winged or not, but he kept his opinion to himself. Jogslen seemed pleased to see them return so soon, standing and wriggling like an overgrown pup. S'ton pat and stroked her face, which she obligingly lowered.

Shail felt a sliver of envy, remembering his time with Stendow. "I can help you scrub her down again," he offered.

"Doubt she needs it so soon."

Shail said primly, "Tabirc cleaned our dragons twice a day at least."

"He the uncle they said you looked like?"

"No, we're not actually related. I call him uncle because he's a close friend of the family. I was staying with him during my apprenticeship."

"Healer Baker's a good master to have, you should consider taking his offer."

"I'm *not* staying," Shail insisted stubbornly.

"You'll learn as much here as there. Probably more."

"And how do you figure that?"

"We have a lot more need of our healers than some regular place. Things like with Feninon happen all the time."

"You're not exactly filling me with confidence."

S'ton sighed, "You talk to him Jogslen."

S'ton stepped back to retrieve the brushes from before, and the dragon transferred her attention to Shail. She was every bit as beautiful as when he'd last seen her. The light played along her scales, making her look like a sparkling scarlet jewel. Shail stared into eyes that were as big as saucers and liquid black, like water at the bottom of a well. She blinked slowly, and Shail was reminded of his cat at home. "Stendow liked it when I scratched under her chin. How about you skylady?" Jogslen purred her approval, closing her eyes completely in apparent bliss.

472

"If you don't fancy working at the healer's tent, you could be my assistant instead," S'ton said as he handed Shail a brush.

Shail began the delicate process of cleaning Jogslen's face, "Do you ever ride her?"

"When it's been awhile between targets and she gets a bit shifty the Chief will let me take her out to stretch her wings."

A plan had begun to form in Shail's mind, "Could she carry two?"

S'ton eyed him curiously, "Probably. Why?"

"What if you and I went to see this homeland of yours?"

S'ton shook his head sharply, "Can't leave camp without orders. Besides, it would take us half a week to get there. We can't make camp too close, or their own scouts would spot us. We don't want to give ourselves away before we're ready."

"Maybe I could ask the Chief. If I he says yes, will you go with me?"

"Sure, but you'll never convince him."

"Will you take me to him?"

"Soon as we've finished here."

473

Shail turned his attention back to his task, and between the two boys Jogslen was soon spotless and ready to sleep again. Shail followed S'ton to the Chief's tent. S'ton scratched at the entrance, and they waited for acknowledgement.

"Enter," barked a voice." S'ton pushed past the hanging opening, Shail on his heels.

Seedruf was standing beside the Chief looking surprised, but pleased. "I didn't expect to see you so soon. Is there something you need?"

Shail said politely, "I'd like to talk with you, if you can spare a minute. Sir," he almost forgot to add.

Seedruf exchanged a look with Chief Omagroef, making a question of his next statement, "We can pick up where we left off later?" When the Chief nodded, Seedruf addressed Shail, "What's on your mind?"

Shail chose his words carefully, "You've told me your group's aim is to return to your homeland."

Seedruf nodded, "Yes."

"And you think that the people who are living there now will try to keep you out?"

Seedruf grimaced, "I know they will, they're the same people that kicked me out in the first place."

"I would like proof of what you say."

Seedruf's look became guarded, "Proof? How?"

"Let S'ton take Jogslen and me to this place, get their side of the story."

Seedruf cut his hand sharply down and across, "Absolutely not. I didn't go to all the trouble of finding you and bringing you here just to hand you over to the enemy."

Shail crossed his arms, "You can appreciate my needing something more than a stranger's word to go on. How do I know this place you speak of is as wonderful as you say? Is it even worth the trouble?"

The Chief gave a feral grin, "Boy has a point. I'd think we were crazy too."

Seedruf cast a disbelieving eye at the Chief, "You'd actually consider sending your only tracker?"

Omagroef stroked his chin, "I don't have a need for her at the moment, and if it convinces your grandson to join us, I'd say it'd be worth it. Why not meet him halfway? Let him visit Kynareth. Almost all of their Denied are Birthrighters."

"Are what?" Shail asked.

Seedruf answered, "People like me, born and raised in our homeland, and then forced to leave when they became adults. They see our cause as a way to regain what should have been theirs." He eyed Shail, "And what

475

guarantee do we have that you won't run off once you're there?"

"I promise I'll stay with S'ton and Jogslen."

"You will promise to return here, by the terms given you by your chief, or this discussion ends."

Shail glared at Seedruf, making Chief Omagroef belly laugh, "We're not *quite* that stupid." Shail felt his ears burn with embarrassment. He hadn't realized he'd been so obvious.

Seedruf crossed his arms, "Well?"

Shail saw he'd been cornered, "I will swear to your terms."

"Your oath as a healer."

Shail was shocked at the implication, then realized with a sinking dread that Seedruf could read him as easily as a book. A promise given under duress could be broken, but a healer's word must be inviolate.

Feeling sick, Shail whispered, "I will swear to your terms, by my oath as a healer."

Seedruf actually looked relieved to have won so easily. He looked to S'ton, "Do I have your word you'll keep him safe, and return him to me?"

S'ton clapped a fist over his heart, "You have it sir."

The Chief pressed a finger to the map, making a circular motion, "Fly to our sister camp, here. They're positioned closest to the abbey, and can tell you the lay of the land, answer your questions. You have my leave to be gone nine days. Three to get there, three back, leaves three days to stay and make of it what you will. When you return, you will join Healer Baker in his work." At Shail's startled look, the Chief chuckled, "Yes, I had word about your little escapade. Patched up one of my fighters." He made a dismissive gesture, "Gather your things and get some sleep. You leave at dawn. Nine days."

Shail was gratified to see S'ton looking completely bewildered, "Aye sir."

"Thank you," Shail offered before making his exit. *'One step closer to freedom,'* he thought to himself, determined to find a way out of this mess.

Chapter 40

The Last Day

Leeinn had thought packing would be a fairly straightforward affair, but every time she thought she was done, Gira would mention another item Leeinn had not even considered. Leeinn would pack her winged horse plush, then put him back on her bedside table, determined to leave him behind as a sign of her maturity. He would seem to watch her as she slowly circled the room, a wistful look in his button eyes. Leeinn would resist for as long as she could, but eventually her resolve would crumble, and she would hug Flappy to her chest, loving the feel of his soft, squishy body. She breathed in, glad that he still smelled like her father after all this time. She set him back on her bed, gave him an affectionate pat on the head, then went to get breakfast.

Leeinn had a confusing mixture of emotions when she saw Tal sitting alone in the dining room. On the one hand, she knew that Tal was family now, and should be cherished as such. She was helpful and considerate and, and … and was responsible for putting ideas in Trader Nassine's head. Without her meddling, Leeinn would be bidding farewell to the guests from the abbey gates, not waving goodbye to everything she'd ever known. Still, Leeinn had never been one to dwell on the dark, instead focusing her attention on the good. She was going on an adventure, and she'd be with her friend Gira, and when it was over she would come home and never have to leave again. So she set her shoulders straight, forced herself to smile, and joined Tal at her table. They talked about inconsequential things; the weather, the food, sticking to safe topics rather than straying into the potentially awkward. They soon lapsed into silence, pretending to slowly chew their food or blow on their already cooled chococafe.

Leeinn half stood to wave when Tiny and Tancer strolled into the hall. The conversation was more organic with four people, Tancer providing impressions of different Accepted he'd met so far. He broke a loaf of black bread in half, then used one of either side of his nose like a drooping mustache, "Trust me, you *want* to take the stairs. Good for you, keeps you trim doncha know."

Leeinn laughed and slapped the table, "Liftmaster Loprosono!"

Tancer took a bit from the left half, "*chewchew* Got it! *swallow* Try this one." He gathered up their forks, arranging them in a line, then bent close to one that was

479

slighter lower than the others, "Back into line you laggard! If you're not spot perfect by the time I count to three, you'll be on muck duty for a week!"

Tiny shivered slightly, "Stablemaster Wyntrin. I wouldn't want to get on his bad side."

Leeinn said, "Don't let him fool you, his bark is worse than his bite. He just acts like that to keep the cadets from doing something silly. They can be a reckless bunch."

Tiny relaxed, "That's good to know."

Tal fidgeted, looking at Leeinn, opening her mouth as if to speak, then closing it while her eyes darted away. After the second time she'd repeated the set of motions, Leeinn asked, "What is it?"

"I was thinking we could do something special for dinner tonight, to celebrate your leaving."

Tancer smacked his lips, "You had me at dinner!"

Leeinn found it hard to swallow, "That's …. A good idea. If everyone else wants to, that is. And we have to invite Gira, and maybe her sister."

Tiny offered, "I can get enough food to feed all of us. I'm sure the kitchen's will lend me a couple of baskets to carry it all."

Tancer bunched a bicep, "I'd better go with you, I *am* sworn to carry your burdens. I could act as a taste tester too."

480

"Right, I'll be sure to pack a decoy basket as well. Stuff it with things that will take you a while to chew through."

Tancer crossed his arms and raised his eyebrows, "I am Accepted, and so is your challenge! I've not yet begun to nibble!"

Tal said, "I can gather up the girls and meet you all there."

Leeinn looked around for confirmation, "Walltop at sunset?"

"Deal," Said Tiny, Tancer, and Tal.

"Then I'll see you all later."

Leeinn took her time walking about Del Abbey, appreciating the simple beauty. Leaves blowing in the wind, dappling the earth beneath with dancing shadows. The long trill of a bird upon a low branch, answered by a neighbor in a nearby bush. The joy of recognizing every face she saw, every voice she heard.

Word had gotten around that she would be leaving to go Abroad, and more than one person pulled her aside to offer advice. *"Don't keep all your money in one place." "Make sure to memorize the address where you're staying, in case you need to ask for directions." "If you run into trouble, find a member of the City Watch."*

To this last wrinkled woman Leeinn responded, "How will I know them?"

"They all wear the same uniform, grey with the City's Silver Spire on the front and back, and they carry stunning glypbats at their waist."

Leeinn's eyebrows raised in surprise, "Their only weapon is non-lethal? The guards I've seen with the caravans wear swords."

"No swords allowed in the City, 'gainst the law."

Leeinn cocked her head to the side, "Well, a criminal wouldn't exactly be worried about the law."

The woman cackled, "They're effective enough. I once saw two hot bloods pull knives on one another. The Watch showed up, got one in the chest, he went down a'hollerin, and the other in the hand what held a sticker. Heard he couldn't use it for a full day after. Course him and his *friend* were taken up and put to work to help cool their tempers."

"But they couldn't have *really* meant to kill each other …."

Her kindly advisor cast a sympathetic look over Leeinn, "People here are peaceful. Some in the City are of a different mind."

"My friends made it sound so nice."

"And it can be, plenty of nice folk in the world. Just keep aware of your surroundings. Predators like easy prey."

Leeinn's head began to spin, "So much to think about. I hope I manage without embarrassing myself too much."

"The family you're staying with knows you've never left the abbey. They'll keep you safe."

"I've never been a guest before either."

All her worries were met with reassurances, "You've a sharp mind, and manners enough to manage."

The day progressed, and Leeinn looked for her father, to tell him she'd be missing from the dining hall that evening. She was not surprised to find him in the orchard, sitting in his favorite sunning spot. He had a stack of apples beside him, and Leeinn knew without looking that each one was perfect. Her father's sense of touch and smell ensured he chose only the best for his basket. When he heard her tread, he picked up three and began to juggle them with both hands, tossing them high into the air before catching them as they dropped. Leeinn giggled, and he switched so two were juggled in one hand, and he calmly began to eat the third. "Show off."

"Would you like one?" he asked, pitching one of the juggled apples to her.

483

Leeinn caught the fruit, admiring it's red skin before taking the first crunchy bite, "*Mmm*, these are good."

"They're going to make excellent pies."

Leeinn sat beside Rumaru, leaning her shoulder against him, "I can't eat more than one, I need to save room for supper." She explained her friend's idea.

"That sounds like fun."

"You won't mind me missing our last meal together?"

"We'll have breakfast before you go, not to mention all those we'll share when you return."

"I really am leaving, aren't I?"

"Maybe think about it like a bird's migration. You fly away for a little while, then come home to roost, and have lots of stories to tell."

"I hope it won't be too much trouble to manage our pool alone."

"I heard I'll have help from your brother and sisters. I must admit, I was a little surprised to hear you agreed to their aid."

"I couldn't think of a way to say no without being rude."

Rumaru sat up straighter, "But you don't need a reason not to do something you don't want to. You're allowed to say no poppet."

"Not after saying yes," sighed Leeinn.

"My offer stands. If you really don't want to go, I will tell Nassine the change of plan."

Leeinn shook her head, "I couldn't disappoint Gira, not after getting her hopes up."

Rumaru settled back, "Told you, you've a heart of del nectar."

"Everyone else has advice for me. Have you anything?"

Rumuaru pursed his lips, "*Hmm*, let me think." He hummed to himself, rocking very slightly from side to side, "Nassine likes to use her flyers early, so the *father's feint* is effective, though I know you prefer the *del distraction*."

Leeinn made a moue, "I was hoping for something a little more universal than fivefs strategy."

"I've already taught you all that."

"Brother Septibb says there's always more to learn."

"He's a teacher, it's job security. You really want my best advice?"

Leeinn stared at Rumaru curiously, "Yes, I would."

485

Her father placed an admonishing finger at the tip of her nose, "Don't forget my cologne."

Leeinn pretended anxiety, "Or else?"

Rumaru waggled his eyebrows impressively, "If you show up without it, I'll send you right back."

"But who will you get to play my part in the midwinter pageant?"

Rumaru made a definitive gesture, "See? It *is* vitally important you remember. I call that sage advice."

Leeinn finished her apple, then buried the core at the root of their shading tree, "I suppose if that's the best you can do."

Rumaru stood with the aid of his cane, which he leaned against the trunk as he slapped the dirt from his seat, "Well, I have one more tiny scrap." He helped her to her feet, then hugged her breathless, "Hurry home, because I will miss you every moment you are gone from these walls." The only possible answer to that was a return embrace every bit as fierce, and maybe a whit tighter. When the moment had passed, Rumaru held Leeinn at arm's length, "I'm going to take my harvest to the kitchen and make a few early pies to take with you."

Leeinn left her father to toddle off with his basket, committing the image of his retreating form to memory. She hoped it would help with the loneliness she knew she'd feel without him, no matter how kind her hosts were.

The day seemed to fly by, and Leeinn made her way to the walltops. She was greeted by Tiny, Tancer, Gira, Challi, Shealah, and Tal, all sitting on a large fluffy blanket. Gira jumped up to take Leeinn's hands in her own, "You're finally here! We've been waiting!"

"I'm glad you could all make it."

"Of course, anything for you! And you'll never get *just* Challi, she and Shealah are joined at the hip. Sit here by me. Are you hungry?"

"I am," said Tancer, "Let's break open those baskets!"

"This one is all for you," Tiny said, pulling a brown box in front of Tancer.

He eagerly accepted the gift, opening it and taking each item out one by one, "Caramel candy, celery with peanut spread, pistachios, baby carrots, molasses bars, sunflower seeds. And what's this?"

"Dried mango, recommended by the cook." Tancer took a curious bite; chewed, and chewed, and chewed. Tiny smiled with satisfaction, "Works like a charm." Tancer pretended to glare for a minute, then shrugged with a grin, popping another piece of fruit in his mouth.

Everyone helped themselves, and they ate as they watched the sun sink into the west. Gira teased her sister for feeding Shealah with her fingers, to which Challi responded by grappling Gira until she sat upon her sibling. Leeinn laughed so hard her sides hurt. She wouldn't have to worry about boredom with traveling companions like these! Gira eventually admitted defeat, and Challi took the win with smug satisfaction.

"Oh look," Shealah point upwards, "First star of the evening!"

Tancer looked, "That's a bright one. Anyone know which it is?"

Tal answered, "It's the South Star. It marks the end of the Damaged Dipper. See the three stars that make up the crack?"

They passed a pleasant time together, eventually moving the baskets to the edge so they could all lie down and stare at the sky. When they began to yawn, everyone worked together to gather up their things. Tiny and Tancer hefted the now empty baskets, "The cook that gave me these said we could bring them back in the morning. We'll see you all at breakfast."

Tancer smiled dreamily, "Breakfast. Such a lovely word."

Gira, Challi, and Shealah waved their goodbyes, and then it was just Leeinn and Tal.

Tal flashed an enigmatic smile, "I hope you enjoyed your last night here."

Dismissing the look as a trick of the moonlight Leeinn said, "I did, thank you. Will you come to see us off in the morning?"

"I wouldn't miss out on the fruits of my labors."

"What?"

"Never mind. Goodnight, sister."

Leeinn was left staring after Tal's retreating form. She returned to her room, climbed into her comfortable bed, and found it hard to fall asleep.

Chapter 41

Plums

Shail was dragged from a fitful sleep by the gradual increase of camp noise as the people within woke to face the day. For a few moments he laid curled on his cot with his eyes closed, pretending he was back in his bed at home.

His respite was short lived. Shail heard S'ton calling him from outside the tent, "Oy, Shail! We flying today or what?"

Shail pressed his palms against his temples, then let his arms drop and lie slack as he shouted back, "Yes, just a minute please!" Shail washed up as best he could, grabbed his pack, which someone, likely S'ton, had moved to Shail's tent, and met S'ton outside.

"Figured you was gonna sleep all day."

"It's barely an hour past dawn!"

"And that's an hour of flight time we can't get back. You're gonna need to toughen up if you ever want to be a Denied soldier."

"You're right, I'm not cut out for this sort of thing. Should probably just take me back…"

S'ton rolled his eyes, "Are you still on that? Leave off will you? Chief is doing you and Seedruf a favor. Me too, since I'm going with you. I'm packed. What about you?"

"I never *un*packed."

"Good, then let's get some tuck before we go."

Shail and S'ton were treated to a generous breakfast by Nan, and when they had scraped their plates clean, S'ton fetched Jogslen's saddle from the Quartermaster. Seedruf had come to see them off, giving Shail an awkward farewell pat on the shoulder. "I know I've made of mess of things, but I hope you will at least *listen* to the Birthrighters. They all have stories just like mine, and they want to go home just as badly."

"Like I want to go home?"

Seedruf pursed his lips, "We'll talk when you get back." With S'ton and Seedruf's help, Shail was soon strapped tight to the tracker. "S'ton, take care of my grandson."

"Yessir! See you in nine days!"

Jogslen leapt into the air, then circled the camp once, and Shail heard cheers and clapping from below until they'd cleared the tree line. The tracker's wing strokes were so smooth it felt more like sailing than flying. The wind made conversation difficult, so Shail and S'ton mostly flew in silence. They traveled like this until their luck turned when a brief, but violent, storm kept them ground bound overnight.

When the clouds cleared the next morning, the sun made all the tiny droplets sparkle. The second day went by much like the first, minus the storm, and on the third morning S'ton still had hopes that they would reach their destination by nightfall. They broke camp, mounted Jogslen, and took to the sky.

Their flight was uneventful until Jogslen suddenly banked hard to the left. Shail was about to complain in S'ton's ear, but the other's startled cry made Shail realize it'd *not* been S'ton's idea. Jogslen flew back and forth, then turned in a tight circle, eyeing the ground. S'ton cried, "Jogs! Whatcha doin? Fly on, hear!"

Jogslen landed, despite S'ton's protestations, and began a low crooning noise, pointing her nose first one way, then another. "What's she doing?" Shail asked.

S'ton released his safety straps, and his feet made a slight thump as he hit the ground, "Dunno, never seen her break from her training."

Shail peered into the surrounding trees, "She must have a reason for landing here. Why don't we look around?"

S'ton helped Shail down, and they both turned in a circle to study the forest around them. Shail could not see anything that would mark the place as unusual. A squirrel chittered a warning call overhead, and after a minute or two some birds resumed twittering from the shaded trees. Jogslen was testing the air about her with deep indrawn breaths, like a hunting dog searching for a fox. When she reached a spot about twenty feet from where'd they'd landed, Jogslen dropped her snout to the dirt. She made a shrill noise that brought both boys over to stare into a shallow hole in the ground.

They stared in shocked amazement as the smallest foal Shail had ever seen. "What's a baby horse doing in the middle of the woods? And how did Jogslen even know it was here?"

"Beats me. Is it alive?" S'ton stepped down to stand beside the foal, which was a mottled brown that blended beautifully with the earthen background. He nudged it with his foot, causing it to bleat in alarm. S'ton dropped into a squat so he wasn't towering over the creature, holding up a hand and making a soothing motion, "Here now, you're alright. We won't hurt you."

Shail glanced nervously around them, "Where's its mother? She might not like us getting so close to her baby."

"Looks a little undersized, maybe it's been abandoned." Jogslen interrupted their speculation by pushing a nose towards the infant. She sniffed it, then made the same crooning noise as before.

Shail rubbed his neck in bewilderment, "But what do we do with it?"

S'ton said, "I'm thinking." Dragon and newborn were completely engrossed with one another. "I don't think we'll convince her to leave it. She *could* carry it, even with both us riding, but with the extra weight, I'm not sure we could make it to Kynareth by nightfall."

"But what if its mother comes back here looking for it?"

S'ton tilted his head up at Shail, "What do *you* suggest?"

Shail's mouth twitched in thought, "What if we stayed until tomorrow morning? If she's going to return, she'll do it by then."

S'ton sniffed, turning his attention back to the babe, "That's a long time to wait for a maybe, and we're already behind schedule because of that storm." Shail made an

494

affronted noise, which S'ton ignored, "I wonder if it can walk yet." He moved to the other side of the depression, leaving a clear path between dragon and foundling. To their delight, Jogslen gave her new friend a lick from nose to forelock. It double blinked, then stared with wide eyes. It had not yet mastered walking, teetering in the attempt. S'ton put out a steadying hand, and Shail watched him go still.

Shail took a step towards S'ton, "What's wrong?"

S'ton's face split into an ear-to-ear grin, "It's a foaling."

"A what?"

"It's a *winged* horse. Of course! I didn't notice at first because they're just stubs. This changes things! We're leaving *now*."

"But what about its mother?"

"Her scent is probably what got Joglsen's attention in the first place. Maybe she was injured, and had to leave it. I don't know why she's not here, but I do know I'll never get another chance like this."

"You said there were lots of winged horses in your homeland. Better to wait and have one proper."

"Why wait, when I can have this one? My father would *have* to be impressed if I came back with a winged horse."

495

"And how are you going to take care of it? Dragons don't make milk."

"I'll get one of the mares at our camp to nurse it."

Shail asked in a skeptical voice, "Can foalings even drink horse milk?"

"One way to find out." Jogslen made the crooning noise, then reached out to gently stroke the foaling's side. It curiously lipped her, but did not struggle or seem at all scared. Shail studied its movements, but other than its smallness, it seemed in perfect health. S'ton began making overtures to the foaling, "Hey now Plumules, let me have a look at you."

Shail quirked an eyebrow, "Plumules?"

"Well, it doesn't have them yet, but it'll grow feathers soon enough. Maybe just Plums for short?"

"I suppose that name would work for either sex."

S'ton gently untangled the foaling's tail with his fingers, using the opportunity to peak underneath, "Looks like Plum is a coltling." Plums switched his gaze between boy and dragon. When Jogslen made no objections, the coltling relaxed, even turning his nose to scent S'ton's hand. S'ton began patting down Plums' sides, "Hard to imagine these as the wings of a future stallion." The foaling turned his head to nibble on S'ton's sleeve.

Shail said, "I wonder how long it's been since he last nursed."

"We'll get him to a mare as soon as we get to camp," S'ton repeated.

"Are winged horse foals usually this small? He's not much bigger than my dog at home."

"Never heard of a runt horse."

"Maybe he was premature."

S'ton nodded, "Could have been the storm yesterday, might have spooked the mare into dropping early."

"In which case, we need a winged horse specialist. Does your camp have one?"

S'ton hedged, "Not that I know of."

"Your camp is supposed to be close to your homeland, right? You said they have lots of winged horses there. *They* must have a specialist."

S'ton crossed his arms, "I'm not turning Plums over to the enemy."

"But what if he dies without the proper help?"

That got S'ton's attention, "He looks fine to me."

"How would you know what *fine* looks like?" Shail asked accusingly.

S'ton listed off, "He's walking, well wobbling, his eyes are bright, and he's *looking* at everything, not just staring off. Plus, I think Jogslen would be acting more worried if there was something wrong with him."

"Has *she* ever seen one before?"

"No, but it's an instinct for dragons to look after foalings. Let's see if we can make it to camp tonight."

"I thought we were waiting 'til morning."

S'ton was the picture of impatience, but to his credit, he closed his eyes and just breathed for a minute. When he opened them and looked at Shail, he said, "If we wait, will you go with me in the morning, no fussing?"

Shail nodded gravely, "Yes."

"Fine, let's make camp. We might as well wait in the tent."

They built a small campfire with the help of Shail's starter pouch, and decided that S'ton would take first watch, then wake Shail when the night was half over. It turned out not to be necessary, because shortly after midnight there was a sudden, loud trumpeting that startled both boys wide awake.

Jogslen was crouched over the coltling, which had not left her side since their arrival. Shail ran out of the tent to see S'ton peering upwards. It was next to impossible to

498

see beyond their fire, but Shail heard a sound similar to the location calls he'd heard between Stendow and Lowkrist.

His guess was spot on, for two dragons, the typical brown, instead of tracker red, landed on the outskirts of their camp. When he saw the symbol on their saddles, S'ton warned, "Those aren't our flyers!"

Shail whispered back, "It's two dragons to one, *and* it's dark. Not good odds."

The dragons in question made inquisitive noises towards Jogslen's tail, where Plums could not be seen but gave away his location with a nervous nicker. A set of riders jumped down from their mount's backs. They pulled off helmet and goggles, revealing features similar enough to mark them as closely related blood.

One stepped forward, projecting his voice to be heard over Jogslen's low growl, "Peace, all. Let us talk." He motioned for his partner to take control of both their dragons, freeing both his hands. "I'm Rintin, and this is my cousin Rena. I think you've stumbled across something that's ours."

"We found this coltling by himself. What business is he of yours?" S'ton challenged.

"One of our pregnant mares came back having given birth. It was too soon, and we feared her babe dead. We've been out searching for it, just in case. Seems we've found it. Or *he*, did you say?"

S'ton scowled, "Yes, and he's mine now. Your mare didn't want him."

Rintin offered diplomatically, "More like she's young and inexperienced. Since it's dragons that do most of the rearing, not all mares have strong maternal instincts. Have you given him a name?"

S'ton lifted his chin defiantly, "Plums."

Rintin nodded affably, "Well, *Plums* will need our Stablemaster's care if he's to survive."

S'ton said obstinately, "I've helped raised horses all my life, I can take care of this one."

Rintin spread his hands in a conciliatory manner, "Big difference between those with wings, and those without."

S'ton dropped his stance, widening his feet and raising closed hands, "Jogslen can take your overgrown lizards easy, and we," he indicated Shail with a jerk of his chin, "can take you."

"I don't want to fight!" Shail yelped, pulling on S'ton's sleeve and getting shrugged off.

Upon hearing Shail's outburst, the rider named Rena gasped in astonishment, "What the? Rin, you seeing this?"

Rintin studied Shail's face, "*Yeeeees*," he said slowly, clearly just surprised.

"What? What is it?" Shail asked nervously.

Rider Rintin frowned slightly, "Nothing that changes our orders. We were to retrieve this foaling if it was alive, but I won't be the cause of dragon-on-dragon violence."

S'ton growled, "Then let us be on our way."

Rintin sighed, "Can't do that either."

"What other choice is there?"

Rintin folded his hands, "Follow us to our abbey, and sort things from there."

"You mean go to where there are enough of you to steal Plums from us," S'ton accused.

The other rider raised an eyebrow, "If you force us to fight, you will lose."

"Please listen to them," Shail begged.

S'ton cast an angry, hurtful glance at Shail, "Course you want me to listen to'em, it's just what you wanted."

Shail strove to keep his voice low and even, "What I *want* is to get out of this in one piece."

S'ton scowled, eyeing the area as if he were really considering rebellion. Shail held his breath, only letting it out when S'ton furiously dropped his fists, "Plums is mine. We'll go with you to this stablemaster, but when he's ready, we're leaving."

501

Rintin bowed his head, "That's not up to me, you'll have to speak with our abbot. If you'll ask your dragon to follow us, Rena and I can each take one of you on our mounts."

"Don't trust I won't try to fly off?" S'ton sneered.

"Ours were bred to carry heavy burdens, like multiple riders. And I think yours has her mind occupied with her new coltling." S'ton sniffed audibly, but made no further comment. Relieved, Rintin said, "Then you'll be with me, and your friend with Rena." Both riders remounted, and each boy took up position accordingly. "Ask your dragon to carry Plums and follow us, please. Rena, take point."

S'ton repeated the orders to the tracker dragon, "C'mon Jogs, we gotta get Plums some help." Jogslen cradled the coltling in her front claws, and for his part Plums behaved as if this were all routine.

Rena and Rintin gave their dragons the fly command, and Jogslen leapt after them. After they were back in the air and had steadied to a glide, Shail's rescuer turned her head to talk with him. He could only hear her because the winds blew her words to his ears, "I'm Rena."

"Shail!" he shouted.

Rena jerked her head away, "Not so loud, I can hear you fine." With the side of her head pointed towards him,

Shail could see that Rena's helmet had been modified with ear slits to allow her to hear normally. "Sorry. My name is Shail."

Rena eased her head back, "You'll be alright once we get you home. Your friend should meet my brother Randoi. He's partnered to a stallion too."

"Will they really let S'ton keep Plums?"

"If he became Accepted, and went through the training."

"I don't know what that is."

"I'll explain everything when we get back to the abbey."

"You live in an abbey?" That did not fit the picture the Denied had painted for Shail. "Do you kick out people you don't like?"

Rena jumped slightly with surprise, "Where in the world did you hear that?"

"The one you caught me with, his name is S'ton. He and his people kidnapped me because they want to be allowed in your abbey."

"Why would they kidnap *you*? You're not from there."

"It's a long story."

"I can't wait to hear it."

Shail could not believe his luck, for Rena proved to be exactly what he needed. She eagerly answered all of Shail's questions. "Your abbey sounds like a big place."

"I'll show you around if you want. We're nearly there now. Look! That's the roof of the belltower shining in the sun."

Shail saw the sparkle Rena had pointed out. "The walls are even taller than I thought they'd be. Do they really go around the whole abbey?"

"Sure do! They don't look like much from here, but just you wait 'til we're inside."

"Why are the gates opening?"

"We had a lot of visitors that are returning to the City. Want to give them something to talk about when they get there?"

"What do you mean?"

"Let's do a flyover. I'd never seen a red dragon before, I bet they haven't either. Then it's straight to the stables for little Plums, and you'll be wanted by the abbot."

"Would he help me, do you think?"

"I'm certain he will."

"What makes you so sure?"

Rena coughed a laugh, "Let's just say ..... you have *a lot* in common."

Chapter 42

Lyhupa festo

Leeinn woke later than was usual, for she had slept poorly. She dressed in a fog, preparing to leave her room when there came a knock at the door. She opened it to find a beaming Gira bouncing on her toes.

"Good morning!"

"Good morning. I'm surprised to see you up so early."

Gira leaned forward, "I wanted to make sure everything was perfect for our trip. Have you finished packing?"

"Almost," Leeinn offered guiltily, "I can finish up if you want to go to breakfast."

Gira stood straight again, "I can wait until you're ready."

Leeinn brought out the two traveling bags she'd put together, "There's just one more small one."

"That's all you're bringing?"

"How many bags do you have?"

"Thirteen. Didn't help my luck much." Gira stared down ruefully at the tattoo on her hand, "This either." Then she looked up at Leeinn, "Or maybe it did, since you're coming with us."

Leeinn felt flattered, "I didn't realize you wanted me to go that much."

"I know we haven't known each other long, but I can just tell you and I are going to be friends forever."

Leeinn wrestled with the weight of her question, "Can I ask you something about Tal?"

Gira looked surprised, "Tal? Sure."

"Does she ever say odd things that don't make sense when you hear them?"

"Like a foreign language?"

"No," Leeinn said with frustration.

"What did she actually say that's got you ruffled?"

"She said she would be seeing me off today because she didn't want to *miss out on the fruits of her labors*."

Gira made a thoughtful noise, "I suppose that is an odd way to put it."

"You mean it makes sense to you?"

"Well, I suppose that she attached herself to our family because we attend a lot of the abbey's celebrations. It was a long shot, but it paid off, didn't it? She was able to travel with us here, and now she gets to stay. Tal's just trying to put the best spin on how things worked out."

"Maybe …"

"Why, what did you think she meant?"

"I don't know, but it didn't sound good."

"Why would Tal say something bad to you? She likes you. She threw that going away picnic last night. You're just nervous about leaving."

"Thank you, that helps."

"What are friends for? Now let's go eat, I'm hungry!"

Breakfast was a boisterous affair. Those who were leaving were making their goodbyes to those who would stay. Leeinn made her way to her usual seat. Her father sat in his next to Nassine, the two of them chatting as they drank hot tea. Gira waved to her mother in passing, and was rewarded with a smile and slightly raised cup. They made up their plates, Leeinn feeling her appetite return in spades.

Rumaru had pat Leeinn on the shoulder when she first sat down, then returned to his conversation, "You're sure her chit will be accepted everywhere?"

"There's no place in the City that doesn't recognize the Del Abbey trademark, nor is there a bank that would refuse to pay out should she inquire. Not that she will need to, she will be well tended while with us."

"What is it you're fond of saying? '*Always have a backup plan.*' Besides, she's going to be buying oodles at Batista's."

They shared a good-natured laugh. "I'll see that at least one bottle of a suitable scent reaches you."

Rumaru pretended to huff, "It's my favorite cologne. My father wore it all his life, and his before him. "Tis a tradition."

"Well you can switch it up when I visit and wear mine."

Rumaru set down his cup and folded his hands on the table before him, "And what do you offer in the bargain Trader?"

Nassine peered up at the ceiling as though for inspiration, "Hmm, another pair of qwikwarm socks?"

"Deal! Shake on it?" They did, both looking pleased with their share.

"Did he just ask for *socks*?" whispered Gira with a disbelieving shake of her head.

When the food was finished, Rumaru rose and offered Leeinn his hand, "Shall we walk to the gates together?"

"Sounds good to me, though I need to stop by my room and get my bags."

They took the long way, Rumaru reminiscing as they went, "There's the corner you nearly broke your toes on. They told me your little foot was bruised for days. And there's where you accidently turned over those tubs of drink. Every bee in Trumpet Vine Valley came to visit us."

"Speaking of accidents, there's the patch of mismatched tiles everyone calls the *abbot's mark.*"

"They asked a *blind* man to lay tiles, they get what they get. Don't know what they expected."

"It was supposed to say *stay hopeful.*" Rumaru waved a hand in front of his face, his blue eyes staring straight ahead. "You couldn't feel the letters?"

"I missed the point of the lesson, I was still too angry to *stay hopeful*, and just stuck the pieces in without caring about their order."

"No one who visits and sees your work can decipher it, *Lyhupa festo.*"

510

"Think of it like a secret message. We say, '*Lyhupa festo*,' and people will think we're speaking another language, but we'll know what was really meant."

"Or they'll think we're having a brainbleed."

"Then it would be especially important to *lyhupa festo*!"

They reached Leeinn's room and Rumuaru offered to help with her travel cases. They had only walked a few paces out the door when he said, "Wait, I think I dropped my towel. I'll be right back." Leeinn stood by her luggage, and did not have to wait long before her father reappeared, "Found it, thank you for waiting."

They made their way to the gates where there was just a fraction of the bustle from when the multiple families had left in convoy. Gira was standing with Tiny and Tancer. Rumaru pat Leeinn's shoulder, "Go say goodbye to your friends, I'll see you in a minute."

Leeinn joined her group, greeted with wide smiles and good cheer. Gira said, "I've been waiting for you. Here, let me have a servant see to your bags." She motioned to young man in dark plum colored livery bearing a set of golden bells across the chest, which Leeinn knew to be the Sulnvoc crest.

"I prefer to keep this one with me," Leeinn said, holding the smallest bag in her hand. The servant bowed to

511

everyone present, took Leeinn's two larger bags, and hurried off to see them stowed.

Leeinn was left feeling off kilter, but willing to roll with it. She shouted after the retreating form, "Thank you, sir!"

Gira tittered, "You really are the nicest person."

"He's doing me a good service."

"He's a servant, he's paid well to be of assistance."

"He's still a person, and praise is appreciated. Do you know his name?"

"Veranst. He's fairly new, like Tal, but he's wonderfully attentive."

"I'm used to doing everything for myself, it will take getting used to having someone else do things for me."

Gira said, "I can't wait to get back to the City! We're going to have such fun!"

Leeinn was glad that Gira seemed in good humor, seeming to have forgotten her recent failure. "I'll need you to help me as we go, I've never traveled before."

"Our carriages are Cadalaxe, they're the best there is, for all kinds of travel. Even with the four of us, there will plenty of room."

"Are Challi and Shealah already on board?"

"I think so, they try to stay out of mother's way. Speaking of, here she comes with your father."

Tancer adopted a severe air, "Chin up, shoulders back, prepare for inspection!"

Tiny followed her husband's instructions with suppressed amusement, and Leeinn was reminded of the height advantage her friend had on all of them. She wasn't just taller than everyone, her shoulders were broad, and she was well muscled. When Tancer stood on tiptoe trying to match her, she simply reached out with her long arm and gave his head a tousle.

"Not the hair!," Tancer complained.

"But it's so soft, and it smells like sandalwood and cinnamon. Now my hands do too." She gave him a saucy look, "Besides, I thought you liked it when I pull your hair."

Tancer blushed until you could almost feel the heat from his face, and the women tittered around him as Rumaru and Trader Nassine joined them, "Something funny?" she inquired.

Tancer was quick to answer before anyone else, "No ma'am, just full of high spirits for the day."

Nassine gave a tight smile, "Well, good. Though it's a far less impressive send off than then last time. At least we're returning to the City with the same number of

513

people we arrived with. Quite the trade off, a servant for the abbey's darling."

Leeinn shook her head, "I'm hardly that special."

"You *are* the youngest to ever be Accepted."

"An accident, because I got away from my father. He wasn't used to having a child, and didn't know how quick they can be. And I wanted to pet the Trinity."

They laughed, and amidst their merriment, Tal joined then, making them a group of seven, "I came to say goodbye."

Gira went to give her a hug, "I'll miss you! No one ever does my hair like you."

"I'm sure you'll find someone new soon, and they'll be as fond of you as I am."

Tal released Gira to curtsey before Nassine, "Thank you for taking me into your household."

"As Gira said, we shall miss your expertise. But if you must leave us, you could find no finer reason to do so."

"Father Abbot," squeaked a voice.

The group turned to look at the little girl who had spoken, Rumaru easily dropped to a knee to speak with her, "Yes Ayelean, what is it?"

"I have a message for you."

He reached out his hand, "It was wonderful for you to bring it to me, thank you." He unrolled the scroll of parchment, which was covered in lines of raised dots.

Gira peered curiously at the paper, "It doesn't have any words written on it, how is it a message?"

Rumaru smiled in her direction, "The abbey has glyphstones that take a written message and translates it into Lraillou, which I read with my fingers." He began running his fingertips over the message. He frowned slightly as he got to the end.

"Trouble?" inquired Nassine.

Rumaru's face resumed smiling, "Nothing that need concern anyone." He recurled the pages and stuffed them into a pocket. "If everyone is ready to leave, I believe our goodbyes have lasted long enough."

Gira pulled at Leeinn's sleeve, "Our carriage is this way."

"Could you wait outside it for me? I want a moment with my father."

Nassine checked her pocket watch, "See that you make it quick, we need to leave soon if we're to make it to our first inn stop by dark."

When they were alone, Leeinn said in a hushed tone, "What was in that message?"

Rumaru was silent for a moment, as though wondering if he should share the secret, "One of our patrols looking for a lost foaling ran into two strangers with an even stranger dragon."

"Strange how?"

"For starters, it's red."

"Brother Septibb told me dragons were either green or brown. Or white, if they grow old enough."

"I shall have a chat with the strangers when they arrive. I'm hoping they can shed some light on the situation, not just about their unusual dragon, but what they were doing in the area to begin with."

"Maybe I should stay …"

"No, you go have your adventure. I'll tell you all about it when you get back. Is there anyone looking at us?"

"No. Why?"

"I have one more thing for you." Rumaru reached into his robe, and pulled out Flappy. "Seems you left him behind, and I know you'd miss him if you did."

"But when did you …. You didn't go back to my room for your towel!"

"Silly of me, it was in my pocket the whole time."

Leeinn snorted a laugh, taking the plush and putting in into her bag, "Thank you."

"One last hug?"

"One *more* hug, not the last." They embraced, and when they pulled apart both had tears in their eyes. "Goodbye father.

"Goodbye daughter. Be well. And remember, *Lyhupa festo."*

Leeinn joined Gira outside a rather plain looking transport, "This is a luxury carriage?"

"Mother says it's better not to boast of your wealth on the road. Our City carriages are much more impressive."

"Besides," Challi called out, "It's not the outside that matters. Come see." Leeinn climbed in, Gira behind. They were right, the inside was roomy, well lit, and all the sitting surfaces felt as soft as they looked. Leeinn took the empty seat next to Gira, across from Challi and Shealah. They both smiled and greeted Leeinn warmly. "You can lean out the window to wave if you want."

Leeinn took the offer, and her goodbye was echoed back to her from all the Accepted present. Her father shook both hands in the air, and as they pulled away from the abbey gates, Leeinn shouted back to him, *"Lyhupa festo!"*

"Liehuppa what?" laughed Challi.

"It's, uh, just another way of saying, '*Stay hopeful*'."

"Good advice," Shealah said.

"Will you say it again?" asked Gira. Leeinn repeated the phrase a few times until everyone had it right. Gira's face became serious as she looked back at the abbey. "A year and a day .... Can I stay hopeful that long?"

A commotion from the leading carriage's drivers drew the four girls attention. Challi commented, "Wonder what that's all about. Can't be raiders this close to the abbey."

Shealah squinted, "They're not looking at the road, but the sky." Two brown forms passed overhead. "Guess a couple of your riders wanted to make a fancy goodbye."

Leeinn was about to agree, then double blinked, "Not a couple, there's three! The last one must be the same as was in the message my father received right as we were leaving." All eyes followed in the red dragon's wake. Leeinn felt the almost over-powering urge to jump down from the carriage and run back to the abbey, to home.

Gira linked her arm through Leeinn's, "It won't just be you with stories to tell when you get back."

Leeinn swallowed hard, "When I get back."

Challi offered, "I brought my fivefs set, fancy a game?"

Leeinn agreed, firmly putting Del Abbey out of her mind. She was going on an adventure, and since it was going to be the only time she ever left the abbey, she figured she should make the best of it.

Epilogue

Rumaru waved even though he could not watch the carriages leave. He heard the clatter of their wheels on the road and the hoofbeats of the horses that pulled them. He made sure to keep the muscles in his face loose, his expression open and easy for those who might be watching.

Inside, the Father Abbot was feeling that strange, stricken panic common to parents when their nest becomes empty for the first time. Should he have argued harder against Tal's suggestion? Nassine had been so pleased with the idea, and Tal had been most persuasive. It had all made sense at the time, but now? Now, his daughter was riding away, with friends true, but still ....

"Father Abbot?"

"Hmm, yes?"

"Stablemasters Dooreg and Wyntrin got their messages and will meet you at the treasure infirmary."

"Thank you, I'll go there now."

When Rumaru arrived at the hospital for winged horses, a stablehand met him at the door. She said, "Oh good, I was just about to go look for you sir."

"You knew I was coming here."

"Yes, but, well, we thought it best to expedite."

"Why, are they giving you trouble?"

"No sir, though one has a temper. But it's the other one you really need to meet."

"Yes, the message said there were two boys with the red dragon. Is the other one causing a problem?"

"No, sir. He's, well … just follow me, please."

Rumaru and the stablehand approached the largest stall in the infirmary. An angry voice said from the left side of the stall, "You said Plums needed help!"

Rumnaru heard Rider Rintin reply from the rightside of the stall, "And that was true, from a certain point of view. Plums needs his mother's milk, and a father dragon to watch over him, and teach him to fly. Things no human can do."

"I can take him to another mare, and Jogslen is as good as any dragon of yours. Better, even!"

Rumaru picked out the sounds of shuffling feet as everyone became aware of his arrival. "Father Abbot, thank the Twins you're here."

The unknown voice spoke again, but this time in utter bewilderment, "Shail, look!"

Rumaru whispered, "*Shail?*" Louder, he repeated, "Did you say Shail?"

"Uncle Wengsper! What are you doing here? What did you do to your hair, and what are you wearing? Is mother here? What about Gran Rox?"

Rumaru staggered as a small body hit him, "Dooreg, does he … look like he sounds?"

"Aye Father Abbot, he could be your son."

"Father Abbot? Uncle, what is he talking about?"

"He seems to think you're an uncle of his called Wengsper, sir."

"I know who he means, though that was not the name he was born with."

The pressure left Rumaru's side, "You're not my uncle?"

"Oh yes, Shail," Rumaru finally answered, "I *am* your uncle."